PRESS
OFFICIAL
CORRESPONDENT

CW01203138

VIP

WDCN SPORTS

THE PLAYBOOK OF EMMA

THE KILLERS NEXT GENERATION

BRYNNE ASHER

Text Copyright
© 2025 Brynne Asher
All Rights Reserved
No part of this book may be reproduced, scanned, or distributed in any printed or electronic form without permission from the author. It is not legal to scan any part of this work into artificial intelligence. Please do not participate in or encourage piracy of copyrighted materials in violation of author's rights. Only purchase authorized editions.

Any resemblance to actual persons, things, locations, or events is accidental.

This book is a work of fiction.

THE PLAYBOOK OF EMMA

The Killers Next Generation

Published by Brynne Asher
BrynneAsherBooks@gmail.com

Keep up with me on Facebook for news and upcoming books
https://www.facebook.com/BrynneAsherAuthor

Join my reader group on Facebook to keep up with my latest news
Brynne Asher's Beauties

Keep up with all Brynne Asher books and news
https://bit.ly/BrynneAsherNL

Edited by Hadley Finn

ALSO BY BRYNNE ASHER

The Agents

Possession

Tapped

Exposed

Illicit

Winslet

Winslet

Killers Series

Vines – A Killers Novel, Book 1

Paths – A Killers Novel, Book 2

Gifts – A Killers Novel, Book 3

Veils – A Killers Novel, Book 4

Scars – A Killers Novel, Book 5

Souls – A Killers Novel, Book 6

Until the Tequila – A Killers Crossover Novella

The Killers, The Next Generation

The Chemistry of Levi, Asa's son

The Playbook of Emma, Asa's daughter

The Carpino Series

Overflow – The Carpino Series, Book 1

Beautiful Life – The Carpino Series, Book 2

Athica Lane – The Carpino Series, Book 3

Until Avery – A Carpino Series Crossover Novella

Force of Nature - A Carpino Christmas Novel

The Dillon Sisters

Deathly by Brynne Asher

Damaged by Layla Frost

The Montgomery Series

Bad Situation – The Montgomery Series, Book 1

Broken Halo – The Montgomery Series, Book 2

Betrayed Love - The Montgomery Series, Book 3

Standalones

Blackburn

CONTENTS

1. Heavy on the Dirty	1
2. God Bless the Flu	19
3. Moonstruck	37
4. Best Day Ever	53
5. Worst Day Ever	65
6. Hostage	79
7. Homies Resurrected	91
8. Viral	113
9. Queen of the Mean Girls Club and Leader of the House of Fake	123
10. Sex Lottery	143
11. Commando In My Sweats	163
12. Drama Llama	179
13. Breakfast of Losers	197
14. Pet A Goat	209
15. Exclamation Points	223
16. Helpless	235
17. Daddy Asa Aura	253
18. Monkey Sex	263
19. Resourceful Guy	273
20. Middle-Aged Badasses	283
21. I Like Chubby Babies	299
22. Daily Multivitamin with Extra Iron	313
23. Lovely. So Lovely	331
24. No One is Killing Anyone	351
25. Open-Faced Sandwich	365
26. End Game	377
27. Jack Hale Is in Love	391
28. Shriveled Peas	411
29. Seven Degrees from Drama	421
30. A Plan … ish	431
31. Red Zone	439

32. Sponge Bath	453
Epilogue	467
Also by Brynne Asher	477
Acknowledgments	479
About the Author	481

This book is dedicated to those who make their own fate and don't let the world pass them by.

You are the true badasses.

1

HEAVY ON THE DIRTY

Emma

I had one goal.

Do. Not. Suck.

But it wasn't that simple.

It also wasn't easy.

And, quite honestly, not sucking was hard. I'm the third string for a reason. I'm new, young, and never worked in sports.

The stakes could not have been higher.

And, not to toot my own horn, but I killed it.

A new job at a new station, working in a new department, in a not-so-new city.

After years of doing my time bouncing around jobs in the smallest markets in the country, I got a big break.

Huge.

I'm back in the District.

I'm home.

Well, home is actually an hour west in the boonies but unless I want to be a counselor, work at a winery, or do scary secret stuff off the grid, there are no jobs there for me.

For the last few years, I've waded through the trenches. Literally.

I trudged through feet of snow and fought blizzards as a community reporter in small-town South Dakota. In the summer, I reported on bison and motorcycle rallies.

After that, I thought I was going to die of heat exhaustion in southern Arizona when I focused on important issues to the community like filling local jobs. It wasn't because people didn't want to work, it was because there was a lack of housing.

And trust me, I felt the pinch when I moved there. I had to rent the small room over Mr. Coolidge's diner. It wasn't even a real apartment. But when I got the job and couldn't find a place to live, he offered it to me when I might or might not have broken down in tears while sitting in one of his booths while eating a stack of fluffy pancakes.

It was not my proudest moment, but at least I ended up with a modest room to rent.

I miss talking to Mr. Coolidge, even though I smelled like bacon the whole time I lived there.

Then there was my last job in a small town in southeast

Kansas. Ask me if I dreamed of riding with tornado chasers when I decided to major in broadcast journalism.

The answer to that would be a big, fat no.

Never crossed my mind.

Definitely not something Emerson Hollingsworth had on her bucket list to live life to its fullest.

But that's how it goes in this profession. You have to be willing to bounce around smaller markets and hope for your big break. Heck, I would've been fine with a mid-size break where I didn't have to trek through snow, sweat my ass off, or run from twisters.

Working in a major market is a dream I knew I wouldn't attain for a long time.

But I got my break.

A big one.

I landed an interview at the highest-rated station in one of the biggest markets in the country.

Washington, D.C.

A talent agent reached out to me after seeing my posts on social media. The job was for a sideline reporter in their sports department.

Okay, so a few important things to know about me ... never have I played sports—past or present. I can confidently state that joining a team of any kind will not be in my future. My brother, Levi, is the one who excels in that area.

Who am I kidding? Levi shined in every area. He still does.

Perfect freaking Levi.

But I do not enjoy sweating, running, or hiking up a hill. I'll make exceptions for escaping a wild buffalo or an F-5 tornado.

I do enjoy a good power walk. I can tear up a mall with the best of them. Take me to an outlet, and I'm straight-up fire. I'll trailblaze it like the best of them.

Get out of my way. I'm on a mission.

That's beside the point.

The point is I landed an interview at WDCN Channel 8 in the District!

Washington-freaking-D.C.

Getting an interview is one thing. I never thought I would land the position. I used the interview as an excuse to go home, see my family, and love on my niece and nephews.

Apparently making a mall my bitch isn't my only talent. I got the job.

I started two weeks ago and didn't have time to look for an apartment, so I moved back into my high school bedroom, living with my dad and stepmom in the boonies.

My first few assignments were exactly what I expected. High school basketball games and a scandal at a small local college where a female professor was having affairs with her male students in exchange for better grades.

Note the multiple.

I excelled at that assignment. Who knew all my hours of watching BRAVO for the drama would come in handy?

My questions were spot on and direct without being aggressive.

My producer was impressed.

I thought high school sports and low-level athletics drama would be my life until I did my time for a few years. What I didn't know is that *my time* would only consist of fourteen days.

All I can say is God bless the flu. Amen.

Every string ahead of me went down hard. Like they couldn't get out of bed kind of hard.

I should have felt bad.

Really, I should've.

But I didn't. Timing is everything. It sucked to be them. It also sucked that they all went out for happy hour and didn't invite the new girl.

Hello.

That would be me.

That was a blessing in disguise. I was as healthy as a horse, and they were at home, feverish, and coughing up a lung.

And that is how I got this opportunity—my big break.

Emma Hollingsworth, sideline sports reporter at *the* game in Las Vegas.

The biggest game of all the games. The one with the best commercials and extended halftime show that seems to divide our country on if it's good or not. And our home team, the Washington Founders, earned a spot to play in it.

The game was close. It came down to the very last second. The quarterback had to zip around so many players, the world was beside themselves. And when he dove into the point zone, the entire stadium erupted.

End zone. Whatever.

The secret element to this story is that I don't speak football.

Despite the fact I was freaking out in my head, I never let on that I'm as clueless as I am.

Dad and Levi gave me a crash course on the game the night before I flew out. I was so nervous about my big break, it was hard to focus.

This brings us full circle.

I wasn't invited to happy hour, the bitch and asshole gang are on their deathbeds because karma is king, and I am in Vegas and just reported on the sidelines of the biggest game of the year.

It's worth mentioning twice, the stakes could not have been higher.

So, yeah, I will toot my own horn. I killed it.

I set aside my sheer aversion to running and raced through the celebrating giants to the winning quarterback, Brett Sullivan. I thought I was going to die, but I was on a mission and got there before anyone else.

Even my cameraman was impressed.

Sullivan was sweaty and acted as surprised as the rest of the world that he scored the winning ... eh, points. He was also an absolute joy to interview. There's a boyish charm to him that was easy to mesh with. He was so ecstatic, he gave me a hug after I congratulated him and before he ran off to find his mom. He even swung me around in circles so fast it made me dizzy

Heck, I was having the best time.

My producer was figuratively kissing my ass. I can only hope that my cliquey coworkers spiked a collective fever when they watched it.

"Fuck, that was exciting. You're the shit to work with, Hollingsworth. After all this time, today has to be a top five for me, and I'm ancient compared to you."

Ross is my partner in crime and fellow track team member. All I had to do is run with my microphone and cheat sheet of football terms and questions. He had to keep up with me while lugging his big-ass camera.

And we're riding that high together. We walk through the front doors of Nebula. It's owned by the Black Resorts and is by far the ritziest in Vegas. It's not on the Strip. I'm not used to staying at places like this for work, and Ross said this is unusual. But the station wants us to stay where the Founders are staying, so here we are.

I pluck another piece of confetti from my hair, slip it into my pocket to keep as a souvenir, and glance over at Ross. "Today was the best day. I still can't believe it happened. Thank you for making me look good."

Ross is a veteran. He's been behind the camera for more than two decades. I was worried about traveling with someone I'd never worked with before, but he's been nice and supportive and not at all cliquey.

"Your secret is safe with me. I'd never know you're clueless about football. You're a natural, Emma." He hikes his enormous equipment bag up his shoulder. He should be tired. He's been hauling it around all day. "I'm hitting it. I'm exhausted. You want me to walk you to your room?"

"Thank you, but I'm good. I've never seen a place with this much security and cameras everywhere." We start to part ways when I call back to him, "And thank you for not telling anyone back at work that I'm clueless about the game. The mean team would have a heyday with that."

He laughs and presses the button for the elevator. "Never. They're fucking annoying, and I'm too old to gossip. You earned your stripes tonight, no matter if you know what a touchback is or not."

I roll my eyes. "Hey, I will never forget what a touchback is for the rest of my life."

"Don't lose all your money in one spot," he warns as he steps into the elevator.

The doors close before I have the chance to tell him that I couldn't gamble if I wanted to. I finally have a decent salary and have put myself on an aggressive savings plan to buy a condo close to the District. As much as I love being close to my family again, I don't want to commute that far.

But what I will do is buy myself a drink to celebrate not sucking.

I stuff my credentials in my backpack before setting it at my feet as I settle on a barstool. It's late. We stayed at the stadium until the teams came out of the locker rooms. I was able to talk to a few more players, but I'm glad I got to Brett Sullivan when I did. He was a sought-after man, and there was no way to get anywhere near him again. He was swarmed with national correspondents.

I wave the bartender down when he glances my way.

"Welcome to Nebula. What can I get started for you?"

I think for a moment before settling on something I rarely have. "A dirty martini, please. Heavy on the dirty."

He smirks. "The dirtier the better. Coming right up."

"Well, if it isn't little Emma Hollingsworth."

That voice.

There's no way I'd ever mistake it for someone else. It's cocky and deep. And sexy as hell.

One of a kind.

My spine straightens, and I twist faster than a Kansas tornado.

When our eyes lock, I shouldn't be surprised.

And still, the shock of seeing him overwhelms me.

Here. In Vegas.

At Nebula.

On the night of the biggest game of the year.

"Jack Hale." His name slips through my lips on a whisper.

Tall, broad, and his thick dark hair is perfectly styled. He looks like he walked off the cover of a magazine created to make the regular people jealous.

His dress shirt is open at the neck. His suit is blue, modern, and he wears it well. It's a touch brighter than navy, and somehow it makes his eyes shine brighter in the moody bar.

There's always been something about his bright blues. Combined with his sexy smirk, the two combined scream *I'm up to no good and you should join me.*

We don't get to choose our eyes. I didn't get the interesting hazel shade that Dad and Levi share. Mine are the color of freshly turned dirt.

Boring. Basic. They don't scream anything.

It's been years since I've seen him. Jack looks as good as ever.

He spreads his sharp jacket without one wrinkle in it so he can slide his hands into his trouser pockets. He cocks his head and doesn't hide the fact he's taking me in from my boring eyes to my even more boring, yet comfortable, shoes. He shakes his head when his blues focus on my browns. "It's been a long time. You're all grown up."

I shake my head. "The last time I saw you was at my college graduation party. I was plenty grown up then. You flew by so fast, you made my head spin."

He shrugs a shoulder as he approaches me to claim the barstool next to mine. "I'm a busy guy."

I swivel to face the bar. "You didn't say a word to me. You talked to Levi and left."

He throws me a smirk. "You remember every detail. And here I thought Levi got all the brains. If I didn't know better, I'd think you were a martyr in your own love story."

I roll my eyes. "Hardly. You know better."

"I'm shitting you." His knee bumps mine under the bar. "Sort of. Don't get me started on your drama-queen days in high school."

"Once an asshole, always an asshole," I say through a smile.

"Your martini." The bartender sets my glass down on the napkin in front of me. "Dirtier than ever."

"Just how I like her," Jack adds and lifts his chin to the bartender. "Manhattan."

"*Please*," I add and turn to Jack. "So you are still an asshole."

The bartender shoots me a concerned frown. "Are you good? Say the word, and I'll have this guy thrown out before you can blink. Mr. Black doesn't stand for women being harassed."

Jack leans back and puts his hands out. "Whoa. I've known her since before she was in a training bra. In fact, I knew her when she was in diapers. If anyone knows there's no bite to my assholeness, it's her." Jack turns his gaze to me when the bartender's frown deepens. "Em, throw me a lifeline."

I wave my hand up and down, motioning to all that is Jack Hale and speak to the only man in my presence with manners—the Nebula bartender. "I appreciate you. Despite the fact he has horrible manners and just talked about my training bra, he's right. He has no bite."

Jack gives the bartender a ridiculous mini bow from where he sits. "A Manhattan, *please*."

I'm not sure the bartender is buying it. He glares at Jack before turning back to me. "Let me know if you change your mind."

Jack leans to me, and I feel his deep timbre as his breath brushes the skin on my ear. "Damn. The Black Resorts are my favorite. If you get me kicked out, I'll never forgive you."

"Never being forgiven by Jack Hale?" I pick up my martini and look at him as I take a sip. Mmm. Salty and bold, just the way I like it. "Whatever will I do with my life?"

"Exactly. How you've made it this long in my absence is nothing short of a miracle." His gaze angles down to my drink before his blue eyes focus back on mine. "Who knew I'd find Emerson Hollingsworth in Sin City all by herself only to learn she likes it dirty."

I lift my glass to him. "Extra on the dirty. And this is one of the best I've ever had."

"The best you've ever had, my ass. How dare you say that when I sit in your presence."

"In your dreams."

He clutches his chest as if I just stabbed a dagger through his heart. "How did you know?"

"Jack Hale is a dreamer?" I mock a surprised expression. "I thought you only created your own realities."

"Some of us have no choice. Not all of us have a Daddy Asa."

I pick up the tall-stemmed crystal. "You were always afraid of my dad."

He rolls his eyes. "Who wasn't? Or should I ask, who isn't? I always thought your dad was a badass, but he proved it the day he bagged Keelie Lockhart now Hollingsworth. She was fucking fire back in high school."

I cringe. "Do you really have to describe it like that? How do you think I felt back in the day when my dad hooked up with my much younger counselor. And with all the other stuff I was going through? It was horrific. I was a freshman when it happened, and it was the talk of the school. Levi was oblivious. He was too busy falling in love and planning out his life at the ripe old age of eighteen."

"How long are you going to play the victim, Em?"

"It's something you never get over," I mutter. "It's a good thing I know better than to take anything you say seriously."

"Hey, I can be serious." He motions to himself. "Look at me now. One does not go from driving the Love Machine to staying at a Black Resorts property without being serious."

"Manhattan." We both turn back to the bar when a highball appears in front of Jack with a clank. The bartender shoots Jack one more glare before turning to me. "You okay?"

I do everything I can to appease him. "I'm fine. This guy is my older brother's best friend. If he throws a frog at me, you can ban him for life."

The bartender barely looks convinced as he moves on to another patron a few seats down.

"My mom would kill me if I threw a frog at a woman. I was raised better than that," Jack mutters.

"I know you were, and yet you still threw frogs at me," I tell him the truth. "It's your mouth that gets you in trouble."

He picks up his glass with amber liquid and puts it to his full lips. "I've never had any complaints. I can demonstrate if you'd like, but that'll get us both kicked out of the Nebula bar."

"Oh, I've heard."

He shrugs. "My reputation precedes me. Trust me when I say, nothing has been embellished. I'll lay my hand on the Bible to attest every word is true."

"Still larger than life. You and Levi are so different, but you managed to run the school."

He takes another sip. "I let Levi ride my coattails."

I roll my eyes. He knows that's not true. "How you two were ever best friends, I'll never know."

Jack turns to me with his glass in his hand. He rests one arm on the bar and the other on the back of my barstool. His legs are wide. He's completely open to me.

"Levi needed me back in the day. I was the yin to his yang. The defense to his quarterback. The Laverne to his Shirley."

"I've never watched it, but I suppose you're right."

He leans in closer. "You've never seen *Laverne & Shirley*? My grandma made me watch that shit when we lived with her."

Jack has been in my life for as long as I can remember. He and Levi have been best friends since before preschool—which means I've known him my entire life.

Levi is a doctor now.

Not just a doctor. A neurosurgeon.

I always said that Levi would heal the world and Jack would charm it.

I was so right.

Don't get me wrong. Jack is no slouch. After college, he went to law school and became a sports and entertainment attorney. But he doesn't practice law. He wheels and deals for athletes. The last I heard from Levi, he's made his niche in pro football.

I shift in my seat to angle myself to him and lift my drink. "Here's to a lifetime of friendship and *Laverne & Shirley*—however they represent you and my older brother."

Before he clinks his glass with mine, he adds, "And annoying little sisters who used to tell on us when we weren't doing anything wrong."

"Jack Hale, not doing anything wrong. That's a lie and you know it."

He smirks because he knows.

His glass clinks with mine, and before I bring my dirty drink to my lips, he downs the contents of his.

All of a sudden, the bartender appears out of nowhere. He must realize Jack isn't here to torment me and asks, "Another round?"

Jack looks to me and hikes a brow.

I take a bigger sip before I answer. "Sure. Why not?"

Jack lifts his chin to the bartender. "And a menu, *please*."

The bartender disappears, and Jack turns back to me. "I'm tired of talking about Levi. I want to talk about you."

I lick my lips. "What about me?"

"I'm here because my client played tonight. What I don't know is how Emma Hollingsworth landed a job as a sideline sports reporter for WDCN. And what I really want to know is when did you start running? I want to know everything there is to know about the grown-up Emerson Hollingsworth."

I toss back the last swallow of my dirty martini, lick my lips, and slide an olive off the toothpick.

Jack Hale.

No.

The Jack Hale.

What the hell am I doing?

2

GOD BLESS THE FLU

Jack

Emerson Hollingsworth.

It's been a fucking minute.

I might get invited to random cookouts at Levi and Carissa's, but it's not like I'm attending Hollingsworth holidays. And she's right, I flew by her grad party years ago like a military jet at the climax of the national anthem. I'd just landed my first client after leaving my old firm to go out on my own. I had to move back in with my mom so I could invest every penny back into my new venture.

I dropped off a card with a generous gift I could not afford at the time. I had no desire to talk about my new business or the fact I had to move back in with my dear mom because times were tight.

Not a time in my life I wanted to face Emma.

Emerson Hollingsworth had one shit year in high school. Other than that, from everything I heard from Levi and Carissa, she thrived. She lived her best life throughout the rest of her high school days and more so in college. She reported the non-news in the middle of nowhere, a place where literally nothing happens besides a herd moving through, followed by months and months of nothing but snow.

I'm in the business of representing talent. I might have struggled through college and law school and passed the bar exam by the skin of my teeth, but I had an end goal.

And I'm fucking good at my job.

I knew if I could jump over every hurdle required to do it, I'd succeed. I'm so good, I gave the double bird to Alfred C. Pike, my old boss, and left Pike Sports Agency because I refused to work the way he told me to.

Fuck him.

I quit in a blaze of glory. It's one of my fondest memories.

One of a few.

It didn't matter that my only clients included a random third-rate golfer and a champion bowler. I might not have had a winning quarterback or star pitcher back then, but that didn't mean they deserved second-rate service so I could spend my time searching for bigger and better. If I'm going to make a living off my clients, I'll treat them like fucking royalty.

Every single one of them.

When I started on my own, I landed a third-string tight end for the losingest team in the league. Injuries suck, but when they're not your client's, they're like hitting it big at a roulette table.

He got his shot near the end of the season and helped send his team to the playoffs. Not only did I get to renegotiate his contract, but I also landed him a sweet marketing deal. It wasn't for anything remotely as romantic as shoes or cereal, but it was a local car dealership.

The next year, I leveled him up to a national insurance company and a basic line of shampoo. After all, he does have great hair.

It took one client to spread the word. The rest followed.

I now represent eleven professional football players in the league, and I'm making my name in baseball.

It took four years on my own, but look at me.

I have one client in the big game.

And the star of the show is mine.

If I don't do anything more in my lifetime, I can say I made it in the profession I always dreamed of.

My grandma always says I was born with the gift of gab. Being raised solely by women didn't hurt.

What I should be focused on is renegotiating my quarterback's contract since he's now a free agent.

Or landing the deals that are romantic as fuck to someone like me. Shoes. Clothes. Fast food. Faster cars.

Hell, I'll take a regional grocery store if they're big enough and willing to shell out the cash.

I might only make three percent of my client's salaries, but I make ten to fifteen when it comes to marketing deals. That's what allows me to live my life—one I do not take for granted.

My phone blew up the moment the refs called the last touchdown and the clock hit zero. Timing is everything. But they can stew until tomorrow. I'm not above pitting corporate reps against one another. They're not the ones with the star quarterback in his back pocket.

I was too on edge to eat at the game, and I never drink when my clients are playing. After the game, I was too busy fielding phone calls and making sure my client could live his best life and celebrate. Everyone wants a piece of my guy. He's about to become a much richer man in the coming days.

Which means I am too. Time is money, and these are the moments that count.

I should be making lists and crunching numbers.

Instead, I'm laser focused on my best friend's little sister.

Emma and I grew up together.

We're friends ... sort of.

Not the kind of friends who go out or talk on the regular. Our definition of friends is because her brother has been my ride or die since we were shitting our pants before she was born.

Emma and I are familiar. Or we were.

But this is not the Emma I'm familiar with. Not at all.

I was not kidding when I said she's all grown up.

Even so, the memories don't suck even if they were short-lived.

There's nothing wrong with having a drink, right?

Hell, if I saw Levi in the middle of a casino, we'd do the same thing.

Though, if my best friend stepped inside a casino, it would only be during daylight hours. Levi is the most responsible person on the face of the earth. He'd never be three drinks into it with my little sister—if I had one—at two in the morning in a bar even if he weren't married with three kids.

We're halfway through a fancy-ass pizza, and Emma proves she's a freak and went crazy over the spicy brussel sprouts and crab cakes. She's told me all about her last couple of jobs. How this one fell into her lap like a freak accident. She went on and on about how she doesn't know shit about football and about moving back to the farmhouse into her high school bedroom, living with her dad, Keelie—the hottest high school counselor on earth—Knox, Saylor, and the shit ton of goats they still keep.

Rest in peace, Jasmine. The most talkative donkey on earth is no longer with us.

My glass hangs from my fingers as I motion to her. "You're telling me you landed the spot on the sidelines of the biggest game of the year, and your camera guy had to teach you what a touchback was during the second quarter?"

Emma's long, dark hair is messier than it was when I found her sitting alone. She's run her fingers through it more times than I can count. She's either eaten her lipstick off or wiped it away, and she's ditched the short blazer that didn't even hit her slim waist. She's down to a thin tank with no bra in sight.

My jacket is on the barstool behind me, I've released another button on my shirt, and my cuffs are rolled.

It's been an hour and a half since I found her alone.

She leans forward, and her hand lands on my thigh—closer to my knee than my dick, but who am I to complain—as she laughs out loud. "Right? I mean, when you think about the whole thing, it's ridiculous. You should've seen Dad and Levi trying to teach me about the game. They even found an old white board for visuals. All those Xs and Os might as well have been hearts and cupid arrows. I was so nervous, I couldn't focus." She leans in farther and squeezes my quad. "Let's be real. The chances of me screwing this up and making a fool of myself on the national stage were probable. Hell, this is Vegas. I would've taken that bet."

I take another sip and smother her hand with mine. "I don't know if you're a masochist or just plain lucky. I saw your interview after the game."

Her eyes light up. "You did? Why didn't you say anything?"

"Too busy catching up."

We stay connected, her hand being one with my thigh and all.

I might be holding it hostage, but she's not complaining. The damn bartender stopped glaring at me over an hour ago. I think I'm safe from being thrown out of my favorite resort in Sin City.

It wouldn't be the first time, but at least I can say I've been on my best behavior unlike the night I barely passed the bar.

Damn, that was a fun night in Georgetown.

"Yeah." She sighs and picks up her dirty drink. "It has been a long time. How are your mom and grandma?"

"They're good. Mom moved to The Plains last year. Grandma is still making waves at the assisted living place."

She takes a sip. "I've kept up with your mom, but I was so little when we were neighbors. Even so, I remember your grandma. I have no doubt she's the life of the party. She did help raise you."

"True."

No one from my present knows my past. It's not something I dwell on, and it sure as shit isn't something I share. I did what I had to do to get to where I am. There's no point in looking back. Besides Levi and a few others who have stayed constant in my life, no one knows my past.

To be with someone who does is…

Odd.

Asa was still a cop and wasn't divorced yet when we lived next door to the Hollingsworths. With a single mom and grandma, we were quite the threesome.

She picks up another piece of pizza, and for some reason that's refreshing. The last woman I dated picked at vegetables and looked like she was starving to death.

Emma plucks a cold artichoke smothered in feta sauce off

the top and pops it in her mouth. "Where did you land? Do you still live out in the country?"

"No way. I like to be close to the city. I'm in Old Town Alexandria. I bought a brownstone last year. I'm on the road most weeks during football season, but it's more than I've ever had. Hell, it's more than I need."

"Look at us." She takes another bite before setting the slice on her plate and pulling her other hand away from me. "All grown up one way or another. You're doing the real thing, and I'm faking it as I go. And still, we ended up across the country in Vegas at the same bar."

I lean back in my barstool and gulp the last of my drink. "Who would have guessed?"

She leans back in hers, but also hikes a foot up to her ass and hugs her leg. "Not me."

I bump her other knee with mine again since we're just that close. "You would've made it eventually even though you can't talk football. You got a break and took advantage of it."

"Because of the flu," she amends, not giving herself enough credit.

I mimic the words she used earlier when telling the story. "God bless the flu."

A smile breaks across her beautiful face. "They had it coming. Karma was my friend in this instance."

"Good for you, Em. Karma is never my friend."

"But you're Jack Hale," she goes on. "You don't need Karma."

I narrow my eyes. "What's that supposed to mean?"

It's late. It's been a never-ending day. I was up at the crack of dawn for my client—but I don't feel it.

I'm in an Emma trance.

She leans forward and lowers her voice like she's telling me something I don't know. Like it's a secret from the universe about my inner-self—my every demon, insecurity, and assholish ways personified.

She returns her hand to my thigh again as she leans in. Her dark hair is disheveled around her olive-skinned face. She's a Hollingsworth through and through, yet so different from Levi and her dad who are both tall and built like brick shithouses. She's even different than her mom who's tall and lanky.

Emma is not tall or short. She's also not skin and bones. Her hair is long and dark, but her eyes are darker. On any scale, she'd be … average.

But there's nothing average about her.

The curves that she does have are perfect. There's a glint in her eyes that makes you question what's going on behind them. And her hair is thick and heavy and soft.

I remember, even though that memory is from another lifetime.

"Jack Hale," she echoes my name that she just uttered, but this time softer, like a secret. "Your personality. Charisma. The fact that you're larger than life and demand attention from sea to shining sea."

"That doesn't sound like a statement. If I didn't know any

better, it sounds like you're trying to talk yourself into all those things."

She shakes her head and tips it to the side. "No. Never a question. Not about you."

I mirror her stance and place my hand on her thigh.

A smile touches her lips.

Fuck.

I give her a squeeze. When she doesn't move, I take the chance and ask her what I've wanted to ask her for what feels like decades, even though neither of us are that old. "Are we going to do this?"

Her dark eyes flare. "There's the old Jack. So presumptuous. What is it that you want to do?"

I lean in so far, I lose her dark eyes when I put my lips close to her ear. "Are we going to talk about the big, fat, fucking elephant that's been wedged between us?"

She leans back far enough to catch my gaze. When she does, she's biting back a smile. "Do you mean the big, fat elephant that happened over a decade ago?"

"Don't play coy." I give her thigh a warning squeeze on the last word. "You know what I'm talking about. The kiss."

"Oh," she drawls like she doesn't remember. But from the look on her face, she remembers perfectly. "You mean my *first* kiss?"

My tongue sneaks out to wet my lips at the memory as I lie. "How was I supposed to know it was your first?"

"Look who's playing coy now?" She shakes her head like she doesn't know what to do with me. Hell, I don't know what to do with me most days either. "And let it be noted that only you could use the word coy and still hold onto your man card."

"It's a gift. And stop deflecting. So I was your first kiss?"

She rolls her eyes. "As if you didn't know."

I shrug. "For all I knew, you went around kissing everyone. Maybe you're just a shitty kisser. I'm not one to judge. How was I supposed to know? You threw yourself at me and then ran away in the middle of Levi's graduation party."

"Whoa." She sits up straight and gives me the palm of her hand. "You went straight to *I'm a bad kisser*? What the hell? I was fifteen, Jack. And let's be real—I had a bad year."

"It was just a drive-by shooting," I deadpan. "There's no need to be so dramatic."

The toe of her shoe connects with my shin. She has the nip of a puppy, not that I'd know. I've never had a dog. "Don't make me call the bartender over and get you black-balled from Nebula."

I shake my head. "Don't talk about my balls unless you're willing to prove you're not a shitty kisser."

Her teeth find her lip, and her nose crinkles. "Was it that bad?"

I shake my head. "I'm just shitting you. You know that. Though, the smell of goat shit will always be laced with the memory."

She licks her lips like she can taste said memory. "My first kiss, tucked away in the barn at Levi's graduation party. Dad's friends were roaming the place trying to make sure no one got drunk or pregnant, and you were the rake who stole my first kiss."

I jerk back and act like her words are bullets to my heart. "I was hardly the rake. I saved you that night, Em, and you know it. I don't remember his name, but that guy was a tool. No way did you want that to be your first kiss. He was shorter than you and covered in pimples. You should be thanking me for saving you from what would have been the shittiest memory in the history of kissing."

She tries to frown.

Unlike her epic interview with Brett Sullivan, she fails. In fact, the last I checked, the interview is on its way to going viral if it hasn't already. But I haven't checked since I found her at the bar. Neither of us have glanced at our phones.

And since I'm in the business of relationships and sales and she's in the business of news, I know it's not the norm for me, and I can't imagine it is for her either.

"I feel judged," she states before going on. "Unfairly judged. For years, you've carried on through life thinking I'm a shitty kisser. Is that why you avoided me at my graduation party and made sure to never attend events at Levi and Carissa's if I was in town?"

This time it's my turn to wet my lips.

"Emma, Emma, Emma," I drone. "You think I've been avoiding you because you're a bad kisser? You were barely fifteen. I'm Levi's ride or die. Why do you think I was avoiding you?"

She leans in closer and lowers her voice to a mock whisper. "We've been over this. You're scared of my dad."

"You're the reporter. Do I have to announce the newsflash that everyone is afraid of your dad?"

She laughs.

"See?" I reach up and twist a chunk of her hair around my index finger. "You know everyone is afraid of Daddy Asa. Not to mention, I was not anxious to go to blows with Levi because I kissed his sister. It's probably the only secret I've kept from him in my entire life."

"Levi is harmless." She tosses those words out like she doesn't give a shit that her brother would've disowned me forever over it. "Since when do you care what anyone thinks?"

"I cared what Levi thought then." I shrug. "Now, not so much."

She tips her head with a smirk. "I don't believe you. But I do care that you've thought I was a bad kisser all these years."

We've touched each other on and off since I found her, so when I reach out and wrap my hand around the middle of her thigh again, it doesn't feel new even though it is.

"This is a conundrum," I note. "What are we going to do about it?"

"That depends on how scared you are of my brother."

I tighten my hand around her thigh and lean in closer. Her big, beautiful eyes are alert, and she hasn't slurred one word. She's had three drinks over a matter of hours with a shit ton of food.

"Tell me the truth," I demand. "Are you tipsy?"

She shakes her head. "Not even close. But I am high on football and high school memories."

"Fuck," I mutter. "Why do I have a feeling you're luring me into something I may regret?"

Her playful expression takes a hike into the desert, and a frown touches her eyes. "You think you'll have regrets?"

"Regret for me? No fucking way. I'd never regret a moment with you. But if this is something you'll regret? Then, yes. I'll fucking hate myself forever."

She looks into my eyes and there's nothing playful or teasing or sarcastic about her now. "I'd never want you to hate yourself over me. I'd never do that to you."

That's so fucking Emma.

She can be hell on wheels one moment and sweet as fuck the next.

That's it.

Right here, in the city of sin and at a bar that proves it with the amount of people eating and drinking in the middle of the night, I claim her face.

But I don't kiss her.

Not yet.

"Emma."

We're so close, our noses almost touch. We're breathing the same air.

She licks her lips, and her dark eyes flare. Those thick lashes flutter as she pulls in a deep breath. "Hmm?"

I brush her cheek with my thumb. "I remember everything about that moment. You weren't a bad kisser."

I feel her swallow hard. "Everyone remembers their first kiss. And mine was with Jack Hale."

"Tell me to stop." My gaze sweeps every feature of her face before focusing back on her eyes. "Say *thanks for the drinks, it was good to catch up, and goodnight*. Say it, dammit."

She shakes her head in my hands.

I brush the tip of her nose with mine. "We're not in high school sneaking around in the dark shadows. This is your last chance. Say goodbye or else."

"I'll take *or else*."

That's it.

I can't wait another second.

I pull her lips to mine.

I didn't lie about her not being a shitty kisser, but it was years ago.

We were fucking kids.

This is different.

When I slide my tongue between her lips to taste her again, she's not tentative.

She's an active participant.

I pull her closer, and she proves how much she wants it. She slides off her stool, and I pull her to me. She grips my shirt and wedges herself between my legs.

When she presses herself to me, she feels even more perfect than she looks.

She can't get close enough.

And I can't keep the blood from rushing to my dick.

"Ah-hem."

Emma tenses in my arms. I want to kick someone's ass for interrupting a moment I was not expecting.

Our eyes open at the same time we hear the bartender. "I know this is Vegas, but Mr. Black does have standards for Nebula."

I don't look away from Emma when I demand, "Check."

Emma's breath fans my face. "Yes. Check, please."

Damn.

And just when I thought this day couldn't get any better.

3

MOONSTRUCK

Emma

At least we didn't get kicked out of Nebula.

Though, after Jack's lips touched mine, I'm not sure either of us would have cared. I don't want to think about what's on the security feed.

Especially the cameras in the elevator.

Jack paid the bill and tossed the bartender two Benjamin Franklins.

Wow. Jack is a big tipper. It was either for the good service or for not kicking him out when he first sat down.

It better not have been a tip to make up for his bad manners. There's no amount of money to make up for a lack of please or thank yous in life.

I know Jack enough to know that would never be the case. If anything, he was overly polite to my mom when we were growing up. So much so, she'd roll her eyes and tell him to quit sucking up.

Still, we couldn't get out of the bar fast enough.

When Jack pulled me into the elevator, I had no idea where his room was, but we went up and up and up, so many floors past mine that's being paid for by the station. So high, he had to use his keycard to select the floor.

Jack pinned me to the elevator wall and claimed my mouth more possessively than he did in the bar.

Damn.

Was he holding back down there?

If Jack ruins sex for me forever, I'll kill him myself.

We were all hands and lips and desperation with a dash of teenage angst from back in the day.

I was able to push my hands between us enough to yank his dress shirt from his trousers and make quick work of the buttons. When I placed my hands on his bare, muscled chest for the first time, my head swam and goosebumps spread over my arms.

How many times have I seen him like this?

Working out.

Swimming.

After a lacrosse match back in high school. If they won, Jack would rip his jersey and pads off and go caveman in celebration.

He's always been one to demand attention. I was always happy to give it to him, but quietly.

Secretly.

From the sidelines where no one knew.

When the elevator doors part, Jack doesn't move other than jutting his muscled arm out to hold the elevator and focus his bright blues on me. "You sure you want this? Say the word, Em. I'll walk you back to your room. We'll forget this ever happened just like that first kiss back in the barn."

I slide a hand up his abs, over his peck, and flick his nipple with the blunt nail of my index finger.

His lips part, and his breath fans my face. His thick, dark hair isn't perfect and styled like it was when he surprised me at the bar. It's disheveled and mussed and looks like he's already had sex.

"Don't you dare take me to my room."

He stares down at me like he doesn't believe me or is trying to talk himself out of this.

"Jack," I call for him. "I'm not fifteen. I want this."

He leans down and presses his lips to mine once more before he aims a heated gaze at me that looks more like the Jack I know.

I get a smirk and a chin lift.

I think he just melted my panties.

He pushes away from the wall and claims my hand in his big one. "It's go-time, baby."

Okay.

Panties?

What panties?

Officially disintegrated.

I bend to grab my blazer and the bag I dropped to the floor when I needed all ten fingers to get a head start undressing him. He takes my bag from me and heads out of the elevator, pulling me with him.

Jack is on a mission. I laugh when I'm forced to skip to keep up. "And here I thought I was done running for the day. Had I only known I needed to conserve my energy for this."

A playful smile hits me when he looks back as we turn a corner and head to the end of the hall. "It's Vegas. We won the big game, and I get you. I'm on a winning streak, baby. There's no stopping us now."

He stalks all the way to the end of the hall and digs a keycard from his pocket one last time. I think my nipples go hard, or harder, when the door beeps and the lock slides open.

Me and Jack.

I'm really doing this.

And I can't fucking wait.

The hotel door bangs against the wall in a rush of sexual energy.

Holy shit.

This is nothing like my room.

I have no idea if this is a suite or a penthouse. Everything about Nebula screams class, money, and sophistication. I thought my room was elegant, but it's nothing like this.

I hardly have time to look through the vast living area through the floor to ceiling windows. We're not on the Strip, but I can see it lit up on the horizon framed only by the mountains and full moon.

I love the moon at every stage. Dad always said I was moonstruck when I was little. I remember thinking it would follow me wherever I went and always return, no matter how big and fat it was or skinny or disappeared altogether. It always returned to me.

Some people check the weather daily because of the sun.

I want to know if the night sky will be clear.

In the whirlwind of the last few days, I haven't checked once. I forgot that tonight was a full moon.

After my entire life of loving the moon, tonight feels different. Like it showed up just for me.

Surprise, Em. I'm back.

Congrats on your big break.

You made it.

And you're even bagging Jack Hale in the same day.

Look at you soar, just like me.

There's something so beautiful and not Vegasy at all about the view. Like I've fallen into an alternate universe where reality isn't a concept and I'm someone I don't recognize.

Like being a runner.

And hooking up with my brother's best friend.

Jack tosses my bag across the room, and it lands next to the full bar with a thud. His suit jacket isn't far behind, leaving him standing in the middle of the opulent space looking like a mouthwatering delicacy with his rumpled dress shirt hanging open.

Unimpressed with the moon and view, his focus is solely on me.

He claims my face again, and I can't get over how good it feels. "Anytime you change your mind, say the word."

I shake my head, but my words are very different. "This could get messy."

He hikes a brow. "Oh, this is the dirtiest cluster I've ever gotten myself into, and I'm me. The thing is, I'm here for it as long as you are. Maybe longer if I have anything to say about it."

I press myself to his bare chest and tell him the truth. "This is crazy."

His dazzling smile hits me. I'm sure it's won over women like me, charmed old ladies, probably gotten him out of trouble more times than he can count. Jack is so full of life, he brims with charisma.

But right now, high in the sky in the Vegas desert with only my moon as a witness, he's all mine.

I'm not sure what will happen after tonight, but I don't care.

"I've never wanted anything crazier." When he says it, it sounds like an admission. Like it's something out of his reach or something he thinks he doesn't deserve.

I wiggle out of my shoes, kick them to the side, and push up to my toes. He meets me halfway for a kiss that's different than the few we've shared so far—the bar, the elevator, and even the one in the barn years ago.

Its intensity is deep. Its tenderness is meaningful.

It's more than a kiss.

It feels like a promise.

But no kiss can guard against how crazy or messy this might get.

Only my heart can do that.

And, still, there's no way I'd stop.

I lose his hands on my face. He wraps his arms around me.

Jack stands at six feet tall, and from the feel of him, he still lifts like he did in high school. I feel like a feather when he picks me up. We never break our kiss when I wrap my legs around his trim waist and my arms around his wide shoulders.

My focus isn't on the view, his suite, or asking why he needs such an elaborate room in Vegas.

The only thing I can think about is this. Jack, me, and his long, hard cock pressed between my legs.

His hands on my ass squeeze, his fingers digging into my flesh through my pants.

And it feels so damn good.

He breaks our kiss just long enough to reach for the hem of my cami with the built in bra when my feet hit the floor. He pulls it up and over my head, leaving me bare from the top up.

His gaze stutters on my breasts, but his fingers don't miss a beat.

They go straight to my waistband.

"Best day ever," he mutters before looking up at me as he makes quick work of my button and zipper. "And I'm going to make sure it ends even better for you."

He pushes my pants down, taking my panties with them.

And, just like that, I'm standing in nothing but my jewelry and a couple random tattoos I got in college that you can only see when I'm in a bikini or naked.

Like now.

He rips his dress shirt down his arms followed by his belt. But he never takes his eyes off me. "Ask me what my goals were before I walked into that bar, Em. It was to have deals signed for shoes, a cell carrier, and maybe beer. Ask me what my goal is now."

I can't answer. All I can focus on is watching him rip open his trousers and reach inside his boxers to adjust himself.

He doesn't wait on me to make a guess. "My new mission in life is to rock your world. And I'm going to do it more than once."

My eyes widen as my gaze shoots from his bulging boxers to his face.

Jack Hale has a personality bigger than a super moon. Part of that is his sarcastic, smartass humor.

But there's nothing funny about him now.

He's dead serious.

"Jack—" I start, but he surprises me when he picks me up again.

This time, we're nothing but skin on skin. My breasts to his pecs. My sex is bare and open and pressed to his abs. This time when his hands come to my ass, they don't just squeeze, they roam.

"Damn," he hisses. "You're so fucking wet. I can't wait to taste you."

I suck in a breath from his words and his actions. My head falls back when he spears me with two fingers and spreads my wetness to my clit.

I draw my knees up to sink down onto his hand.

Instead, I lose his touch when he tosses me on the bed. I land with a light bounce on the soft mattress and luxurious bedding.

Every nerve in my body is aware of the sensations happening around me.

There's a lot going on.

I fist the white duvet as Jack drops to his knees at the side of the bed and parts my legs. I barely get to glance down my bare body when his mouth lands on my sex.

"Oh my—" My choked words call out through the quiet space before my gasps and moans take over.

My thighs are lifted high and wide, his fingers this time biting into the skin of my hamstrings where he holds me in a vise.

His lips and tongue.

Talented and strong and full of energy.

He fucks me with his tongue before lapping his way to my clit.

I get a circle.

A flick.

A suck.

I have a vibrator. I've even had a couple long-term boyfriends. But nothing has been like this.

This is new and different.

And we haven't even done the deed yet.

Every thought of what's to come escapes my brain. Maybe I should be embarrassed that I'm too anxious or merely turned on by the thought of being right here with Jack. But when my orgasm washes over me from top to toe, I can't think of anything other than what's going on between my legs.

It's all consuming.

I hope the walls of Nebula are soundproof, because when I call out, I don't care how loud I am. All I can think about is the feeling of falling off the ledge and Jack not letting up.

Jack doesn't allow me to move. He's driving my orgasm at his own will.

And his determination is second to none.

He finally lets up when my body is limp and one with the bed. I jerk when he surprises me and nips the inside of my thigh. Then, what I'm quickly learning is that Jack has a whole side I don't know.

In a complete one-eighty from the bite on my delicate skin, his lips make their way up my body in soft kisses.

Like a breath, teasing me, making me want more.

His chest covers mine as his big hand smothers my sex in a grip that's possessive and is like nothing I've ever had before.

"So fucking sweet," he murmurs against the skin of my neck where his nose and lips hover.

I drag my limp arms up his body and run my fingers over his lats. His back is as rock hard as his chest, and his skin is smooth.

He presses his lips under my chin before looking down at me. "If I don't have a condom stashed away in my shaving kit, put me out of my misery fast so I don't die a slow painful death from a case of Emerson-induced blue balls."

He has me pinned to the bed so I couldn't wrap my legs around him if I wanted to. "Do you mean to tell me *the* Jack Hale doesn't travel with a mega-sized box of condoms?"

He narrows his eyes and gives my sensitive sex one more squeeze. "You're not the only one who's grown up. I'm fucking selective."

"Well, then." The effects of my orgasm slowly wear off. I drag my hands up his sides, over his shoulders and neck, until they land on his face where I frame his strong, square jaw. "I'm the lucky one."

He shakes his head before pressing his lips to mine.

He's a cocktail of bourbon and me and a dream.

The tip of his finger flicks my sensitive clit before he says with a demand laced in his tone, "Do not move. Not one fucking inch. I want to see you just like this when I come back."

My fingers tense on his jaw. "God's speed. If you die of blue balls tonight, I'll feel really bad."

A smirk touches his lips as he releases my sex. I let out a yelp when he gives me a smack on my left ass cheek. "Women have all the fun."

"Only with generous men like you," I amend, giving credit where credit is due.

He kisses me one more time before I lose his heat, and he stalks through the dim space to the bathroom.

I don't obey his orders. I tuck my legs into myself and pull a pillow into my chest.

I lift my head when I hear him return to see a satisfied expression.

I also see nothing but Jack holding up a square foil between his index and middle fingers.

And when I say nothing, I mean *nothing* else.

I toss the pillow to the side and push up to my forearms to get a better look.

Because Jack naked deserves my undivided attention.

Jack has always been a brute. There was a reason he was a goalie in high school. There's nothing lithe or lanky on him. He's solid, thick, and rugged.

And as he stalks toward me with nothing but a condom and a promise, I'm taken aback by all that is him.

I can't tear my eyes away.

His wide shoulders, chest, and waist narrow down to a V that points directly to his erect cock.

It bobs and sways as he stalks toward me. The closer he gets, the details of his beautiful body become more defined.

A vein.

A bulging tip.

And manscaped everywhere.

Jack is not lacking in any department.

I lick my lips and squeeze my thighs together.

He bites the foil between his teeth and rips. When he rolls the condom down his thick shaft, jealousy eats at me.

"I want to do that next time," I admit.

"Next time, we'll play. Go slow. I'll savor you." He bends at the waist, and his hands land on either side of my head. He dips and takes my mouth one more time before gazing into my eyes. "I haven't even had you yet, and I can't fucking wait for next time."

I try to bite back my smile.

I fail.

I don't know what's happening or where this is going. If it ends here, it is what it is. I didn't chase Jack to his fancy suite with any thoughts beyond tonight.

I was too caught up in the moment. Jack has a way of demanding that from everyone around him.

But tonight is different.

The energy crackling between us feels different.

He doesn't break our gaze when he hooks an elbow under my knee. I feel his engorged tip right where I want it.

Jack gives me an inch, then stops.

I pull in a breath, anticipating him. All of him.

"Emma," he calls for me, as if he doesn't have all my attention into the next decade.

"Hmm?" I hum, not able to form words.

His hand comes to the top of my head to stroke my hair as his next words hit me low and gruff. "Mark my word, there will be a next time."

He doesn't give me a moment to let that sink in.

He surges into me in one go.

4

BEST DAY EVER

Emma

My eyes fall shut as I take in the feel of him. My body has no choice but to form to his.

His hand on the top of my head fists, and he gives my hair a little pull. This time his tone is tense when he demands, "Are you okay?"

"Okay?" I bring my hands to his face. He doesn't move a muscle and stays planted deep inside me. I lift my head far enough to press my lips to his and learn something about myself I didn't know—I'm not above begging. "I've never been this okay. Ever. Please."

His blue eyes intensify as he gives me what I want.

He pulls out and pushes back in.

Again.

And again.

The more he moves, the wetter I get, and our bodies become one. He lifts my leg higher and wider the harder he moves. Every time he takes me with more force, he rocks into me in a way that hits my clit just enough, I need more.

I arch my back.

I've never come during sex. Not like this.

"Harder."

When the word slips from my lips, it ignites the man above me.

He gives me what I want. Every muscle in his body goes taut as he takes me.

When my second orgasm washes over me, it's different than the first. It's unlike anything I've ever had before. Maybe it's because Jack is inside me. Maybe it's his sheer strength or girth or his intensity.

Maybe it's just Jack.

All I know is when I come, I don't see anything but stars when I call out for him.

Either he was waiting for me, or it pushed him over the edge. He groans when he comes. His last two thrusts are the icing on the cake I didn't know I needed.

The luscious dessert to top off a perfect day.

I hope it was half as good for him.

Let's be real, he did all the work.

That's proven by the fact his warm skin is covered with a light sheen of perspiration.

Sex sweat.

Jack can work me out any day of the week.

Way better than running sweat.

Or any other sweat-inducing activities for that matter.

And it's proven by the fact I'm spent. As I lie here in a relaxed state of sexual exhaustion, my brain slowly starts to come back to reality.

And I can't help but wonder what's next.

Do I leave? Do I roll over and pass out and deal with the talking portion of the hookup in the light of day?

Lips hit my neck for a little suck. Not enough to leave a mark, but enough to tell me that the man I've known all my life isn't tired.

Either he's still hard or half-hard. Hard enough to press into me before he murmurs in my ear, "I need to deal with this condom. Come with me."

I force my eyes open and shift my gaze to his dazzling blues that shine through the dimmed space. "Do you need help?"

His immediate smile is the only thing in my world.

Forget being moonstruck.

If I don't guard my heart, I might be Jackstruck.

Jack

"Jack, I don't think I can," she says.

I twist her nipple. "Your body says otherwise. You're so fucking wet again."

"Mmm," she moans. "You're mistaking me for the fancy-ass shower."

The shower is huge. Bigger than the one I have at home, but I don't have this many shower heads and jets. The thought of having Emma like this makes me want to go through the hassle and expense of ripping the thing out and starting all over so I can recreate this moment with her whenever I feel like it.

Okay, when we feel like it.

I am a giver.

Water washes over us as her head falls back to my shoulder. Her hands are pressed to the marble wall. Despite coming as hard as I ever have, my dick hasn't had enough. I'm pressed to the small of her back and on my way to giving Emma her third orgasm.

I might be a giver, but usually not this much.

But fuck. I could watch her come all day.

And all night.

Even if we are exhausted.

The Playbook of Emma

She might say she can't go again, but her body doesn't agree.

I pulled her from the bed and into the bathroom. She didn't even try to hide the fact she enjoyed watching me ditch the condom. So when I turned on every jet and shower head, she didn't complain. I took her hand, and she followed with as much enthusiasm as she did when we left the bar.

I washed her hair and took my time lathering her up. There's not a hesitant bone in her body because she did the same to me. By the time I turned her back to my front and reached between her legs, she leaned into me and gave me the space I wanted.

I've been teasing her clit ever since. But I'm only teasing.

I didn't plan on fucking her as hard as I did. But when she asked for it, things got out of control. In a way I'll never forget.

"Jack." She shifts her hips forward to find my touch.

I run my nose along her temple. "I thought you said you couldn't."

"You're too much." She tips her face to me. She's makeup free and her hair is almost jet black from the water.

And she's all mine.

While I've got her right here. If the saying goes that what happens in Vegas stays in Vegas, I'll be forced to take action.

"Forget golf or rowing. Edging you is officially my new hobby."

"Rowing." She mutters the word like a complaint when I trace the bare lips of her pussy without touching her where she wants it most. "That sounds horrid."

"Not on the Potomac," I argue and drag my nail across the tip of her hardened nipple. "I'll take you."

"Only if you do all the work." Water droplets dot her thick eyelashes when she looks up at me. "We can act out our own Victorian postcard. I'll ride, drink wine, and eat cheese with my sunshade umbrella. A lady can't get too much sun."

I lick the water from my lips. "No one has ever asked me to recreate a postcard."

"I've never had three orgasms in a row. Reality and dreams are two different things."

I stop what I'm doing and cup her like I have before. The tips of my fingers dip into her pussy as I press my hand into her needy, swollen clit. "Is that a dare?"

Her eyes fall shut, and she presses into my hand. "To recreate a postcard? Yes. I dare you to be that gallant and chivalrous."

My hold on her tightens. "Like this?"

She arches her back. "This is anything but gentlemanly."

"You didn't complain when I had my mouth between your legs."

"That was orgasm number one. I was too swept away in the moment."

I pull my hand from her and spread her with my fingers, careful to touch her everywhere but where she wants it most. "You didn't complain about the second when you came from me fucking you."

She opens her eyes and smiles. "You're really going to suck at recreating the postcard if you talk like that."

"Yet here you are." I move the tip of my finger close enough to her clit to tease her. "You might be talking about another era, but your body is begging for a third orgasm."

"I've not begged once…" She shifts her hips and presses her back into my chest. "…this time."

"I don't know how much hot water we have, and we could use a couple hours of sleep after today. You, especially, since you're not used to running."

Her dark eyes fly open and her body tenses against mine. "Sleep? Here?"

This time I give her what she wants.

I circle her clit with the lightest pressure. "Do you really think I'm going to send you on your way after tonight?"

She licks her lips and lifts a naked shoulder. "I didn't want to assume…"

My view does not suck looking down at her bare body. Her tits rise and fall in tandem with her breaths. Feeling her and seeing her wet and pressed bare against me is something I could get used to.

And definitely something I'm not giving up. Especially not tonight.

I lean down and take her mouth as I stop teasing her. Her moan vibrates against my tongue. When I finally break our kiss, I murmur against her lips, "Are we going for a three-peat or what?"

Her head falls against my shoulder once again as she leans into me, enjoying every touch I offer. "Maybe you can teach me sports lingo. I'm going to need it with my new job."

I add two more fingers and give her what she wants. "A threepeat it is. And I'll teach you things you never knew you needed to know."

I don't waste another moment.

She lets go of the shower wall and only hangs onto me. I hold her tight as we go for a third.

Her first kiss.

Her first threepeat.

I missed all the firsts in between, but I'm back.

As she falls apart in my arms for the third time tonight, I wonder how many other firsts I can invent just to say they're mine.

Emma

I stare out the floor to ceiling glass at the moon as Jack climbs into bed behind me.

His chest hits my back right before he spoons me in the middle of the big, soft bed.

He swipes away my wet hair. "You want me to shut the drapes?"

I shake my head quickly. "No. It's a supermoon. I'm a little obsessed."

"I think I might be too." He drags a hand down my bare body until it lands low on my hip. "But not with the moon. How long are you in Vegas?"

I stare at the engorged amber-hued ball floating in the sky. "I leave tomorrow. We take off at one-thirty."

"I wonder if we're on the same flight." His voice is low and hoarse. He sounds as tired as I feel. "My guy is headed out for commitments tomorrow, and I have a million meetings lined up with potential endorsements. I'd usually follow him, but I trust him. Of all my clients, he handles himself the best. Hell, after today, I'll probably have more knocking on my door. I need to get home and work."

I stare out at the dark sky and think about home.

"I've barely had a chance to breathe since I got the job at WDCN. I assume they'll send me back to high school sports. Maybe a chess match."

I feel a smile form against my hair.

I yawn. "Maybe not chess. But it is a game, so who knows."

"If they assign you to the chess circuit, they're idiots. Your interview with Sullivan went viral. Who the hell knows? It's probably still circulating. There's good viral and bad viral. As an agent, I know the difference. I'm sure you'll be upgraded to at least … I don't know, ping pong."

I nudge him in the shin with my heel. "Don't piss me off, Jack. I'm relaxed and sated from my threepeat."

"Hey, I'm not knocking ping pong. My grandma plays at the assisted living center."

I yawn. "That's because your grandma is a badass."

"True."

"I did my job. I'm still a newbie. I'm sure I'll go back to bowling, and that's okay. I liked it." Then I contemplate what I haven't had a chance to since we've been naked and busy since we got here. "Why are you staying in such a fancy suite?"

"I've been here all week, and my guy is a star. I've hosted meetings and get togethers about details I'm not willing to discuss in the bar or lobby. I don't need competitors watching or the media reporting on shit before it's announced."

"The media," I murmur. "They're pesky like that."

I feel and hear the deep chuckle come from his chest. "I love and hate the media, but after tonight, I have a newfound appreciation for beautiful sideline reporters."

"At least you're not referring to me as your best friend's little sister."

There's no chuckle this time and his tone lowers an octave. "About that—"

"I'm tired, Jack. The last thing I want to talk about while we're naked is Levi."

"Fine." He presses his lips to the top of my head. "But whatever happens, we're exploring this at home."

Home.

I smile at my trusty friend once more—the big, beautiful moon—before I let the activities of the day and night push me into sleep.

Despite his mention of Levi, it's the best day ever.

5

WORST DAY EVER

Jack

I feel something shift on top of me.

Fuck, I'm hot.

I bring my hand up at the same time I open my eyes. I feel bare skin and see a mess of wavy dark hair.

When I stretch, she lifts her head and her dark, sleepy eyes hit me. "Hey."

My hand constricts on her ass. "Hey, yourself."

She gives me a weak smile before burying her face back into my chest. "I have morning breath."

"I don't know anyone who doesn't when they wake up." The sun shines brightly through the windows, and I have to squint to look over her head to check the time. "Checkout is in two hours. You want a ride to the airport?"

She rolls off me and reaches for her phone. "I'm traveling with my cameraman. I can't exactly ditch him to ride to the airport with a strange guy. That will surely get back to the station. I'm already not invited to happy hour. I can't have it getting around that I hooked up with someone on a work trip."

I lean up on an elbow and frown. "But we're childhood friends."

She fists the sheet at her tits and turns to me before unlocking her cell. "Correction, you're Levi's childhood friend. We have never been friends. You threw a frog at me on the school bus when I was in kindergarten."

I don't try to bite back my smile. "I forgot about that until you mentioned it last night. We had to pull over so the driver could find it."

"Right." She does not smile at the memory. "And Levi threatened to cut off the hair on all my barbies if I told on you."

"And still I was your first kiss, gave you a threepeat, and fucked you to the moon and back last night—wait, no. The supermoon. Talk about an epic comeback. The fact I wasn't awarded MVP in Sin City is, in fact, a sin."

She rolls her eyes, turns back to her cell, but doesn't make a move to get out of bed.

I push the sheet down to my waist to get some fresh air since I spent the last two hours being deliciously smothered by Emma.

"Tell your cameraman you'll meet him at the airport. Make up something. I've got a limo scheduled. There's no need to waste it all by myself."

Emma gasps.

"No need to be impressed," I go on. "Limos are a dime a dozen in Vegas."

"Holy shit," she exclaims as she yanks the sheet off me. "I've got to go."

She scrambles out of bed with the sheet, and I'm left naked.

Don't get me wrong. I don't mind being naked, but I'd rather not be naked alone.

"What's wrong?"

Her hair is a mess from drying overnight as she feverishly scrolls her phone. What she doesn't do is answer me.

I stand, not at all concerned about my state of nakedness. I work out fucking hard to look as good as I do.

"Emma, what is it?" I demand.

"I've got to go," she repeats, but doesn't make a move. She keeps reading while she pushes her messy mane from her face. "There's a story. It's breaking. My producer wants me there, in like… Shit, thirty minutes ago."

All of a sudden, my phone vibrates with a phone call.

I look down at the nightstand and tense when I see the name flash across my screen.

I look at the time.

What the hell? He's supposed to be on a theme-park float with princesses and dogs and mice for fuck's sake.

I don't let it ring a second time and slide my finger across the screen. "Hey. Tell me you're calling me from a fucking princess float."

"Jack ... um, I don't know what to say."

I look up and Emma is staring at me from where she stands on the other side of the bed.

I grip the cell and narrow my eyes. "You can say you're at the fucking parade acting like the fucking superstar you were last night. Because when I left you after the game, you were on your way to a private jet to fly across the fucking country on a red-eye to get there."

"Um, yeah." He takes a deep breath. "I'm at the parade, but you're not going to be the happiest person on earth. I'm fucking not."

"Man, I'm getting ready to toss a mountain of endorsements at your feet today. Why am I not going to be happy?" I hiss.

Emma gathers the sheet so she doesn't trip over it when she tries to run to her clothes.

I move in front of her for the block and put a hand to her abs to stop her.

Brett Sullivan keeps talking even though he does it through a wince. "I had a bit of a problem last night."

I look at the clock again, as if the time has changed drastically in the last few moments. "And you're just now calling me? We've been over this. You get a parking ticket, you call me. You have a breakup, you call me. You fart in the wrong direction, you fucking call me. If you had trouble last night, why am I just now hearing about it?"

"I know, Jack. But the thing is, I don't know what happened. I blacked out at a party. When I came to and realized what time it was, I grabbed a cab to the airport. I'm here, but everyone around me is talking. I don't know what to do. And now … pictures. They're fucking everywhere."

"Brett." Emma's eyes go big when I bite out his name. I realize in our sex-craved cloud, I never verified that my client is none other than her viral interview. I drag a hand down my face and pull in a deep breath for patience. "Tell me what happened."

"I don't fucking know!" he growls across the line.

In fact, he yelled it so loud, Emma heard. She purses her lips together and slowly turns the screen of her cell to face me.

I take in what I see. It's one picture even though Brett said there were multiple.

There was a time in my life that I was a drama magnet, so I know.

This one picture is bad enough. If there are more to corroborate what's going down in this graphic, it can only get worse.

But I've also been doing this long enough to realize there's not much I can't manage, spin, or just outlast.

It's a modern-day miracle, but I've become more patient than the American public. My third-rate tennis star with a temper gave me the deep-dive lesson on patience. Sure, fans and the media can get up in arms about throwing a camera across the net, but they also forget just as fast.

I call it the SpongeBob Effect.

The lack of long-term memory coupled with the lowest standards in the history of humans is a good thing for people like me with clients who fuck up.

But never in my life did I think Brett Sullivan would be one of them. That's why I felt good about leaving him to celebrate last night instead of babysitting him.

Sidebar...

Brett Sullivan is a midwestern boy who grew up on a farm outside of Omaha, Nebraska. He helped his school win two state championships in a row thanks to a stellar high school coach. He killed it in college before being drafted. I picked him up two years ago and got him signed with the Founders. He was a second-string quarterback, but I had a good feeling he'd get his shot.

I was right.

Ironically, Brett got his big break when the starting QB, Mark Morse, went down with an injury. He was out for the first six games of the season.

Morse isn't immune to drama or injuries. He's played in the pros for years. I knew it would only be a matter of time.

Brett took advantage of all six weeks to prove himself. He went undefeated. Six weeks passed, Morse's doctors and therapists glued him back together, and he demanded his starting position back.

The Founders not only lost the next two games, but those losses were so epic, I was jumping with fucking joy.

Brett was put back in, and the chemistry returned to where it was the first six weeks.

Not only that, the press ate it up.

So did the fans. Brett is a single, good looking, professional football player. I'm as straight as they come and even I'll admit, the man could melt butter in the arctic.

He also manages a foundation that offers more than a million dollars in college scholarships every year. Ten lucky kids get a different start in life than they would have because of him.

Brett Sullivan is America's homecoming king and wet dream rolled into one.

What he's never done is gotten a parking ticket or farted in the wrong direction.

But all that flies out the window as I stand here buck-naked staring at the graphic on Emma's cell.

A graphic that has over two million views and is clicking up as I stand here naked and flabbergasted.

I drag a hand through my messy hair. "What the fuck did you do?"

Emma's dark eyes flare.

"I'm sorry, Jack," Brett says. "I'm so fucking sorry."

Emma

The man I had life-altering sex with last night stands in front of me like he's wearing a custom three-piece suit rather than the one he was born with. It's hard not to appreciate his beauty and the way he's confident in his own skin.

I had no idea Jack represented Brett Sullivan. I went on and on about my epic interview last night, and he never said a word.

I pull my cell to my chest, grip the sheet, and try to move around him, but he side steps me with a curt shake of his head.

My phone vibrates again. When I look down at it, three little words that make up a force in my life appear.

Dad is calling.

I cannot talk to my dad while I'm naked with Jack. Hell, I can't talk to my dad while I'm naked with anyone, but especially Jack Hale. Dad always gave Jack the side-eye in high school. And I haven't been around in years to see if those feelings have lived into adulthood, but now is not the time to find out.

I send him to voicemail.

Jack's expression turns from shocked to angry to something else wholly that I don't recognize. He's not the playful, charismatic man who I couldn't wait to rip my clothes off for last night. Hell, he might as well be a snake charmer. I would've followed him anywhere.

He looks like his whole world is falling apart around him.

He drags a hand down his face before pulling in a deep breath. "Listen to me, Brett, and listen closely. Forget about the pictures. Forget about what happened. We'll deal with it when we get back to D.C. The only thing I want you to do is get on that damn float and look like you're the happiest person on earth. Wave and smile. I don't give a shit if you do a dance. The moment you look like anything is wrong, the fucking media will have ammunition. Do you understand me?"

The fucking media.

Huh.

That would be me.

Which drags me back to reality. I need to call my producer and Ross. Now that I know Brett Sullivan flew across the country while I was doing the dirty with his agent, I'm not sure what more we can do in Vegas besides report a quick update before catching our flight back home.

But I know where Brett will be by the end of the day.

I cannot miss my flight.

Brett must not be arguing about pretending to be happy, because Jack adds one last demand, though it comes out as a warning. "And for fuck's sake, do not talk about this to anyone. You have no practice with shit like this. No one is your friend right now besides me. Got it?"

Brett must get it.

Because Jack doesn't say goodbye. He slams his cell on the bed where he just rocked my world a few short hours ago. "Fuck!"

"I've got to go." I hurry around the man who I've known all my life, while not having any idea how comfortable he is standing around naked. "I've got to call my boss back and head to the airport. It seems you have…" My words trail off as I collect my clothes from every corner of the room where Jack threw them last night after he ripped them off me. "Things to do too."

It's a miracle I haven't tripped over myself on the way to the bathroom when Jack blocks the door I'm about to slam in his face. The fact I'm looking for some privacy when he washed me from head to toe in this very space is ridiculous, but the sun making an appearance and quarterback drama has a way of humbling a gal.

There's no way I can shut the door when his thick arm holds it high over my head. "You cannot report on this. I know my client. There's got to be an explanation behind what happened. Do not make this worse, Emma."

I drop my clothes to the floor and put my free hand on my sheeted hip. "You think I could make this worse? Do you remember anything I said last night? Just last week, I barely got any airtime at a high school basketball game. I'm a nobody who just wants to keep her new job. Anything I do in the next twenty-four hours is nothing compared to what your client did to himself. You saw the pictures. I mean, we're in Vegas. Lots of shit is legal here that isn't in other places. So many other things he could have celebrated, but he chose the illegal ones."

Jack brings his hand up and enunciates every word that spills from his mouth as he points at me. "Trust me, I know what it's like to push the boundaries, but Brett Sullivan is not that guy. His only goal in life is to score touchdowns, put youth through college who wouldn't normally have the opportunity, and work on his family farm in the off-season to help his dad. Whatever you think you just saw on the internet is not what it is. I just need to prove it."

"Jack." I lower my voice and do everything I can to keep my gaze from taking a trip south for one more souvenir from my entire experience with him. "I have to get dressed. If anything, I can't miss my flight, and it sounds like you can't either. Your quarterback isn't even in town for me to run after. I mean, thank goodness. Running two days in a row sounds like hell, even though I'd do it to keep my job. Please, let me get dressed. We're running out of time."

His expression intensifies when his tone lowers to something that sounds like a threat. He leans in closer and captures the tip of my chin between his index finger and thumb. "This isn't over, Emma. Not by a long shot. Now that this has started, there's no way it'll end until I get what I want. And I never lose."

My chin gets one last squeeze before Jack, in all his naked glory, takes a step back.

He's not the only one with moves.

I slam the door. He and all his extremities are lucky they don't get caught in the crosshairs.

His deep voice bellows from somewhere far away in his fancy suite when he growls, "Worst day ever."

After I lock myself in, I freeze when I catch a glimpse of myself in the mirror.

Holy sex on wheels, I'm a mess.

In more ways than one.

Well then.

Time to move on.

I pull in a breath and reach for my panties.

I might not have known what a touchback was yesterday, but I do know drama. And when it comes to professional sports, it seems that what goes on off the field is as big as what happens on it.

Maybe bigger.

6

HOSTAGE

Emma

"Oh! Lookie here, I have great news! You've been upgraded to first class."

I blink at the agent who's checking in my luggage. "Excuse me?"

"Damn. I didn't get bumped," Ross mutters behind me. "Maybe you should move to Vegas. You're killing it here."

"It's not like I have points or tons of miles." I look from my new travel bestie to the agent. "I don't understand."

She narrows her eyes on a frown and stares at me like I'm crazy. "You don't question the first-class gods. You bow down, thank them, and accept the glass of champagne they offer you when you board."

I glare right back. I know what first class is like. I was raised by Asa Hollingsworth who does not mess around when it comes to travel accommodations. If he doesn't charter a private jet, we ride in first. "I know that. What I mean is, I feel bad. I'm traveling with my work associate. Can you upgrade both of us?"

"Sorry," she sing-songs and goes back to pecking on her keyboard. "That was the last seat. And since you're in first class, I won't charge you for your suitcase weighing in two pounds over the limit. You should get on your way. You're late. Your plane will be boarding soon."

"It's fine, Emma. I'm so tired, I'm going to sleep the entire flight. Let's get through security."

"Next!" The agent looks over my head to the travelers behind us who look like they have the patience of an over-tired toddler.

I have to double time it to catch up with Ross. "I don't know what to say. I'm so sorry. I'm half your size. You should be able to stretch out. I'll see if they'll let us trade when we get to the gate."

He waves me off and proves that a long week in Vegas chasing around professional football players and their coaches hasn't worn through his kindness, even though he continues to tease me about my viral interview. "I'm not worried about it. Maybe they know you're the next big thing in sports broadcasting. It hasn't even been twenty-four hours yet, and you're already being treated like a superstar."

"Hardly. Whatever luck I had yesterday in front of the camera wore off. Not one player or any of the Founders staff will talk to me today."

Ross shakes his head. "Their star is in a shitload of trouble. Yesterday at this time, they were talking about his new contract. Today, a suspension is the least of his troubles. Don't get your feelings hurt. They weren't talking to anyone."

Yeah, I know intimately from Brett's agent how much trouble he's in. "I tried my best. That's all I can do, which means my big break is about to come to an end. When we get home, I'm sure I'll be sent back to hauling around my own camera at high school games. It's what I was hired on for. That's fine, but I'll miss you. I'll always have my days in Vegas."

Ross glances down at me as we walk past a slew of passengers heading to precheck. "I'll put in a good word for you with the big boss. You've got a knack for getting people to talk."

Ross and I get through security and hurry to our gate. We hung around the resort as long as we could hoping to get a few words from anyone in the Founders organization about Brett Sullivan. I have a feeling everyone is utilizing the Jack Hale approach to manage the storm created by his client.

Silence.

Ignorance.

Complete and utter disregard for reality.

When we arrive at the gate, there are only a few stragglers in front of us boarding. I turn to Ross one more time. "I feel horrible sitting in first class."

"I bet you're the only news reader at the station who would feel bad about that."

I give him a light punch on the shoulder. "Wow. You just

called me a news reader. I see how it is. And here I thought we were friends."

He laughs as he steps onto the plane before me. "We are, but you're still a news reader."

I'm about to tell him how happy I am about being in first class while he sits in the back and eats flavorless pretzels and stale cookies with the commoners when I stop dead in my tracks.

Sitting on the aisle of my row is none other than the man I can still feel between my legs.

Having three orgasms and sex two times in the matter of a couple hours will do that to a girl.

He looks up at me with a hiked brow. "Is this your seat?"

I forget all about Ross who's continued on to the back of the plane and double check my seat number.

Yep.

That's my seat.

Instead of taking it like a normal, gracious person would, I stand here and block the aisle. "Did you do this?"

"What? Pay a premium to upgrade your ticket at the last minute so I could have your undivided attention for the next four hours?"

"Yes," I hiss. "Did you?"

"Fuck, yeah, I did."

I hear a gasp from the seat behind Jack. An older woman with jet black hair glares at me.

I apologize for Jack. "I'm sorry. I promise he'll be on his best behavior throughout the flight."

"The hell I will," Jack spouts and throws back the last of a Bloody Mary. He slams the glass down on the wide armrest, plucks a limp piece of celery from it, and chomps half of it in one bite. He looks up at me and talks with his mouth full. "Sit down so we can get this show on the road. I'm having a shit day and need a plan of action by the time we land on the other side of the continent."

The woman's frown deepens just as the flight attendant bends next to her and says, "May I offer you a set of complimentary headphones?"

Jack raises his voice but doesn't bother to turn around. "I'd take those if I were you. My business imploded with one fucking internet post. This is going to be a long flight."

I glare at Jack before turning my apologetic gaze to the woman who clearly isn't used to R-rated passengers. "I recommend you accept the headphones."

"Lady, take a seat so the rest of us can move through."

I look back at the man behind me wearing an ugly expression. "Sorry."

Jack doesn't shift to make room for me, so I have to maneuver over him stepping between his legs as I go. When my ass falls into my wide, plush seat, the attendant leans down and directs her words at Jack. "I should kick you off since we're still at the terminal. Consider this a warning to be on your best behavior."

Jack smiles sarcastically. It's not sexy or dazzling and it does nothing to make my panties wet.

Quite the contrary.

It makes me angry. And I rarely get angry.

He leans in close—which is a big lean since our seats are wide and spacious—and puts his lips so close to my ear, his breath caresses my skin. It's warm and familiar and reminds me when I felt it elsewhere on my body last night. "You and I have unfinished business to talk about."

I lean toward the window and frown at him since he's boxing me in. "I can't believe you upgraded my ticket. I feel like I've been kidnapped and am being held hostage for exactly four hours and forty minutes."

His smile is triumphant, like he's the one who scored the winning touchdown last night and not his client who's up to his ears in drama—both the viral and legal kind. "Maybe lady luck will be on my side, and we'll get stuck on the tarmac. Make it an even five hours. Maybe six if she's not on her period."

I glare at him. "Have you been drinking since I left you this morning? Lady luck hates you. The proof is all over the internet."

He reminds me how comfortable he got with my body last night and wraps his hand around my thigh and slides it up two inches. "Lady luck was on my side last night."

I grab his wrist and throw his hand back into his expensive seat. "That's over. The moon is gone, and the sun shines bright. Welcome to reality, Jack. I've been running around Nebula trying to get someone to talk to me or utter some type of statement. But not one word. Not even a glance in my direction. Do you know how frustrating that is?"

"No one's going to talk to you. Professional sports is a *business*. When shit hits the fan, the last thing any business is going to do is blab to the media. You're spinning your wheels, Em."

Speaking of wheels, the ones on the plane start to move. I realize the attendant is giving Jack and me the side eye for bickering during her entire safety presentation.

Like anyone pays attention to those anyway.

I lean back in my seat and close my eyes. The guilt nibbles at me since Ross has at least six inches and probably eighty pounds on me, but first class is so comfortable. I let myself sink into the seat and decide not to think about Jack holding me hostage for almost five hours.

I've been running on pure adrenaline since our phones blew up this morning. Chasing down professional football players, no sleep, and hours of flirting followed by vigorous sex sink in.

I'm exhausted.

The pilot breaks into my bubble to announce takeoff right before we start to speed down the runway.

"Em," Jack calls for me right before his fingers touch my jaw and force me to face him. When I open my eyes, he's right here in my space. I know for a fact how much sleep he got last night, but he doesn't look the least bit tired when he announces, "I have a plan."

"Good for you." I yawn. "So do I. I'm going to put on my noise-cancelling headphones and shut my eyes. My plan is to catch up on my sleep and pretend I'm not grateful for this comfortable seat. Do not touch me or talk to me until we enter the Commonwealth's airspace."

He hikes a brow. "I wore you out, huh?"

His words remind me of last night and how much I enjoyed every moment. I don't break from his hold or his intense gaze. "I was worn out before you found me in the bar. Let's say you were the nail in my coffin."

"I prefer to be the cherry on your sundae. You'll like how I taste if you give it a try."

Jack's seat jolts as it's bumped from behind.

"Enough up there!" the old lady pipes. "I'm going to tell the pilot, and you'll get kicked off the plane.

I bite back a smile.

Jack doesn't hide his. I wonder if he threw back espresso martinis before he boarded because he doesn't look tired in the least. He looks like he could go another four rounds in the sheets. His smile is dripping with sexual energy.

My ears start to pop as the plane leaves the earth. I lower my voice to barely a whisper since we're so close our noses would brush if we experience one bump of turbulence. "We'll be at thirty-thousand feet soon. Don't get yourself kicked off the plane now."

"Have you ever had sex at thirty-thousand feet?"

I shift in my seat to face him as best I can without loosening my seatbelt. "Something to know about me, Jack. I'm a germaphobe. I will hold it until I'm blue in the face before I'll even think about walking into an airplane bathroom. The only reason I didn't flip out about walking around barefoot in your hotel room last night is because it's a Black Resort property, and they're just that clean and perfect. Otherwise, my bare feet do not touch a hotel floor. I even have hotel shoes."

His lips tip on one side. "You were so distracted by me, you forgot all about the germs. I could do the same for you high in the sky if you give me the chance."

I shake my head. "My guess is you paid a pretty penny for my seat. I don't plan to leave it until we're touching the earth again. I might sleep on your shoulder, but that's all the action you're getting from me."

His fingers on my chin slide toward my jaw to cup my face. "Action with Emma ... that's something I can't stop thinking about."

"Please don't think out loud. The woman behind us will bust a vein."

He leans in and presses his lips to mine.

I don't argue or try to stop him.

I'd say it's because I'm too tired, but really, it's because I like it. The morning has been too much of a whirlwind for me to process last night.

Jack and me—what a night it was.

He breaks our kiss but doesn't say anything. Instead, he contemplates me, like he's rethinking this plan of his.

When he finally breaks our silence, he announces, "You're lucky I have fires to put out from coast to coast. Take a nap, but I'm not letting you sleep until we get to the Commonwealth. I'm waking you up over Kansas. You're a part of my plan in more ways than one. And when we land, you're coming home with me so we can put that plan into action."

My eyes widen as I shake my head. "My dad is picking me up from the airport. There's no way I can tell him I'm going home with you instead."

His jaw goes taut. "Fuck. I can't compete with Daddy Asa."

"Can I get you something to drink?"

Thank goodness the attendant breaks into the conversation. I do not want to talk about my dad with Jack.

I smile. "Water, please."

"I need my vegetables—one more Bloody Mary," Jack demands.

I glare at him.

He turns to the attendant and settles back into his seat. "Please."

Then he flips up the wide arm rest between us and reclines his seat. If we weren't in first class with more than enough space, I'd berate him for being rude. He puts his arm out and motions to himself. "Come here."

My frown deepens.

He rolls his eyes. "You slept on me last night. I'm here for you. But only until Kansas. Then we have shit to talk about."

As much as I don't want to admit it, I did enjoy the short time we slept together last night.

I tuck my feet in my chair and lean into him. His thick, heavy arm drapes down the side of my body, and his hand lands on my ass.

I'm too tired to complain.

And it feels good.

It must feel good to him too. I get a squeeze.

His lips hit the top of my head as he pulls out his cell and hooks up to Wi-Fi. "I'll see you when we're over wheat fields."

I snuggle in deeper and ignore the fact Jack thinks he can tell me how long I can or can't sleep.

I'll deal with that when he tries to wake me. It's been years since Jack and I spent time together. He has no clue who I am or what he's dealing with.

7

HOMIES RESURRECTED

Jack

We're long past wheat fields.

In fact, the farther we travel east, the worse my day gets.

It started out with one picture.

One viral picture of Brett Sullivan who looked nothing like the all-American golden boy I represent.

I saw his potential. The agent he signed with right out of the gate was shit. I've already renegotiated his contract and was about to make him a much richer man with the long list of companies who were salivating to get him to sign with them.

And when my clients become richer, so do I.

But that was yesterday.

I've spent the last four hours doing everything I can to salvage those deals.

I thought it was miserable working for the firm before I went out on my own.

That was bad, but this is hell.

And I know why Brett says he has no idea what happened, because none of it makes sense.

Drugs—and not the mild shit that's legal in small doses. The hardcore shit that is very illegal in all fifty states and around most of the world for that matter.

Women—plural. Not illegal, especially not in Vegas if there's a tab at the end of the night. But they are fucking toxic when it comes to Sullivan's image.

Finally, guns—lots of them. And not the legal kind. Especially not guns that any American can get a license for.

When it comes down to it, I'm a salesman. I wheel and deal for a living. I'm one hundred percent personality and lip service. Sure, I count on my good looks to get me through the door, but after that I need to convince them—*them* being the world around me—to do what I want.

What I am not is a gun guy.

But from the viral picture from hell, even I can see some of the guns surrounding Brett are not legal.

Drugs. Women. Weapons.

A triple whammy. Brett doesn't even have a manager. He's never needed one. When he's not playing football, practicing football, farming his family's land, or putting kids through college…

Well, I'm not sure what else he does, but it's so fucking wholesome, it doesn't require a manager to keep his shit straight.

He can do that all on his own.

All he has is me—a pissed off agent who hung his hat and reputation on a star player who was supposed to be my golden ticket to the next level.

Hell, I'm about to sign an up-and-coming pitcher from Texas based on what I've done for Sullivan. I just leveled up, and this could implode my reputation and entire business right along with Brett's.

Not that it's all about me. I'm not that much of a selfish asshole. I like Brett and give a shit about what happens to him.

Not just one.

Many, many shits.

It is why I left Pike.

I told Emma I have a plan, which I do.

It sucks, but it's a plan.

My phone vibrates where it's sitting on the wide armrest. I stopped scrolling social media an hour ago. It was like watching my career slowly spiral down a dirty gas station shitter.

I can't do anything until I land anyway, so I'm choosing to ignore it. I need a mental break and decide to take it. Besides, Emma curled into herself to fit across her seat and mine.

During the entire flight, she's slept in so many various positions, I had no idea anyone could fit in a first-class seat in so many different ways. Her head is now resting on my lap so close to my dick, I've had to adjust myself twice and had a long conversation with the guy downstairs that he had his moment last night. I need him to cooperate until I fix my professional drama so I can get back to the drama with my best friend's little sister.

I can't even think about the drama this will lead to with Levi.

But that one notification turns into a chain of them so demanding, there's no way I can ignore them.

I sigh when I glance at the screen.

I should've guessed.

A text string that isn't used much anymore, but every once in a while, someone resurrects it, even though I was the one who created it back in the day.

The Homies—a group of friends from high school. Collectively we could not be more different, but teenage drama had a way of bonding us back in the day and it never broke. Levi, Carissa, Cade, and Mason.

Levi married Carissa when they were so young, it was on the verge of creepy. Okay, that's only a slight exaggeration, but seriously, who gets married before the legal drinking age? She wasn't even pregnant nor were they in a cult, which are the only acceptable reasons to get married that young. But then again, Levi Hollingsworth was born with the maturity of a middle-aged man as opposed to yours truly, whose maturity level is still questionable every third week of the month.

The Playbook of Emma

Cade Collins is Carissa's twin and might be smarter than Levi. So smart, I'm not sure what he actually does for a living. Every time he tries to explain it to me, I zone out and start to wonder about the weather. All I know is he makes a shit ton of money to make sure corporations are safe from hackers. He lives behind a computer screen in Boston and only comes back to Virginia when Carissa puts her foot down and demands twin time.

Mason Schrock might be the glue that holds our weird group together. He moved back to his family farm when his parents decided to retire where they could plant their asses in the sand and toes in the water year-round. Mason married a Virginia Tech cheerleader he met in college. He sat front and center at every football game of the student section for Enter Sandman, and not because he loved football.

He just loved her.

It took until his junior year to make an impression, but now he's married to his redhead bombshell, Jessica. She even agreed to live the farm life with Mason when his parents gave him the farm. They have one kid with another on the way.

But the kicker is, they're famous—and not because the strait-laced, slightly-nerdy-nice guy landed the flexible hottie.

No, they are riding the coattails of their famous chickens.

So famous, Mason and Jessica Schrock retired from their D.C. corporate jobs for a slower life in the country, but thanks to the viral chickens, they're documenting their lives for millions of nosy fuckers all around the world. Mason has put his computer science brain to work on the algorithms. He's made "nice guy" cool again and brought back flannel shirts and cargos. They're making bank on product partnerships and even started their own line of candles, each scent named after a different chicken.

They don't even need someone like me to help them get endorsements. Companies are knocking on their door, waiting in line to shovel money in their bank accounts to get in on the action.

My friends are thriving, as opposed to me who's sitting in first class at thirty thousand feet hoping I make it to next week. I have a huge mortgage and an assisted living facility to fund.

Yeah, the Homie thread is hopping.

This is not what I need right now.

> Mason – I can't believe it's taken this long, so if you jerks are talking on the side and not including me in the drama, then we're going to have words at the birthday party. I know you're all busy. Heck, we're in the middle of a chicken condominium reno and need to get the heat on before the next snow, but I'll be the first to bite. Jack, what happened to your client? Did Brett Sullivan lose his mind last night?

> Carissa – Thank you for breaking the ice, Mason! We all want to know. You'd better spill, Jack.

> Levi – I'm in the clinic today, and everyone is buzzing about it. It's bigger news than the last-minute win. But can we talk about that dive into the endzone? Maybe Sullivan took a hit last night and no one knows. If you need me to examine him, I'll fit him into my schedule.

> Cade – I'm in over my head with a deadline that was due last week. I have no idea what anyone is talking about.

> Mason – At least Cade hasn't left me out of the loop. I can always count on him. Thanks, man.

> Carissa – Cade never watches the news and is allergic to social media. He wouldn't even know about your chickens if it weren't for me. I should've filled you in when the story broke, bro. Sorry.

> Cade – What story?

> Levi – I told the staff that I have an in. I need to come through for them, Jackie.

> Mason – Spill, Hale. We know you're never an arm's length from your phone. You're worse than me.

> Levi – I'll ask Emma. She'll answer. Brett seemed to be into my sister in a big way after the game. Maybe she has an in…

Fuck that.

Brett has nothing to do with Emma and never will.

> Carissa – Oh my gosh, can you imagine? Everyone is talking about the interview and wants to know everything there is to know about the new-girl sports reporter. I've seen tons of chatter about her and Brett.

Damn. I'm usually the one demanding information. It's not fun to be on the hotseat with The Homies.

They brought their A-game today.

> Carissa – Jack, we know you're here. You're always here. We want answers.

If I don't answer, they'll never stop. I refuse to be the reason the chickens freeze to death. They'll kick me out of the club.

I type with one thumb since my other hand is securely planted on Emma's ass. I do not plan to move it until we touch down in the Commonwealth.

> Me – You fuckers are demanding. I'll tell you what I can so you can get back to babies, chickens, hackers, and saving lives. Sullivan's brain is just fine. Something went down that isn't what it looks like. I'm working on damage control. But if there's one thing I know, Brett and Emma are not a thing. There. You can get back to your lives now.

> Mason – Whoa. That's it?

> Carissa – That can't be it.

> Cade – He said what he said. I don't have time for this.

The Playbook of Emma

Levi – Defensive much?

Carissa – You're treating us like the media.

Mason – Exactly. We're not TMZ. We're The Homies—Homies for life. If I remember correctly, you're the one who made us swear to it back in the day, and you're going to hold out on us?

Me – I'm not holding out on anyone. Brett is in Florida with a mouse who's only slightly more popular than Mason's chickens these days. I know what you know, but I do know it's not what it looks like.

Me – And what the fuck? I thought you were my friends. You should be more worried about my career than my client's. Thanks for having my back. Homies for life, my firm, rock-hard ass. Bounce a quarter off it—I dare you.

Cade – Deflecting with his own ass … Jack is always upping his game. Never saw that coming.

Mason – He hasn't let himself go. Maybe I need to install a home gym this year. My workout is working on the farm, but I'm not sure Jessica could bounce a quarter off my butt. Now I have new goals.

Carissa – Can we stop talking about everyone's asses?

Cade – Remember Jasmine? Now that was an ass.

> Mason – Rest in peace, Jasmine. She lived a long life with the goats.

> Me – Everyone loved Jasmine. She could've been as famous as your chickens. Daddy Asa and Keelie really missed the boat on that one.

> Carissa – Would you please stop referring to my father-in-law as "Daddy?" It gives me the ick so hard.

> Me – He's the ultimate Daddy. But I guess Levi's your Daddy now.

> Carissa – Stop. Just stop.

> Cade – I just threw up.

> Mason – And Jack is the ultimate deflector. We still don't know what happened to Brett. But we do care about your career. Sorry you're going through this. Levi, text Emma.

I have more important things to attend to at the moment. I need to be done with this.

> Me – I shit you not—you know what I know, and I'm not happy about it. Once I get home, I'll get to the bottom of this. When I find out, you and your fluffy friends will be halfway down my list to tell. I do not have the energy to stroke egos today.

> Cade – With the words ass, Daddy, and stroking tossed into the convo, I'm out. If anyone can manage drama, it's Jack. Good luck. But if you need someone to break into a system for old time's sake…

> Carissa – Shut your mouth, Cade. We're not doing that again.

> Mason – Wow. It just got real.

> Me – I might need to call you off the bench, Cade. Your mad skills could come in handy. Appreciate you.

> Carissa – Nope. Not happening.

> Cade – Good times.

> Carissa – Scary times.

> Cade – I'm out—putting you on do not disturb.

> Mason – I'm not sure I want to know if Jack puts Cade in the game…

> Me – If it comes to that, you'll all know. Until then, keep my career in your thoughts. I have a grandmother who likes her butter cookies and buying shoes.

> Levi – Emma isn't answering, guys.

> Me - I'm pulling a Cade and putting you on do not disturb. Peace out, Homies.

I've had enough. I drop my cell into the cup holder and return my attention to the woman on my lap who I grew up with. After last night, friend is the last category I want to be lumped into when it comes to Emma.

I need to fix the drama with my biggest client not only to save my career, but so I can focus on her.

I put the Homies out of my mind and return my energy to getting my client and my business back on the straight and narrow.

I've come up with something so brilliant, I even surprised myself.

"Hey." I bop the tip of Emma's nose with my index finger. "Wake up, you little narcoleptic beauty."

She doesn't open her eyes but bats my hand away like I'm a pesky fly.

I've never seen anyone sleep in such contorted positions.

"Emma," I call louder over the hum of the jet engines. "Open your eyes. We need to talk."

She stretches and lets out a little moan that reminds me of all the ways I made her moan last night.

I need to build more of that into my plan.

Her dark lashes flutter open and sleepy brown eyes gaze up at me. She unbuckled somewhere over Kentucky and twisted so her head rests on my lap.

She yawns. "Did you call me a narcoleptic?"

I brush the dark hair from her face. "I call 'em like I see 'em. Normal people don't sleep like this on planes."

She rubs her eyes. "Maybe not where the commoners fly. This is first class. What else am I supposed to do with all this space?"

I trace her bottom lip with the pad of my thumb. "I can think of more titillating activities than sleeping."

She pulls my hand away from her face and holds it between her tits over her heart. "Just when I think I know you, you say things like titillating."

I force my hand open and drag my fingers over her nipple. "I like titillating you."

"There's the Jack I know." She pulls my hand back to her heart. "Are we over Kansas already?"

"I let you sleep all the way home. We have about forty minutes until we land."

Her eyes widen, and she pushes to her ass. "You let me sleep the entire time? Thank you."

"I might go cross-eyed I have to go to the bathroom so bad, but anything for you."

"I appreciate it." She digs in her backpack until she produces a box of mints. She pops one in her mouth before offering another to me.

"Speaking of bathrooms, we still have time for me to rock your world at thirty thousand feet."

She rolls her eyes and settles back into her seat. "As good as you think you are, there's no number of orgasms that would make me forget about the germs."

I shift in my seat to face her. "Then door number two, it is. When we land, we're going straight to my place."

She hikes a brow. "That's awfully presumptuous. Sorry, no can do. My dad is picking me up from the airport. I'm sure he's already on his way. I might not be in high school anymore, but I'm still not anxious to tell my dad to turn around and go home so I can shack up with Levi's friend again. That will make dinnertime straight up weird."

"Look at who's being presumptuous now. If you want to hit it real quick, you're going to have to take me up on it before we land. That's not why you'll drop all your immediate plans and tell Daddy Asa to turn around and go back to the boonies."

"And why would I do that?"

"Because we need each other. And when I say *need each other*, I mean in every way ... professionally and carnally."

She frowns but doesn't question the carnally part.

I lean in and take up half the space of her pricey seat. "Our lives are on the brink. Your career might've been jump-started by the flu, but you said yourself you'll be demoted back to high school sports. I was about to become a quick multi-millionaire the moment Brett Sullivan signed the deals I've been working night and day on since he got his chance to shoot his shot. Not only that, but I have potential clients I'm about to sign that might walk on me if I don't get this shit sorted."

She swipes her thick, dark hair on top of her head and wraps it in a high messy do. It's sexy as fuck. I can't wait to wrap it around my fist again while I'm balls deep inside her. "It sucks for both of us. But there's nothing you can do to protect me from the mean ladies at the station, and there's really nothing I can do to save your millions. If I could do that, I'd be cashing in myself and not spending my evenings in high school gyms that smell like dirty jock straps."

"That's a shame," I say. "Even back in the day, I perfected the art of a good manscape and knew the need for deodorant."

A smile touches her lips.

"As you know since you couldn't keep your hands off my cleanly shaved balls last night."

"And what does your perfected art of manscaping have to do with my career and your millions that are on the line?"

I reach up to tag her around the neck and pull her the rest of the way to me. I lower my voice to barely a whisper when my lips brush the lobe of her ear that I very much liked the taste of last night and tell her my plan. It's my best bet at the moment, and one I know that will have her salivating the way she did when she saw me naked last night for the first time. "I can land you the interview everyone in the country wants at the moment. You won't have to do a thing besides show up."

Emma jerks back far enough so I see nothing but her sharp dark eyes. "What are you saying?"

I tell her exactly what's going to happen, because it's the only path to fixing what Brett Sullivan somehow managed to fuck up last night. "I'm saying I can get you the exclusive interview that will make all the bitches at your studio green with envy. Your producers will drop to your feet with gratitude. Your ratings will soar. And it will all be because of you."

Her eyes flare. "And what do you want in return?"

"I see I have your attention. The only thing I want in return is for Brett to be able to tell his side of the story, and for you to spend the night."

Her frown returns in an instant. "No way. I'm not going to just let him say what he wants and not ask any questions. I might be a reporter, but I'm also not an idiot and that's how I'll look if I give him an avenue to spew his side of things without pressing him for answers that the world wants."

"Then press him. He'll only tell you what he knows, which is what I need to happen. But I need it to happen in an environment where the press isn't chasing him down the street screaming demands at him. I need him calm, cool, and controlled when he tells his side of the story. I do not need agitated and panicked news clips going viral around the world."

She lifts a finger to poke me in the chest. "I will not allow you to use my position or manage me."

I knew this was going to happen. Emma might be a beautiful face and a reporter, but she's certainly not stupid and she's not a pushover. She got over that back in high school. "Look, I need you, Em. And if you want to capitalize on your big break yesterday, you need me. The last thing I want is the world coming at my client for some pushover PR stunt. I don't need this interview to *look* legit—I need it to *be* legit. Do your job, ask your questions, but be fair."

She pulls in a deep breath and thinks about it for a moment. "You could offer this to anyone in the world. Why me?"

"Are you seriously asking me that?"

"Yes, Jack. It makes no sense why you'd offer this to me right now instead of the top sports reporter in the country." She leans in closer and glances between the seats at the old bitty behind us before adding, "Unless you're just trying to get in my pants again."

I can't help it. It's been since before we fell asleep last night since I've tasted her. I take advantage of the space she just erased between us and drag my tongue up the column of her neck before sucking the skin behind her ear. "Baby, I got in your pants last night on pure charm and wit. I plan on doing it again very soon and don't need to resort to blackmail to see your clothes on the floor."

She puts a hand on my chest and gives me a push so we're nose to nose. "That's a definite no-go since I'm staying with Dad and Keelie. Saylor is still in high school. Despite the fact they still can't keep their hands off each other, they do keep a PG home."

"Oh, it'll be my floor, Emma. And I can't wait."

"Let's get back to Brett Sullivan. If you're not trying to get into my pants, then why would you hand over an opportunity like this to me?"

I cock my head to the side and wonder if she has amnesia. "For someone who works in the news, you sure don't keep up on things. The video of you racing onto the field to get to Brett has only slightly fewer views than the one of my client with a shit ton of drugs, guns, and prostitutes. The very one where he picked you up and swung you around like you were the stars of some sappy Hallmark moment reenacted in real life. You are the obvious choice."

She bites her lip like she's actually considering my Hail Mary plan to save my ass, my client, and to throw her a bone in the process.

"Say yes," I demand. "You have nothing to lose—unlike me, who stands to lose everything."

Her expression falls. "Will you really lose everything? Stop being all Jack Hale for a second and tell me the truth."

"Fuck, yes. And it's going to happen in a nanosecond if I don't do something about it. Not only me, but Brett Sullivan is not an asshole. He doesn't dabble in drugs, and the only gun he owns is the one he went hunting with as a kid. I know this because we've talked about it. He blew up overnight and has little to no security to speak of. He still lives in a rented condo he signed for on the fly when he moved to town."

The pilot breaks through our negotiations to announce our descent. She sits back in her seat again to stare out the window.

"Em." Everything about her is familiar yet so fucking new, my blood rushes south at the thought of her and me. "Please. This is a no-lose situation for you. Tell everyone at the station you reached out to Brett and got the interview on your own. Beyond that, it's all you. This is the right thing to do. He's a good guy. Someone set him up, and he needs to clear his name. I trust you to be fair."

"Of course, I'll be fair," she spouts quickly before closing her eyes on an exhale. She rubs her eyes before muttering, "How did I go from chasing tornadoes to star quarterbacks?"

I pull her hand away from her face and wrap it in mine. "You're a fucking rockstar."

She shakes her head. "I've never been a rockstar, and you know it."

I do what I've wanted to do since she boarded the plane and sat her fine ass next to mine. I lean in and press my lips to hers. When she doesn't pull away, I slip my tongue between her lips to deepen the kiss. When I let her up for a breath, I tell her the truth. "Yeah, you're a fucking rockstar, and I'm going to make sure the rest of the world knows it."

I feel a jab from behind, and the old lady spouts over the noise of the landing gear, "Can you not wait until we're off the plane?"

We both ignore her.

I stare into Emma's eyes. "What do you say? Are you going to capitalize on my spiraling career as a sports agent?"

She doesn't move from my hold. "Do you mean am I going to save you and your client's ass?"

"I always knew you loved my ass."

She pulls that lip I'm becoming obsessed with between her teeth again before relenting to me and my every desire. "Yes. I'll do it."

I lean in and press my lips to hers again to seal the deal.

Well, maybe not my every desire. She hasn't agreed to spend the night with me yet.

Ask me twenty-four hours ago what my desires were, and the answer would've been my bottom line.

Now that's a tie with Emma Hollingsworth.

And Emma might be pulling ahead in the race.

I need to get Brett's shit figured out so I can figure out how to make this thing with her more than a one-night hook-up in Sin City.

I have a feeling a normal old plan isn't going to cut it.

I'm going to need a whole fucking playbook to make sure this doesn't blow up in my face.

One thing I know for certain, Emma is coming home with me so I can get this shit going.

8

VIRAL

Emma

I do not go home with Jack.

There's no way I'm telling my dad to just turn around after trekking all the way to the airport.

Besides, I'm out of clothes, I need a shower, and it's not like I can interview the man who is the hottest topic on the internet about being a winner—or a criminal, depending on what camp you're in—without both. I don't know anyone who can do that on the fly. I'm also not Ross and, therefore, don't lug camera equipment around with me.

As much as I know this is a priority, I need a minute to get my shit together.

Jack will just have to deal.

Dad has been grilling me nonstop all the way home about the game, my viral interview, and how lucky I was to have him and Levi teach me all the things about football.

"Proud of you, Em. I knew you could do it," he says as he turns into the long drive to the house that's seen its share of changes over the years. This place looks nothing like the run-down, century-old farmstead we moved into before Dad and Keelie were officially a thing.

"I'm glad you knew I could do it, because I didn't have that confidence in myself." I collect my things as he comes to a stop in the driveway and opens the garage door. "I bullshitted my way through the entire week. I'm counting on Ross to keep my secret that I barely know anything about the game I just reported on."

He throws it in park and kills the engine. "You were perfect. There's plenty of commentators who specialize in breaking down every play. You did what you were sent there to do. Your producer must be happy."

"I hope so. I knew there would be a learning curve with this job, but last week was Mount Everest steep. I'm sure I'll be sent back to stinky high school gyms, so now is the time to learn everything."

I climb out of the car as Dad gets my bags and proves he's all in no matter what his kids are interested in. "We'll start on basketball rules right away."

"Emma! You're famous!"

I turn to the garage to see Saylor come barreling at me from the house. I have to brace when my younger sister throws her arms around my neck and jumps up and down. "I don't know about famous."

"You are!" she squeals and finally steps back. "Everyone was talking about it at school today. And I don't care what Brett Sullivan did—he's hot. And the way he picked you up for a big, sweaty hug was unreal. Please, make my dreams come true and tell me he asked for your number when the camera shut off. That would be, like, a fairytale love story for the ages."

"How many times have I told you to quit talking about love stories?" Dad says before turning to me. "She's been going on about this since the game last night. She's been sixteen for two seconds. I'm running off high school boys left and right these days. I do not need her going on and on about love stories."

"Whatever. I'm almost seventeen." Saylor beams like nothing could make her happier than a drove of high school boys knocking on her door. "Dad just can't handle that I'm the baby and he'll have no one else to fuss over."

Saylor is not wrong. When she leaves for college, Dad might have a mini-alpha meltdown. If I can find a man who loves me half as much as Dad loves his family, I'll be lucky.

Dad fell in love with my high school counselor when I was going through the worst patch of drama that could ever be thrown at a girl. As mortifying as it was at the time, there's no one more perfect for my dad than Keelie.

And he didn't just fall in love with my counselor, he embraced Knox and Saylor as his own and adopted them on their wedding day. Their dad might have died when they were young, but Asa Hollingsworth has loved them like they're his own. Knox is away at college being the best brainiac he can be, and Saylor is a junior in high school.

We're a blended, all-American family from Levi down to Saylor.

My sister grabs me by the arm and pulls me into the house. "Tell me everything, and don't leave out one single detail. I want to be you, so I've decided to follow in your footsteps and go into broadcasting."

"That's interesting," Dad mutters and follows us into the house with my bags. "Yesterday you wanted to be a physical therapist. The day before that you wanted to be a vet."

I don't have time to start in about my rollercoaster of a week. Keelie flips the water off to the sink and comes straight for us. "Why are we talking about Saylor's ever-changing career choices when all we want to hear about is Brett Sullivan?"

"You too?" Dad complains. "I need to invite the guys over. There's a lack of testosterone in this house."

"You're the love of my life, Asa." Keelie lifts to her toes and kisses Dad, as if that will soften the blow from her next words. "But that doesn't mean I'm not curious about the quarterback like every other woman in the country."

Dad shakes his head and moves through the kitchen. "I can't listen to this any longer. After I dump your bags in your room, I'm out of here. I'll hit the gym or go to the range for target practice."

"We love you," Keelie calls in a sing-song voice as he walks away. Dad grumbles something under his breath, but Keelie only has eyes for me and says through a huge grin, "Tell us everything."

I drop my backpack to the counter and have no plans to tell them everything. "There's nothing to tell besides what you saw on TV. The game was amazing. I got the thirty-second sound bite from Sullivan that you saw. But you know me—I'm way more interested in the drama. I've reached out to Sullivan to see if he'll talk to me about the photos that were leaked overnight." What I don't tell her is that the interview was set up for me by Jack, but I at least need to pretend I'm trying. "It's a stretch, but you never know."

Keelie loses her grin. Her expression returns to one I became way too familiar with when we first came to live here over a decade ago. It's her adult counselor face that screams concern. "Guns and drugs ... the whole story is surprising. He comes across as friendly as a golden retriever, not to mention, he's the hottest thing in football right now. Why would he dabble in anything illegal?"

"Does it matter, Mom? He's hot. I mean, those dark, moody eyes and thick, dark hair." Saylor turns from Keelie to me. "I think Brett is into you. He hasn't said one word to the media since those pictures were leaked. I've been watching all day."

I narrow my eyes. "He just won the biggest game on the planet. He was so happy, he didn't realize what he was doing. Brett Sullivan is not into me."

Her eyes widen, and she stares at me like I'm the world's most profound idiot. "Well, you won't know if you don't try. What's wrong with you?"

"There's nothing wrong with me," I snap as my mind goes back to Brett's agent, who I'm now carnally familiar with ... the same man who kissed me so deep and long before we got off the plane that it made my knees weak and the old lady behind us yell one more time for good measure. I pull in a deep breath and look at my cell when it vibrates with a text. When I see who it's from, I slide it into my pocket without reading it, and lie, "That's my producer. I need to call him back and then shower off the airport germs. I might need to go into the studio tonight."

Keelie glances at the clock. "Tonight? Can they not give you a travel day? You've been gone for a week. You haven't even had dinner."

"Oh, I forgot to tell you. They upgraded my ticket, so I ate on the plane and took a mega nap. I'm good to go for the night."

Keelie frowns and Saylor doesn't let up about the football player who's in trouble up to his *dark, moody eyes*. "Is it about Brett Sullivan?"

I grab my backpack and head for the stairs. "I'm positive he only wants to give me the high school basketball schedule for the week, Saylor. You need to focus on boys your own age. Maybe, if you're lucky, Knox will bring some friends home from college during spring break."

She rolls her eyes. "Knox's friends are smarty pants, just like him. I want a hot jock."

Dad comes stomping down the stairs to pass me just in time to hear Saylor. "If you don't stop talking about hot jocks, I'll come unglued."

The last thing I hear are Keelie and Saylor's laughter when I shut the door to the room that's been mine since my freshman year of high school. I pull my phone out and toss my backpack to the bed.

> Jack – I don't know what hurts more since you ran out on me at the airport, my pride or my feelings. You're embarrassed to be seen with me, aren't you? Especially in front of Daddy Asa.

I can't help the smile that forms on my lips as my ass hits the edge of the bed.

> Me – I'd never be embarrassed of you, even if we aren't "a thing."

> Jack – Oh, Emma. We will talk about all the "things" we are when you get to my place, which better be soon. We have a football player's reputation to resuscitate, a career to save, and a certain new-to-town sexy broadcaster to ride her viral rise to stardom.

I flop back on my bed.

> Me – I just got home. How are we going to do all that?

> Jack – My biggest client just landed in the Commonwealth on a private jet. I drove by his place on my way home. There's so many paparazzi and media outlets staked outside it makes the flies pestering your goats look friendly.

> Me – Wow. Whose feelings are hurt now? I am the media, Jack.

> Jack – Yes, but you're going to use your powers for good and not evil.

> Me – I'm neutral to good and evil. I only report the truth, even if it's just high school basketball at the moment.

> Jack – Enough of that. My public relations nightmare and I are promoting you to hard-hitting news. You might get an Emmy when it's all said and done. An Emmy for Emma.

> Me – I forgot how dramatic you can be. You weren't like this last night.

> Jack – Last night, my life wasn't falling apart. Last night, I had nothing to focus on but you. My goal is to fix everything else so I can get back to recreating last night.

> Me – You assume I want more of last night.

> Jack – I know you do. Now, get your fine ass to my place stat. And pack a bag. It'll be late when we're done. We'll work on recreating last night right after you interview my client.

I sit up, equally intrigued by Jack's client and recreating last night.

> Me – Brett will be there?

> Jack – Don't make me jealous, Em. It's not a pretty sight. Brett can't exactly go home with everyone wanting a piece of him. I told him to come straight here after he lands.

I glance at the clock on the screen. The network is still open. The late-night news doesn't go live for another two hours.

Jack is not a patient man.

> Jack – Do not ghost me, Em. I need you … in all the ways.

The Playbook of Emma

> Me – I'm not ghosting you. Just thinking things through. I need a camera.

> Jack – For fuck's sake, I have to do everything. Where do I get a camera?

> Me – I can get my own camera, jackwad.

> Jack – That's always had a different meaning for me. No one's called me a jackwad in years. I feel like I'm back in high school.

> Me – Okay, you talked me into it. Send me your address. I'm going to take a shower, so I don't look like hell, stop by the station, and I'll be there.

> Jack – Was it my promise to elevate you to a new level of viral or my magic cock?

> Me – I'm tired of mean girls and stinky high school gyms. My answer is viral.

> Jack – Get your sweet ass over here, baby. I can't wait to convince you how wrong you are.

9

QUEEN OF THE MEAN GIRLS CLUB AND LEADER OF THE HOUSE OF FAKE

Emma

"Well, well, well. If it isn't the shiny, new superstar. What are you doing sneaking around the supply room?"

I jerk when I hear the smooth, condescending tone hit me from behind.

I flip around and do my best to not show that I'm startled. My heart that had been beating too fast for my health or my age goes into overdrive. Still, there's no way I'd let on that she unnerves me at every turn.

"Hey, Molly. Are you feeling better? You look great. And what are you doing here on a Monday?" I deflect through lies.

Molly Minders, queen of the Mean Girls Club and leader of the House of Fake.

At least that's what I named her in my head on day two of working at WDCN.

"Thank you," she quips as she looks down her skinny nose at me. "That nasty bug is still working its way through the station. I'm filling in on the main desk until Drew is better."

Molly looks like shit. The karma flu really did a number on her. She's more gaunt than her regular boney, and if she contoured her pale skin any heavier, she'd look like the taxi runways at Dulles International.

Mean-mean Molly isn't quite the Queen Bee at the station, but she does sit in the number-one chair on the weekends. Drew is the face of WDCN and has been for over a decade. He's been nothing but cordial and professional to me, even though we haven't worked together. It's notable because I'm the newbie high school sports reporter, and he's logged five hundred years in the industry by now.

"You get to anchor the news during the week." I shoot her a fake smile. "What a great opportunity for you."

She frowns, and unlike my smile, hers isn't fake. "I am the official stand-in when Drew is gone. Everyone knows that."

"Sorry," I offer and give my hand a slight raise. "Everyone but me. But you set me straight."

"What are you doing here?" she demands.

"Picking up my equipment. I've got an assignment first thing in the morning. You know, back to the grind—high school sports and bowling alleys. Maybe I'll get some pickleball tournaments tossed my way this spring. A girl can dream, right?"

She crosses her arms and narrows her eyes on me. "Everyone assumed you'd come back from Vegas and demand higher profile stories."

"*Everyone* ... wow. I'm honored so many people are thinking of me. You know, I'm just happy to be here. I'll go where the station needs me."

An ugly sneer curls her ruby-red lip. "So selfless. You'll never get anywhere with that attitude."

"I don't know. It got me to Vegas. I'm just going to do my thing and ride the wave." I glance at my watch. "It's getting late. I'm sure you want to re-contour and empty a bottle of hairspray. I've got to drive all the way back to the country, so I'm just going to grab my equipment and let you work your magic."

She doesn't move. "What's wrong with my makeup?"

I wave my hand between us. "Nothing. It's perfection. You have to go heavy so the lights don't wash you out. You're a pro. I should take some tips."

She rolls her eyes like she'd rather rip her fake nails off with pliers than teach me how to paint runways on my face. She turns for the door to the equipment room and holds her head high as her heels click on the floor with almost as much attitude as her helmet hair. "Enjoy the attention while it lasts. The world will forget about you in no time."

I can't help myself. "I hope so. I got a hand cramp signing autographs in the airport today."

She lets out a loud grunt that sounds like she might actually be in pain before she slams the door.

I exhale. If this interview turns out the way I hope it does, Molly Mean Face will be grumpier than ever.

I need to get the hell out of here. I called and told my producer, August, that I planned to stake out the Founders main offices at the stadium first thing in the morning to see if I could get a statement from anyone. He approved it and wished me luck. I could tell he thought it would be a wasted effort and told me not to spin my wheels too long.

What I didn't have the nerve to do was tell him about the actual interview Jack promised me. There was no way I was going to promise anything like that and underdeliver. If this turns out the way I hope it will, August will be the happiest employee at WDCN by this time tomorrow.

After me, that is.

I grab the bag, a light, and tripod. Working with Ross all week was a treat. I'm used to being a one woman show and lugging my own camera around for things like this. The impending interview might be monumental, but working on my own is old hat at this point.

I might not be skin and bones or have every plane on my face defined like a mountain range, but I did shower and blow out my hair. I told Dad, Keelie, and Saylor not to wait up for me since I was working on a story that couldn't wait since people are still out with the flu.

Little white lies for the win.

I pull out my cell and bring up the text string that sits at the top of the list.

> Me – I'm on my way. Looks like we're doing this.

> Jack – You bet your sweet ass we are, baby. Let's make you more famous and get my guy off the hook so I can figure out how to tell my best friend I'm into his sister without him murdering me.

Jack

"This isn't like you. Don't hesitate when answering," I bite.

Emma shifts from where she's sitting and glares at me. "If you don't shut up, I'm going to kick you out of your own house. Brett is doing fine—honestly, great under the circumstances, but every time you interrupt, we have to start over. Are you going to let me do my job or not?"

Brett drags a hand down his tense features. I've never seen him like this. I doubt he's slept since he woke up from his drug-induced stupor. "You're stressing me the fuck out, Jack. And that's saying something since my life is in shambles at the moment."

I stop mid-pace and hold my hand out low. "We have one chance for you to make your post-apocalyptic appearance and statement to the world. We need to get this right."

"If it's too rehearsed, no one will believe him," Emma counters. "Look, in this day and age, no one wants to believe that anyone is innocent. If the story dies, there's nothing to talk about. He needs to be genuine and authentic in his answers, but that won't happen if you're interrupting us every twenty seconds. Not to mention, this isn't *60 Minutes*. I need to get to the meat of the story in a short amount of time."

Brett shakes his head. "This is a bad idea. You negotiate contracts and shit. I never thought I needed a PR manager, but maybe it's time to hire one."

I motion to Emma who is behind the camera for the fourth time to restart the recording. "No one wants to see you get off the hook more than me. I'm all you need at the moment, other than her. The fact that the two of you are reunited since going viral after the game is nothing short of brilliant."

Emma turns to glare at me. "Not one more interruption, got it? In fact, go sit back there in the sunroom where Brett can't see you. He doesn't need the distraction."

"She's right," Brett agrees. "I can't focus with you pacing behind the camera."

I open my mouth to argue, but Emma interrupts. "The sunroom or the sidewalk, Jack. It's your choice."

I stare down at the woman who let me do delicious and kinky things to her just yesterday. "You're really going to put Baby in the corner?"

She sighs. "Don't micromanage me. If he didn't do what the world thinks he did, it will show. He'll be just fine."

"This isn't me being a selfish asshole, Em. I might've been in bed with you while shit was going south with my client, but I know him. Hell, do you know how many people never go down for doing shit and get away with it? I don't want to see him go down for something he did not do."

Her dark eyes saucer. "Did you really just reference our one-night stand in front of your client?"

I glare down at her. "Do you know the definition of a one-night stand? We're not strangers. I've known you your whole life. And there's nothing *one* about it, Emma. There will be more."

"There won't be if you try to tell me how to do my job."

"You do know I'm right here," Brett mutters from where he's sitting by the fireplace. He's elbows to knees with his head resting in his hands.

I look back at Emma and motion to Brett. "Look at him. He's such a wholesome kid, it makes him uncomfortable talking about one-night stands."

"Whoa." Brett sits up and glares at me. "I might not have a collection of illegal firearms or narcotics, but I'm not wholesome. What the fuck?"

"That's enough," Emma bites. "Jack, stop puppeteering this interview. I know what needs to be done. Go sit over there out of Brett's line of sight and keep your mouth shut." She looks back to the camera and flips a menagerie of buttons before reclaiming her seat across from Brett.

"I don't care if you're wholesome or not. You need to convince your fans that whatever happened in those pictures was against your will. Say what you need to say."

"The truth," Brett says. "I'm going to tell the truth."

"Even better." Emma pulls in a breath like she's willing it to give her the patience she needs to deal with my shit. "Let's do this."

I move to the sunroom where Brett can't see me, but I can still see Emma. She looks nothing like she did when I kissed the hell out of her on the plane and said my goodbye at baggage claim.

That was it for me. The damn airline lost one of my suitcases, not to mention Asa was waiting outside for her.

Asa Hollingsworth...

Okay, I'm just going to put this out into the world: I am a successful, grown-ass man. I've built a business in the matter of a few years that has pushed me into seven digits. If I can dig Brett out of the hellhole he buried himself in, that number will be even higher this year. I have professional athletes in my inbox daily begging me to take them on as a client.

Also, let's not forget, high school was a lifetime ago.

Even so.

There's always been something about Asa Hollingsworth that puts me on edge. It doesn't matter how old I am, that I was in a fucking suite at the biggest game of the year yesterday, or that I have a financial advisor because I have no fucking idea what to do with my money.

Asa Hollingsworth was intimidating back in high school. Becoming a grandfather to Levi and Carissa's kids hasn't softened any edges either.

I mean, I guess it has when it comes to Levi's rugrats, but not to the rest of the world.

I know he worked with the CIA back in the day. And there's the fact Levi has never told me what he actually does for a living. All I know is it seems like he has a bottomless pit of money and always gave me the side eye like he knew every move I made.

Even the next three I was thinking about making.

The only thing that was transparent about Asa Hollingsworth back in the day was that he loved his family. That was easy for someone like me to see. I never had a dad. Not even an absentee one who showed up to every third birthday. My sperm donor isn't even listed on my birth certificate. My mom and grandma never minced words about the man who helped give me life—and every single one of those words were bad.

We were all better off without him.

Not that I'd know the difference, but I think someone like me who's never had a father notices when one stands out in the masses.

That would be Mr. Hollingsworth.

And since I bedded Daddy Asa's daughter last night and plan to do it again soon, I wonder if he's as much of a scary motherfucker as he was back in the day.

I can't think about that right now.

I have a client to resuscitate and a career to save.

Which brings me back to Emerson Hollingsworth. Who knew she'd be the key to every fucking thing in my life.

Her dark hair falls down her back in smooth waves. I remember how soft it was last night brushing against my skin and fisted in my hand. She's wearing a cashmere sweater that fits her like a second skin even though it shows very little of it. It does highlight every swell and curve I burned on my brain.

It doesn't matter how much I focus on the interview in front of me, my fingers itch to touch her.

Questions and attempted explanations bounce back and forth between her and my client. I'm not so sure I'd go as far as calling them answers from Brett. Emma might be giving him a platform to tell his story, but that doesn't mean he's offering any facts. Not any that the public will want anyway.

He was casino hopping with players. Since he was the MVP and had a private jet headed to the happiest place on earth, he had some time to celebrate. The last thing he remembers telling his teammates was he had to get back to Nebula and leaving.

Alone.

The next thing he knew, he woke up in a strange hotel room surrounded by drugs, guns, and naked women. He doesn't know how he got there and didn't recognize anyone.

There are no useful details and even less proof he was taken advantage of.

Emma tips her head to the side and lowers her voice a notch. "Is there anything else you want to say?"

"What you saw in those pictures isn't who I am," Brett bites with more conviction than I've ever heard from him. "I don't do drugs or pay for female entertainment. The only guns I've ever used are to hunt on my family's land back in Nebraska, and that's with an old bolt-action rifle. I fund and personally run a scholarship foundation. We've put more than one hundred students through four-year universities and trade schools who might not have had the opportunity otherwise. The foundation, football, and my family are my only passions in life. Don't trust anything else you see online."

Emma pauses for a dramatic second before standing to move to the camera.

I move to the woman I'm currently obsessed with in more ways than one at the moment.

"That's it?" I ask

She flips the recording off and turns to me. "That's it. I think he did great."

"Thanks." Brett sighs and stands to move to us as he drags a hand through his hair. "What's next?"

I tip my head to Emma who's taking the camera down. "She puts it on the news."

"Hardly," Emma says. "I'll bring it to my producer. I can't imagine he won't be interested in it, but he's the one who will make the final decision. You forget that I just report the news. I'm not the one who decides content."

I shake my head and refute her. "You're the only person in the country to land an interview with Brett Sullivan. Your producer would be an idiot not to run with this. And the fact you're the one whose interview with Brett went viral to begin with makes it even more lucrative for whichever news organization hits the airwaves with this first."

"I'm fucking exhausted," Brett says. "I've barely slept since before the game."

"You can't go home," I say. "I'm sure the press is parked outside waiting for you. You don't even have a security system in that condo."

Brett sighs. "Well, it's not like I can check into a hotel. Where else am I going to go?"

I look around and realize this will probably fuck up my plans with Emma, but there's no other option. "You can crash on my sofa."

Emma glances from my sofa to me and frowns. "He's six-five and as wide as a Mack truck. There's no way he'll fit on that thing. You should give him your room and you sleep out here."

I cross my arms. "Then where are you going to sleep?"

If she could shoot daggers at me through her narrowed eyes, I bet she would. "I'm going home."

"So you two really are together?" Brett asks.

"Yes," I say.

At the same time Emma shakes her head. "No. And I'm not joining your slumber party. I'm going home."

I shake my head. "We're pretty damn good together, and we have shit to talk about. You're not going anywhere."

"I talk to you every day," Brett says. "I thought we were friends. What else don't you tell me?"

I turn to him and defend myself. "It's a new development. Not to mention, I've been a little distracted with your drama."

"They're going to find out that he's here eventually. Old Town Alexandria isn't exactly hidden away or private. If he wants to avoid the press," Emma pauses and places her hand over her chest, "the evil press—not the press like me—he needs privacy."

Brett contemplates that. "I could go back to Nebraska."

"No way," I say. "You're in the middle of a PR nightmare. I need you here."

Emma pulls her phone out and starts tapping the screen. "I have an idea."

"Are you calling Daddy Asa?" I ask.

"Who's Daddy Asa?"

Emma rolls her eyes. "Ignore Jack. Asa is my dad, and no I'm not calling him. Be quiet."

She puts it on speaker. It only rings twice when a woman answers but doesn't do it with a normal greeting. "Well, if it isn't my famous friend, Emma Hollingsworth! We saw you on TV! Are you home?"

Emma spears me with a warning glare to keep my mouth shut as she talks. "Hey, Addy. I got home earlier today, but I'm working again."

Ah. Addy, Crew Vega's wife. Asa and Crew work together. Levi and Emma have known Crew Vega most of their lives.

If I'm honest, Crew used to freak me out more than Asa back in high school. I haven't seen him since we graduated.

Addy keeps talking. "Vivi and Aimeé have watched the video no less than a million times. They told all their friends at school that the woman who interviewed Brett Sullivan used to babysit them. I think Aimeé told everyone you're her BFF, so be prepared for that. You know her—she's the attention seeker of the two."

"It's been crazy since I've been back. I promise to drop in to see them soon," Emma drags on the reunion that's playing out in front of us.

"We'll see you at Hudson's birthday party, right?"

Emma's dark eyes fall shut, and she pinches the bridge of her nose. "I forgot. I'm the worst aunt ever. It's his first birthday, of course I'll be there."

I vaguely remember a text I got from Levi before I left for Vegas saying something like if I could make time for anyone other than my clients, I should actually stop by for a beer and a piece of cake for Levi and Carissa's youngest.

All of a sudden, I'm hungry for cake.

"I can't wait to see you," Addy goes on. "You have to stop by the tasting room so we can really catch up. I want to know everything there is to know about Brett Sullivan. He's in a mess of trouble."

Emma's eyes angle to me. "Since the game, I've talked to Brett again."

"Really? The news says he's MIA," Addy says.

Emma bites her lip and glances at Brett and me before she keeps talking. "Honestly, Addy, my gut says he's innocent—for more reasons than I can go into at the moment."

I doubt Addy Vega would talk like she is if she knew the subject was standing right here listening. "You think the pictures were generated? Like artificial intelligence?"

"No," Emma says. "I think he was set up."

Addy laughs. "I'd believe AI before buying that story."

Shit. If Addy is a sampling of what the public thinks of Brett Sullivan, this isn't good.

Brett starts to pace.

I widen my eyes and motion to Emma to get on with it.

Emma pulls in a breath. "This is actually what I'm calling you about. Is the bungalow available right now?"

Addy doesn't even pause. "Goodness, the bungalow has sat empty for years. I'd have to freshen it up for you and stock the fridge. But it's yours if you want it. Is it that bad moving back in with your dad and Keelie?"

"No, no," Emma says. "It's not for me. I have a friend who needs a place to crash for a bit. A private place."

For the first time since she answered the phone, Addy sounds suspicious. "Who needs privacy?"

"Um…" For as articulate as I've seen Emma be in front of the camera about shit she doesn't know what she's talking about, she stumbles over her words. "See, I have a gut feeling, Addy. I don't think he did the things they're accusing him of. He just needs a minute for the press to forget—"

"The quarterback?" Addy interrupts. "Emma Hollingsworth, are you and Brett Sullivan a thing?"

Fuck. Here we go again.

I don't know Addy Vega well, but I'm about to rip the phone away from Emma to set her straight, even if it will get back to Emma's dad and Levi.

Emma must sense it because she holds a hand out to me to cool it. "No. It's not that. Not at all. I just know him through a friend. Please, Addy. Trust me on this one. He needs a place to get away from the press for a minute. There's no better place than Whitetail."

Addy sighs. "Of course, I trust you. Okay. But when everyone hears I'm hosting Brett Sullivan in the bungalow, I can't promise that there won't be fanfare. If my tweens and your younger sister find out, he might have the privacy he needs, but not the peace."

"Can we just keep this on the downlow for a while? There's no need to tell the whole group."

"That's a nice sentiment, Emma, but I doubt that's going to happen."

Emma shrugs, like it's no big deal that Addy refuses to keep my client's whereabouts a secret. "True."

Daddy Asa and his friends are intimidating because no one knows what the hell they really do. For that reason alone, even I know I'm not in a position to argue with Addy Vega.

"Explaining to Crew why a quarterback who just found himself in a heap of trouble will be staying in the bungalow will be fun, but he won't say no to me. When will he be here?" Addy asks.

Brett finally has something to say and whispers to me in a hiss. "Are you sure about this?"

I don't whisper. "It's the first thing I've been sure about since you called me this morning."

"He'll be on his way soon. I can't tell you how much I appreciate you," Emma says.

"I know you're a mover and shaker these days, but if you're not sitting at Whitetail with a glass of wine and filling me in on your exciting life soon, then we will have a problem." Addy delivers her warning with the claws of a kitten. "I'll get the bungalow ready and explain to Crew that we'll have a guest on the property. Give him directions and tell him not to freak out when my husband looks like he doesn't trust him."

Brett's eyes widen.

Emma isn't fazed. "Sounds good. I'll touch base tomorrow."

"You'd better," Addy says before they both disconnect the call.

Brett doesn't speak in a whisper this time. "Why wouldn't her husband trust me?"

Emma answers before I can. "Because there are pictures of you plastered all over the internet with illegal drugs, guns, and probably prostitutes. And there's the fact he doesn't trust anyone outside of his circle."

"Maybe I should just go home. Dealing with the press might be better than that guy," Brett says.

"You're fine." I dig my fob out of my pocket and toss it to him. "Take my ride. If anyone is onto your whereabouts, they won't recognize it. Do you need anything?"

"No. I've still got my shit with me from last week." Brett flings his keys at me to trade cars. He turns to Emma. "Thanks. Even though I have no idea what I'm walking into. If Jack trusts you, then I'm good."

"My car is in the garage. I'll move your suitcase. You'll be in the middle of nowhere sitting in the woods by yourself in no time."

It's late, dark, and cold as I lead them through my garage. I get his shit dumped in the back of my Porsche, and Emma sends him a pin to Whitetail. "When you get to the vineyard, don't follow the signs for the tasting room. There's a dirt lane that veers off to the right after you enter the property. You'll have to pay attention, or you'll miss it. The bungalow is small, but it has everything you need. Addy is the queen hostess. I'm sure the place will be stocked by the time you get there, and you'll have privacy. I'll call my producer first thing in the morning and see what he says about the interview. I'm sure Jack will keep you up to date."

For someone who should be on top of the world at the moment, Brett looks like his dog died. "Thanks. I appreciate everything you've done."

Emma crosses her arms and hugs herself to keep warm in the cold night. "I'm happy to help. You'd better not turn into a drug dealer who collects illegal guns."

"Don't worry," Brett mutters and slides into the driver's seat. He's so big, he makes my Panamera look like a clown car. "Thanks again, Jack. Call me when you know something."

"Will do," I say.

Emma and I watch him back out of the garage and disappear into the night.

I turn to Emma. "Let's go inside. There's no way his SUV will fit in the garage. It'll have to be okay on the street."

I was lucky my place came onto the market when I was looking. It's the shit and not many places here have garages. I bought it from a politician who lost her reelection bid.

After growing up in the boonies, I like being near the city. My brownstone is narrow as hell and three stories tall, and the woman who previously owned it was delusional about how her constituents felt about her. She gutted the place. Everything is new and shiny and looks like a magazine.

Her loss, my gain.

I follow Emma to the family room where she goes straight for her coat.

I cross my arms. "Where do you think you're going?"

She shrugs her jacket on. "Home. I have to get up early and be back in the city if I'm going to pitch this interview to my boss."

I move in front of her and block the stairway. "We have shit to talk about. You're not going anywhere."

10

SEX LOTTERY

Emma

"Stay," he insists like a crazy man. "Spend the night. You'll be closer in the morning and can leave from here."

I level my stare on him as I hoist the camera bag up my shoulder. "Our one night was off-the-charts amazing, but I do have a certain level of decorum to keep at work. I can't walk into a meeting with my boss looking well sexed and wearing clothes from the night before."

"It's late," he argues. "Too late for you to drive back out to the country."

"You didn't give a shit about Brett when you sent him off into the dark night."

"Brett can take care of himself. He's not a beautiful woman who I give a shit about."

I hitch a foot and remind him of why we're here right now. "Excuse me, but I'm not the one who got roofied. And have you forgotten that I've lived all over the country in the last few years and fared just fine on my own coming and going at all hours of the day? I do not need a man telling me when I should and should not be driving in the dark."

His expression screws up into a wince. "Okay. You've got a point. But I'll bet my retirement fund that won't happen again to Brett. Work with me here, Em. I'm being possessive and protective. Women love that."

I glare at him. "You're telling me what to do when I'm smart enough to take care of myself. Women do not love that."

He pauses before taking a step and eats up what little empty space there is between us. I don't move when he frames my face in the same hands that are familiar with every part of my body. His thumb is firm when he drags it over my bottom lip, never taking his eyes off his movements.

When his gaze finds my eyes, his voice is low and meaningful. Nothing like the Jack Hale he's been since we woke up together on the other side of the country earlier today.

Damn. That was actually today. I'm tired.

"Emma." My name is a hushed breath. "The thought of you leaving me and driving off into the night makes me crazy because I give a shit about you, but I'm also desperate for you to stay. When it comes down to it, I'm just desperate to be with you. Please stay."

My shoulders slump, and I feel what little energy I have left drain from my body. "Do you see how that's so much nicer than telling me what to do?"

A slow, small smile spreads across his full lips. It doesn't quite touch his eyes when he nods. "Bare my soul and fall at your feet ... that's your love language. Now I know. I wouldn't do that for just anyone, but I will for you."

I pull in a deep breath. "Actually, sleep is my love language. It's been a long day."

His soft smile dissolves. He hikes a brow as his hold on my face becomes firm. "May I remind you of the cross-country nap you took spread across two first-class seats while reclined all over me? If anyone should be tired, it's me."

I don't move from his hold, but I do let the camera bag slip down my arm and set it gently on the floor. "Emotionally, Jack. I'm emotionally exhausted."

His hands slip from my face to my shoulders where he drags my coat down my arms and lets it fall to the floor. "All the more reason to stay. Let me fill your emotional coffers ... while I fill you."

I shake my head. "No one has ever given me whiplash by being an asshole and sweet at the same time. Pick a Jack. I need to know which one I'm dealing with."

His hands come back to my face. Without another word, he pulls me to him with such force, I stumble into his wide, muscled chest when our lips meet for a searing kiss. It's not like the one on the plane this morning. It's like the one that happened the moment we stumbled into his suite last night when we couldn't keep our hands off each other.

I feel the desperation he just admitted to.

And it feels good.

So good, I push aside all thoughts of how I'm going to get ready for work tomorrow and what I'll wear so I don't show up in the same clothes I interviewed Brett Sullivan in.

When Jack drags a hand down my back and lands on my ass for a firm and delicious grope, I decide getting ready for work is a tomorrow problem, definitely not a tonight problem.

The hand on my face slides into my hair and pulls at the roots to break our kiss. Then Jack Hale surprises me and proves me wrong.

I might actually have multiple love languages, because when his possessive side surfaces again, I feel it in places where love languages are not spoken.

Like, in my wet panties.

"Stay," he demands again, but this time it's different. "I want you here in my house—in my bed. I don't want you in some hotel room that screams one-night stand. I want to smell you on my sheets to remind me of how fucking lucky I am that the universe did me a solid for once and put me in a position to beg you for one more day. I don't have a crystal ball, but I really fucking like having you here. Tomorrow, I'll beg for another day. From there, we'll see how Wednesday goes."

I let my weight sink into him farther.

"Give me one more day," he echoes his own words. They're rough and demanding and fierce.

And, yes, they're even desperate.

I pull in a breath. "Is there a Target close by?"

He frowns. "Why?"

"If I stay, I'm going to have to go shopping before work for a new outfit. You're just lucky I work in TV and don't go anywhere without a full makeup spread for touch up."

His gaze studies every feature of my face. "As if you need any."

"The camera washes you out. I need makeup."

His eyes settle back on mine. "I'll buy you enough clothes for the next month if you stay."

"I really like clothes. I might take you up on that."

"I dare you," he goes on. "But it won't be at Target."

"I love Target. And I'm on a Target budget and it will be the only thing open before my meeting."

"Fair enough. As long as you stay, but I'm buying."

I can't keep the smile off my face. "I will have to text my dad. Should I tell him I'm staying with you?"

Jack's hold on me intensifies. "If you think that's a good idea."

My smile widens. "I think we've had enough drama to deal with today. I might not be in high school anymore, but I'm not sure that's the best idea. I'll tell him I'm crashing at a friend's place to save myself the drive."

"I'll take it," he mutters before taking my mouth again. He lets go of me, claims my hand, and pulls me toward the stairs to a level of his house I haven't seen yet. His place is gorgeous and looks like a magazine rather than a bachelor pad. This is a different side of Jack than I've ever known. He's just as confident and charismatic as he always was, but this polished side of him is new. "I'll take anything as long as you stay. Not that I'm afraid of your dad."

I follow him up the narrow stairway to the top floor. Anticipation swirls inside me even though I've already been with Jack.

Vegas was Vegas.

It felt right, so I went with it. Even if I thought it would be one night.

I knew I'd see him eventually since I was back in the District. Maybe at Levi and Carissa's for a cookout or birthday party. I assumed Jack and I would always share one secret night together. A secret to celebrate his big win for a superstar client and my once in a lifetime career-changing experience.

Icing on the cake.

The proverbial cherry.

I did not expect to be in Jack's home, seduced by his beautiful blue eyes, or being led to his bedroom for a second night together.

I haven't been in any type of relationship for a long time. There's been no time. I knew my last few jobs weren't long term. There was no reason to invest time in anything just to complicate moving on.

I have goals, dammit, and they're important.

But I'm back in D.C., a goal I reached faster than I ever thought I would. I'm home where I wanted to be. Jack Hale might've been my first kiss and a soul-wrenching crush in high school, but he was never a goal.

He would've been a pipe dream—even for me.

We hit the top floor, and he leads me around the corner to a large room for this size of home. The walls are bright white and trimmed in wainscoting from floor to ceiling. Double doors lead to a bathroom, but other than that, there's nothing else on this floor.

Everything is new, shiny, and as perfect as the rest of the house.

Just like the new Jack.

I wouldn't say he's improved. I was obsessed with the younger Jack back in the day. As shiny as the new version of this man is from the man-boy I remember, I see hints of him. And I didn't think he needed to be improved, but here we are.

The best of both worlds.

He comes to a stop at the foot of his bed and pulls me to him. But he doesn't claim my face or take my mouth like he did downstairs. He goes straight for my sweater.

I've never been happier to cooperate.

I lift my arms for him to rip it over my head and toss it behind me as he talks. "What you did for Brett tonight means a lot to me."

Standing here in my bra and slacks, I toe my loafers off and kick them to the side. "Brett seems nice, but I didn't do it for him."

Jack proves he can multitask and starts to work my belt as he keeps talking. "This will be good for your career. As long as this nightmare continues, and after, I'll make sure you have first access to him."

He rips my belt from the loops and tosses it behind him this time.

My fingers go to his shirt.

"I appreciate that," I say as he works the clasp on my slacks, and I claw at his buttons to get to his smooth, chiseled chest. "But I didn't do it for me either. I landed a job at WDCN. I work hard—I'm proud of where I'm at."

The zipper on my slacks slides south. Before I know it, I'm standing before him in nothing but my bra, panties, and bared soul.

"Must I teach you everything, Emma?" he teases. "The sports industry is tough. Sports broadcasting is an extension of it. I've been around long enough to know everyone in your industry wants the sports gig. You're not battling hurricanes, reporting on drive-bys in the middle of the night, or fighting your way through a damn political rally. You have to make your move and take advantage when the opportunity arises."

I push his shirt wide and watch my fingers trail over his pecs, rippled abs, and down to the smattering of hair that sits above his waistline.

"Emma," he calls for me and claims my chin to force my gaze to meet his. "You okay?"

I don't answer that question, but I do tell him the truth. "I did it for you."

He freezes.

My insides tense at the expression that settles in his features.

"I mean, you own your own business. It's not like you roofied your client. None of this is your fault. And I might not know what a touchback is, but I do know that if Brett Sullivan goes down for this, it can't be good for you." I glance around the immaculate bedroom and wave my hand at the opulence surrounding us. "Everyone knows how expensive it is to live in Old Town, and this place is amazing. It's easy to see you've worked hard. If I can help, I want to."

His hands drop to my ass and squeeze where he pulls me flush to him, but he says nothing.

"It's not because of the sex," I blurt, desperate to fill the dead, stifling silence that fills the perfect room.

It is perfect. The bed isn't just made, but the pillows are perfectly placed. They've even been karate chopped.

The image of Jack fluffing pillows does not reconcile in my head, but the proof sits before me in fine linens and Egyptian cotton. It has to be. It looks that lush.

The intensity dissolves and his blue eyes might as well sparkle with a touch of humor. "Damn, Emma. I must have misread the vibes. Are you telling me the sex wasn't good?"

My hands tense where they've worked their way to his lats. "No! I mean, yes. It was good. But that's not—"

I yelp when my body defies gravity.

His hold on my ass tightens as he lifts me from the floor. I'm forced to hang on for fear of falling.

I shouldn't have worried.

My back hits his perfectly made bed and he comes down with me. His bare chest is pressed to mine as his forearm rests on the fluffy duvet the color of sand.

I was right about the Egyptian cotton. It's so soft on my bare skin, I might move into Jack's bed and never leave. It's big, and I sleep like the dead. Once I settle, I hardly move for the night. Heck, I slept just fine on a lumpy twin mattress in the studio above Mr. Coolidge's diner.

Jack won't notice me.

His bright blue eyes shine through the dimmed space. "Don't throw hate like that at me and expect it not to be a challenge."

My fingertips grip his wide shoulders. "I hardly threw hate at you. I would never."

His hand drags down my body until it lands on my hip at the thin string of my thong. I hate these panties, they cut into my skin.

But they look damn good on me. The smart, rational part of me did not come here tonight planning for more sex.

But the other part of me, the part who still feels where Jack fucked me last night and likes it, wanted to look good in my panties just in case.

"I told you I did this interview with Brett for you and the sex was good. How is that throwing hate?"

"Because I give better than just *good* sex. Especially to you. You just laid a gauntlet at my feet. Now I'm going to be forced to rock your world at a whole new level."

I had no idea there could be a level better than last night.

His fingers trail down the crack of my ass until they dip beneath the slip of fabric. No surprise here, his touch slips through my sex easily from my arousal. In fact, *arousal* has new meaning next to it in the dictionary since Jack sauntered back into my life.

His lips land on my collarbone and slowly make their way between my breasts. I suck in a sharp breath when his teeth drag along my skin before they catch the lace of my bra as he pulls

One.

Then the other.

My breasts are bare and lifted with my bra taut below them. His lips wrap around my nipple as his teeth sink into my delicate skin with just enough force that I feel it below the waist.

I grip his thick, dark hair and hold him to me. "Holy shit."

He sucks my nipple before letting go with a pop. "Holy shit just *good* or holy shit *Jack is about to rock my world?*"

As if Jack Hale could be average. Still, I force my gaze down where his tongue drags down the center of my body and work hard to catch my breath as I keep giving him shit. "Whatever you do, don't be a quitter. You should keep trying to redeem yourself."

He glances up with narrowed eyes, but they're paired with the sexiest, cockiest smirk I've seen in…

Well, the last twelve hours.

I could get used to that smirk.

I think I like the cocky as much as I like the sexy.

"I haven't had the luxury of quitting anything. And since you're a luxury, I don't plan to stop now."

He proves to be a man of his word. The thin material at my hips drags down my thighs, over my knees, and past my toes. They're a whispered memory when he pushes my thighs apart and his lips land on delicate skin inside my thigh.

Another suck.

And a bite. This one harder than the one on my nipple.

I put my feet flat to the bed and lift my hips. I'm desperate for his touch. His fingers, lips, tongue.

I'll take anything he'll give me.

I'm greedy.

Jack proves he's not a quitter, and I feel like I won the lottery. The sex lottery.

I get his tongue.

He laps me from sex to clit. I shudder when he circles the most sensitive spot on my body. Every part of me is acutely aware of the magic being spun between my legs. My breathing shallows and I think this is it.

That's when he rips the rug out from under me. I lose his touch and everything perfect and sensual.

I push up to my elbows. "What's wrong?"

Jack is standing at the foot of the bed looking down at me with heated eyes. He rips his belt from his pants before going for the button and zipper like they're strangling him, and he can't wait to get them off.

"Roll," he demands.

I pull my knees together and cross my feet at the ankles. "Why?"

"Because when you come, you're going to do it with me inside you."

His pants and boxers hit the floor, and he moves to his nightstand to yank open a drawer.

I do not move or roll because I can't take my eyes off him. The sight of Jack bare is a sight to see.

I stare at his cock. Thick, long, and hard. It bobs as he stalks back to me, demanding my attention.

"Roll over, baby," Jack croons, ripping the condom open between his teeth.

I sit up in front of him and drag my fingers from the base to the tip of his cock.

His skin is silky but what lies beneath it is hard and masculine.

I run the tip of my finger over a drop of precum. I look up and find him staring down at me.

I slip my finger between my lips and taste him on my tongue.

Then I suck.

"Fuck," he hisses.

I smile around my index finger and suck once more before pulling it out with a pop. "That's what you get for stopping."

"You're trying to kill me," he mutters as he slides the condom down his thick length. "No way am I coming before you. But the next time you do that, you'd better be ready to follow through."

He bends at the waist and grabs me by the hips. The next thing I know, I'm tossed onto his mountain of perfectly chopped pillows and find myself yelping a second time in surprise before pillows fly left and right through the air. Then he flips me to my stomach, and my bra goes slack.

"Next time," he says. His words come out on a rushed breath near my ear, and his heat hits my back. His chest is heavy when he gives me just a sliver of his bulk, and his long, hard cock presses into the crease of my ass. "I can't wait to fuck your sweet mouth, Emma. It's not going to happen tonight, but it's going to happen soon."

"Soon," I echo and let that word trail off. It sounds like a promise.

I guess there's no one-night stand when it comes to Jack Hale and me.

His thick forearm tucks under my waist and lifts. His knees nudge mine apart, and my ass is in the air.

But Jack…

He's everywhere.

His lips hit my neck.

His chest presses to my back.

And the tip of his cock teases my sex at the same moment his fingers find my clit.

I moan when he gives me a hint of a touch there.

"Please." I turn my head to the side and beg for something … anything. "You've already taken me to the edge once. Who's trying to kill whom here?"

This time, his answer is in the form of an action.

He takes me in one firm thrust.

Jack Hale.

A dream that's now a reality.

Jack

I groan into the side of her face when I slide inside.

I'm not sure how it can be better than yesterday, but it is. Maybe it's because we're here. In my house and in my bed. The first place that's been all mine.

Who am I kidding?

It's none of that.

It's all her.

I feel her arch and tip her ass into me, so I press into her harder and put my lips to her ear. "You like it deep."

Her voice is breathy. "I haven't experienced anything with you that I don't like."

I pull out and press back in, teasing her clit. "I think I could stay right here forever, baby."

I give her clit more pressure as I slide in and out, slow and steady. She's not the only one I'm edging. There's no way I'm coming before her. I want to feel her everywhere.

"Please," she begs. "So much teasing. I can't take it."

A small tremor moves through her body when I give her clit more pressure. I feel it through my chest and all the way down to my cock. "I'm not sure you have a choice what you can take."

I spread her knees farther and thrust. She might not have a choice on how fast or slow this goes, but my cock is begging me to let the reins go so he can have his way with her.

When her pussy clenches me, I realize I can't hold out much longer.

"Fuck," I groan. "It seems I can't deny you anything."

"That's good for me," she mutters on a moan and tries to move on my hand, but I have her pinned.

Her body is mine to control.

The more pressure I give her clit, the quicker her breaths come and the harder it is for me to fight every animal instinct within me.

She fists the bedding as her jaw goes slack. Just like last night, I take in every gorgeous feature.

I may never get enough of her.

I thrust into her again and stay planted as I give her what she wants, and it doesn't take long. A little more pressure, and she falls. Her entire body convulses, but especially her pussy.

And I can't hold on any longer.

I keep working her clit as I start to move.

Faster.

Harder.

Deeper.

She's not quiet and doesn't hold back. Her moans fill my bedroom. It's like music for the soul.

And it feeds me like I've never been fed before.

When I really let go, she moves with me. Rocking into me harder.

I slam into her two more times before I come. It's like I didn't just have her less than twenty-four hours ago.

Staying planted deep, I slide my knees out from under me and take her with me, giving her as much weight as she can handle without leaving her.

I press my lips to her temple. "Thank you for staying."

She drags her eyes open, and a lazy smile touches her lips. "Did you just say thank you? The way you balance your sweet and cocky amazes me."

I press into her harder and take her mouth. When I finally break my kiss, I shift my weight to the side as much as I can. "I'll thank you every time for that."

"I misspoke the first time. I'll never use the words good and sex in the same sentence when it comes to you again."

I press my lips to hers once more. "If I have to keep proving it to you, I will."

"I'll hold you to that."

"You'd better. You deserve it."

Her voice dips to a whisper. "There you go again … sweet."

I press my lips to her forehead this time. I can't be this close and not kiss her. "I'll find you a toothbrush and whatever else you need. I need a good night's sleep. I didn't have a marathon nap like some people."

"And there went the sweet." Her smile swells proving there's no bite to her words.

"Can't let you get bored with me, baby. I've got to keep you on your toes."

11

COMMANDO IN MY SWEATS

Jack

"No. He hasn't skipped town, and he doesn't need a PR manager. He has me, and I'm on top of it."

"You listen to me, Hale. You might represent him, but I'm the one signing his paychecks and writing his contract. He's a free agent and had the nerve to shit all over my big win. Tell your boy that when I call him, he'd better answer his damn phone."

I don't take my eyes off Emma as Eric Oliver, the general manager of the Founders, rips me a new asshole. Emma has inspected every pair of pants in the store and has moved onto a rack of dresses. If it weren't for the fact nothing else is open this early, there's no way I'd be here. I can afford the best now and that's what I buy. My mom couldn't even afford to shop at a big box store when I was little.

"Respectfully, Brett Sullivan is my client, not my boy. I've talked with him at length about what happened. He was framed. I believe every word he says. And since he is a free agent and MVP of your big win, everyone and their dog is going to want to make a run for him. If he needs a minute to recover, I'm going to make sure he gets it."

"There's only so much bullshit the franchise can deal with when we know nothing," Eric bites. "If you have this handled, the least you can do is keep me in the loop. The media is eating me alive. They're all over my ass like a fucking STD that won't respond to antibiotics."

"My skinny latte won't be the same after your graphic metaphor just made me throw up a little in my mouth. You're reimbursing me. I'll negotiate it into Brett's contract."

"Fuck that," he growls. "I refuse to pay for even a shitty cup of coffee until Sullivan proves those pictures of him are AI generated or he produces the medical records that he really was roofied."

"Unfortunately, Brett hopped on a plane to make his appearance for the parade with mice. It's too late for a blood test."

Emma plucks a dress off the rack, turns to me, and holds it up to her. It looks like it'll cover every inch of her and still show off every curve she's got. It'll look fucking great.

I'm about to nod with my approval and make dinner reservations so I can look at her all night in it, until it dawns on me whatever she wears to work won't only be seen by her associates, but also the millions of people who tune into the nightly news. Not only that, but she's gone viral, and that's likely to happen again when they post the interview with the most-talked-about man in the country.

I frown and shake my head.

Emma frowns back and doesn't take my advice. She tosses the damn dress into the basket and moves onto the next rack.

Eric keeps interrogating me. "Then what are you doing to make this shit go away with the media?"

I follow Emma and her ever-growing pile of clothes she pushes around the store. "I arranged an interview. It happened last night and should go live today. My *client*," I stress the word to the asshole on the phone, "held his own."

Eric lowers his voice and tries to be menacing, but it comes off desperate. "Make sure he does better than that. The celebration parade in the District is tomorrow. He can't hide any longer. He needs to show his face and be on the fucking open-air bus."

I sigh. The only thing I'm thinking about more than Emma and shoring up Brett's contracts is the parade.

If Brett skips the celebration, the media will do nothing but talk about him.

If he shows up to the parade, the media will do nothing but talk about him.

Either way, it won't be good.

I just need Emma's interview to go live sooner rather than later. If there's some sort of explanation out there, that will give the talking heads something to chew on other than the leaked photos.

I give in and confirm what I haven't talked to Brett about yet. "He'll be there. I'll make sure of it."

"He'd better be. And you'd better be as good at PR as you are strong-arming me out of more money."

I follow Emma out of the clothes and straight to the shoes. "I'm going to take that as the compliment it was meant to be. I appreciate it."

"Agents," he mutters. "You think you rule the world."

"Only when we represent the star of the show," I amend. "Good talking to you. Enjoy your day."

"Enjoy my ass."

That must be his form of a farewell, because he disconnects the call before he can utter the second S in ass.

The damn parade.

One more thing for me to worry about.

"Are you planning on moving in with me?" I ask as I watch Emma push the cart through the aisle of socks.

She throws me a look like I'm a mutant from Mars.

"What? If that's the case, you won't get a complaint from me. But I thought we were here for one outfit so you don't look like you shacked up last night or live out of your car."

"I'm not feeling anything at the moment. I can't decide."

"You might be feeling it if you would've let me shower with you this morning," I announce.

I say this as we pass an older woman inspecting a rack of knee socks. She glares at me.

"What?" I hold out my free hand since my other is holding my almost cold cup of coffee. "It's true."

Emma stops and grabs my hand to pull me around the corner, hissing, "Would you stop? How many times do I need to explain that I couldn't get my hair wet?"

"What do I need to buy you so shower sex is always an option? Let's go to that aisle."

She lets go of my hand and picks up a pair of panties clipped to a hanger. "My dad asked me a million questions last night about where I was staying, which means this cannot become a normal thing. That's the last conversation on earth I want to have. I'd rather walk into work wearing yesterday's panties, and you already know how much I don't want to do that."

I rip the hanger from her hand and inspect the garment that looks nothing like the panties I almost ripped to shreds when I tore them off her last night. "These are … interesting."

She yanks them back and tosses them in the cart. "These are comfortable."

I smile, take a step closer, and hook a finger in the waistband of my sweatpants she stole from me this morning when she got out of the shower. She refused to put on her panties from yesterday. Her hair is slicked back and pulled into a high ponytail and her makeup might be perfect, but she's commando in my sweats. "I vote you don't buy any of this shit. I like knowing you aren't wearing anything beneath my clothes. If anyone asks, I'll give you a stack of my business cards so everyone will know who's responsible for the state of you. I've never been more fucking proud of anything."

Emma glances down at herself. "Your client is Brett Sullivan, and *this* is what you're proud of?"

I feel bare skin beneath the cinched waistband that's folded over twice when I yank her to me. Her hands land on my biceps, and we're pressed chest to chest under fluorescent lights in a sea of bras and panties. I slide my hand around her waist and dip my hand inside until the tips of my fingers kiss the crack of her ass. "I got to rock your world two days in a row. I'm very fucking proud of that."

She smiles but changes the subject. "Who were you talking to?"

"Eric Oliver."

Her brows rise. "The general manager of the Founders?"

I tip my head to the side. "I'm impressed. And you said you knew nothing about football."

"I was in Vegas for an entire week covering the team. I know who Eric Oliver is. What did he say?"

I press into the small of her back to hold her to me. "Are you just using me for my professional sports contacts?"

She hikes a brow. "Are you just using me for PR to get your client out of the doghouse?"

"Touché, my beautiful lover."

It seems Emma can dish it out as good as she takes it. She looks pleased with herself, which she should be.

"Brett isn't answering Mr. Oliver's calls, and the GM is pissed. He expects Brett at the championship parade tomorrow. I'm not sure how that's going to go, but in the end, The Founders organization is Brett's employer. He needs to be at that parade. Which means we have one day for you to release that interview."

Emma's dark eyes light up. "Maybe they'll let me cover the parade once they see the interview. You need to stop groping me in the middle of Target so I can get to work."

"We could hit the dressing room for a quickie," I offer.

It almost takes me off guard when Emma raises up on her toes to press her lips to mine. "Nice try, but I refuse to go to work smelling like sex."

"Then you're back at my place tonight," I demand.

She leans into me farther and lowers her voice. Gone is the teasing tone in her voice. "What are we doing, Jack? One night in Vegas is turning into tonight and tomorrow—"

I stop her right there and interrupt. "And the next day. If I get my way, you can add the one after that. While you're at it, keep your calendar clear for next week too."

She opens her mouth to say something, but my cell vibrates in my pocket. We both feel it since she's pressed to me. Since I've got more drama swirling than the old soap operas my grandma used to watch, I can't afford to let any call go to voicemail. I set my cold coffee on a shelf next to us and dig my cell from my pocket.

"Shit," I mutter.

"Who is it now?" Emma asks without pulling away.

I hold her tight and answer her question when I connect the call. "If it isn't Dr. Hollingsworth taking time out of his surgical schedule to call his best friend."

Emma's eyes widen. The mention of her brother is enough for her to pull away from me. Or at least try to.

I hold tight and shoot her a wink.

"What the hell are you talking about?" Levi bites. "Outside of the Homies string, I texted you five million times last week with no answer, so I had to actually dial your fucking number like we're retired or some shit. When all I got in return was crickets, I kept calling—four fucking times. I even broke our high school pact and left you not one, but two, unnecessary voicemails. I watch the news, Jackie. I know you've had a big week, but did I do something to you? Are you pissed at me? This silent treatment feels like I got dumped, and you won't man up and say why."

It's not lost on me that my making a mental list of all the ways I want to fuck my friend's sister while talking to said friend might be fucked up on a level that's new even for me.

But here I am, going through the physics of dressing room sex with Emma in my head while on the phone with Levi.

That's some challenging shit since I skated through physics on nothing but sparkling charm and quick wit.

"Trust me, Dr. Smartypants, if I broke up with you, you'd know. You don't have some ball-less lame excuse for a bestie. If you piss me off that much, I'll hire a plane to write that shit in the sky for all to see."

"You would do that," Levi mutters. "But now that I've got you pinned down and know we're not over, I want to know what's new with your big-name client. You have to know something by now."

Emma's eyes are as big as the bullseye on the front of this store. "He's not into anything. He was framed. The truth will come out soon enough. I'm actually working on that now."

"I listened to a sports podcast on the way into the hospital this morning. There's speculation he won't show up for the parade tomorrow."

"Are you admitting to filling your big-ass brain with something other than medical journals and motivational books?"

"Fuck you, Jack. I work long hours and have a family. I don't have time to sit around and watch game after game like we used to. By the way, did you run into Emma while you were in Vegas? She's not returning my messages either. You had to have been close since she interviewed Sullivan."

"Yeah, you could say I ran into your little sister." A small smile finds its way to the corner of my lips. "It's been forever, but we definitely made up for lost time."

Emma bites back a smile, and her hold becomes firm on my arms. It feels like a warning.

As if I'd heed any warning as soft as that.

"For someone who doesn't know offsides from three seconds in the lane, she found a way to hold her own. She's got the gift."

"Don't sell her short," I warn. "She's fucking killing it."

"She is. Carissa even thinks there's something between her and Sullivan. I can't think about my sister with anyone. I thought I might be able to buy into that until shit hit the fan.

If he's bad news, he'd better fucking stay away from her. Carissa doesn't give a shit. She can't stop talking about, and I quote, the spark that sizzled between them after the game."

The fact that anyone thinks they saw a spark during that interview pisses me off. I didn't think my hold on Emma could get any tighter. But at the mention of Emma and any man other than me, it makes me want to put a fist in someone's face.

And I'm not a violent guy. I might be all man in every other way, but I was raised by women.

It's impossible to cover the bite in my tone, but I'm sick of hearing the Emma and Brett rumor. "I know for a fact there's nothing between him and your sister."

"That's good." Levi sounds relieved. "She doesn't need to be with anyone in professional sports."

My defenses go up, and I hold Emma tighter.

"What's wrong with professional sports?" I demand.

"Drama," he states, as if he double majored in it alongside molecular and cellular biology when he was at Hopkins. "Always drama, but under the microscope of the public. Hollingsworths like their privacy. It's the way we grew up. Hell, after the shit Carissa and Cade's dad put them through, we value it even more."

Not that I'm trying to justify a reason that Emma should hook up with my fucking client, but I feel the need to defend my industry or, more accurately, myself. "Unless you've been living with your head buried in the sand, your sister went viral two days ago. Her job literally puts her under that big, bad microscope you mentioned. That's her own doing. And look at yours truly—I live and breathe professional sports."

"Then you of all people know the difference between working it and having the world picking apart your life choices or your outfit. I don't want that for Emma."

"Look at Daddy Levi taking after Daddy Asa. Emma is a grown woman. If she wants drama, she can choose drama."

Emma hikes a questioning brow.

I shake my head.

"You know what I mean, and this isn't what I called about. I'm pulling into the parking garage at the hospital. I have a full day in surgery. Hudson turns one next week, and we're having a party at the house Friday night. We haven't seen you in months. The season is over, so there are no excuses. Everyone will be there. If you skip the way you have the last few events, Carissa will hold it against you forever. She said so. If she starts up on The Homies group text again, I'll hold you responsible. That's the last thing I need blowing up my phone."

I slide my hand deeper into my sweats to cup one globe of Emma's beautiful ass.

Her eyes widen, and she whips her hand around to stop me before I go any further.

My smile swells into a wolfish grin.

She shakes her head.

"Yeah, I'll be at your baby's party. Text me the details, but not on The Homies thread. I'm trying to salvage a dramatic professional football career. You're not the only one saving lives, asshole."

Levi laughs as the call goes from his car's Bluetooth to his cell. "You'd better not cancel. This is our last one year old. Carissa's doing it up big."

"Big party at your creepy-ass mansion. I can't wait. And for some reason, I don't believe you two are done popping out babies."

Emma realizes I'm talking about her nephew and yanks my hand from her pants. She turns to the cart full of clothes with the granny panties thrown on top and turns down the main aisle toward the front of the store.

"I don't know about that," he says as I follow his sister to the checkout.

"Oh, one more thing, Levi."

"Make it fast," Levi says. "I'm about to get on the elevator and will lose you."

"Just to set the record straight, when you see Emma going viral again with an exclusive interview with Sullivan, you can rest your head tonight knowing she's not bumping uglies with him. No drama with the quarterback star."

There's a pause over the line. I'm about to disconnect the call so I can pay for the damn cart full of basic clothes, when Levi's tone turns to one that sounds like it will erupt into World War III. "What the fuck are you talking about?"

What I do not tell him is that she's not bumping anyone's ugly but mine, or the fact my ugly is damn obsessed with his sister and intends to do everything in my power to make sure the bumping continues well past my client's drama. "When you're done cutting brains open, check the news. You'll see. Gotta go."

"Wait—" Levi bites, but I've had enough. I hang up on my friend who's smarter than humans should be and slide my cell into my chest pocket of my blazer that isn't from a big box store, but from Bloomingdales.

Emma doesn't look at me as she sifts through her choices. She tosses the dress, a pair of pants, and sweater on the conveyor belt along with the panties. Apparently, she needs two outfits for the day. "How is Levi?"

I ignore her question and pick up the panties. "These are nothing like what you wore last night. I had no idea you liked grandma drawers."

She shakes her head. "They're bikini panties. They're hardly grandma underwear."

I toss them back on top. "I prefer the other ones."

"Then I can't wait to see you in a thong. These are cotton and comfortable," Emma says.

Beep.

The checkout lady wearing red tosses them in a bag on the carousel and butts into our conversation. "She's not wrong."

"Seems I was out voted fair and square. I'm not one to question a democracy."

Beep.

Beep.

Beep.

There goes the rest of Emma's outfits for the day. Apparently one or two are not enough.

I dig my wallet from my pocket and pull out my platinum-colored credit card. I'm considering this purchase an investment in Brett Sullivan's career, which means Emma's granny panties are a tax deduction.

I dare Uncle Sam to argue this point.

I will win.

I also add shopping for real lingerie for Emma to my list of shit to do after I get Brett's career—and mine—back on track.

I'm shocked when the lady in red announces the grand total. Fuck, I forgot how cheap this place is. I swipe my card, happy to be done, so we can move onto digging Brett out of the pile of shit he was shoved into.

I grab the receipt and hand it to Emma. "Next time, I choose where we shop, and I get to pick out your underwear."

She beams up at me. "Thank you for my new clothes. I'm so excited to go to work and show my producer the interview."

I lean down and kiss her before claiming her hand so we can get out of this place. "Me, too, baby. Me too."

12

DRAMA LLAMA

Emma

I stand behind August. He sits in front of an oversized monitor hanging on every word throughout my exchange with Brett last night.

It's the evening news. Prime time for breaking stories—late enough that people are getting off work and early enough that the story has time to fester and gain momentum for the rest of the night.

In addition to my start with Jack, the day has been a whirlwind.

When I sat down with August this morning and explained the interview I carried out on my own, he looked at me like I was an alien who just told him the world was flat. I'm not sure he believed me.

Until he saw it.

He watched the interview three times before he finally moved into action.

The District is a busy place.

Politics.

Finance.

Crime.

Scandals.

There's always a breaking story.

It's not lost on me that the big wigs at my network always have a laundry list of choices to lead the evening news.

And tonight, that story is mine.

Mine!

They've teased it all day. Expectations are high. Not only is D.C. watching, so is the world.

I prerecorded a bit with the main anchors about my interview. I'm not on live, but I am watching myself on the monitors in the control room with my producer.

I try not to act nervous and tense as it comes to an end as Brett Sullivan makes his last dramatic statement about who he is.

And, more importantly, who he is not.

The feed switches back live to the anchor who promises that WDCN is committed to be the go-to network for breaking news on the Brett Sullivan story.

Then they break to the next political scandal playing out on Capitol Hill.

Those are a dime a dozen, so I turn to August who leans back in his chair, drags a hand down his lined face, and looks up at me. "This is like old-school shit. It's not every day we can break a story that you know without a doubt no one else has information on. Nice work, Emma."

My cell is buzzing my ass in my back pocket, but I ignore it. "Thanks. I was at the right place at the right time. I'm lucky he trusted me enough to do the interview."

August stands and moves out of the control room to let the staff do their thing for the rest of the show. I shut the door behind us and follow him to his office as he talks. "We're going to continue running bits on it through prime-time programming and rerun the interview on the late-night news. You've been here all day. Go home. You need to be ready for tomorrow."

I take a seat across from his desk in anticipation. "Tomorrow?"

He reclines in his office chair and levels his gaze on me. "The parade. We had a meeting this afternoon and decided you're officially the face of the Founders championship era. We need to run with it. You'll be there all day tomorrow. But you're not going to be in the temporary booth at the end of the parade route. You're still too new, and we need to play on your fresh energy. We're putting you back on the sidelines, but of the parade this time. You'll have press access to move through the route and do what you do best—improvise in a live situation. Ross will be with you again."

I can't keep the enormous smile from my face. "Thank you. I'll do my best to deliver quality content. You won't regret choosing me. I promise."

He lifts his chin. "Haven't regretted it so far. Be back here first thing in the morning for the production meeting. And whatever you do, keep in contact with Sullivan. He's the biggest story right now, second only to the Founders winning the big game for the first time in decades. The parade will be off the charts chaotic. And the real chaos won't be at the end route where the anchors sit. It'll be on the streets. I want every moment captured."

"I won't let you down, August. I promise." I stand, not sure if I should shake his hand or give myself a high five.

Jack Hale might be the secret tucked into my back pocket who helped set up the private interview, but everything else I did in Vegas was all me.

And tomorrow it'll be back to me.

I can't wait.

I forgo a handshake and high five when August turns back to the TV mounted on his wall to watch the rest of the news. "Tomorrow is going to be a long one—get some dinner and a good night's sleep. You're going to need it."

"Thanks again," I call as I make my way out of his office down the hall to my cubicle to get my things. I need to go home and figure out what to wear.

I pull my cell from my pocket. The notifications are adding up by the moment. The family text thread has exploded. I have two missed calls from my mom in California, and it seems viral news makes old friends come out of the woodwork. But then again, I've had this number since middle school.

I open the family text thread, because I can't not answer my family.

The Playbook of Emma

Keelie – I'll never get used to seeing you on the news. You're a badass and beautiful. A beautiful badass. I'm so proud!

Saylor – OMG! Brett is hot!

Knox – I made my entire robotics team stop our meeting to watch your interview. I might be the most popular guy at school thanks to you.

Levi – Only you would find your niche as a sports reporter through drama. You've also officially brought the Hollingsworth privacy era to an end, but you did it with a bang. You're killing it.

Carissa – I'll shout it from the rooftops of the Boyette mansion—that quarterback is into you! I beg you, tell me it's true!

Saylor – I'm Team Carissa. This would be the best meet-cute and happily ever after in history. Is it true?

Levi – Also, your ability to bullshit the world into thinking you know anything about football is fascinating to the point it makes me question everything you do and say. I'm equally impressed and suspicious of who you've become.

Dad – My smart, articulate, beautiful girl. Love you, Em. I'm a proud dad right now.

Saylor - I DEMAND FOR THIS LOVE STORY TO BE TRUE!

Levi – Tell me it's not true.

> Carissa – Ignore your brother.

I need to put an end to this so I can get out of here and move onto the text thread I really want to read.

> Me – Thanks, everyone. I've been assigned to the parade tomorrow!

I stuff my laptop in my backpack and grab my coat hanging on the back of my chair. I turn to leave but am stopped in my tracks.

Mean Molly Minders.

She's wearing a form fitting matching set in navy tweed boucle. The jacket barely hits her at the waist, and the skirt definitely doesn't hit her knees. Her heels boost her so high, she looks more like a super model rather than a weekend news anchor.

This woman has really mastered the art of sex-kitten news lady. Her blond hair sits in the perfect shape of a helmet and hardly moves when she shakes her head at me.

Molly has a way of demanding attention when she walks into a room. I doubt she relied on an epic influenza outbreak to make it to where she is today. All she needs to do to look the part is a case of hairspray, a bucket of foundation, and form fitting clothes.

And her fake boobs.

"Hey, Molly. I saw your story on the traffic light glitch that caused gridlock in the Maryland suburbs. Fascinating."

Her green eyes narrow. Between that and her thin, sharp nose, my mind goes to the wicked witch of the west from my favorite childhood movie.

In boucle, sans the broom.

She doesn't acknowledge my compliment on her traffic reporting. "I was bumped from the parade."

Oh shit.

"Oh, no," I feign disappointment. "I'm sorry."

She doesn't feign anything. She's shockingly transparent despite her many layers of foundation and concealer. "No, you're not."

She's right.

I'm not. Not one bit.

I decide to tell the truth. "I don't know what to say."

Her tone dips low enough for only me to hear. "That's interesting, because it seems like you always know what to say and where to be."

I take a step back to put some space between us and try to make light of my recent success. "I think getting somewhere fast has more to do with it. I didn't know I was a runner. I guess all those power walks through the mall really paid off. And comfortable shoes. I'm not as agile as you. I could never work in heels. You make it look so easy."

"Shut up," she snips, not in the mood to talk shoes and lowers her voice to a hiss. "I'm sick of you getting my assignments."

I hitch my backpack up my shoulder and straighten my spine. "It's not like I gave you the flu."

She shakes her head and cocks her hip … the universal bitch stance. I brace. "Who knows what you did to get

Sullivan to do that interview. Where was it anyway? His house? Maybe his bedroom?"

If she only knew whose house it was and whose bed I slept in after the interview, it was absolutely not the drama llama quarterback. "I've never had to resort to that. Is that how you landed your traffic-jam story today?"

"Damn you," she seethes. "You haven't even done your time. You can't waltz into a major market like this and expect to get all the good assignments right away. You've been here for two whole minutes. I've been here for four years."

Instead of fuming back at her in rage, I smile. "Two words, Molly—flu shot. I wish I could stay and chat, but not all of us can wear cute shoes to work. I'm going to be on my feet all day tomorrow and from the weather segment, it's going to be a cold one. I need to dig my shoes out from my time in South Dakota, where I reported on traffic jams, just like you. Though, they were caused by wild buffalo, not an entire grid going out."

I sidestep her, and she tries to stop me, but Ross comes around the corner just in time.

His gaze shifts between Molly and me before narrowing his eyes. "Everything okay?"

I smile. "Yep. Just chatting about football."

Ross crosses his arms. "I bet you are."

Molly mutters as she turns on her pricey heels. "Football, my ass."

Her cubicle is in the next row over, so it's not hard to hear her pissed-off exhale when she sits.

I bite my lip.

Ross chuckles and moves on. "I hear we're teamed up again."

"Just like old times," I say. "Like, a couple days ago."

"Can't wait to see who we chase after tomorrow. I'll be sure to carb up for the marathon."

I smile. Ross not only rescues me with informative football facts, but also from Mean Molly. "I can't wait."

"Do you know if Sullivan will be there?"

I shrug. "I'm not sure. I haven't spoken to him since the interview."

"For the sake of ratings, we can only hope. I'll see you in the morning."

"Have a good evening," I call after him and pull out my cell to read the text I haven't had a chance to open yet.

> Jack – It's official. I'm in your debt for life. Tell me what you want. A shopping spree with my personal stylist, dinner at my place, or an endless string of orgasms? Personally, I'm a fan of the last one, and even though I cook, I'm not in the mood, so I'll order in. I will personally create the orgasms—homemade and to your liking. I was going to say pick your poison, but I just decided you're getting all three and more.

> Me – Hey! I've never had a stylist, so I don't know what I'm missing out on. And as much as I like food and orgasms, I need to go home. I was assigned the parade tomorrow and have to be back early in the morning.

Jack – No, don't go home. We'll hit Tyson's, order dinner, and then get to the good stuff.

> Me – Jack, you cannot buy me clothes every day just to keep me in the city.

Jack – Fine. You can go home tomorrow to pack a bag. But tonight, I get to feed you and spin magic in your loins.

> Me – My loins? I can't believe you just said that. That's just … no. Please, don't say that again.

Jack – More begging. I like it.

I make my way to the front door when Sadie calls out from where she's sitting at the front desk. "Emma! I've been looking for you. You have a call."

I frown because in the few weeks I've been here, I have never gotten a call on the main business line. Everyone I know has my cell. "Who is it?"

She shakes her head. "He wouldn't say, and the caller ID is blocked. But he's insistent. He won't talk to anyone but you."

"I'll take it in the conference room, is that okay?"

"Sure. I'll give you a minute and transfer it."

I move to the conference room and shut the door behind me. The phone rings twice before I have a chance to pick it up. "Emma Hollingsworth."

The caller says nothing, but I can hear a rustling on the other end of the line.

"Hello? Is anyone there?" I ask.

"Yeah." It's a man, and his tone is low. I also hear wind in the background. "Is this the chick who interviewed the quarterback?"

I look around the empty room as if someone's watching me. Like someone will jump out of the walls and yell *you've been punked*.

"Yes. I interviewed Brett Sullivan. How can I help you?"

"Shit," he says. Somehow, I know it's not directed at me. It's a muttered frustration. "I knew this was going to go bad. I just knew it."

I look down at the bare conference room table and trace the vein of the wood with the tip of my finger. "What did you know?"

"I knew this was going to blow up in my face."

I freeze before asking, "What's your name?"

"No fucking way. I'm not telling you who I am."

"Then why did you call?" I press.

His exhale sounds almost violent. "Dammit. Look, I can only do so much. Who knew I'd have a fucking conscience?"

My insides tighten with anticipation.

Conscience.

"If you need to tell me something, I'll listen. We can meet if you'd like—"

"No," he interrupts. "You can't see me in person."

It's my turn to exhale, but mine is nothing but relieved. There's no way I'd meet with anyone by myself. "If you have something to tell me, you can do it now."

"He didn't do it. He didn't fucking do it. He's telling the truth. He was drugged."

I pause before demanding, "And how do you know this? Can you prove it?"

"No, I can't fucking prove it. Even if I wanted to, I don't have a death wish. If anyone finds out I made this call, I'll have the biggest fucking target on my back. It's your job to prove he didn't do it. You can do that, right?"

Whoever this man is, he's anxious and in a rush. I need to get all the info out of him that I can while I have him on the phone. "I'll try. I want to do everything I can. But right now, it's just his word versus photographic evidence. That's hard to disprove without more information … or someone else to prove it's untrue."

He says nothing, but I can hear his breathing pick up like he's walking or moving in a light jog.

"Did I lose you?" I ask.

"Dammit," he seethes. "I don't know what to do."

"Look, if you give me your name or your number, I can get in touch with you. We can work together."

"No fucking way. You'll call the cops."

"No. I promise I won't."

"Right. I have a shitload of promises that were ripped out from under me. I don't trust anyone."

"Okay. I get that. Let me earn your trust. I'll give you my number. My personal cell. You called the main line to the station. If you call here too often, people will notice. But you can call me. Or text, whatever you're comfortable with. But I always have my cell. Please help me. Tell me what you know so I can expose the truth. I can tell you want to."

More walking.

More breathing.

More thinking.

Finally, he gives in. "Fuck. Give me your number but do it fast. I need to get off this call."

I rattle off my number. Then I do it again just to make sure he gets it right.

"I feel bad not addressing you by name. Can you give me anything?"

He huffs one, single laugh. It's the farthest thing from humorous. "There's no fucking way I'm giving you any more. Just answer your fucking phone. I'll be in contact."

With that, the line goes dead.

I place the receiver in the cradle in the middle of the conference table. What the hell was that?

I pick up my cell that's been going crazy with notifications.

> Jack – Are you really giving me the silent treatment?

> Jack – Fine. It's my turn to beg, dammit. Please, Emma. Bump uglies with me again.

> Jack – Wow. You don't seem like the silent-treatment type of woman, but here we are. Fine, I won't refer to sex with you as bumping uglies.

> Jack – Emma, you are the most beautiful woman in the world who knocked me on my ass when you walked back into my life. Please forgive me for throwing frogs at you when we were little. Even though it was fucking fun, if I could go back to my childhood and not be an asshole to you when it came to amphibians, I would do it in a heartbeat.

> Jack – There's nothing more I want to do than take you shopping, feed you, and make sweet love to you until you pass out so I can stare at you like the freak I'm turning into.

> Jack – Holy shit, you're really trying to be a badass here, aren't you? Fine … again. I'm sorry for all the ways I might've been an asshole, not just when it came to amphibians. Don't make me scream at you through text by using all caps. I will if I have to.

> Jack – Emerson Hollingsworth, TALK TO ME!

Holy shit is right. Does anyone ever make this man wait two seconds to answer a text?

> Me – Change of plans, drama queen. I'll take you up on food and maybe other extracurricular activities. Definitely shopping. But something big happened. We need to talk.

> Jack – What the fuck, Em? That was the most painful four minutes of my life.

> Me – I had to take a call. I do accept your apology for the frogs. Don't ever do it again.

> Jack – Fucking fabulous. Come to my place and we'll go from there. I'll be waiting out front for you.

I can't wait.

I grab my things, hurry out of the conference room, and through the front door. I don't want to talk about this over the phone.

What I do know is nothing like this has ever happened to me before.

And because of that, I'm slightly—or more accurately, immensely—freaked out. I scan the parking lot as I hurry to my car. Whoever called me, knows I'm at work. The sooner I can get out of here the better.

I can't help the excitement simmering within me. I'm a genuine reporter. I know this about myself.

Even so, I'm chasing star quarterbacks on a football field, conducting secret interviews, and now have my very own Deep Throat, even though his tone isn't that deep. He's more of a middle C.

The stakes are high.

This is exciting.

But since I was raised by Asa Hollingsworth, I'm no idiot…

It might be exhilarating, but it's equally scary.

13

BREAKFAST OF LOSERS

Jack

"This is miserable, Jack. People are shouting at me. I'm either a drug-dealing low life or their hero. And the hero shit isn't because of football—it's because they think I'm a drug-dealing low life. It's all about the scandal. There's no in between, and the parade hasn't even started yet. This was a mistake. I should've stayed in the country with the cows who don't judge me."

It's a sea of people as far as I can see. The streets are packed, and most players are drunk, but it's nothing compared to the crowd. They've been congregating since yesterday, and the police are everywhere. I badged my way into a VIP tent at the end of the parade route. It's enclosed, heated, has a full buffet, and bar service.

"Eric Oliver demanded your presence. I'll remind him of your loyalty when this is over and I'm negotiating your new contract. Don't drink. Not even one beer. We need you to look the picture of who you said you were in the interview that aired last night."

"I don't need to look like anything or pretend I'm something I'm not," he growls through the phone. "I know who I am. That doesn't change the fact I feel like I have a target on my back. I was about to back out until you told me about Emma's mystery caller. It's my only hope at the moment. If there's nothing to it, I don't know what I'm going to do."

I lift my chin when I see an agent from my old firm, Gary Acosta. He represents Mark Morse, the quarterback Brett replaced when he went down early in the year. Gary isn't a dick by nature, per se, but he does roll over when the agency tells him to.

Which makes him a limp dick, just not an asshole dick.

The parade is about to kick off. The whole thing might be managed by the District, but it's televised nationally.

I turn away from the crowd that's growing by the moment and give my client my full attention. "You're not going to do anything. No charges have been brought forward. It all seems worse because it's not you or your brand, but there are some who wouldn't blink an eye if this shit happened to them. All you have to do is wave for the next hour, stand on stage for fifteen minutes or so, and the whole thing will be over. Then you can go back to your new cow friends."

"If my dumpster-fire career can't be extinguished, I'm moving to the country."

"One step at a time, Brett. Get through today and let me work on the rest," I say as I look up when I sense someone by my side. Gary the limp dick is standing next to me sipping an amber-colored cocktail. "I've got to go. Find me after the party."

"You bet your ass, I will," Brett mutters.

I disconnect the call and turn to Gary. "Good morning."

He takes a large sip of his whiskey. "Trouble in paradise, Hale?"

"My client is the Championship MVP and not a washed up half-broken quarterback. And my breakfast consisted of a spinach protein smoothie. I'm feeling like a winner, Gary."

"Is that why your client is in hiding and only doing selective interviews?"

I could keep my expression bland, but I don't bother. I can do that no problem for my clients or during negotiations, but with a limp dick like Gary?

Wasted energy.

"Are you drinking your problems away for breakfast since your client is washed up and being outperformed by his back up? Maybe you're shopping around for a trade. That's what I'd be doing if I were you." I lean in and lower my voice. "Oh, wait. I forgot you're still a puppet for the agency. You must not have been given the green light to think for yourself yet. You never know. It might still happen."

He glares at me and throws back the last of his cocktail, the breakfast of losers.

I take a sip of my coffee.

He sticks a finger in my chest. "Morse will get back in the game. I've been talking to Eric Oliver over the last few days. He doesn't like the drama Sullivan has brought on the team. Your boy is out next year. Morse is back on the field."

I bat his hand away. "The only field Morse will see next year is during warmups. Sullivan is a free agent. And after the season he had and his performance in Vegas, there's no amount of drama that overrides stats on the field. Maybe it's time to grow a pair and do what's best for your client and you—look for a trade. There are plenty of mediocre teams out there who would be drooling for your quarterback. If you're lucky, a wild-card team will give him a sniff."

Gary looks around at the A-list group surrounding us. Actors, singers, retired players. They're all here for the party.

I'm never here for the party, which is ironic since prior to becoming an agent, I *was* the party. The fucking party didn't even start until I said so.

Gary grasps the back of his neck, like he's trying to ward away an early hangover. The stress is evident. Gary Acosta is not well.

I bring my hand up and slap him on the shoulder. "Don't frown too deeply. Those lines will stick. If you need an aesthetician, let me know. No one wants to look prematurely old and washed up—you know, like your client."

The creases between his eyes deepen. "Fuck you, Hale. And fuck your client. He dug his own grave. All I have to do is sit back and watch the system bury him in it."

I smile and shake my head. "Grab another drink and keep dreaming. Your future is bleak, just like Mark Morse's career outlook."

I've had enough for more reasons than one. But the biggest is what catches my attention from across the enclosed tent. The enormous monitors televising the parade live flip to the crowd.

The weather has taken a turn in the last couple of days. The temps haven't only dipped, they took a dive the day we arrived home from Vegas. The crowd is nothing but a sea of winter clothes in the Founders colors. The parade has started, and the open-air buses make their way through the Capitol streets.

The camera is focused on my client. Brett might be the only one not chugging beer, throwing back shots, or dressed in couture. He's wearing a ski jacket, a ballcap with the logo of his foundation, and a generic smile. The only thing he's sporting of any significance is a pair of shades from one of his endorsements.

He waves to the crowd while talking to one of his receivers.

The main sports anchor from Emma's station, WDCN, is reporting the activities when he gains my complete attention.

"Let's see what's happening on the streets with the fans. Our own Emma Hollingsworth is doing what she does best —reporting from the sidelines." I take a step closer to the big screen when the woman I've become more and more obsessed with as the days go by fills the screen.

She's wearing the heavy winter coat, hat, and gloves I bought her when we hit Nordstrom last night. It was too late to make an appointment with my personal shopper, but Emma didn't need one. She knew exactly what she wanted. Even in a thick coat and furry hat, her long dark hair billows down her shoulders and her dark eyes shine bright in the cold, morning sun. Her cheeks are pink, and it has nothing to do with her makeup. The wind bites like a bitch today.

The crowd is in rare form, even for this city. Some are playing off the team name, dressed up like founders of our country to other crazies who are in full-on body paint, even in these temps.

But the weather doesn't tamp down her bright smile as she interviews fans in the crowd. I'm not sure which they're more excited about—being on TV or talking to her.

She has a way of putting you in a trance, making you forget about everything else. I might as well be Exhibit A. She's been doing it to me since I tracked her down at Nebula.

A group of guys who look like they've been partying for way too long come up behind her to get in the camera. They're rowdy, cheering, and crowding her.

Her smile is big and fucking bright as she continues to do her thing.

And I don't like any of it.

She's doing her job, and the idiot drunk fans are doing what they always do. It's nothing I haven't seen before. Hell, it's nothing the world hasn't seen. And she's handling it like a pro.

But something simmering inside me drowns out the surrounding chaos. The cheers, the jeers, and even the back and forth between Emma and her interviewee turn into white noise.

It's not jealousy. Hell, I'm me. I've never been jealous a day in my life.

Fuck.

But possessiveness...

That's something new for me.

This woman is not mine.

I mean, I sure as hell made her mine the last few days. But that doesn't make her mine. And it sure as hell doesn't put me in a position to demand that she doesn't do shit like this when it's her job, which is exactly what I want to do right now. I want to run out there and punch the assholes in the face who are too close to her. Especially the ones who are touching her.

But she keeps on while I'm here in the VIP tent. I need to focus on networking and other things, like piecing Brett's reputation back together and saving my career.

"Here they come." Gary breaks into my possessive haze and mutters, "Let the drunk speeches begin. I just want this day to be over so I can get back to business."

My attention is pulled away from the screen where Emma continues to report the celebrations on the street. I look out the windows of the heated tent where I'm protected not only from the weather, but the crazed fans. The beginning of the parade is inching its way around the corner.

Finally, one thing Gary and I can agree on.

I can't wait for this fucking thing to be over.

But my reasons are more than saving Brett Sullivan from whoever framed him and the mainstream media.

"Here they come." Emma's voice resonates through the space where she's only a block or two away from where we stand. "The team is coming around the corner."

The drunks hear what she says and move on. I start to release my tense breath until another group moves in.

The idiots who are stripped from the waist up and risk frostbite to decorate their bodies in team colors.

A glass landing on the banquet table next to me pulls my attention from Emma. Gary Acosta wipes his bottom lip with the back of his hand and slurs, "I'm headed to the back of the stage to corner Oliver when this shit wraps up."

"Good luck with that." I cross my arms and turn to him. "But do what you need to do. It must suck that the general manager of your bread-and-butter client's team won't take your call. A bit of advice—don't breathe on him. He already doesn't take you seriously."

Gary's eyes blink nice and slow. "And how would you know that?"

I tip my head to the side and tell him the truth. "Because no one takes you seriously."

His face reddens with anger, but he doesn't waste any time. He pops a mint in his whiskey-marinated mouth and turns to exit the tent, stumbling down the stairs.

Mark Morse has more problems than he can count, and what's sad is his shitty agent isn't even at the top of the list.

All thoughts of Gary and Mark disintegrate when I turn back to the screen.

Fuck.

If I thought the drunk bastards were a lot, they're nothing compared to the body-painted crew.

But there's one in particular who makes the hair on the back of my neck stand straight.

He's close to her.

Too close.

And he's angled away from the camera. Not that I could see his features through body paint if I wanted to. He might be painted from the waist up like the rest of them, but he's wearing a ski mask.

A ski mask in this weather wouldn't be weird if he weren't bare from the waist up.

Emma's attention is on the camera as she continues to do her job. She puts her hand to her ear, and you can tell she's listening to her producer give directions. "The fans are electric today and are about to get what they have waited long hours in this weather for. The team is right in front of us."

I take a step closer to the screen. For the first time this morning, my attention isn't on Emma.

I can't take my eyes off the masked man.

He's not like the rest. He's not cheering or watching the parade. His focus never wavers from her.

As the open-air busses round the corner, the crowd pushes

toward the street. But they have nothing to do with the proximity of him to Emma.

That's all him.

And he's fucking close.

She does her best to stay focused on the camera as she continues to talk, but when she senses him, she tries to shift away.

But there's nowhere to go.

That's when it happens.

My coffee hits the table in front of the big screen, as I feel the word vibrate on my breath. "No."

I feel pathetic and helpless as I watch panic form on Emma's face.

Then she's gone.

The feed shifts back to the anchor in the booth. It's clear to see that he saw what I saw. Tension lines his face when he says, "Thanks, Emma. We'll check back soon."

I don't bother to see what he says next. I'm out of the tent and down the stairs with my phone to my ear.

As I push through the gate and move out of the secured area, I enter the general population. With the team making the turn, fans are crushing the barriers at the edges of the streets. I'm going against the grain and barely hear her voice come across voicemail.

"Hey, this is Emma. Leave me a message, and I'll get back with you as soon as I can. Be kind and have a fab day."

"Dammit," I growl and don't bother leaving a message.

"Watch it, dude," a guy yells as I push past him.

I ignore everyone and everything.

I'm on a mission for Emma.

Even though I have no fucking idea where that might be.

14

PET A GOAT

Emma

One second, I was less than five feet from Ross, reporting on the parade and listening to August tell me to throw it back to the booth, and the next, I was grabbed from behind and swallowed up in the crowd.

"Shut the fuck up and cooperate."

That voice…

The words are growled into the side of my head through a ski mask. I caught a glimpse of him right before it happened. He's tall and strong even though his frame is lanky. And since he's not wearing a shirt and is covered in body paint, that's easy to see.

"Emma!" August yells into my ear. "Are you okay? Tell me where you are."

The transponder is hooked to my belt under my coat and my earpiece is hidden beneath the thick beanie. There's no way this guy can know I have contact with anyone unless he starts ripping my clothes off.

He has my arms pinned to my chest where I grip my mic like it's a lifeline.

Which, at the moment, it is.

"It's you," I say loud enough that August might hear. "You're the one who called me. What are you doing in D.C.?"

"I said shut up. And if you want me to trust you, you'd better not do anything to attract attention."

"Who in the hell is that?" August bites into my ear. "Dammit, tell me where you are."

I ignore August and do everything I can to keep Deep Throat talking. "I'll talk to you, just tell me where we're going."

"We need to talk alone." His tone is sharp and controlled. Unlike most everyone else I've encountered today, this guy isn't drunk or high.

"Please, let's just stay here. People will see you pulling me away. I'm willing to talk to you, but we don't want to attract attention."

"Who are you talking to, Emma?" I wince from August's bursts in my earpiece. "Tell me where you are so we can come and get you. Ross is looking for you."

Deep Throat finally comes to a stop. We're deep in an alleyway tucked behind a dumpster. It reeks of trash, urine, and stale pot. It basically smells like the city.

He lets me go and forces me against the brick. Our first conversation was exciting, but that was over the phone. This is pushing the boundaries for someone like me who only signed up to report the news.

His voice ... I recognize that voice when he bites, "Don't you dare fucking scream. You'll be sorry."

I shake my head. "Okay, but this isn't necessary. I told you to call or text me."

"There's no fucking way I can trust you. Look, I'm trying to do the right thing, okay? But we need to do it my way."

"Tell me where you are, Emma," August demands.

"I was reporting on a national event," I say. "If you don't want attention, then dragging me into an alley behind a dumpster while I was on camera isn't a good idea. A phone call—that's lowkey."

"She's in an alley," August says, talking to someone else in the control booth. "Call 9-1-1 and tell Ross."

Damn. I don't have much time.

I mean, that's also a good thing.

But I need to get this guy to talk.

"You've got me here," I say. "Did you come all the way to Washington just to talk to me?"

He looks up and down the alley before turning his masked face back to me, but he doesn't answer. "I have proof."

I push away from the wall and ignore my panicked producer in my ear demanding to know who I'm talking to. "Tell me. I can protect your identity."

"There's no way. Not with the guy I work for. He'll know I'm the rat."

I ignore the fact I'm in a desolate alley with a stranger who sort of kidnapped me and close the distance between us. "Then why did you drag me back here?"

Even though I can't see his expression behind the mask, frustration bleeds through his tone. "It seems no matter how much bad shit I do, I still have a fucking conscience."

"The cops are looking, Emma. I don't know who the hell you're talking to, but keep talking so I know you're okay," August demands.

"Tell me why we're here. I'm a journalist. It's my job to report the news and protect my sources. I'm doing everything I can to report the truth about Brett Sullivan. If you have evidence, I need it."

He leans in and lowers his voice. "Sullivan was framed."

"I need more than that."

"Who the hell are you talking to?" August bellows.

I take a chance and turn my mic off, rip the earpiece from my ear, and stuff it in my pocket so I can focus on the masked man who, for some reason, I trust. "Who framed him?"

"It was an inside job—or close to it. That's all I can give you. If you're looking anywhere but there, you're off track."

My insides seize. "You mean ... the team? Someone inside the Founders?"

He doesn't answer me, but his voice bristles further to a low, threatening tone. "I'll know if you fucking rat me out. You'd better find another way to take them down."

"How would I rat you—"

But I don't finish the sentence. We both freeze for an instant when the sound of sirens whirl from a distance.

"Fuck," he bites and turns in the opposite direction of the parade. "I've got to get out of here. Don't fuck me over, Hollingsworth. I proved I could get to you once—I'll do it again."

"Wait," I call after him, but he's fast. He turns the corner and is out of sight.

Dammit. I'm in fluffy winter boots, not the shoes I wore last weekend when I raced onto the football field. There's no way I can catch him.

All of a sudden, my adrenaline rush is gone. I force myself to pull in a deep, calming breath. I shiver from the cold I didn't feel during the drama. Now every cell of my body feels like the heat was leached from it.

I rip my glove off and dig my earpiece from my pocket. When I get it back in my ear, I switch my mic back on. "August, are you there?"

"She's back!" I wince when August shouts in my ear. "Are you okay? Where are you?"

"I'm okay. I'm headed back to the parade."

I'm about ten feet from the street when I see him come to a skidded stop as he sees me, fighting to catch his breath.

The look on his face is something I'll never forget. His wide chest rises and falls with labored pants, and I don't know if his cheeks are red from running or the cold.

And I have no idea how he knew I was in trouble or that I needed him.

I don't care.

All I know is he's here, and I've never been happier to see him than I am right now. And that includes the moment he showed up back in my life in the middle of the night at the fancy Nebula bar.

Jack drags a hand down his face as he stalks toward me. When he's the only thing in my vision, I hear Ross say from a distance through a winded tone. "Damn, there you are. August, we found her."

But all I see are Jack's tense blue eyes right before his hands claim my face. When his lips hit mine, I feel every ounce of anxiety and stress written in his expression.

Just when my lips are warmed by his, he breaks his kiss and pulls me to his chest. Jack isn't even wearing a coat, just a wool blazer over a sweater. His cashmere is soft and warm, but even better because it's on him.

Being wrapped up in him makes me feel safe.

"Fuck, Emma. That scared the shit out of me," Jack murmurs against my hair.

I press into his chest deeper and decide that the next time I spend the night with him, I'm going to steal this sweater and never give it back. I never want to forget how I feel at this moment. "I'm okay. How did you know to look for me?"

He puts a hand to the side of my head and forces me to look up at him. "The live feed cut out right when that guy grabbed you. I'll never forget the look on your face. I had to make my way against the crowds to where I thought you were. That's when I found your camera guy."

I look to the side where Ross is working way harder to catch his breath than Jack was. The camera is hanging from his hand, and his other is supporting his weight against the brick building. "I don't know what it is with you and running. Had I known I needed to condition to work with you, I never would've agreed to go to Vegas in the first place."

I press my cheek into Jack's chest. "This isn't normal. I hate running more than anyone."

Ross lifts his chin and motions to Jack. "I have no idea who this guy is, but I took a chance and trusted him when he grabbed me and asked which way you were taken."

"This is Jack. He's my…" I look up to find my new lover who's also my brother's best friend staring down at me with a hiked brow. I shake my head and turn back to Ross. "I'm not sure what he is, but I'm stealing his sweater."

Ross shakes his head and puts his cell to his ear. After he tells August where we are, he adds, "She's okay. Yeah, I'll ask and see what she wants to do."

"What I want to do about what?" I ask.

Ross doesn't move the cell from his ear as he answers. "Your non-boyfriend here isn't the only one freaked about what they saw before they were able to cut the feed. The station is flooded with calls about what happened to you.

They want to know if you feel like going back on air to show that you're okay."

I didn't think Jack's arms could constrict tighter than they already are, but they match his words when he bites. "No fucking way. She was grabbed by someone in the crowd. She's not putting herself out there again."

I fist his jacket to get his attention. "It's okay. We can talk about this later, but I'm fine. I can go back on air."

"You don't have to do anything. All they give a shit about is ratings," Jack argues.

"Hey now, *Jack*." Ross bites his name like a curse word. "You saw me running through the crowds with my equipment. I give a shit and so does my producer."

I ignore Jack and turn my attention to Ross. "Tell them I'll do it. I just need a moment to fix my lipstick."

"I don't like this," Jack says. "I'm not taking my eyes off you this time."

"She'll do it," Ross says to August. "You'll hear from her when she's ready." Ross glares at Jack. "Since her lipstick is smeared all over your face, maybe you should tend to that first."

Jack drops his arms and wipes his mouth with the back of his hand. I dig in my pocket for my lipstick but find my cell vibrating instead.

"It's my dad," I mutter.

Four missed calls and even more texts. Most of them are from Dad, but others are from Carissa and Levi.

I ignore the calls and open my texts and read the most recent one.

> Dad – Don't make me drive there to find you myself, Em. Let me know you're okay or your old man is going to send a search party, and you know what that means.

Shit.

I do know what that means. The last thing I need is a secret team who contracts with the CIA searching for me. They would've found me faster than the cops.

> Me – I'm good. It was all a misunderstanding. I'm going back on air and will call you when I'm done.

Bubbles appear immediately.

> Dad – Damn. It took you long enough to answer. If I don't get a call from you soon, I'm coming.

> Me – Go pet a goat and relax. I'm fine.

> Dad – I know you did not just tell me to pet a goat.

> Me – You'll feel better. Gotta go.

> Dad - At least I know no one kidnapped you and stole your phone. No one would tell me to go pet a goat but you or Saylor.

> Me – Ignoring you now. Don't freak out again.

"I'm not kidding when I said I'm not leaving your side," Jack says.

I pull up my camera to use it as a mirror to apply a fresh coat of lipstick. "Don't you need to be at the end with the team?"

That gets Ross's attention. "You're with the team?"

"Not exactly," Jack mutters.

I check my hair and fix my beanie before I stuff everything back into my pocket. "Can I have a moment before we go on, Ross?"

"Sure. We just need to get you on before we have to cut to the team at the end of the parade." Ross looks down the street. "I'll be on the sidewalk waiting. You good here with your non-boyfriend?"

I smile. "Yes. I just need a minute."

Jack moves in front of me and puts his hands to my hips, pulling me to him. "Are you really okay?"

I turn my mic off as I peek around him to make sure we're alone. "It was him, Jack—the caller."

His stare on me intensifies. "You're sure?"

"Yes. It was the same voice. He knew the details about our phone call. Because of the mask, I still have no idea what he looks like. Call me crazy, but there's something about him … I don't know. For some reason, I trust him. I definitely trust what he says. I don't think he's innocent in what happened to Brett, but there's someone else behind it."

Jack's blue eyes intensify. "Why do you think that?"

"Because he said so. He said it was someone on the inside. When I asked him if he meant the Founders, he didn't confirm it, but he did tell me he'd know if I told anyone."

"Fuck," Jack hisses.

"Exactly," I confirm. "Whatever we do, we have to be careful."

"*We* are not doing anything. Look at what just happened to you. I shouldn't have gotten you involved. You're done."

I push out of his arms. "I'm hardly done. I'm the one who interviewed Brett when everyone else in the world wants a piece of him. Quite literally, I might add."

Jack crosses his arms. "No more. It was the moment when I saw that guy put his hands on you when I thought I was going to lose my mind."

I mirror his stance and add a hitched boot. "But nothing happened to me, and he made it clear he didn't intend to do me harm. He wants to talk."

"Then he can talk to someone else in the future. I'm the one with access to Brett and the team. I'm cutting you off."

"Emma, you ready?" Ross calls from the sidewalk. "August wants to get this done before the team hits the stage. Some of them are so drunk, we want to make sure and get footage if they fall off."

Jack rolls his eyes.

I do not.

I take a step closer and poke my gloved finger into his chest and glare up at the man who is as infuriating as he is hot. "You might have access to the team and quarterback in question, but I'm the one in contact with the quasi-bad guy. He has my number, not yours. If you try to cut me out, Jack, I'll do the same to you. We'll see how far you get when I quit sharing information with you."

He catches my wrist when I try to move around him to prove to the world I'm fine. "You can't do that. It's dangerous."

I pull my hand away. "Watch me."

This time I do sidestep the man I've had more sex with in the last few days than I have in the last few years.

I stalk straight to Ross and turn on my mic. "Can you hear me, August? I'm back and ready to roll."

Before he speaks, I hear an exasperated sigh in my earpiece. "Emma Hollingsworth, you are officially the biggest drama magnet I've hired in my entire career. And I hired Molly Minders, if that is any comparison for you."

I smile at Ross who hears the same thing I do. "That's not the compliment I was hoping for."

August goes on. "You're good for ratings. But I've got kids older than you. Consider me the bonus dad who wants you to come home in one piece."

"That's sweet," I say. "But my dad is enough for me to deal with. And that doesn't include my bonus uncles."

"Alrighty then," August says. "Let's do this. The world wants to make sure their new darling of sports is alive to report another day. I'll have the desk throw it to you. Be ready."

I glance at Jack who wasn't kidding when he said he wouldn't let me out of his sight. He's barely out of the camera frame and looks like he'll pounce if anyone so much as bumps into me on accident.

"I'm ready, August."

Jack's jaw tenses.

"For anything."

And with that, the anchor reporting from the makeshift booth at the end of the parade route throws the live feed to me.

I force myself to ignore Jack Hale and convince the rest of the world—most specifically my dad and family—that I'm okay.

I don't care what Jack says.

I'm moving forward.

And he can't do anything to stop me.

15

EXCLAMATION POINTS

Emma

"I swear, it was nothing. I was caught up in the crowd. Everyone was drunk and happy. I was fine."

Dad pulls in a deep breath and leans back in his chair at the dining table. He's giving me that look he did when I was a teenager, which screams he can read through my bull shit, and that I'm a big, fat liar.

He would be correct, just like he was back in the day.

"It didn't look like nothing," he states.

But Keelie proves she's not just the best stepmom of all time but also has my back. "If she says she's fine, I'm sure she's fine, Asa. She's been doing this for years and we didn't watch every moment she was on air. I'm sure there are many things we missed."

"You're fine, blah, blah, blah." Saylor's glass hits the table and water sloshes in dramatic fashion as she leans forward and levels her gaze on me. "You were at the parade today, and Brett Sullivan came out of hiding. After chasing him down on the field and the private interview, you can't tell me that you didn't see him today. Please," she drawls. "Tell me the two of you met up in a dark corner and made plans to hook up."

"Saylor!" Keelie yelps.

I gape at her. "Are you asking me if I scheduled a hookup while we're eating dinner?"

"Holy shit," Dad mutters as his eyes fall shut. He pinches the bridge of his nose like he feels a migraine coming on, and that's a lot for him since he rarely gets a headache. When he opens his eyes, he reaches over and grabs Keelie's hand. "Why are teenagers like this?"

"I didn't mean it that way. I meant like a date." Saylor is annoyed with everyone but still shoots me a sly smile. "But if you did schedule a *hookup* hookup, you can tell me later. Apparently, the 'rents are too old to handle this kind of talk over ziti."

Keelie stands and picks up her plate. "I'm declaring dinner officially over before our daughters prematurely age us any further."

"Thank goodness." I follow suit and start to do the dishes. "Between the trip to Vegas and the Founders win, I haven't had a chance to look for an apartment in the city. That's on the top of my to-do list."

Dad loads the dishwasher before pressing his lips to the top of my head. "Just got you back, Em. I'm not in a hurry for you to leave. Saylor will age me one way or another."

Saylor wraps her arms around Dad's middle for a big hug. "You wouldn't have me any other way."

Dad shakes his head and gives her a squeeze. "You're right about that."

"Thanks, Dad. But driving from the country every day is a lot. I can't crash on my friend's sofa every night." My thoughts go straight to Jack, whose sofa I've never crashed on. I go willingly to his bed when I'm at his house. But today, we didn't leave on good terms. I was done reporting and had to get back to the studio with Ross. Jack had to tend to the mess Brett found himself in. We didn't even say goodbye.

Keelie spoons leftovers into a glass dish. "You'll be at Hudson's party, right? I can't believe he's already a year old."

"Yes. My producer gave me a few days off. I've missed so much the last couple of years, you couldn't keep me away if you tried. I need to go shopping for a gift."

"Have you been to Levi's lately?" Dad asks. "Those kids don't need anything else."

Keelie elbows Dad on her way to the refrigerator. "Says the grandpa who just ordered an entire addition for their play equipment. Did you even tell Levi or Carissa that will be arriving?"

Dad does his best to bite back a grin. "Why would I tell them? It's a surprise."

"The creepy old mansion gets less and less creepy with each kid they have," Saylor says. "I remember when Carissa and Cade lived there with their grandmother. I was scared to be there even with you guys. She died in that house. I'm not sure how Levi lives there."

"Levi and Carissa made that mansion into a beautiful home. It's not at all creepy like it used to be," I say. "Plus, it's private. What's not to love about that? No drive-by shootings. Right, Keelie?"

"You had to bring that up," Keelie mutters.

"We don't talk about that," Dad states.

I look at Saylor and shrug. "See? Creepy old private mansions are good for something, right? And the percentage of people who experience a drive-by shooting has to be low. It's not like it's going to happen again—statistically speaking."

"I don't want to know the statistics of living through that again." Keelie shuts the fridge and turns to us. "Changing the subject from the event that shall not be mentioned, Knox called me today. He's coming home for Hudson's party. Everyone will be together. I thought it would be normal family time, but he said he's bringing a girl home."

Finally, Saylor has something else to focus on besides me. "A girl?"

Dad crosses his arms. "Good for him."

"Did he tell you anything about her?" I ask.

Keelie pulls her lip between her teeth and shakes her head. "No. He was in a hurry to get off the phone. All he said was he met someone, and he wants to bring her home for a visit. They'll come straight to the birthday party Friday night."

"He never tells me anything lately." Saylor says and crosses her arms. "It has to be because of her. There's no other explanation."

Keelie's tone is sharp, and she sounds more like a teacher than a mom. "You don't know that. None of us know anything. I just want everyone to be prepared."

Saylor is annoyed. "We know nothing. How can we prepare?"

"She's not wrong," I point out even though I'm distracted. My cell vibrates three times straight where I stuffed it in my back pocket.

Keelie sighs. "The first thing I need to prepare for is a place for a guest. Despite how Saylor talks at the dinner table, we still run a PG home. There's no way they're sharing a room. We converted Levi's old room into a library and Emma is home. That was our guest room."

"She can sleep on the sofa," Dad says.

Keelie gives him an exasperated look. "I can't put a guest on the sofa."

"Is she really a guest?" Dad asks. "We didn't invite her."

"Put Knox on the sofa," Saylor suggests. "That's what he gets for not telling us anything."

"I'm not putting my son on the sofa when he's home from college."

I ignore all talk and the eeny-meeny-miny-moe of the Hollingsworth Inn. Someone is rapid fire texting me again.

Jack -- You left.

> Jack – You left before we could talk. We're so not done for the day.

> Jack – Where are you? Remind me to figure out a way to track your phone. That would've come in handy today when DEEP THROAT FUCKING KIDNAPPED YOU.

> Jack – Dammit, where are you, Emerson Hollingsworth?

Wow.

I knew Jack was a big personality but when he gets like this, he's too much.

> Me – Did you just scream at me in all caps and address me by my full name?

> Jack – I wouldn't have to do that if you'd answer me in a timely manner. Like, immediately.

> Me – Possessive much?

> Jack – Much. Very much.

> Jack – And for your information, I was not screaming at you. I was emphasizing my words. There's a big difference. Screaming would include exclamation points. Note: Caps plus exclamation points equals screaming. I would never scream at you.

> Jack – Not unless I really needed your attention. Like IF YOU'VE BEEN KIDNAPPED. Note: no exclamation points.

"Who in the hell is texting you?" Dad asks. "Your phone is buzzing nonstop."

I look up and shake my head. "A friend. Friends. It's a group chat."

"I have an idea," Saylor pipes in, dragging me back into the who-sleeps-where conversation. "Emma can stay with Brett Sullivan so mystery girl can have her room. You can boobytrap her door to make sure Knox doesn't go sneaking around in the middle of the night."

I plant my hands on my hips and ignore Jack Hale. "I am not staying with Brett Sullivan. We are not a thing."

Saylor flips her long blond hair over her shoulder and picks up her backpack on her way out of the kitchen. "If you say so."

I turn to Keelie. "I'll stay with Levi and Carissa. Good luck keeping Knox and the new girl apart. I should be surprised, but I'm not. Knox has that wholesome cute thing working for him. He reminds me of Mason Schrock. I knew the girls would be all over him at school."

Keelie drags her hands through her hair. "Don't say that. Please don't say that. Knox isn't old enough to get serious about anyone."

I take a cue from Saylor and escape the kitchen. "Might I remind you, Levi was secretly engaged to Carissa when he was younger than Knox."

Keelie gasps. "Stop it."

"Come here, baby," Dad says softly. The last thing I see is him pull his wife to his chest and wrap his arms around her. "It'll be okay."

"No, it won't," Keelie cries. "My baby is serious about a girl."

That's the last thing I hear before I round the staircase to my old room that I'm being kicked out of. Sort of. Levi and Carissa have a million bedrooms in that old mansion. I just need to remember to tell them to dust one off for me.

But now is not the time. The man I invited into my life and my pants is so demanding, I can't see straight.

> Me – We need to work on you texting entire thoughts together. And I was not kidnapped, Jackson Hale.

> Jack – Ha, joke's on you, EMERSON. My name isn't Jackson. It's just Jack.

> Jack – Unless you're my best friend, aka, Levi, then you can call me Jackie. No one else is allowed to call me that other than my grandma.

I flop down on my bed and stare at the screen. The man is as sweet as he is obnoxious.

> Me – I'm at home. I haven't been here in days. I had to show my face. Dad freaked out when he saw what happened today on TV. I'm twenty-six. I really need my own place.

> Jack – Pack a bag. I'll share my place with you any day. Wait. Every day. I want you in my bed. And in my kitchen. And on my sofa. Hell, I'll take you in my creepy-ass basement that you haven't seen yet. It's the only part of the brownstone that hasn't been touched since the twenties—the nineteen twenties. How's that for a complete thought?

> Me – We've been together for five minutes. And four of those minutes have been filled with quarterback drama and Deep Throat drama. Sharing a bed with no expiration date is too much to think about.

> Jack – I refuse to put an expiration date on you.

> Me – I'm staying at Levi's this weekend. I've been kicked out of my room for Knox's girlfriend.

> Jack – Emma, Emma, Emma. I'm wounded. You can stay with me.

> Me – Next time.

> Jack – You've shown your face at home. Come back. Brett is coming over for a quick meeting before he heads back to Whitetail. I'll fill you in if you come.

I knife up to a sitting position.

> Me – Why is Brett coming over?

> Jack – Now you're interested. Should I be worried?

Me – Don't be ridiculous. I'm invested in his story. The fact you'd even ask that is crazy.

Jack – Are you going to tell me if Deep Throat calls you?

Me – Are we really doing this? Tit for tat?

Jack – I'll take your tit any day, baby. One of them … both of them. If you can't tell, when it comes to you, I'm pathetically desperate.

Me – There you go again.

Jack – What's that?

Me – Being sweet when I should be mad at you.

Jack – I'm hard to be mad at.

Jack – Or, I should say, I'm hard to stay mad at.

Jack – Sorry about the random thoughts. I'm trying to do better. I have an itchy trigger finger.

I roll to my side and pull a pillow into my chest.

Me – It's okay.

Jack – Gotta go. Brett's here. I'll call you.

Me – You'd better. I'm jealous I'm not there, and you get to talk to Brett.

> Jack – Now you're making me jealous again. I'll call when he leaves. I might update you on what he has to say, but it depends on certain sexual favors.

I can't keep the smile off my face.

> Me – You've officially lost it.

> Jack – For you, I have. DO NOT LEAVE YOUR PHONE. I'll call. Note: No exclamation points.

I don't answer him. I toss my cell next to me on the mattress and roll to my back.

I'm exhausted. It's been one long day after another. Maybe I should've made an excuse to stay in the city. I've gotten used to being with Jack.

Sure, he pissed me off when he tried to tell me what I could and couldn't do.

No one tells me what to do.

Still…

My obsession when it comes to him is becoming stronger every day.

Damn.

All there is for me to do now is wait.

16

HELPLESS

Jack

We're almost in the same position we were the last time Brett was here, sans my new favorite sports reporter, also known as the most frustrating woman on the planet.

When I saw that guy grab her, I thought I was going to lose my fucking mind.

Never have I felt so damn powerless. I've been a lot of things in my life. I was the kid with no dad. The kid with shit clothes and holes in his shoes and my bedroom was the sofa until I was in middle school.

Hell, I never would've known that wasn't the norm had I not spent half my childhood at Levi's to know that other kids actually had their own bedrooms, or that they weren't raised by a grandmother so their moms could work two and a half jobs to support an unconventional family.

I was too busy being smothered in sappy love by two women who were more determined than the Pope to make sure the long line of asshole men in my ancestry stopped with me.

Don't get me wrong.

I know I can be an ass of a different variety.

Growing up, I was never where I was supposed to be. I drank too much and experimented with drugs just enough to realize that my mom and grandma were right—that shit will fuck you up so fast it's like getting hit on your blind side. All I had to do was look around to see it play out in front of me.

But I was never helpless.

Hell, if anything, I was the opposite of helpless. I made sure I was in absolute fucking control of every aspect of my life. I was not going to sit back and watch the universe pass me by. I was already behind the eight ball with no father while skating the edge of poverty.

I was the kid who got free lunches at school and handouts from the counselor whenever there was something to hand out. Mom and Grandma made sure I was grateful and never looked a gift horse in the mouth. I heard those words growing up over and over and never knew what they meant, I just knew the women in my life were serious and would get out the wooden spoon if I showed my true ass by not being grateful.

But being an asshole to a woman?

I would never. To say I'm in touch with women is an understatement.

Every aspect of the female psyche was ingrained into me so deeply, even I'm surprised I turned out straight.

Am I proud of myself that I went caveman on Emma and told her what to do?

Not really.

Am I proud that I got pissed at her for not doing what I told her to do?

Again, no.

But this is where helpless has gotten me, dammit. It's hitting me from all angles of my personal and professional lives, blurring into a dark sea of emotions I cannot get under control.

"You're sure you can't think of anyone on the team who would do this?" When I told Brett what Deep Throat said to Emma today, he was as shocked as I was.

Brett shakes his head. "No way. I've been in the organization for a year. I've done nothing wrong. I did what I was hired to do."

I stop pacing and turn to him. "You did more than that. You killed it. There's no way they'll replace you next year."

"There will be if I've been charged with drug possession and stolen weapons. Drugs and guns on their own ... idiots get off all the time for being stupid. But you mix drugs with the guns, and the charges go through the roof."

"How do you know that?"

Brett juts to his feet, throws out his arms, and raises his voice. "What do you think I've been doing for days? Drinking wine and playing with cows? I've been researching my future, Jack, and it's not looking good. In fact, it's looking pretty fucking bleak."

I drag a hand through my hair. "There's one rule in life: when you have a medical or legal emergency, stay off the internet. Everyone knows that."

He gapes at me. "Really? That's the only rule in life? Well, I'm pretty sure you can add to that list possession of illegal drugs along with stolen, fully automatic weapons. That's pretty bad in the state of Nevada and anywhere else I looked it up—just because I've got time to kill."

"I've rarely seen those rules apply when it comes to celebrities. Trust me, I know. I'm a lawyer—even if I don't argue daily in front of a judge. If this goes south and charges are filed, I have the best of the best in my back pocket when it comes to representation. She might cost nine hundred dollars an hour, but she's a fucking shark. If it comes to that, you'll be fine."

For the first time since this all went down, Brett finally loses it. "If it comes to that, I promise you I WILL NOT BE FINE!"

I pause and lower my voice. "Did you just yell at me in all caps?"

"What the fuck are you talking about?" he bellows.

"Nothing." This time I add tossing my stress ball into the air and catching it rhythmically as I continue to pace. "I'll call the lawyer tomorrow in case it blows up—which it won't, but it won't hurt to be prepared. What I'm more worried about is who has it out for you from within the organization. Especially after you delivered the trophy. If they did it once, they'll do it again. Have you talked to anyone else today?"

Brett falls to his ass once again. "Morse checked in with me a few times. We're tight and he's been supportive of me since he went down early in the season. There was no reason for me not to take his calls. Other than that, I've gotten messages from a lot of players, but I let them go to voicemail. At first, I didn't have the energy or want to deal with anyone. Now I'm glad I ignored everyone."

I stop mid-pace and fist the stress ball so hard, my knuckles go white. "Acosta."

Brett narrows his eyes. "The agent?"

"Gary Acosta represents Mark Morse," I add. "Acosta has had it out for me for years since I left the Pike Agency. I ran into him today in the VIP tent before the parade. He was more stressed than I've ever seen him. I put it out of my head after what happened to Emma. He all but threatened me that Morse would be back on the field next year and you'd be on the sidelines. I barely had a chance to set him straight when I saw our anonymous informant grab Emma."

"If it is him, there's no way to prove Mark is in on it. Acosta could be acting alone to get his client back on the field."

"Going to the police ... that would be the logical thing to do. But it happened in Vegas. Whoever set you up was smart enough to figure out how to kill the surveillance. And it's not like the cops are knocking on your door with an arrest warrant. I'm not sure we want their attention. Then there's the fact Deep Throat warned Emma. I can't risk anything coming back on her."

"I don't want that," Brett says. "She's been helpful and cool."

I pull in a deep breath before exhaling my only idea that feels questionable at best, but it's all I've got. "Let's test Morse. You said he's been calling you. Give him something. Something that only he'd know. We can see what happens."

"What am I going to tell him?"

"Start with something small. Something innocent. Lie about where you're staying. Hell, tell him you're with me strategizing how to crawl out of this shit show. We'll see if anyone shows up. Like the fucking media. Your behemoth monster is parked out front if I'm home. That'll make it easy. The press knows your ride from coming and going at the games."

"You really want the paparazzi at your place?"

I toss the ball one more time and shoot him a wide grin when it lands back in my hand. "Look at me, Brett. I was born to handle the press. If it reveals the fucking traitor, bring it on."

Brett stands and digs his keys out of his pocket—my keys since he's still driving my car. "Let me get out of here and I'll call him on the way back to Whitetail. Unlike you, I'd very much like to avoid the media right now unless it's your girlfriend."

My girlfriend.

It's been a long fucking time since I've referred to any woman as my girlfriend. Hell, I'm not even sure I was in college the last time I did that.

I follow Brett through the family room and kitchen to the garage where he parked so he wouldn't be seen coming and going from the busy street.

"Let me know what he says," I call for him as he makes his way to my car through the cramped garage.

Brett lifts his chin before he fits his large frame into my driver's seat. "If he answers. He might still be partying after the parade today. I was the only one who didn't want to be there."

"If anyone deserved to party today, it was you. You made the winning touchdown. I'll wait for your call."

Once he's gone, I waste no time.

Her cell rings exactly once before she bypasses a traditional greeting. "Are you going to talk to me like you text me—in all caps?"

"Emma," I call her name in a low, smooth tone. "There are a few things in this world that require all caps. Kidnapping is at the top of that list."

She sighs. I've been with her enough in the last week that I can tell she's very fucking horizontal. I'm very fucking pissed I'm not horizontal with her.

"Hang on, baby," I say.

I touch the screen a few times before going back to her. "I want to see you."

"So demanding," she mutters, but doesn't hesitate.

The next thing I know, my screen is nothing but big dark eyes, messy hair, and Emma. And I was right. She's horizontal.

So fucking beautiful.

"I knew it."

"What did you know?" she asks.

I lean back in my favorite leather club chair. It's the only place I sit in the whole place, and it's not often. If I'm not sleeping, I'm pacing. "That you're in bed. I could tell by the sound of your voice."

She tries to bite back a smile. "Oh, do I have a bedroom voice?"

"You very much have a bedroom voice. I like it better when it melts across my skin than when it comes through a small screen."

"Mmm," she hums, right before she licks her lips. "I do like that."

"Are you done being mad at me?" I ask.

She settles into her pillow farther. "Was I mad at you?"

It's my turn to smile. "You know you were. But I couldn't help it. You bring out the monster in me. You needed me, and I couldn't get to you. It didn't sit well."

"Has anything sat well since we ran into each other at Nebula?"

"I think our first night went really fucking well. And every other time when it's just you and me and we shut out the world. You don't agree?"

"It's been a little manic. I need to mentally compartmentalize the good from the bad, but when I do, you're at the root of it all."

I shrug. "I'll admit I'm not surprised by that. Probably not the first time a woman has thought that about me."

"But the bad isn't your fault. Other than texting me in all caps. I don't like that."

"You've made that clear. The last thing I want to do is something you don't like. Can we agree that I will only talk to you in lowercase letters as long as there is not a kidnapping involved?"

She changes the subject. "What did Brett say? Does he have any ideas who might want to frame him?"

"We have a hunch, but we're not sure. Mark Morse's agent was acting more awkward than normal today. It could've been the whiskey he was drinking for breakfast, but my gut says it's more. Brett's going to call Mark, feed him some lies. See what comes of it."

"That makes me nervous. I'm not sure that's a good idea. I wish there was something more I could do."

"You've done more than anyone else. We have the ever-so-charming Deep Throat because of you."

"Charming," she echoes. "He could use some chill when contacting me. Otherwise, delightful."

I'm sick of talking about Brett or the informant. "This shit show won't last forever. When it's over, it'll be just you and me. I can't wait for that."

Her expression softens. "What will we do without the drama swirling around us?"

My blood rushes to my cock just thinking about uninterrupted time with Emma. I adjust myself as I speak. "I'd book the most private table I could find in all of Northern Virginia and the District. Then I'd tell you to put on the sexiest dress you own. I'd wine and dine you the way you deserve. Depending on how private the table was, I'd touch you in every place your dress allowed. Because when I'm with you, I can't not touch you."

"That sounds scandalous." Her chest rises and falls with a quick breath. "I like it."

A smirk touches my lips. "For some reason, I thought you might. You're a brave one."

"It seems I am for you."

"I like that even better." My tongue sneaks out to wet the crease of my lips. "That you're only brave for me. That's a theory I'm not willing to allow you to test with anyone else."

"Allow." She wastes no time quipping back, but this time she does it with a smile. "There you go again thinking you can tell me what to do."

I lean forward as if I can get closer to her through the damn screen. "When it comes to the thought of you doing anything with anyone besides me, you bet your sweet ass I will. And, trust me, that's not me being an asshole. That's me wanting you and only you."

"This is fast, Jack."

"That's me—fast Jack."

Her dark eyes flare. "You know what I mean."

"I've known you your whole life. How is that fast?" What I do not think about is Levi. No one knows me better than he does, which does not bode well for me when I finally break the news that I'm into his sister in a big way.

She's about to argue with me again, probably about the fast track we're on that I refuse to acknowledge, but I get another call.

"Hang on, baby. That's Brett."

"I'm not going anywhere, but you'd better tell me what he says."

I flip over before I lose the call. "Hey. Did you get hold of him?"

"I did," Brett says with highway noise humming in the background. "I did what we talked about. He didn't seem interested in where I'm staying but offered to get together with me soon for a drink. He expressed again how what happened sucks and no one on the team believes it. Like that matters."

"We'll see what happens." I get up and walk to the bay window that overlooks one of the most historic streets in Old Town Alexandria. "I'm here for the rest of the evening and night. Bring it on."

"I hope we don't regret this," Brett says.

I turn and start pacing again. "I'll let you know if something happens. Enjoy the wine with a side of cow."

"I think this'll be the last night. I appreciate your friends letting me stay, but I'm getting antsy, and quite honestly, pissed. I'm tired of hiding out."

"Let's see what happens in the next day or so. I happily take the heat for my clients. I'll touch base if anyone shows up."

"Thanks, man. I don't know whether to hope we talk soon

or not. It's hard to wrap my head around my teammates doing this to me."

"Time will tell."

"Later."

Clicking back over to Emma, I have too much pent-up energy all of the sudden. Knowing this is the best I'm going to get tonight, I wonder when I became the guy who's anxious to Facetime anyone.

I don't even do that for my grandmother, and I'll do anything for her.

I don't have a chance to tell Emma all the things I'd do to her in the back of a limo when she starts in with her journalistic inquisition. "What did he say?"

Emma

"You know, if I didn't know how much you're into me, that would hurt my feelings," Jack drawls.

I smile. "Sorry. This is like some crazy mystery game that I'm itching to solve. I can't help it."

He acts like he's put out, but he tells me in detail about Brett.

"Thank you," I say when he's done. "More wait and see, I guess."

"Now we can get back to what I'm going to do with you in a restaurant. Or in the back of a limo."

"You didn't tell me there was a limo." I can't keep the stupid smile off my face. "Would I hike my fictional dress and straddle you?"

"Baby." His voice dips. "Only after I slid your panties to the floor."

"You know how weird it feels having this conversation as an adult woman in my teenage bedroom with my dad and stepmom downstairs?"

"No weirder than it does having this conversation with Levi's younger sister."

My smirk grows into a smile bigger than it should. Just a few days ago I never could've imagined this conversation would be a reality. I thought Jack Hale would only be a one-night experience. "I'll protect you from my brother. I'm brave that way."

"I'll gladly take a beating from Levi if it means I can have you. Whatever it takes for him to get over himself. But I don't want to talk about him. I want to talk about you riding me in the back of a limo."

Wetness pools in my panties at the thought. "That sounds like I'm doing all the work. What is your part in all this, and what do I get out of it?"

His blue eyes close a touch. I recognize the lust in his features as he talks about me. "I get to feel you. Inside and out. I get to watch. And you, baby, get to come."

I turn the volume down a notch on my cell and hug my

pillow tighter. My nipples are hard and there's nothing I want more than a limo ride with Jack.

"I want that," I whisper.

Jack stops pacing. "Not as much as I do. I can't fucking wait to make that a reality."

My cell beeps with an incoming call.

Not just any call.

An unknown caller.

I let go of the pillow and sit up straight.

"Jack, I've got a call."

Gone is the lust. "Who is it?"

"Unknown. Shit. I need to answer in case it's him. Shit. Shit-shit."

"Answer it," he bites. "I'll be right here when you're done."

I touch the screen and put the cell to my ear. "Hello, this is Emma."

"What the fuck did you do?"

It's him. Every nerve ending in my body goes haywire. "Wh…what do you mean? I didn't do anything."

"You did something," he bites. This is just like his first call, but this time he's angry. "I'm trying to help you. Fuck, I'm trying to do the right thing for once in my fucking life, and you fucked it up."

I jut to my feet and do everything I can to keep my tone from sounding as panicked as I feel. "No, I swear. I didn't do anything. What happened?"

"They know where he is. I got a call with a job. I had to lie and tell my guy I wasn't close enough. I guess I do have boundaries. I'll drug a guy but I'm not killing anyone. Not for any amount of money."

My free hand goes to my hair and fists it. "Kill him? No. You have to stop it. How did they find him?"

"They found out where he's staying. Who the fuck would let that information out?"

"Jack," I whisper.

"Who?" my anonymous informant growls as I hear feet hit the pavement in the background.

"Oh no. I've got to go. I need to warn him. Please, whoever is doing this, make them stop. Please! And call me back."

My fingers tremble. I'm afraid I'm going to disconnect the call on accident, but I finally manage to switch to Jack on FaceTime.

His warm blue eyes are intense when he sees me. "Now it's my turn to demand—"

"Jack!" Tears streak my face. "Get out. You have to get out. They're sending someone for Brett. Get out!"

Jack frowns. "What the hell did he say?"

"Get out! Please," I beg. "They're going to kill him. They think he's at your house. Someone is coming. Listen to me!"

"Emma," Dad yells for me from across the house. "You okay?"

I ignore him and don't take my eyes off my screen. "Jack, did you hear me?"

He drops his cell and moves across the room. I can't see him. All I see is the damn ceiling.

"Jack!" I scream.

My bedroom door bursts open. Dad stands there with Keelie pulling up the rear. Their expressions are as confused as mine is horrified.

"What the hell is going on?" Dad demands.

I shake my tear-streaked face and turn back to my phone.

I think my heart skips a beat when I see Jack's face. He shakes his head and shrugs. "Em, there's no one here. I swear. I'd tell you if there wa—"

And that's the last thing he says before it happens.

Gunshots.

And not just a few.

Memories fill my mind from a moment in time long ago, but a moment I'll never forget.

One of the worst in my life.

"NO!" I scream.

My cell falls to the floor when I drop to my knees.

Helpless.

Scared.

And empty.

More so than I've ever felt in my life.

17

DADDY ASA AURA

Jack

I saw it right before it happened.

Had I not been looking, I'd be dead.

A car so nondescript and basic, I didn't even know how to describe it to the police other than dark but not black, small but not too small, and with four doors. It happened too fucking fast. And the only reason I remember what I do is because there were two barrels pointed toward the front of my house. One through the front window and the other from the back.

Yeah. Two.

You know, in case one wasn't enough to get the job done.

Well, it turns out when you know it's coming, two isn't enough.

I dropped to the floor heavier than an anchor. The only

thing I could hear through gunfire and glass breaking were Emma's cries through the cell that fell next to me.

It seems my century-old brownstone brick was built to withstand the test of time.

And drive-by shootings.

The original antique windows … not so much.

And my home, the only one I've ever owned—the one I bought based on pictures alone the moment it came on the market and paid top dollar for—is a fucking disaster.

Cops are everywhere. Up and down the street, in and out the front door, and collecting every bit of evidence they can find. I found the one spot on the main floor to sit that isn't shot to shit or covered in glass.

An EMT cleaned the gash on my hairline where I hit a table on my way down. She said it could use stitches, but it's borderline. I told her I'm not going anywhere. There's no way I'm leaving my house the way it is.

I hear commotion from outside, which is easy to do since there are no windows.

"Sir, you can't go in. No one can. This is an active crime scene."

A deep voice—one I recognize and was afraid of in my youth—is just as firm and authoritative as I remember. "Son, my security clearance goes back before you were born. The U.S. Government says I can enter the premises, and she's coming with me."

"But—" the cop starts to argue as I pull away from the EMT and turn toward the front door.

"Dude," another cop jabs him. "Did you see his credentials? You don't argue with that shit. You step aside and let him do what he wants."

Asa Hollingsworth demands attention when he walks into a room.

Normally I'd give it to him.

Daddy Asa's aura is that commanding.

But not when she's in the room.

All I see is Emma being ushered in with her father's arm around her shoulders.

Her olive skin is ghost white, and her dark eyes are swollen.

The moment our gazes meet, tears form. That's when I lose her dark eyes.

She stops in the middle of the room, glass crunching under her winter boots. They're the same ones I bought her to wear to the parade to keep her warm.

Her face falls to her hands where her body wracks silently.

The EMT tries to get my attention. "Sir, I'm not done."

"You're done," I mutter and go straight to Emma.

I had no idea she was holding it in until I wrap her in my arms. Her tears and sobs flow freely. I've never seen her like this.

I put my lips to the top of her head. "Shh. It's okay."

She shakes her head against my chest. "I can't believe this happened. I was so scared. I thought…"

"Hey." I dip my hand in her hair and tip her head back to look at me. She might be more of a mess than I am, and I just survived a drive-by shooting. I've hardly been able to think about what that means. I did call Brett after the police got here and told him to stay put and not to think about going home. "You warned me. It's the only reason we're standing here."

Asa breaks into our dramatic moment. "Hold up. What did you say?"

My attention is pulled from the woman in my arms to her father. But that doesn't mean I let her go. If anything, I hold her tighter as Asa Hollingsworth crosses his and spears his daughter with a glare.

"You told me what happened. It seems you left some stuff out." He points between the two of us. "But we'll get to that later. What you did not seem to share with me is that you warned him this was going to happen. How in the hell did you know that?"

"I can explain—" I start.

But Emma interrupts, and her tone is firm and clipped for her father. "Not now. I'll tell you, but not here."

Asa glances around the rubble that was once my home. "We had an hour in the car on the way here. You didn't think that was a good time to share?"

"I'll tell you everything later," I say and lower my voice so no one around us can hear. The moment the words come out of my mouth, Emma presses into me tighter. "Whatever happened tonight was directed at my client. Very few people knew that he was supposed to be here. The suspect list just got very short, but I need to regroup. I'll tell the police when the time is right, but I'm not sure that time is now."

Asa drags a hand down his face before looking around and shaking his head. "You have cameras outside?"

"Yeah. Detectives already have the recording. The shooters wore masks. There weren't plates on the car. Seems this wasn't their first rodeo."

"Send me that video. Then we need to talk." Asa focuses his gaze on Emma. It's not scary, but it is serious. "And you need to tell me everything." He glances at me before turning back to his daughter. This time he sounds exhausted. "And I mean everything. Does your brother know about this?"

Emma wipes the tears from her face. "No."

Asa's head falls back and stares at my ceiling, which oddly enough is the one spot in my house that is still in good condition.

One thing to be thankful for.

"That's going to be interesting," Asa mutters.

Emma ignores him and looks up at me. "You're coming home with us."

Asa's exhale reeks of more drama than it has a right to. It's not like he was shot at tonight. If anyone has the right to be melodramatic, it's me.

But I'm too tired for that shit and focus on Emma.

"I can't leave my house like this."

"I'll make a call," Asa offers. "We'll get it boarded up tonight. You can deal with insurance tomorrow. If whoever did this thought your client was here, you can't stay. You can…" He jabs at the screen on his phone and puts it to his ear. "Sleep on the sofa."

"See?" Emma's eyes brighten a touch as she does her best to form a small smile. "You're coming home with me. I'll pack you a bag while you deal with the police."

And she proves she doesn't give a shit what her dad thinks of me or me being with her. She presses up on her furry boots and presses her lips to mine.

Her kiss is a balm after the shit I just experienced.

And I want more.

I cup the back of her head, hold her to me, and take over the kiss. Her hands frame my jaw, and my hold on her turns into a vise.

I can't get enough, and it seems she can't either.

"Thanks," Asa bites out louder than necessary to whomever he's talking to.

The last thing I want to do is let go of Emma, but her father is glaring at me.

Emma licks her lips before pushing away. "I'll pack you a bag."

She bypasses a slew of cops and hurries up the narrow staircase.

I turn to Asa and listen to him finish his call.

"There's a stack of plywood in the back barn. Bring all you can with the tools and more cameras and do it fast. You can start as soon as the officers give you the all clear."

He disconnects his call, and there's something reminiscent about him that makes me feel like I'm eighteen and got caught kissing his daughter in the barn.

Not that *that* happened.

Thank God.

He turns square to me and rests his hands on his hips. "I've got a team coming. They're going to board up the place and put more cameras up. It's a busy street, so we'll have to set the sensors close to the house, but we'll know if anyone tries to fuck with the place."

The emphasis he put on *fuck* did not go unnoticed.

I cross my arms, impressed and only slightly intimidated. "You've got a team? A whole team?"

He lifts his chin. "I do."

That's it. No further explanation.

For all I know, he could coach a lacrosse team of second graders. He was my first coach back in the day and made me run since I was the one always fucking around.

Daddy Asa has me locked in a zone. But I've already survived a drive-by tonight. What's the worst that can happen?

His son is my best friend, which should give me some leeway, even if I am fucking his daughter, even though he doesn't know that.

Yet.

"This team," I start. "Do they normally clean up after shootings and install surveillance?"

"They install surveillance all the time. I make sure they're damn good at what they do, but..." Asa pauses on that thought and looks around before leaning in so close, I fight the instinct to step away. I win the battle only to hear his next words delivered with more force than the bullets that took out my windows tonight. "They're usually the ones doing the shooting. Remember that."

He takes a step back and offers me the scariest smile I've ever seen before slapping me on the shoulder so hard, I struggle not to rock to the side.

"And I do not want to fucking think about why my daughter knows where your shit is to pack a bag for you. I don't care how old she is. That said, I'll do anything for my kids. The sofa is yours for as long as you need it."

I clear my throat. "I appreciate it."

"Mr. Hale?" I turn to find the cop in charge waiting to talk to me. "We have a few more questions."

"I'll let you get to it," Asa pipes and slaps me one more time. "I'll just stay out of your way while I wait for *MY DAUGHTER*."

Well, fuck if he didn't say that in all caps.

Asa goes straight to the window to look at the damage. Even the cops give him a wide berth.

"Hey, isn't that the chick who interviewed Brett Sullivan?" the cop asks.

I sigh and turn to him. "Yes. Can we get this done? I'll tell you anything you want to know."

That last part is a lie.

I'm not telling them shit about the Founders, or the fact the dried-up quarterback who was put out to pasture by the team should be high on their suspect list. He might not have pulled the trigger, but I'd bet my retirement fund that he made the order.

We need to get this figured out fast. I'm not sure how long I'll survive sleeping on Asa's sofa after I just learned he has an entire team who probably takes orders to do illegal shit. And I doubt they think twice when doing it.

Brett's SUV was shot to shit tonight. So, for the time being, it looks like I'm homeless and relying on Daddy Asa to carpool me around.

Helpless is a fucking heavy word and has an all new meaning tonight.

18

MONKEY SEX

Emma

By the time we got home, it was after midnight.

Saylor was asleep, but Keelie was waiting up in the kitchen even though she has to work tomorrow.

I'm not sure if Dad filled her in on the current situation, but she proved to be as cool as always. She hugged me, kissed me on the cheek, and greeted Jack like she's still his high school counselor.

But the main hint that Dad filled her in on everything was the sofa. It was covered in sheets, fluffy blankets, and topped with two pillows.

Keelie's hostess skills rival Addy's. I remember the day we moved into her house when she and dad were barely dating. Ironically, that happened because of a drive-by shooting too.

Who knew lightning could strike twice?

But that was an hour ago. I kissed Jack goodnight, came to my room, and have tossed and turned ever since.

I exhale and stare at my shadowed ceiling. My brain is wired and my heart aches for the man on the sofa.

Fuck it.

I throw back the covers and grab my robe tossed over the chair in the corner. On bare feet, I tiptoe down the stairs as lightly as I can and avoid every creek in the old staircase. Keelie's farmhouse is from the last century. Every inch of the place has been renovated or updated, but there's no quieting these stairs.

My old, trusty friend, the moon, might not be full like he was in Vegas, but he's still winking at me through the windows, giving me a full view of Jack's bare muscled back.

I must make enough noise as I pad through the family room because Jack twists to his back in a flash.

He looks me up and down in my short robe that barely hits the tops of my thighs. "You're trying to get me killed one way or another today, aren't you?"

I don't hide my smile.

But I do pull the tie loose on my robe.

It falls open and I drop it to the floor at my feet.

I'm left standing in a tank that scoops so low, it barely covers my breasts, and a pair of panties so small they barely cover anything else—nothing like the ones he bought me at Target.

"Fuck," Jack hisses. "I don't know what gave you the idea that I have a death wish, but I do not."

I ignore him and pull back the covers to join him. "I'm a grown-ass woman. My dad isn't going to do anything to me. They made you sleep on the sofa because Saylor is here and she's only sixteen. They have to set the right example."

Jack is down to his boxers. We're skin to skin in all the places except the ones I want when I cover his body with mine. My legs fall to the sides to straddle his hips, and it's evident he misses me as much as I miss him. His cock is already thick and growing by the moment.

For me.

I press my lips to his and gaze down at him through my messy hair that tents us in a beautiful quiet spot. "Together again."

His hands come to my ass. I'm instantly wet when he squeezes each globe in a firm grip that feels so good, I rock my sex against his erection.

He lifts his hips to meet me even though his actions do not match his words. "This might be the lamest and least masculine thing I've ever said, but I'm not worried about you when it comes to Daddy Asa. I'm worried about me meeting my maker in an early demise. Don't make my eating vegetables as an adult mean nothing because your dad takes me out with the snap of his fingers."

I shake my head and keep moving. "He would never."

Jack's brows rise. "Baby, he would. He told me all about his team. I was right to be scared of him in high school.

Apparently my keen sixth sense is on point. I've always known he was a scary fucker."

I run the tip of my tongue across his bottom lip. "He's a teddy bear. You just have to get to know him. Nothing but a family man. And if you stick around long enough, he'll love you too."

Jack's grip on me tightens where I'm pressed to his cock. "Do you plan on me going somewhere? Or walking away from me? Because I can tell you right now, Emma, that kind of talk does not make me happy."

"Relax," I whisper.

"You're the chick and I'm the guy in this affiliation. I'm supposed to be the one to tell you to relax."

I try not to laugh. "This is an affiliation?"

"Hookup. Kinship. Liaison. Despite the fact I'm comfortable enough with your body to perform medical examinations, whether I'm qualified to or not, you haven't given me the go ahead to call it a relationship."

I rub up and down his cock right where I want it. I wish I'd taken my panties off. After tonight, this is exactly what I need.

Him.

"We can try that word out next week," I say.

Jack slides a hand down the back of my panties after he reaches up for a lingering kiss. "If your dad hasn't killed me by then."

I moan when he dips a finger into my sex from behind. "Until then, we can liaison."

"Is that what you came down for, Em? A little Jack Hale liaison?"

I nod, not at all embarrassed about wanting him. Not after tonight.

I drag my fingers across his strong jaw. "I was so scared."

His touch on me turns gentle as he reaches far enough to take my mouth. His kiss is firm and long and lingering. "I know, baby. It's how I felt when I saw that guy grab you on TV."

"That same guy saved you."

He nods. It doesn't matter that we're discussing life-and-death scenarios. He never stops the magic he's spinning between my legs. "He's a complicated guy. I hope to meet him one day."

I feel all the tension and angst melt away. It's replaced with pure, hot lust.

For him.

"I don't want to talk about anyone but you and me. The last thing I remember before all hell broke loose was you describing what you'd do to me in a limo. I want to go back to simple times like that."

The side of his lips tip up. "Limo … sofa. What's the difference?"

"I'll take it as long as we're together."

"You're going to have to be quiet," he murmurs against my lips.

I give him a quick nod. "I will."

He puts his hands on my hips and rocks me up and down his cock as he presses into me. "You're going to have to move."

There's nothing I want more. Even though he told me what to do, Jack does all the work. With his hands firm on my hips, I have no choice but to move at his command. My swollen clit gets all the friction it needs from his rock-hard cock with only my thin panties and his boxers between us.

"There you go, Em. I could watch you do this every day for the rest of my life."

Those words. I get lost in them.

I've never thought about that with anyone else.

My fingertips press into his wide shoulders, and I hang on as he moves me faster. I press my face into his neck, his whiskers bristle the delicate skin of my cheek. Every sense is heightened. Jack is everywhere, and I love it.

When it comes over me, I gasp. His hand lands heavy on the back of my head and pulls my mouth to his. He drinks my moans and groans all the while holding me tight to prolong my orgasm even longer.

When I become limp, he lets my head go, and my cheek falls to his chest. My breathing is shallow as my heart speeds from my high.

A hit of Jack Hale is a strong drug. One I'm quickly becoming addicted to.

He zapped the energy clean out of me as I allow gravity to do its thing and fuse me to him.

I bring my hand up and lightly flick his nipple with my

fingernail. "Now it's your turn. We might have to get creative on this sofa."

He presses his lips to the top of my head. "No, baby. Tonight is all about you."

I lift my head to look at him. "No. I can't leave you like this."

He kisses the end of my nose like I'm a cute little puppy or something. "We can and we will. I'm not fucking you on the sofa with your family asleep upstairs. Tomorrow night I'll get us a room. We can have all the crazy monkey sex you want."

I rest my cheek on him and press into his neck. "I never dreamed of wild monkey sex, but now I want to see what it's all about."

His fingers play with the ends of my hair as his other hand tucks itself to bed for the night inside my panties on my bare ass. "I'll make sure you love it."

I close my eyes. "I think I love everything with you."

He's still hard below me.

"I feel bad," I say. "I can't let you suffer like this."

He pulls in a breath, and I wonder if it's to calm himself. "I'm good. Better than I deserve with you here. You'd better go back to bed soon."

"Later. I can't leave you right now. I have an internal alarm clock. I promise I'll wake up."

Jack takes a deep breath. "If your dad sends his team after me because your internal alarm jams up, I'll haunt you forever. You'll never have decent sex again."

I press my lips to his pec. "That's the blue balls talking. Don't be dramatic."

"Trust me, that's not what my balls are saying. They're begging me to forget the scary ass team your dad keeps in a barn and fuck your brains out."

I smile. "I love your balls. I'll make it up to them during monkey sex."

"You're killing me, Em. Set your damn alarm clock and take a nap. I'm here to serve as your bed … again."

I shut my eyes. The longest week has turned into the longest day. I got kidnapped and Jack was shot at.

Tomorrow has to be better.

19

RESOURCEFUL GUY

Jack

"Um, what in the actual fuck?"

Emma shifts in my arms.

I feel nothing but a bare tit in my hand.

Hmm.

Nice.

I like Emma's bare tits.

It deserves a squeeze.

She presses her ass into my morning wood.

"Emma!"

We both jerk at the same time my eyes fly open. Emma might've fallen to the floor if I weren't so obsessed with her tits.

Emma's little sister, Saylor, is standing in the open space between the kitchen and family room staring at us.

"Jack?" Saylor gapes before turning her attention to Emma. "I thought you were going to hook up with the quarterback!"

Emma grips the blanket and pulls it to her chin. "Stop yelling. It's too early. And, no, I'm not with the quarterback."

"I can see that," Saylor states as she hitches a backpack over her shoulder.

Damn. Why is the universe trying to keep me from this woman?

The teenage girl just shrugs as she hands me the most back-handed compliment ever. "No offense, Jack. You're no slouch, but you're not famous."

"None taken," I mutter as I slide my hand out of Emma's thin tank and think about how miserable it'll be to settle my dick down so I can actually get up from this sofa.

Emma hangs on for dear life as she rolls to her back and smirks up at me. "Don't take her seriously. You're way better than a quarterback."

"Way better is a stretch," Saylor drawls as she proves how unimpressed she is with me and disappears into the pantry but doesn't stop talking. "Aside from the initial shock of seeing you with your hand up Emma's shirt, I've known you forever, so this is way less than exciting."

Emma's smirk grows into a satisfied smile. I lean down and press my lips to hers and proceed to kiss the smile off her lips despite morning breath. Her hand presses into my bare chest, and I wish we were on a secluded island with no teenagers and no gunmen.

Saylor was right—we have known each other forever, and it seems that nothing has changed. The girl can demand attention and run her mouth like none other. And coming from me, that's saying something.

She yells so loud from the pantry, she'll rouse the goats. "Does Levi know about you guys?"

"No, and I'll be the one to tell him," Emma bites before whispering for only me, "I'd better get up. Dad and Keelie will be down at any moment."

I put my lips to her ear. "Then you'd better hurry up, because I'm hard as a rock. It's going to make coffee with your dad awkward."

She leans up and kisses the tip of my nose before practically rolling off the edge of the sofa backwards. She barely has time to tag her robe off the floor and slip it up her shoulders when we hear heels clicking down the wooden staircase.

Emma ties her robe shut and digs a pair of sweatpants out of the bag she packed and tosses them to me. Getting caught in my underwear by my high school counselor is so far down my bucket list, it's hanging out around almost dying during a drive-by shooting.

I barely have a chance to adjust my cock when Keelie starts barking orders to her daughter. "Hurry up, Saylor. If I'm going to make it through the day after that late night, I need extra coffee."

"Good morning," Emma greets her stepmom.

Keelie is standing there in a fitted dress that hits her above the knees with a pair of heeled boots. Her hair hangs down her back in strawberry blond waves. Keelie has aged well.

I bet every boy in that high school still lusts over their counselor. Just one more thing that hasn't changed. Hell, I was one of them back in the day.

Keelie comes to a stop in the middle of her kitchen and glances from Emma to me and back to Emma. "It's an interesting morning, that's for sure. From what your dad told me when you got home, there are all sorts of things to talk about."

I pull a t-shirt over my head and do everything I can to keep my gaze off Emma's bare thighs as she reaches for a mug.

"As you and I both know," Emma says as she heads for the coffee pot. "It was horrible, but Jack is okay. That's all that matters."

"You're very lucky," Keelie says before following Emma to the cabinet and grabbing a thermal to go. I take this opportunity to move to a barstool while my blue balls suffer a slow death. "Asa told me everything when he got home last night. And I mean everything."

Saylor comes out of the pantry and cracks open a protein drink. "Did you know about Emma and Jack? I'm always the last to know anything."

Emma slides a mug of black coffee across the island to me with a private smile. "You're going to need this."

"You're not wrong. Thanks." I think of my house, my client, and the few options of where Emma and I can sleep tonight that isn't on her father's sofa.

"You're barely the last to know things, Saylor. I didn't know the details about these two or the shooting until after your dad got home last night," Keelie adds. "We're going to have a houseful when Knox brings his new girlfriend home."

I shake my head. "I appreciate you letting me crash last night. I'll check into a hotel tonight."

"Maybe you need to take the same advice you gave Brett and get out of the city. I'm sure Levi and Carissa have room for you." Emma takes a sip of her coffee. "I'm staying there while Knox is home with his mystery girl."

"That'll be a fun way to tell Levi you're shacking up with his life-long bestie." Saylor's smile is wicked. I need to remember to avoid her as best I can. "Please don't tell him until I'm there to witness it."

Emma waves her off. "Levi will be fine."

"I'll handle Levi," I amend.

Emma hikes a brow.

Saylor's eyes go round the size of saucers.

Keelie bites her lip.

I pretend like it's not the big deal that it is. "It's the unwritten bro code. When I signed the best-friend contract, it became my responsibility to announce that I'm dating his sister—should that ever happen."

"How long have you been together?" Keelie asks.

It's Emma's turn to bite her lip.

I take another sip of my coffee.

Saylor barks a laugh.

Keelie pulls in a deep breath and changes the subject. "We need to get to school. You ready, Saylor?"

Saylor grabs her drink. "So close to the weekend, yet still so far."

"You're not going anywhere without saying goodbye." We all turn to Asa as he walks into the kitchen and heads straight for his wife and plants a firm kiss on her lips. "Have a good day, baby."

She smiles up at him. "You too."

Asa and his team … I wonder what they're up to today.

Asa bops Saylor on the head. "Good luck on your geometry test."

Saylor rolls her eyes. "Thanks."

Keelie picks up her coffee and bag. "We'll see you two later. I expect all the details of what's been going on."

"Have a good day," Emma calls.

I'd like to know what I did to make Emma hate me in the last two minutes, because as soon as they're out the door, she picks up her own coffee and leaves me to the wolves.

Or rather, the WOLF—in shouty capitals.

She turns to her father and me. "I'm going to take a shower. They're adjusting my days since I worked straight through while in Vegas. We have a ton to do after what happened last night. Jack, you can get ready in the bathroom that goes out to the pool. It's stocked with towels. I packed you everything else you need. I need exactly fifty-five minutes, and I'll be ready to roll."

And with that, she struts her sexy ass out of the kitchen. I force myself to focus on my coffee so Asa doesn't murder me watching her run up the stairs in her short robe.

I wonder if he knows she slept on the sofa with me.

Shit. I didn't think about that last night when I lulled Emma to sleep with an orgasm. I bet he had his team put cameras in every square inch of his house.

"We need to talk."

I hang onto my chill with the skin of my teeth and focus on the good news that my blue balls have retreated into hibernation. "Look, I know I had a reputation in high school, but I can assure you—"

"I don't want to talk about anyone's reputation," he bites. "I want to talk about the fact it's clear my daughter is comfortable in your house—a house that was shot to shit last night. Emma's a smart woman. She can decide who she spends time with. I trust her in everything. But if she's going to be with you, I need to make sure you're not being shot at, which means I want to know what the fuck happened last night."

"Oh, well, that's easy. They were after my client, Brett Sullivan."

"But he's at Whitetail," Asa counters, proving he's in the know.

"He is," I confirm. "But we planted the information that he was staying at my place. Brett has my car, so his was parked on the street. They had every reason to believe he was there."

Asa crosses his arms and frowns. "Are you trying to tell me that you invited this on yourself?"

I put a hand up. "No way. Someone inside the Founders organization set Sullivan up after the game. We were trying to figure out who that was."

"And how do you know it's an inside job?" he demands.

"Because of Emma's anonymous source."

His tone dips to a scary place. "My daughter has an anonymous source?"

"Look, I know how this looks. Last night was a lot. I appreciate everything your team did, whoever they are. But I can promise you I've never been shot at before. Normally, my life does not invite this kind of drama. Emma is completely safe with me." I stand, pick up my coffee, and feel the need to amend my statement. "Or she will be once I figure this shit out. If you don't mind, I'm going to grab a shower and get ready. I need to check on my house, call my insurance, and touch base with the police."

"Before you go anywhere with my daughter, I want to know all about this no-name source of Emma's. I have access to technology. The next time he calls Em, we can trace it."

I stop and turn back to him. "I might be a sports agent, but I studied all areas of the law. Unless you acquire a warrant, that's illegal."

Asa says nothing.

Not one word.

But he does give me a nod.

Damn.

I guess if he has a team at his disposal who's willing to do the shooting, I should have realized Asa doesn't give two shits about a warrant.

Asa being Emma's dad isn't the only reason to stay on his good side.

I tell him the truth. "You've turned out to be a resourceful guy."

"And you're the weird, adult version of the kid you were in high school. I don't know what to think about that," Asa mutters as he pours his own coffee.

I decide to take that as a compliment.

I also decide to get the fuck out of his kitchen before he brings someone over from his team to good-cop-bad-cop me. Or even worse, waterboard me.

If he wants to tap Emma's phone, I'm down for that. The sooner we can get this shit over with, the better.

I do make a mental note not to sext her from now on.

Disappointing.

Same with my client being framed…

…and drive-by shootings.

20

MIDDLE-AGED BADASSES

Emma

For it being my first day off in almost two weeks, it's been a doozy.

One day you think you're an adult, making your own choices, and independent of your parents.

Then the next, your father and his friends have inserted themselves, and their satellite system, into your life.

Talk about an invasion of privacy in the name of love for me and baptism by fire for Jack.

Dad called a meeting at Uncle Crew's old farmhouse. I've known Crew my entire life. He and dad have worked together since before they retired from contracting with the CIA. Now they work in other capacities on the downlow, which means, they can do things normal people cannot.

Hell, they do things pretty much no one else can — normal or not.

Dad must have filled them in before we got there, because the group my father works with knew everything.

But then again, they usually do.

This is how the meeting went right before I handed my cell to Ozzy, the tech wizard of the team.

"I love you. We need to make sure you're safe." That was Dad.

"Someone snatched you on live TV. What the hell did you think we were going to do?" That was Grady.

"Deep Throat knows all. It's time to uncover that fucker." That was Jarvis.

"I'll figure out who Deep Throat is before the birthday party." That was Ozzy.

"Sit back and relax, Em. I bought an entire satellite system for situations just like this." That was Crew.

And my personal favorite…

"Look at you, love. You're a bloody badass. I'm so proud." That was Bella who joined the meeting over speakerphone since she and Cole are on vacation with their kids.

For what it's worth, Bella's comment pissed Dad and Jack off.

Then Jack confirmed that none of this is legal—not that he wasn't okay with that. He stated that his number one goal was, and I quote, "to get this shit over with, clear his client's name, and move forward with life."

He said that while holding my hand.

It felt good.

Dad had stress lines etched between his eyes. I haven't seen those there for years. In fact, not since Levi went through his own flavor of drama with Carissa's parents. Before that it was the last time our family experienced a drive-by shooting.

The meeting was weird, tense, and quick. It ended with me wearing a new bracelet with a tracking device in it that I was instructed not to remove under any circumstance, and my cell is now controlled by Ozzy Graves. He can see everything I do on it and trace every person I come into contact with. They also took down Mark Morse's number and announced that he'd have an unofficial tap on his phone before lunch.

Not exactly the party anyone wants to start their day off with.

I was done with Dad and his team.

I couldn't tell if Jack was more disturbed or impressed. It was obvious he was a little bit of both.

But we have things to do. The first on the list is to visit Brett.

Jack and I hike through the woods on the worn path to Whitetail. Brett opens the door to the small bungalow the moment it comes into sight through the barren, winter forest.

"It's about time," Brett barks.

"I'm alive and thriving, thanks for asking," Jack deadpans.

Brett stuffs his hands into the front pocket of his hoodie. "Sorry. It's frustrating being out here in the middle of nowhere with my hands tied."

"The alternative isn't great," Jack mutters. "My antique windows and shot-up living room are a testament to that."

Jack and I stomp our shoes on the porch rug before stepping inside the warm, tiny house. I've only been here once before, but it's exactly how I remember it—a cottage that would go viral on social media. It's eclectic and looks like something you'd dream of running across in the English countryside. Bookshelves stand floor to ceiling and flank the old cobblestone fireplace that's crackling with a low blaze. They're dotted with old books and knickknacks—pictures of Whitetail and Addy's cows.

It's cozy and has a way of making one forget about bullets and anonymous callers.

I'm jealous.

Even if my new career as a sports reporter has blown up into something I never expected, I'd rather be hidden away here with Jack.

Brett shuts the door behind us, and I go straight to the fire to warm my hands.

"Do you want anything?" Brett asks as he moves to the small kitchen and opens the packed refrigerator. "I know I'm a big guy, but Addy delivers enough food daily for my entire offensive line."

I turn and put my back to the fire. "I'm good, thank you. Addy is amazing. I knew this was the best place for you until this settles."

Jack reaches for an apple sitting on top of an overflowing bowl of fruit. He takes a bite, points to Brett with it, and talks with his mouth full. "It's a good thing I'm my own brand of baller and create my own destiny in life. Bad luck loves to nip at my heels, but we're going to get past this. Mark Morse can kiss my ass right before he trips into a prison cell. I did not work this hard to get to where I'm at for some jealous, dried-up quarterback to fuck with my life or yours."

Wow.

The fire behind me is nothing compared to the warmth between my legs. "This is new. You've been calm and collected all morning."

Jack bites the apple between his teeth and holds it there while he takes his coat off and tosses it over the back of the sofa. He rips another piece of fruit off and says, "I'm keeping my shit together to make a good impression for your father, but I'm pissed and am ready for heads to roll. I'm also protective of the heads in this room."

Being bottled up has caused Brett to take a cue from Jack, and he starts to pace. "How do you think I feel? I thought Morse was in my corner." He stops mid-step and turns to Jack. "Not just in my corner, but he's been supportive. I sure didn't think he was a murderer. He took the bait really fucking fast."

Jack continues to eat his apple while he talks. "Asa's team of middle-aged badasses who do questionable shit for a living are all over it. Once Emma gets another call from our anonymous friend—who, by the way, saved my life—we'll know who he is. That is, if the badasses are truly badass. We can only hope."

I frown at Jack. "I thought I saved your life."

Jack licks his lips and shoots me his sexy half-smirk. "Sorry, baby. You're right. If it weren't for you, I wouldn't have been able to tempt the gods to experience sleeping with you almost naked on your dad's sofa. That was worth living for."

"Professional football players dream of the big win like I got, but never would I dream the week following would turn out like this. I should be riding the high of pinnacle success in the game and signing historic contracts, not hiding out in the woods forced to listen to you two talk about your sexcapades."

"You weren't paying attention." Jack tosses his apple core into the trashcan like he's shooting a three-pointer. "We were on the sofa with her family sleeping upstairs. There was no sex."

"Can we not talk about us and sex with your client-slash-friend? I think he's more than just a client since you took rounds for him." I shift my glare from Jack to Brett. "I have no doubt that after my informant damn near kidnapped me yesterday then warned me about the drive-by that he'll call again. It's only a matter of time until we know who he is and can connect the dots."

Brett collapses into a club chair. "Until then, I sit here and do nothing?"

"After last night, my house is proof that sitting here is better than the alternative." Jack pulls his cell from his pocket and frowns as he reads the screen before putting it to his ear to answer. "Jack Hale."

The air in the small cottage grows thicker as Jack's frown deepens. He turns away from us as we only hear one side of the conversation. "Yes, he is my client, but I have no idea where he is."

I'd bet my modest salary that the very client he speaks of is sitting in the same room as us. My gaze shoots to Brett as we sit here and listen to Jack tell one lie after another. "I saw him at the parade yesterday. I haven't spoken to him since. Have you tried his home? I can get you the address."

Props to Jack for being cooperative, even if it is only in spirit.

"Absolutely. I have full faith my client was framed. He wants to be cooperative. As soon as I hear from him, I'll ask him to call you."

I brace.

Brett juts to his feet.

Jack turns another one-eighty, this time pinching the bridge of his nose even though his tone doesn't give away the tension that's written all over him. "Of course, officer. Thank you for the call."

Brett waits to make sure the call was disconnected before he exclaims, "Who the hell was that?"

There are times I see bits of who Jack was back in the day. The cocky high school jock who skated by with average grades—sometimes less than average—and had the student body and everyone else in his vicinity in his chokehold based on personality alone. You never knew what he was going to say.

What he was not was controlled or methodical.

That was the guy I crushed on hard. Hell, I think ninety percent of the female student body was in line right behind me.

But as Jack pulls in a deep breath before exhaling it on a slow nod, all I see is the man he is today.

The attorney and agent to the athletic stars of the world, wheeling and dealing salaries and managing careers and egos.

Combined, Jack Hale the boy has turned into a man so complex and fascinating, he's hard to resist.

No.

He's impossible to resist.

And it hasn't even been a week. But when someone you've known all your life crashes into your world, you just know.

The girl in me was infatuated with who he was.

And the woman I am is captivated by who he is to a point I wonder if I can turn back.

Controlled, he's in command of the situation when we all know the situation is nowhere near in control at the moment. "That was a detective from the Las Vegas Police Department. Ballistics reveal that casings from the weapons retrieved from the hotel room have your prints all over them. Apparently, you're in the system from when you were booked for a party they busted up in college."

"Fuck," Brett bites. "It was disturbing the peace. That's it. Who knew that would come back to bite me on something like this?"

"Yeah," Jack agrees, but this time I can tell he has to work at maintaining his cool. "One of the weapons with your prints on it was used in an armed robbery at a gas station outside of Vegas days before the game—during the time the team was in Nevada."

"No," I say. "But he was set up. We know he was. And the shooting last night is just icing on the cake. Mark Morse is pissed he lost his starting spot, and he's doing everything he can to make Brett public enemy number one. When that didn't work, he resorted to attempted murder. Maybe it's time we tell the police everything."

"No way. I'm not going to the cops until I have evidence it wasn't me," Brett says.

"I agree," Jack says. "But, man, I'm sorry to tell you this, you have a warrant out for your arrest. Local officers are helping Vegas with the case. You are a wanted man."

I pull out my cell and go straight to the WDCN website.

There it is.

The headline is top and center.

A Warrant for MVP Founders Quarterback Brett Sullivan's Arrest in Sin City

"I hate to deliver more bad news." I hold my phone up. "It's out in the wild. Your PR issues aren't going to die off anytime soon. I'm so sorry, Brett."

"Fuck!" Brett bellows so loud, I'm sure the walls of the bungalow would rattle if they weren't built of cobblestone.

I should offer my condolences to Jack, too, but he continues to be the controlled man he's become.

"The good news is, no one knows where you are. But you're right, we can't go to the police. Not yet. Now that we have the secret good guys on our side from the neighboring barn, I feel good that this will end sooner rather than later. You just need to stay put."

Brett drags a hand through his hair. "I'm hedging my bets on an anonymous man who we hope will call again. The plan is shaky at best. And I'm going crazy. I can't even work out to let off steam. This has to end soon."

Jack flips through screens on his phone and mutters, "Go for a run in the woods."

"No. I need a real gym. Weights. I want to throw some medicine balls through a fucking window."

"Um," I start. "We've had enough broken windows. If you promise not to break anything, I can ask my dad if you can work out in Crew's barn. They have a whole gym over there. It's not posh or fancy, but by the looks of them, it works."

"Hey," Jack calls. "Don't make me jealous of middle-aged men."

I cross the room and wrap my arms around his waist as I fit myself to him. "Don't make it weird. They're like my uncles."

Jack presses his lips to my forehead. "I haven't been to the gym in two weeks. I can't get soft now that I know you have an appreciation for muscly middle-aged men."

"Hello? There's a warrant out for my arrest," Brett scoffs with sarcasm.

"Not for long," Jack declares. "Your name will be cleared, someone will pay for what they did to you, and I'll use this to make sure the Founders pay up big time in your contract or big time in court. If they want the MVP on board for the next seven years, they'll need some deep pockets, which I know they have. And when you get married someday and birth your first son, you can name him after my greatness since the only reason he'll be in existence is because I made sure you avoided the slammer."

I shift so I can turn to Brett without letting Jack go. "I'll call my dad so you can get into the gym. You might have to sign some autographs while you're there—and maybe an NDA—but you'll be fine. That property is safer than this one."

Brett twists his neck and cracking fills the space. "Thanks. I need it."

"I need my keys," Jack demands. "Oh, and your car was shot up right along with my house. I had it towed off the street. If you send me your insurance information, I'll call it in for you."

"Fucking great," Brett mutters. "Keys are on the table by the door."

Jack lets me go only to claim my hand. "I need to check on my house and then come right back to the country. It's DG and pie day."

"I'm changing so I can hit the gym." Brett leaves us and shuts himself in the bedroom.

"What's DG and pie day?" I ask.

"Once a week we take Grandma to Dollar General to get what she needs for the week and then we go to Frank's Diner for pie. I never miss, except for last week when I was in Vegas. Before the bullets and warrants, I promised I'd make it today. I can't let Grandma down."

I shake my head, and my voice cracks a little with emotion. "No, you can't let your grandma down."

His hand fists my hair and forces my head back.

Then he kisses me.

Like really kisses me.

When his other hand lands on my ass for a delicious squeeze, my insides flip flop with anticipation. This reminds me I still don't know where we're sleeping tonight, but I refuse for it to be on the sofa or in the general vicinity of my family.

I want to go back to simpler times when it was just Jack and me.

Like, two days ago. Before quasi-kidnappings, shootings, and arrest warrants. And definitely before my phone was being monitored by my dad and his friends.

Jack breaks his kiss. "How do you feel about Dollar General and diner food?"

I have to catch my breath. "Dollar General has everything. Totally underrated."

"Then you should come. It's an experience. You just have to promise not to tell Grandma about the shooting. She'll freak. I'll tell my mom later."

"I can't say no to you. In anything, it seems, but I really won't say no to Dollar General. If the diner has cobbler, you might just be the perfect man."

Jack lowers his voice and presses his hand into my ass harder. "I should have the menu memorized after going every week since we moved Grandma into Rolling Hills Ranch, but if they don't have cobbler, I'll raid their kitchen and make you one myself."

I give him more of my weight. "How are you still single?"

His expression freezes.

Shit.

The words just popped out of my mouth.

"You don't have to answer that," I spit. "It's none of my business."

He shrugs. "I've been busy."

"Oh."

That's not the romantic answer my heart hoped for.

"Fate is what they drone on about in romcoms. My life is the farthest thing from a romcom, and there's no way I'm leaving my life up to fate. If I waited for the universe to bestow goodness on me, it would never come. That's why I had to find you after the game in Vegas."

Every cell in my body freezes. "You what?"

He lifts his chin. "I knew you were there all week, but my schedule was packed. After your interview went viral, I asked high and low where I could find the woman who chased down Brett Sullivan. I was just lucky you went to the bar and not straight to your room."

"Jack." I wrap my arms around him tighter. "Why didn't you tell me?"

"Would it have made a difference?"

I don't even have to think about that. "No. Not at all."

"I wanted to reconnect and made my own fate. Though I didn't know I'd be right here or plan to drag you along to solve a whacked mystery involving my client. I feel fucking bad about this. And when you were kidnapped ... I've never felt guilt like that."

I take a chance and tell him the truth. "I thought you were a player."

He hikes a brow. "Why is that?"

"Because you're ... you." It's lame but it's all I've got. "And I assumed our one night would only be one night."

"A few things to know about me, Emma. I don't have time to be a player. That shit is exhausting. I was raised by women to respect women. If I tried to play a woman, I swear my mom and grandma would figure it out just by looking at me. I can't explain it, but it's like they have superpowers. And do you really think I'd fuck my best friend's little sister for a one off? I mean, you're *you*." He mocks me by emphasizing that word. "You're Emerson Hollingsworth. You are not a one-night stand. You're a fucking prize. I do not take that lightly."

Tears spring to my eyes.

His hands claim my face. "I'm pissed that you thought I'd do that to you."

My words are raspy. "I don't know what to say."

His lips tip on one side. "Beg me for forgiveness and promise you'll make it up to me in bed later."

I bite back my teary smile. "See? This is why I thought you were a player."

He shrugs. "Lucky you. You get my winning personality without the drama."

"Without the drama? That's cute." I snort. "But, yes. I am lucky."

"Remember that when we're shopping at Dollar General."

"Who doesn't like Dollar General?" I ask. "And you already bought me couture. Dollar General makes sense with your layered personality."

He pulls me in for a deep kiss. When his tongue plunges into my mouth to dance with mine, the depth of him bleeds into me and settles in a place I've never felt before.

Yes, there are more layers to Jack Hale than I ever knew. Layers that I can't wait to explore.

21

I LIKE CHUBBY BABIES

Jack

"Wow-wee, Jackie! There's a woman in your car!"

I help Grandma to the car with one hand as I wheel her oxygen tank with the other. I also ignore her announcement about the woman in my car. "Mom is going to kill me when she sees you not on your oxygen."

"I'm fine. Magnolia always finds stuff to nag at me about," Grandma bites. "Who's the woman?"

"You know her. It's just been a while."

Grandma's wrinkled hand grips my forearm tighter. "I've never seen that woman in my life."

"Trust me, you have. And I'd appreciate it if you didn't scare her away."

"If I don't like her, I'll damn well do whatever I want."

"I'm sure you will, Grandma." I reach for the back door and open it for her.

"Who are you?" Grandma demands before her ass hits the seat.

Emma twists to greet her with a big smile from the front. "Hi, Miss Maple. We used to be neighbors. I'm Emma, Levi Hollingsworth's sister."

Grandma huffs an exhausted breath when she gets settled in her seat and exclaims, "Emma Hollingsworth? Well, I haven't seen you since you were a toddler. You were always a chubby one. You sure grew out of those fat cheeks and that belly."

Emma laughs.

I do not. "Didn't I just warn you not to scare her away?"

"It's okay." Emma focuses her smile on the woman who raised me while my mom worked night and day. "It's true. I was a chubby baby."

"I'm just telling the truth. The Hollingsworth girl wouldn't want me to lie." Grandma glares at me while I put her oxygen on the floorboard next to her. "What's she doing here?"

"She's here to go to Dollar General just like the rest of us," I say.

"Who doesn't love the DG?" Emma states the most rhetorical question of the day.

"Amen, child," Grandma agrees. "I hate the new fancy grocery markets. The buggies are too big, and the stuff is overpriced. Don't even get me started on the Walmart. The last time I went there, I had to get a scooter. The battery putzed out on me right in the Depends aisle. Jackie had to push me over to the toothpaste. Heck, I'd rather be caught in front of the condoms. And I don't even have to wear diapers. I was doin' a favor for my neighbor. She can't blow her nose without wettin' her panties."

"That's nice of you to shop for your neighbor," Emma says.

It's the last thing I hear before I shut Grandma's door and jog around the back of the car. Grandma is still talking about her neighbor peeing her pants when I put it in drive.

I change the subject. "Mom is meeting us there. She just called—she's running late."

"Well. That's going to mess up our together time," Grandma complains. "It's her day off. I bet she's with Pierce."

My foot hits the brake harder than necessary. We all rock forward against our seatbelts, the oxygen tank crashes sideways on the floorboard, and Emma braces a hand on the dash.

"Jackie!" Grandma exclaims. "If my tank explodes, we'll all be goners!"

I stop in the middle of the parking lot and turn to glare at the old woman who's been front and center my entire life. She tells it like it is—no bullshit, so I'm counting on her to be straight with me. "Who the hell is Pierce?"

Grandma's eyes go as big as her arthritic knuckles clutching her purse.

She says nothing.

"Who. Is. Pierce?" I repeat.

A horn honks from behind us.

Emma lays a light hand on my forearm. "You're blocking cars."

I turn to Emma. "Someone named Pierce is in the same sentence as my mother. The parking lot can wait."

"Shoulda kept my trap shut," Grandma mutters. "Magnolia is gonna kill me."

I turn back to the blabbermouth in the backseat who's never been able to keep a secret in her life. She used to make games of hinting what I was getting for my birthday because she couldn't stand keeping the secret. "So Pierce is a man. And from the way you're acting, he's not her accountant or a coworker. He's a man who's into my mother. Am I right?"

Grandma releases her purse to point a crooked finger at me. "Now you listen here—your mama is a beautiful woman who has spent most of her adult life alone. She works hard. She took care of me so I could take care of you all those years. She deserves this bit of happiness."

I gape at her. "Why didn't she tell me?"

"Because she knew you'd do this!" Grandma exclaims.

The car honks again.

Damn. Senior citizens are impatient. It's not even close to their afternoon dinnertime. They can wait.

"My mom is seeing someone and didn't tell me," I state. "Of course I'm doing this."

"Well, you're seeing the chubby baby next door." Grandma

motions to Emma who is not chubby or a baby. "You didn't tell us. How do you think we feel?"

"That's different," I bite. "And don't call her names. We've been seeing each other for about twenty seconds. Why do you think I brought her to Dollar General Day?"

"Because everyone needs something at the Dollar General! In fact, we're late. Put this fancy car in drive, and let's go. If anyone sees me in here while you're holding things up in the parking lot, they'll talk about me in the dining room. That's the last thing I need."

I shift in my seat and stare out into the cold, gray day.

"Jack," Emma calls for me. "You don't want anyone to talk about your grandma at dinner."

"I like your little girlfriend," Grandma states. "She gets it."

"Has your mom never seen anyone? Dated at all?" Emma asks.

"No. Never." I drag a hand through my hair before giving up on life and putting it in drive to save my grandmother's reputation in the dining room. "Well, damn. At least not that I know of." I glare at Grandma through the rearview mirror. "Has she been doing this on the downlow all these years and not told me?"

"Cool your hotpants, Jackie. Your mama has taken care of her family. Once the sperm donor was out of the picture, she focused on us. Pierce has a good job, and he's a looker. She deserves a little nookie."

"Grandma! You're going to make me throw up."

"Jack Hale, do not yell at me. If I had a wooden spoon, I'd bop you with it."

Emma laughs.

"Was she going to keep him a secret forever?" I demand.

"She was waitin' to tell you until after you got home from Vegas. Dagnabbit, she's gonna get her knickers in a twist when she finds out I spilled the beans."

"Maybe it's better this way. Jack can prepare himself." Emma turns from Grandma to me. "You cannot act like this when she tells you. I haven't seen your mom in years, but she's the sweetest. She's obviously worried about telling you."

"I approve of you, Emma. Bop him on the head for me, will you? I'm also glad you grew out of your baby fat. Some people aren't as lucky."

When I come to a stoplight, I turn in my seat. "If you talk about anyone's baby fat one more time, we're skipping Frank's today."

"I'm eighty-four years old. I can say what I want." Grandma motions to the front of the car. "Keep your eyes on the road. The light's green. And you never know how many more meals at Frank's I'll have. I know you won't rob me of my chicken fried steak and pie."

"I agree," Emma says. "And I've hardly eaten anything today. I'm starving."

"Now that we're past that, I wanna know all about your athlete. Did he really pay for those hookers?"

Fuck me.

"I can tell you all about that," Emma says.

And for the rest of the short drive, I listen to Emma give the condensed version of what's been going on. She proves she's just as perfect as she's been since I barged into her life at Nebula, because she gives the condensed version that doesn't include kidnappings, shootings, or Deep Throat.

So much for a normal day with all the women in my life.

The two old ones and one new one.

I mentally add this Pierce guy to my list of shit I need to obsess over.

Maybe I'll ask Emma's "uncles" for another favor.

Emma

"Gimme a box of those Pop-Tarts. The brown sugar cinnamon ones. Jack gives me grief for these, but I've eaten one a day for the last twenty years, and I still don't even need my oxygen in the Dollar General, so I ignore him."

I'm not sure what Pop-Tarts have to do with her need for oxygen, but the last thing on earth I want to do is argue with Maple Hale.

"You're eighty-four, Miss Maple. You should eat what you want." I put the boxed pastry in her cart and walk alongside her.

Jack's mom is exactly as I remembered from back in high school with a few more smile lines around her eyes. I never thought much about Magnolia Hale when I was growing up. I'd see her from time to time when she'd drop Jack off to spend the night with Levi. I only knew Jack didn't have a dad and his mom worked a lot.

The moment the automatic doors slid open inviting us into Dollar General, Jack proved he has no chill. The interrogation started right there in front of the batteries and seasonal display of Valentine candy.

To everyone but her mom, she goes by Maggie. Jack must not take after his mom by keeping secrets about his love life, so Maggie wasn't surprised to see me join their weekly outing. She gave me a warm hug and told her son she'd fill him in over pie.

Jack refused to wait.

That's when I grabbed a cart, took Miss Maple by the elbow, and led her to the pantry goods.

"What else is on your list?" I ask.

"Toilet paper, triple A batteries, and I want to look at the magazines. I like to read the gossip about the rich and famous, but they don't always get the magazines in. Oh, I forgot to put it on the list, but I need some scotch tape."

"That sounds easy enough. Maybe Jack will have chilled out by the time we get to the office supplies."

"Jackie loves his mama. Don't get me wrong, he loves me, too, but he and Magnolia are close. I kept telling her not to keep it a secret, but she worries. He's just not used to her datin'." Miss Maple grips my sweater and gives it a pull to get my attention. She even lowers her voice which she hasn't done once since she got in the car when we picked her up. "Between you, me, and the Pop-Tarts, I spilled the beans on purpose. I know my grandson. I had a feeling he wouldn't take this well. The last thing we needed was for him to lose his cool at Frank's. Everyone would talk about us!"

If there's one common theme for the day when it comes to Maple Hale—she doesn't want anyone talking about her.

"I'm sure Jack will come around. I can see how much he loves both of you."

"And that's it right there. Since he started that company, he's gone overboard taking care of us. Magnolia has paid my rent at Rolling Hills Ranch since I moved in. That wasn't easy for her. But a couple years ago, Jack bought her that house. His mama told me that he pays my bills now, too, but he doesn't want me to know."

I stop next to the toilet paper and look down at the old woman. "I had no idea. Jack was only slightly sarcastic when he said we've only been seeing each other for twenty seconds. It's been a hectic week. But he's been generous in a way that isn't showy. I'm not surprised."

Miss Maple tosses a package of toilet paper in the cart. "That's how I raised him. I think I need some chocolate. Let's do a U-ey back to the junk food. If you're here, Jack might not complain about my sweet tooth."

I haven't seen Maggie and Jack since we left them at the front of the store. But his grandmother seems like an open book, so I decide to be nosy. She did call me a chubby baby, after all.

"Do you like Pierce?" I ask.

She uses the cart for support as she shuffles back to the candy aisle. It's evident Dollar General is her home away from home. She knows this place inside and out.

"Seems like a good man. And that's something my Magnolia has never had in her life. Her daddy was a jerk. Back then, it was hard for someone like me to get divorced. I wasn't a career woman. I was stuck. When Magnolia got pregnant, her good-for-nothing boyfriend wanted nothing to do with a baby. By then, my husband had run off. I told Magnolia we'd make a life together, and that's what we did. When she had Jack, we were bound and determined to make sure he was a good one. He got the attitude and the good-looking genes from the sperm. Other than that, we take credit for him. I'm not saying it was easy, but we did it. Anyway, she and Pierce have been together for a few months. Magnolia wanted to make sure it was real before she told Jack. She knew he'd react just like he did. It's why I had to break the ice."

"I have a feeling when it comes to Jack, you know best."

We stop in front of the candy, and Miss Maple squints to study her options. "Hand me those chocolate covered pretzels. And pick out something for you. My treat."

"Oh, you don't have to—"

"Don't argue," she snaps.

I shut my mouth and pick up a bag of M&Ms.

"Good choice. I think we've wasted enough time. My knee hurts. Let's finish this list and find my daughter and grandson. Shopping for all these sweets makes me hungry. We need to get to Frank's before someone takes our table. I like to sit in the booth by the window."

I smile. "Sounds good."

When we turn the corner to go back to the front of the store, Jack is still talking to his mom. Miss Maple was right, her grandson just needed a minute. His gaze shifts to me the moment he sees us shuffle to them. Maggie's smile is almost a carbon copy of the one I've become addicted to in the last few days.

Jack might've taken after his father in other ways, but he has his mom's smile.

He might be cocky, but he's a good man. Good to the bone.

And it's their doing.

Maggie's warm expression swells the closer we get. "Once Jack threw his fit and realized I could live my life as I wish, he told me all about the two of you. My Jack and Emma Hollingsworth. I have to say, I like it."

I say nothing, but I do smile.

Because I like it too.

"I saw your interview with Brett," Maggie goes on. "Both of them. Jack filled me in on everything that's happened. You two have had a big week."

"What interview?" his grandmother asks.

"Mom, Emma was the one who ran out on the field after the game. Remember? We watched it together."

Miss Maple looks up at me. "That was you?"

I shrug. "It was."

"Well," Miss Maple exclaims. "No wonder you're not chubby anymore. You're fast."

"Mom!" Maggie exclaims.

"For fuck's sake," Jack mutters.

Miss Maple nudges me with her elbow. "For your information, I love chubby babies."

I smile. "Thank you."

"Which is good for you two if this fling lasts. I'm eighty-four. I don't have time to sit around and wait for great grandbabies. The chubbier the better. You two need to get busy."

"Okay," Maggie says. "Let's get you checked out. We're all hungry."

Maggie pulls the cart to the checkout. Her mother follows, but pokes Jack in the chest on her way. "Watch your mouth, Jackie."

Jack shakes his head. "Sorry."

"You can't talk that way around babies. Might as well go cold turkey now."

Jack pulls in a deep breath and looks at me. "I knew this could be interesting, but not to this level. I don't know what to say."

I try to bite back my smile. "You'd better hope Frank has cobbler on the menu. Blueberry—none of that fake peach stuff from a can. And if it's not á la mode, we're done."

"My future is hanging in the balance, and it's all on Frank. Good to know." Jack stuffs his hands in his pocket and pulls out his key fob. He leans down and puts his lips to my ear. "I don't care what anyone thinks, including your father—we're getting a room tonight. I've had about all the family I can take for the day."

"Don't just stand there, Jackie. Go get the car!" Miss

Maple yells loud enough for the entire Dollar General and beyond. "I feel my knee swellin'."

Jack lifts his chin to his grandmother and turns for the door. "Outings with you are always interesting, but this one takes the fucking cake, Grandma. I'm getting the car."

His grandmother doesn't miss a beat as she pulls a wad of small bills out of her purse and yells, "I love you, Jackie, but that mouth is going to do me in!"

22

DAILY MULTIVITAMIN WITH EXTRA IRON

Jack

Emma's fingers tangled in my hair when she calls out my name is nothing short of fucking unbelievable.

Not that I can tell her that since my tongue is in its new favorite place—glued to her clit.

I force her thighs high and wide to extend her orgasm.

We're not on her dad's sofa and we put off shacking up at Levi and Carissa's until Knox comes home. Mom offered me her guest room, which was also a big, fat fucking no thank you.

There aren't a lot of hotels out here in the boonies, but I couldn't book a room fast enough.

It's no Nebula, that's for sure.

It's not even a boutique hotel.

It's a chain, which I do not do unless it's a five star. Once I started landing endorsements for my clients, I swore I was done staying at mediocre hotels. During football season, I'm on the road almost every week, and I've come to like nice shit.

But tonight, we're at a chain, and I don't give a shit. It's clean, and my tongue is rooting for Emma to be as loud as possible.

She pulls at my roots before her fingers go limp as the rest of her body follows.

I give her clit one last swipe and lick my lips but don't move.

I gaze up her bare body and enjoy the view. "You're fucking beautiful."

Her breaths are shallow as she lies there spent. "You're relentless."

"When it comes to you, I am." I press my lips to the inside of her thigh before crawling up her body. "There was no way I could go another day without having you just like this."

Her tits rise and fall as she recuperates from her orgasm. I press her into the mattress and fit the underside of my bare cock, hard as a rock, to her pussy.

She's slick and wet and warm.

I've never had a woman bare. Never been with anyone that I wanted that with. Hell, I've never been with a woman I've trusted wholly.

Before I made it in this industry, the last thing I needed was an accidental pregnancy or STD.

And after I was successful, the last thing I needed was a woman trapping me with a not-so accidental pregnancy.

And let's just say STDs don't give a shit what your financial portfolio looks like.

Women know women. Mom and Grandma were in my face about all the ways they could trap a man. That shit lives rent free in my brain.

Which makes it monumental that every cell in my body wants nothing more than to slide bare inside Emma.

There has been lots of sex in the last week, and not one conversation that should be had when it comes to giving into my desires.

I rub my cock up and down her wet pussy as she drags a bare foot up my hamstring and tell her the truth, even if it does show her how obsessed I am. "Do you know how much I want to throw caution to the wind and take you just like this? Feel you inside and out with nothing between us. It's all I can think about."

Her dark eyes blink in slow motion, and her fingertips trace my jaw. "Given the fact you have a lot on your plate right now, I'm honored."

I press my cock into her still-swollen clit and enjoy the shutter of her body since I'm pressed to her everywhere. "You should be. I've never done that before."

Her expression comes alive a notch. "You're a bare virgin?"

I fight the desire to rub up and down on her again. At this point, bare or not, I won't last long if I don't slow things down. "I didn't know there was a name for it. I guess I am."

She traces my bottom lip with the tip of her index finger. "Then we have that in common. I, too, am a virgin when it comes to sex the way it was meant to be. Just two people with nothing between them. I've never wanted to."

"Fuck, Em. Now I want to take you bare more than ever. We could be each other's firsts."

"Jack Hale, taking another one of my firsts." She leans up and kisses my jaw. "You're greedy."

"And you're not giving me a reason not to slide inside you the way we were born to do."

"Oh, the awkward conversation. I've never had one of these before."

I slide my hand down the side of her body until I tag her around the back of her knee and yank it up my side to open her wider. "Since you're a bare virgin, I'm glad."

"I'm clean, and I'm on the pill. Your turn."

Iron Man has nothing on me. That's how hard my cock is from this conversation. I've never wanted anyone as bad as I do her right now.

"I'm clean and I take a daily multivitamin with extra iron."

"There you go one-upping me," she mutters. "I don't take an extra anything."

"I win." I press my lips to hers, kissing her slow and deep. Our hearts beat together, and I can't help but press my hand to the side of her neck to feel her pulse.

It speeds.

I like that.

I angle my hips enough that my cock springs free between us. My tip rests where it's meant to be.

Where it's fucking begging to be.

United with Emma. With nothing between us.

Fuck, I feel like a dirty Hallmark movie.

Her eyes fall shut, and her lips part.

"What's my prize?" I demand.

She licks her lips as her eyes roam my features before her eyes reunite with mine. "Me. Just me. I want nothing between us."

I rest my forearm above her head and brace.

Without looking away from her, I take her in one strong, deep thrust.

She gasps. "Jack."

"I know," I agree and don't move. This is so new and different. "So this is what sex is supposed to feel like."

"Only with you. We're perfect." Her eyes deepen with an emotion I recognize, even if it is new and something I've never experienced before.

I can't take it another second. I want more. I need more

I pull out and push back in. "So fucking perfect."

Her head falls back as her neck arches. She lifts her hips to meet me as I start to move in and out of her.

This is one more reason to tie me to Emma. The list is getting longer by the minute it seems.

My heart speeds as we move together. Each time with more force than the one before.

The energy between us is exponential. Some fucking mathematic equation that would make no sense to anyone but me.

And I can only hope…

Emma.

I've never needed someone else to match my level of whacked obsession. But I'm desperate for her to feel it just like me.

Our combined moans and bodies slapping is enough to push me over the edge.

Just before I'm about to let loose, her body tenses. Fingernails bite into my biceps, and my balls draw up.

I thrust into her two more times, then another, before I give her all my weight. We're connected in every way possible as I press her into the mattress.

I don't wait for us to catch our breaths. I lift my head and take her mouth.

When I let her go, I gaze down at her through the dim light of the basic hotel room. "There's something about getting to know someone you already know everything about. I'm thinking things I've never thought before, Em. And things I should not be thinking after such a short time with you. You make my head spin, baby."

She places her hand over my heart and presses in. "Right back at you. I'm not going to lie—it feels good and right … and it's scary."

I shake my head. "Let it feel good. Never be scared with me. I'm laying myself bare for you. And I don't mean this." I press my still-hard cock into her. I place my hand over hers on my heart. "I mean this. There's nothing hidden when it comes to me. Of all the people in the world, baby, I would not have gone here with you if it didn't mean something."

"I believe you." Her smile is small and her eyes glassy. "Who would've thought?"

The last person on earth I want to think about at this moment pops into my head.

Levi.

This might be a fantasy for me, but it very well could be his nightmare.

And since we're going to see him at the party, I'm going to have to take care of that.

"Yeah," I agree. "You're a fucking dream, baby. And I'm not letting you go."

Emma

"I think I need to pack a bag and leave it in your car. Now I've got to go home and do the whole walk of shame in front of my family. Not that they don't know where I am. I am wearing a tracker."

Jack looks from the mirror to me where I sit on the vanity watching him style his thick, dark hair. Mine is drying naturally as I sit here in his T-shirt and boxers. We slept in, ordered food, and watched sports news while lounging in bed.

He leans in and grabs the back of my neck and pulls me to him for a kiss. "I'll take you shopping again if you want. I need to get a birthday gift anyway."

I touch the screen on my phone. "We have two hours before the party. And with this group, it'll go late into the evening. If Carissa doesn't have an entire circus set up, I'll be surprised."

Jack grabs my cell from me and tosses it to the counter. He spreads my legs, pulls my ass to the edge, and presses his chest to mine. "You've checked your phone a million times since we got out of the shower. That doesn't include since you opened your eyes this morning. He'll call."

I wrap my arms around him and dig my heels into his ass. "Like you haven't talked to Brett almost as often since we woke up."

He leans in and kisses the tip of my nose. "Since Brett's arrest warrant was announced far and wide by the Vegas PD, I would argue that's different. Let's just say he's been in Crew's gym nonstop and still has steam to blow. He's pissed."

"It looks like Deep Throat is freaked too. The flames are getting warmer. He can't disappear on us when we have a way of finding out who he is. I feel it in my heart that he wants to help."

Jack shakes his head. "A lot of shit is balancing on the conscience of a guy who drugged and framed my client. I know you're ready to trade friendship bracelets with this guy, so forgive me for guarding my heart in this situation."

I can't help but bite back my smile. "Guarding your heart? Have a little faith, Jack. I believe in Deep Throat."

Jack hikes a cynical brow. "Then you're a better person than me, which we both already knew. I can count on one hand the amount of people I believe in. You might've just rounded that out to number five."

I lose my smile.

"What?" he asks. "Are you surprised?"

"Maybe," I tell him the truth. "I don't save lives like Levi or wipe terror from the world like my dad. I don't even invest in young people like Keelie."

His hand drops to my ass and slides inside the boxers I dug from his bag this morning for something clean to wear. I'm commando, so he has no trouble palming one cheek with a firm squeeze. "You stepped up to help when I needed you. So, yeah, you made the short list that includes my mom, grandma, your brother, and me."

I lower my voice. "You made your own list?"

"I'm at the top of my own fucking list. I told you I don't leave anything up to karma. I make my own fate." He bops the tip of my nose with his index finger. "And I've decided that you, baby, are my fate. I'm just lucky you didn't tell me to get lost when I tracked you down in Vegas."

"And here I thought that was real fate."

Jack shakes his head. "That was me seeing you run out onto that field in the middle of a frenzy, while all I could think about was kissing you in a barn that smelled like goats. There was nothing more I wanted right then than to recreate that kiss. But without the goats."

I'm about to tell Jack that he's grown into a man who hires personal shoppers and can afford the nicest of everything. He's too fancy for goats.

But I don't get the chance to state the obvious.

My cell vibrates on the counter next to us.

Finally.

Jack snatches it before I can and reads the two little words on the screen that make my heart skip a beat. "Unknown caller."

"It's him," I whisper and grab the phone. I press go on the call and put it on speaker. "Hello?"

"Hollingsworth," he bites. "I just saw the news. Sullivan has a warrant out for his arrest in Vegas. I told you where to look. What the hell have you been doing?"

My gaze darts to Jack. "I'm trying to figure it out. I can't just walk into the lobby of the Founders offices and demand to know who tried to frame their quarterback. I'm doing all I can. More information from you would be nice."

"Dammit." He sighs. "The people who arranged this are dangerous. I'm trying to do the right thing, but they'll come after me if they find out. You think that anyone gives a shit about some punk who's willing to do some shady shit for a buck but feels bad about it after the fact? They'll kill me and dump me in the Potomac so fast, I'll never see it coming."

Jack motions to me to keep the conversation going. I have no idea how long Ozzy Graves needs to track this call.

I do what I'm good at and keep talking. "You're really caught in the middle, but the fact you keep calling me tells me that you care about doing the right thing. As you can tell, I haven't said a word to anyone who would compromise you. Please, you have all the answers. I've proven you can trust me. Meet with me. Let's figure out a way to get to the bottom of this, clear Brett's name, and keep you out of it. There's only so much I can do on my own. I need more help."

"It's not like the boss hands me a background file of his customers. He offers me a job, and I take it. All I know is you're not digging deep enough."

"If you can't help, then why are you calling me?"

"Because you're not doing enough!" he bellows.

Jack grips my hip tighter when the unknown caller growls through the phone at me, but I can't focus on that.

A text pops up at the top of my screen.

> Ozzy – I got a hit on the line. Good job, Emma. You can hang up whenever you want.

I look up at Jack and smile but keep my tone even when I keep talking. "I won't stop—I promise. Can you tell me one thing?"

"This is going nowhere," he says. "I'm hanging up."

"No, wait," I beg. "Please confirm one thing for me. Did these orders come from Mark Morse? Because right now, that's all I can come up with."

"You think a washed-up quarterback is going to risk being paid out the remainder of his contract? And here I thought you knew sports. I'm obviously feeding information to the wrong source."

I forget all about the fact Ozzy is about to learn who this guy is. All I can focus on is the fact that Morse might not be the bad guy we assumed he was. "Higher than Morse? Are you talking management?"

"You're getting warmer, Hollingsworth. You're also running out of time. I don't know where Sullivan is hiding, but he can't stay there forever."

That's so true.

I look up at Jack as I plead with my caller. "I'm trying. Just don't ghost me. In fact, you should call more often. Check in. Let me know you're okay."

"Why do you give a shit about me?"

"Because you're doing the right thing. You're helping me, so I want to help you."

"Yeah, I'll believe that when I see it. No one gives a shit about me."

"That's not true." Now that Ozzy can trace his line, I ask the question I've wondered about since the beginning but was too afraid to scare him off. "I do wonder why you give a shit about Brett after doing your part to frame him."

"Let's just say I had no idea who I was dealing with. Had I known, I wouldn't have taken the gig."

"Then what makes Brett different from anyone else you'd be happy to frame for something they didn't do?"

He laughs.

The guy actually laughs.

And he doesn't sound like he wants to come through the phone at me or like he's running for his life. "Lady, I like to eat."

My pause hangs in the air so long, Jack puts his fingertips to my chin. I'm forced to look him in the eyes when I answer. "Fair enough."

"I also like to breathe, so don't fuck me over," he adds.

"I'm not sure what more I can do to convince you … fucking you over is not my goal. I am wholly confident we can prove Brett's innocence and protect your identity."

"That does not make two of us. Keep your phone close, Hollingsworth."

I'm about to beg him to keep in touch for a second time in the matter of minutes when the line goes dead.

"Well, that was interesting. Let's see what Ozzy can do," I say.

Jack opens his mouth to say something when I get another call.

This one is not unknown.

It's my dad.

I put it on speaker as fast as I can but don't have the chance to greet him since he talks first. "You did good, Em. Ozzy says he has what he needs."

A smile pulls at the corners of Jack's lips.

"That's great," I say. "I actually feel bad for him. He's trying to do the right thing, but I can tell he's scared."

"Only you would feel bad for someone who admitted to drugging and framing someone for multiple felonies," Dad states.

"I can't help it. We have a connection."

Jack frowns.

"Maybe it was the kidnapping," Dad deadpans. "Reporting in the face of tornadoes has made you an adrenaline junkie."

"Hardly. I just get the feeling he's a man without a lot of choices." I need to move on, so I change the subject. "I need to stop and get a gift for Hudson. I don't want to be late to the party."

"You didn't come home last night, and you're wearing a tracker. I know where you are, and I know who you're with."

Before I can confirm, deny, or plead the fifth, Jack joins the conversation. "Hey, Asa."

I give him a playful jab to the ribs.

Dad's sigh is louder than it should be over the speaker before he greets the man I just had bare sex with for the first time last night. "Jack."

"I just wanted to thank you and your team again for the work on my house along with the extra security. Insurance is coming next week. The sooner I get windows, the sooner I can move back in.

"Great." Another one syllable word bitten out by my father. He doesn't sound like he thinks anything is great at the moment.

It's time for me to step in. "I texted Carissa this morning. Jack and I are going to stay there tonight."

"That's even…" Dad pauses as if trying to choose his words carefully. "More great."

"We'll see you at the party," I say.

"I'm already here coordinating the play equipment installation."

"See? Best Grandpa in the world," I say.

"Emma, their other grandfather is doing hard time in federal prison. That title is not hard to obtain in this family," Dad jokes.

"Well, I'm sure if that weren't the case, you'd still be the best."

Jack is still standing between my spread legs. He takes this opportunity to swipe my hair to the side and press his lips to my neck.

"Gotta go, Dad. I don't want to be late even though I can't compete with play equipment."

"Love you, Em."

"Love you too."

I disconnect the call before Jack has the opportunity to express his affection as well. If his lips weren't connected to my skin, I wouldn't put it past him.

"We can't be late. I don't want to miss Hudson digging into his cake."

Jack dips his hands under my thighs and lifts me. When he makes it across the small room to the bed, I bounce with a giggle when he comes down on top of me. "Are you going to do the walk of shame or am I buying you yet another outfit?"

"I don't have time to birthday shop and do the walk of shame. Looks like I get more new clothes."

He kisses me quickly and slaps my ass with a light smack. "Put on my sweats. You'll freeze."

"Jack." I grip his shirt and hold him to me before he can stand. "Let me tell Levi today, okay?"

His expression turns serious. "No way. You let me worry about your brother. I can handle Levi."

"I don't know if that's a good idea. At least let me tell him, then you can talk to him."

"Baby, you saved me from a drive-by shooter. I don't need saving from your brother. He'll be fine. And if he's not, he'll be fine eventually. That's the last thing you need to worry about. I'm here and I'm not leaving."

I'm about to argue again, but this time he shuts me up with his lips and tongue.

It reminds me of last night.

And, again, in the shower this morning.

There's meaning to it, and it's laced with desperation.

It feels like Jack is hanging on tight, as if I might slip through his fingers.

If he only knew.

I plan on hanging on so tightly, it feels like my life depends on it.

23

LOVELY. SO LOVELY

Jack

Ten years ago, my best friend for life, Levi Hollingsworth, hooked up with the new girl in school.

No.

That's not right.

He didn't hook up with her.

He fell to his fucking knees, obsessed with the new girl, and didn't stop until he made her his wife.

We were in high school at the time, so you'd think their story of young love would be one with Gilmore Girl vibes.

But not those two.

That spring semester was a straight up made-for-TV Lifetime movie.

Politics.

Adultery.

Computer hacking.

Oh, and the biggie…

Who can forget murder?

It was a fucking trip and not one to the beach.

Most of it played out here, at the Boyette Mansion.

The creepy-ass old house that was owned by Carissa's grandparents. When old-lady Louisa Boyette died peacefully in her sleep—note, in the same room that Levi and Carissa now sleep in, I mean, can it get any creepier?—she left the estate to Carissa and her twin, Cade. Cade chose to stay and work in Boston after he graduated from MIT. That left the mansion that sits high on the hill and sprawling land to Carissa and Levi.

This is where they raise the kids they're popping out faster than horny rabbits.

And they've embraced this mansion for what it is over the years. The walls are brighter, the furniture doesn't feel like two-by-fours stuck up your ass, and there's a security system that's probably monitored by the team of middle-aged badasses.

If I've learned anything this week, it's that once you're in with Crew Vega's group, you're in for life. Asa might've called in those favors to board up my house and put it under their surveillance, but I know he didn't do it for me.

He did it for Emma.

"Emma and Jack! I shouldn't be surprised that my favorite singles got here at the same time. Jack, I have to say, you're usually later than this." Carissa Hollingsworth throws herself at her sister-in-law. When she lets go, she holds Emma at arm's length and looks her up and down. "I can't believe I haven't seen you since you moved back to Virginia. You look amazing! I love your dress. Where did you get it?"

Emma waves her off and slides her coat down her arms. "Thanks. Target. I've been shopping there a lot lately."

Yeah, she has.

And not that anyone cares, I'm sick of having to walk through the dollar aisle, cosmetics, and a movie candy end cap to get to the women's section. I've worked too fucking hard to shop like that.

I not only bought her a new dress and pair of shoes, but Emma also walked out of there with a desk organizer, a bottle of wine, and nail polish remover.

Oh, and a stack of books and puzzles for Hudson.

Never did I dream of purchasing such a lame-ass gift for a one-year-old. It's not at all loud or obnoxious, which goes against every fiber of my being.

It's official.

I cannot say no to Emma when it comes to anything.

I paid for the most boring birthday gifts on earth and slapped my name on the card in the car.

I even did it with a smile on my good-looking mug.

Emma hands over her gift of finger puppets and the wine I thought was for us later tonight. "For Hudson. And the wine is for you. I thought you might need a drink after the party."

"You know I will." Carissa holds my wine to her chest like it's her most cherished possession before she looks at me. "How's it going, Jack? I heard about your house. That's horrible. Talk about a rollercoaster week."

"Ups and downs, that's for sure." I hand Carissa the most perfectly packaged gift that's ever had my name on it, thanks to Emma. "For the birthday boy. It's not loud or obnoxious. Hudson will no doubt nickname me *Dad's boring-ass friend*."

Carissa laughs and moves through the long entryway that spans three stories. Emma follows, but not before she elbows me in the ribs. I follow and can't take my eyes off her ass in that tight dress.

I might not like shopping at the big, red bullseye, but I can't deny their shit looks good on Emma.

Then again, she'd make anything look good. Especially my boxers and T-shirt.

Carissa talks as she walks. "Dinner is in the dining room. Kids are high on sugar and running feral. Ladies are in the kitchen tasting Addy's new batch of wine she just bottled. Asa is still outside with some of the guys even though it's dark, overseeing the playground that's bigger than those at most elementary schools. Between us, it looks more like a miniature tactical course, but it is what it is. We had no idea what was happening when we woke up this morning. It's so Asa. Can I get you guys something to drink?"

There's a low chatter from the family room when we come around the corner.

Emma doesn't give me a glance and follows Carissa. "I'll help you with the drinks, then I need to find the birthday boy and kiss him all over his face."

I spot Levi hanging with a couple of the badasses, Crew, Grady, and Ozzy. Cade and Mason are with them.

Every time I'm here I'm shocked it's the same house we snuck in and out of back in the day.

"I'm going to find my long-lost friend who's always too busy for me," I say.

"Beer, Jack?" Carissa calls.

"Whatever you've got. Thanks."

I make my way through the family room and wonder how this is going to go. Levi's hands are full since he's holding Hudson and a beer. He lifts his chin and smirks when he sees me.

Well then.

I guess Levi doesn't know about me and Emma yet.

I've got work to do.

"What's up, everyone?" I greet Levi and put my hand out to Hudson to see if he'll give me a high five. "Happy birthday, little guy."

Hudson throws himself at Levi since he doesn't know me. "Stranger danger. Smart kid."

"He just woke up from a nap. He'll wreak havoc soon," Levi says before lifting his beer bottle to me. "Thanks for taking time out of your high-profile life to stop by. I'm not sure we can offer the action you're used to."

I stuff my hands in my pockets and tell him the truth. "Give me five minutes, I'll do my best to up the game around here."

Mason leans in and lowers his voice. "I heard Brett is staying at Whitetail. Probably a good thing he went into hiding before they issued the warrants. How long is it going to take you to clear his name?"

"He can stay as long as he needs to," Crew says. "But he might be able to go home soon. Ozzy has news. Cade even kicked in to help."

I turn to Cade. "Seriously?"

"I was bored. I can only sit around this place for so long." Cade shrugs and takes a gulp of his soda and turns to Levi. "No offense."

Levi smirks. "None taken."

"I saw these two at work." Grady motions to Cade and Ozzy. "They're like freak hackers. I'm in awe of their illegal talents."

"Well?" I demand. "Do I have to beg for information?"

Ozzy takes a sip of his beer. "We ID'd Emma's informant. I don't know whether to be surprised or not, but he's got connections to Sullivan."

I forget all about the fact I walked into this room moments ago wondering how I'm going to tell Levi about me and his little sister. All I can do is wonder how Deep Throat is connected to Brett. "Who the hell is it?"

"Rylan Crawford," Cade announces.

That's it? No explanation

"I have no clue who that is," I bite. "It would be nice if someone could fill me in."

"His younger sister is Renee Crawford," Crew says. I'm sure they see nothing but a blank look on my face since that's how I feel. Crew finally gives up the link to my client. "Renee was a beneficiary of Brett Sullivan's foundation two years ago. She graduated with honors from a school in the District and is in the middle of her sophomore year at George Washington. We checked her out. Her GPA is a three-point-nine. She's killing it. Her older brother, not so much."

I drag a hand down my face. Besides showing up to Brett's annual celebrity fundraiser for his foundation and making a sizeable donation, I have nothing to do with it.

"Are you saying this guy did this to Brett because of who he is or he's trying to save him because of his sister? Because the first doesn't make sense," I say.

Ozzy puts in his two cents. "I agree. And from what we can tell, the phone he uses to call Emma is a prepaid. There have been no other incoming or outgoing calls. The guy might not sport a GPA of any sort, but that doesn't mean he's not smart. What he doesn't know is we can triangulate that phone from the satellite. We can pinpoint his location to pick up the other lines. I've got a list we're working through."

I look between Crew, Grady, Ozzy, and Cade. "I sucked at geometry. You lost me at triangles."

"If I didn't work with them every day, I'd be lost too," Grady says. "Oz has a short list of phones in close proximity to the prepaid. They're going through them one by one."

"And by pinging, I'm taking it down to five hundred square feet. If this guy has been in the vicinity of other cells in the last fourteen hours, we have the number. We're continuing to collect data as we sit here drinking beer. It's on autopilot," Ozzy says.

I stuff my hands in my pockets and rock back on my heels. "Impressive."

Mason shakes his head in disbelief. "That's more than impressive. This feels like old times, but we're adults and got to come through the front door instead of having to sneak in the back."

Grady lifts his chin and turns to Crew. "I remember that night. These guys were freaked."

"I wasn't freaked," I argue. "I was ready to step up, but it was Mason's bedtime."

Mason laughs. "Hey, I was fourteen and barely weighed a buck-oh-five. I was not interested in hunting a murderer in the Love Machine."

"The Love Machine." Levi reminisces as he bounces a wiggling Hudson in his arms. "Fun times … sort of."

"It's been a while since I've hacked anyone illegally," Cade says. "Felt good."

Ozzy lifts his bottle to him. "You know your way around a network. Come back anytime."

Cade looks like he might actually consider it. "Thanks."

"This is all great," I snap with sarcasm. "But where do we go from here now that we know who Deep Throat is? I need to know who paid Rylan to drug my client. My number one priority is to prove Brett innocent so I can go back to contracts and endorsements, not kidnappings and drive-bys. They cramp my style."

"Did I hear someone say innocent?"

We all turn to see Emma standing there with two bottles of beer. She hands one to me and takes a sip from the other leaving a drop on her bottom lip.

Damn.

I want to lick it.

It's go time on project *tell my best friend I plan on banging his sister for a very long time*.

Dare I say ... forever.

If we didn't have an audience, I'd take advantage of him holding a baby.

Instead, I tap the neck of my bottle to Emma's. "They ID'd Deep Throat. His sister was a scholarship recipient for Brett."

Emma's eyes widen. "No way. Who hired him?"

"It's only been a few hours, Emma. Cut me some slack," Ozzy drawls.

Emma smiles. "Sorry. But if we know who he is, we can contact him. Right?"

Grady rubs his jaw. "There's a decent chance you'll spook him, and he'll cut off all contact with you and his sources. We'll lose our technical trail of breadcrumbs."

Emma disagrees. "I think he wants to help us, but he's scared. I want to meet with him again."

"Whoa." Levi steps into the conversation with a deep frown. "You're not meeting this guy after what he did at the parade. He's unpredictable."

Emma rolls her eyes. "Hello to you, too, bro."

Levi frowns at his sister. "I don't like that you're in the middle of this."

I can't say that I don't agree, but there's no way I won't have Emma's back.

She proves she doesn't need my help and sets him straight. "I'm the one he trusts. He's not unpredictable. If anything, he risked his own safety to help us help Brett."

"Let's not jump the gun," Ozzy says. "He'll have other cells. Give me a day to track those and study the activity. We'll figure out how predictable he really is."

Crew looks at Emma. "If Bella were here, she'd tell you to do it. Hell, she'd probably offer to be your wingwoman."

"I could use someone in my corner. Where is she?" Emma asks.

"She and Carson went to Winslet to visit her brother," Crew says. "This guy kidnapped you. Your dad—correction, all of us—will lose our shit if you try to meet with him."

"Would everyone quit saying I was kidnapped? It was a conversation, that's it."

That, I disagree with. "I was there. You were kidnapped."

"Let's talk about that." Levi glances between Emma and me. "Ever since Vegas, you're both running from the same drama. It's more than coincidental."

Grady huffs a laugh and glances outside. "Where's Asa? He could probably chime in on this."

"That's true," Mason agrees and doesn't stop there. "The game. The interviews. The parade. Jack was at Emma's kidnapping. Emma warned Jack about the drive by... I could go on. Statistically speaking, Levi is right. It's more than coincidental."

Fucking Mason.

I do not need an audience when I talk to Levi.

I motion between Mason and Levi. "You two and your oversized brains making everything about statistics."

Instead of talking about stats, Emma forces me to take her beer and reaches for her nephew. "Come here, little cutie. Auntie Em wants to kiss you all over your sweet little face!"

Shit. In her effort to change the subject, Emma stole the only shield I had between me and my best friend.

And what is it with adults referring to themselves in the third person when it comes to babies?

Hudson goes straight to Emma and squeals when she tickles him. I can't take my eyes off her and her nephew.

Emma is hot.

Emma with a kid on her hip is even hotter.

But Carissa appears and pulls Hudson from Emma's arms, ruining the vision of my future. "As much as I know everyone would rather discuss football and shootings, it's time to open presents so we can get to the cake. Can you round up the kids, Levi? They're outside with your dad. I'm pretty sure he and Jarvis are running drills and timing them."

Levi leans down and kisses his wife. "That might take a minute. They look like they're having a great time, including my dad. The last I saw, Eze was killing it. I'm pretty sure Jarvis is making plans to build an even bigger set at their house. Knowing him, he'll build another garage and make it an indoor gym."

Levi heads outside and Carissa says, "I'm going to change Hudson. Be right back."

Once they both leave, it's Grady who calls us out. "You know, I remember the day I found out my friend hooked up with my baby sister. I want everyone to know, I'm not leaving this house until someone leaks it to Levi that you two are together. I don't want to miss the brawl."

"Wait a second," Mason exclaims and turns to Emma and me. "You two are doing the dirty?"

Cade looks just as surprised. "You hooked up with Emma?"

"Thanks for that, Grady." Emma grabs her beer from me and takes a big gulp.

Mason goes on, way too loud, "You broke the bro-code?"

"Hell yeah, he did," Grady confirms. "Asa knows, but Levi does not."

"Everyone knows but us?" Cade motions to Mason. "Why were we left out?"

"Because you'd yap to Levi and Carissa, that's why," I bite. "I'm going to talk to Levi. Emma and I have had a lot to deal with this week—give us a break. And Levi will be just fine. Hell, he loves me. Once it sinks in, he'll be so happy, he won't know what to do with himself."

"Keep telling yourself that," Crew mutters.

"Hello?" Emma calls to the group. "I'm standing right here. This isn't some regency romance where my father and brother get approval of who courts me. What century are you people living in?"

I motion to the woman I can't get enough of. "Exactly what she said. Just don't open your big mouths before I get the chance to talk to him."

"I can't believe it." Mason beams and crosses his arms. "It's finally come full circle."

"What does that mean?" I demand.

"Yeah, what *does* that mean?" Emma echoes.

Mason leans in and lowers his voice. "It means we know what you did in the barn at Levi's graduation party."

"Are you serious?" Emma blurts.

Cade looks bored. "It's true."

"Damn." Grady shakes his head. "I remember that party. Our only job was to make sure no one got pregnant. Apparently, we can't be good at everything. We need to stay in our lane."

Emma swats Grady with the back of her hand. "It was a kiss. No one was close to getting pregnant."

I look to make sure Levi is still outside wrangling kids and Carissa is still changing diapers before I put my hand low on Emma's back and glare at Mason and Cade. "The Homies were snooping? What the hell kind of friends are you?"

Mason takes a swig of his soda. "I could say the same thing about you, since you were kissing your best friend's little sister."

"He's here!" Our huddle of Homies and badasses turn to the opening of the family room when Keelie rushes in from the kitchen.

Knox saunters into the room.

He's grown at least six inches since I last saw him and put on some weight in the form of solid muscle.

He's not a kid anymore. He's at the stage between a boy and a man. He's grown into the body of a man, but still has the eyes of a kid.

I doubt he's had to embrace vegetables yet. Lucky fucker. I remember those days when I could survive on fried food, pizza, and beer that someone else bought for me since I wasn't of age yet.

And right now, I know who's buying his beer.

The woman attached to his side.

I lean down and put my lips to Emma's ear. "Talk about all grown up—I haven't seen Knox in forever."

It's like Emma doesn't hear me. Her whole body goes taut. "Who the hell is with him?"

The Playbook of Emma

I look down at her and raise a brow. "You mean the cougar on his arm?"

"Knox landed an older woman?" Grady drawls low for only our group to hear.

"I don't know," Emma whispers. "Keelie said he was bringing home a girl. He lied. That is no girl."

Since every eye in the place is on Knox and some older woman, I slide my hand low on Emma's back and wrap it around her hip. "No offense, Em, but you're more of a girl than that woman."

Emma's dark eyes angle to mine. Her expression is set to shocked. She must not take offense at my comment. "Right? Knox is twenty. What the hell? Keelie is going to have a fit."

We're not the only ones in the room who see it. Once Keelie gets past her excitement of seeing her son, her expression is a million times more shocked than Emma's.

I've known Keelie since she was my high school counselor. That was well over a decade ago, and I've never witnessed her skirt the edge of rude.

Until now.

"Who are you?" Keelie demands as she looks the woman up and down.

Knox puts his hand to the woman's back and ignores his mom's freak out. "Mom, this is Ricki. Ricki, my mom."

Keelie shifts her glare from the female who is not a girl to her son. "Ricki?"

The woman, who I'd put money on is older than me, offers her hand to Keelie. "It's so nice to meet you. Knox has told me so much about you."

Keelie moves in slow motion and takes her hand. "Interesting. My son hasn't told me anything about you."

Knox stiffens.

Grady chuckles.

Crew sighs.

"Who's ready for presents?" Asa bellows as he enters from the cold. Everyone's heads swing to the other side of the room where Asa, Saylor, and Levi come in from outside with a slew of kids in all shapes and sizes. "Good luck topping my gift."

"Dad," Emma hisses and pulls out of my hold to hurry to Asa. "Do something. Knox got here with his girlfriend who is *not* a girl. Keelie is about to freak out."

Asa's gaze moves across the room to the scene playing out. "What the hell did Knox do?"

Saylor comes to a stop next to Asa, and her face lights up when she sees Knox. "This is amazing."

Asa ignores Saylor and moves to his wife on the other side of the room.

Knox takes a small step toward his mother. "Mom, calm down."

"I'm calm," Keelie bites in a tone higher than normal for her. "All I'm saying is you haven't told me anything about…" Keelie turns to the woman who fits herself to Knox's side. "Ricki?"

The woman smiles. "It's short for Erica."

"Asa." Asa introduces himself but we can all see it's a ruse to hold his wife back as he puts an arm around her. "I'm the dad. Nice to meet you."

Ricki glances up at Knox and smiles before turning back to Asa and Keelie. "You, as well. It's lovely to be here."

"Lovely," Saylor mimics. "So lovely."

Asa holds Keelie back to his chest and narrows his eyes at Knox and Ricki. "How long have you two been seeing each other?"

I've got to hand it to Knox, he doesn't look the least bit anxious about bringing an older woman home as a surprise. "A couple months. We met on campus."

Levi butts into the conversation. "I'm Levi. Welcome to our home."

Ricki smiles and tips her head to lean on Knox's shoulder. "It's beautiful."

"Beautiful, right?" Saylor just won't stop and crosses her arms. "Are you a ... professor?"

Keelie gasps. "Saylor!"

"Oh, goodness no," Ricki exclaims and stands up straight. "I work on campus but not as an instructor. Knox and I met at a student government meeting. I work in the Student Affairs office."

"I bet she does," I mutter.

Emma doesn't move from my side and whispers, "This is a nightmare."

Levi must agree, because the moment Carissa returns with Hudson, he announces, "Who's ready for presents and cake? And I think we could all use another drink." He turns to Asa. "Dad, can you and Keelie get everyone a refill?"

"No—" Keelie starts, but Asa doesn't allow her to argue.

He pulls Keelie toward the kitchen. "We have all day to visit, baby. Let's get you a glass of wine. I have a feeling you're going to need it."

Everyone does as Levi says, but Saylor continues to interrogate her brother. I turn Emma to me and lean down to whisper, "Thanks to Knox, no one is paying attention to us. I'll talk to Levi tonight. No more secrets."

Emma takes a sip and exhales like she needs a long winter's nap.

After the last week, I wish I could make that happen for both of us.

"Time to rip off the bandage." She glances around the room before she steps closer to me than she would a friend. This time it's her turn to put her lips to my ear. "Then you can rip off my dress."

My fingers flex on her hip. I'm about to drag her to the third floor and lock us in the attic, when Ozzy interrupts us as he stares at his cell. "Guys, I think we've got something."

"Is it one of the new cells we started to monitor?" Cade asks.

Ozzy looks up to the group. "Sort of. We've got a trail of calls from those cells."

"To whom?" I demand.

"Do you know anyone named Pike?"

Emma grips my arm.

"Jack?" Crew calls for me. "You know him?"

I feel something between rage and a kick in the balls. My old boss and firm … I left for a reason. If he can't be the best of the best through hard work and integrity, he finds another way to the top. It comes from willing to work dirty and being a straight up asshole. Freddy Pike is both down to the bone.

"I know him," I confirm. "And I'm going to kill him."

24

NO ONE IS KILLING ANYONE

Jack

We're back in Crew's old farmhouse with Crew, Grady, and Oz, having followed Ozzy past the dining room they use as a conference room toward the back of the house. Everyone else stayed back at the birthday party but Mason.

He was quick to join and said it was for moral support, but I suspect he's just as curious as the rest of us.

Crew Vega's central command looks like something out of a movie.

The walls are covered with monitors, and there are more keyboards than badasses. I can see why Cade would take them up on the opportunity to come back and hang out whenever he felt the urge to dabble in illegal hacking.

"Find out where Sullivan is," a voice growls over the recording that Ozzy turned up on the speakers. I'm not just pissed,

but I'm pissed in surround sound thanks to Crew's high-tech everything.

That voice belongs to none other than Alfred Pike, the owner of my old agency.

"I don't know where he is. Nobody does."

That's Gary Acosta.

I thought that fucker was too lazy to extend this much effort into anything. He's skated by with talented clients for far too long. New athletes on the block see him as old school and want nothing to do with him.

They want agents who actually give a shit about them.

Like yours truly.

Fred doesn't stop talking. *"There's a warrant for his arrest—fucking finally. It took long enough. If Sullivan goes down, so will Hale. He's been making too much headway. Sullivan getting MVP was the last straw. I'm ready to bury him for good. No one will sign with him if he can't even keep his golden boy out of trouble."*

"I'm not in the business of finding missing persons," Acosta complains. *"How do you expect me to find Sullivan when the cops can't even find him?"*

"I don't know, but if you want to make partner, you'll fucking figure it out."

Nothing has changed. Fred is just as much of an asshole as he used to be.

Hell, he's worse.

Gary makes more excuses. *"I've got my guy looking, but he's spooked. Took him over a day to return my call, and he gave me nothing. I have a feeling he'll go silent on me if I push too hard."*

"I don't give a shit if you have to put up a bat signal. Get him the message that we know where his family is. Hell, we know his little sister's dorm room number. That'll push him over the edge. I don't want to hear from you again until there's breaking news that Sullivan has been read his fucking rights. If that scene goes viral, Hale will be shut down. Do you understand? You're not just going to lose your chance at partner, you'll find yourself without a job. The agency needs this and so does your client. Get it fucking done."

The recording ends, and Ozzy taps at the keyboard. "That took me less than a day. Now we know."

"He's not even after Brett," Emma says from where she stands at my side. "He's after you."

I shouldn't be surprised even though I am. It's not like I stole their clients—at least not right away. Once my non-compete died a happy death, the writing was on the wall. It took that long for my old clients to realize Alfred Pike and company weren't getting them the best contracts, were charging them higher rates, and adding on fees for everything in the book.

I drag a hand through my hair and grip the tense muscles at the back of my neck. "Yeah, I'm going to kill him."

"Hold up." Crew steps in. "No one is killing anyone. We're not in the desert or the jungle, and this isn't the wild, wild west. We don't do that shit in the States."

Mason's eyes saucer, and he pales a shade.

Emma sighs.

I'm not sure I'll ever get used to that as I stare at the leader of the badasses. "I was being rhetorical. I don't do that either … anywhere."

Grady steps in. "Let's move forward. He's using Sullivan to fuck you over. Let's focus on the fact we have the evidence and motive. We need to decide how to use it."

"Not to burst anyone's bubble, but how do you use it?" Mason asks. "I'm not a cop or an attorney, but that recording wasn't obtained on the up and up."

"You're not wrong," I agree. "I can't exactly go to the police with what we have. I need proof, and I need to get it the legal way."

"If we have proof of anything, it's that I was right," Emma says. "We can trust Rylan. He's definitely not cooperating with your old boss. Let me contact him."

I shut her down. "No way. Especially not now that we know who we're dealing with. This shit started because Pike is after me. I regret dragging you into this more than ever."

Emma rolls her eyes. "Let me remind you, I was the one who chased Brett down for an interview. You hardly dragged me into this."

"Ah, guys? Jessica sent me this." Mason holds his cell up and winces. "This isn't good."

A gasp escapes from Emma's lips as she reaches for the phone, but I get to it first. "What the fuck?"

Emma pulls at my arm to see the screen. "Holy shit. What have they done?"

"I can't believe it's from your own network," Mason says. "And it's gone viral. Not the kind of viral that you experienced when you raced onto the field, but my chickens would be thrilled with those kinds of views."

It's Emma and Brett all right, but not after his winning touchdown. It's the interview in my family room that should be old news by now.

"That bitch!" Emma exclaims. "Molly Minders is doing a bit about Brett and me!"

"Huh." Mason crosses his arms and contemplates the situation with not nearly enough gravity as it deserves. "I guess you would call this news about the news?"

"I can't believe her." Emma wipes the cell from my hand and cranks up the volume.

Molly Minders sits at the news desk, front and center, even though it's normally her job on weekends. She looks more smug than she should when reporting lies about one of her own associates. *"In an effort to be one hundred percent transparent with our viewers, there is a shocking turn of events surrounding Founders quarterback, Brett Sullivan. We are coming to you with reports that Emma Hollingsworth, a WDCN field sports correspondent, has been found to be personally involved with Sullivan. The network has chosen to bring you this news first as opposed to covering it up."*

Grady rocks back on his heels and crosses his arms with a smirk plastered on his face. "Well, I'd say that's a shocking turn of events considering you two are trying to keep the fact you're doing the dirty from Levi."

I glare at Grady. "Not the time for middle-aged badass sarcasm."

That wipes the smirk off his face.

Emma ignores everyone and focuses on Molly. "I hate her. I hate her more than I hated her yesterday."

Molly continues to spew lies about the woman I've had in multiple beds at this point and switches to the video of Brett spinning Emma in a circle after the game. *"A warrant has been issued for the arrest of Brett Sullivan in Las Vegas, as he continues to evade authorities. Emma Hollingsworth, an employee of WDCN, has been put on temporary leave from the network until further notice. We will continue to follow this story as it develops."*

Emma shoves the phone at Mason before she does a one-eighty and drags her hands through her hair. "I cannot believe this. I find out they put me on leave through a social media post? This is so messed up. And where did this fictional story come from?"

Mason looks to Ozzy and tips his head. "I think you've got more illegal wiretapping to add to your to-do list."

I turn Emma to me and look into her dark eyes. "We'll take care of this. I swear. They can't spew shit about you that isn't true. If anyone can prove that you're personally involved with Brett is a lie, it's me. This might not be my forte, but I'll slap them with a defamation lawsuit. When I'm done with them, you won't have to work for a decade."

Emma's expression switches from pissed to panicked in a heartbeat. "How are you going to do that? Tell the world I'm sleeping with you but not him?"

"That's enough." Crew puts a stop to all conversation about who's sleeping with whom. He looks nauseated. "I've known you your entire life, and I've got two daughters. I don't care how old you are, I cannot sit here while everyone talks about … that."

"Crew is right. This is skating the edge of weird—even for me," Grady agrees.

Crew pulls in a deep breath. "Mason is right. We need to tap more phones."

Ozzy does not look nauseated or irritated. "Get me the bitch's phone number. I'm all over it."

Mason is the only one in the room wearing a smile, like he somehow solved all our problems when nothing is fucking solved.

Nothing.

Someone keeps pouring gasoline on the dumpster fire that is my life and somehow dragged Emma into the blaze.

"Texting you her number now," Emma grumbles before her eyes flare. "Shit. My producer is calling. I need to take this."

Emma moves to the hallway to take the call as I mentally add her producer to my shit list.

I turn back to the guys. "I need to update Brett on what's going on. It pisses me off more than ever to know he went down because of me."

Crew crosses his arms and glances at his associates. "What do you want us to do?"

"Since you made it clear that killing anyone is off the table," I give Crew the side eye, "I can handle it from here."

Grady frowns. "Are you sure?"

"I can handle Fred Pike and will get the proof I need that he's behind this, but if you could continue to monitor him, I'd appreciate it. I can stay one step ahead. The fact that

Emma is getting fucked over at work because of this pisses me off."

Ozzy is already tapping away at the keyboard. "I've got it covered."

Grady cracks his knuckles. "If you need us to bring Pike to the barn for a talk, we're more than happy to. Nothing we haven't done before."

"A talk," I echo.

Mason gulps and turns his wide eyes to me. "You should be happy they didn't catch you kissing Emma at Levi's party all those years ago. They would've dragged you to the barn for a ... *talk*."

"Asa might've," Crew says before turning to me. "You're sure you don't need our help?"

"I'm good, thanks."

"I've got his back." Mason slaps me on the shoulder. "As opposed to the last time we fought crime together, I have my driver's license. You've got a getaway driver at your disposal."

"The only person who's going to need a getaway anything is fucking Freddy."

Mason's eyes widen. "Maybe I don't want in on this. What are you going to do?"

"I'm going to walk into his house like a grown fucking adult and have a conversation about how he's so bad at what he does that he feels he needs to cut me off at the knees to get clients. Then I'm going to put my fist in his face, but not for what he's done to me or Brett—but for what he's putting Emma through."

Everyone in the room glances around at each other at the sound of my plan.

"Okay, that's a pipe dream. What I'm really going to do is swallow my pride, reach out to him for help with my delinquent client, and trick him into saying something. But first I need to buy a recording device, so I'll have record of everything he says. But once he admits it, then I'm going to punch him in the face for Emma."

"That sounds like a better idea. If you need moral support, I'll call Jessica to let her know I'll be late."

"I can help with that plan," Ozzy offers. "You can borrow a wire. I'll monitor it from here."

"Cool. Hook me up."

"Please don't tell me I need to be worried about you hooking up with someone else. I don't have the energy."

We all turn to find Emma leaning against the door jam.

I hold my arm out for her. "Baby, come here. If you break my heart into a million little pieces, even then I won't want to hook up with anyone but you. You've ruined hookups for me for the rest of my life."

"That's good. One less thing for me to worry about." Emma fits her front to mine and tucks her face into my neck. "It's official, I'm on unpaid leave. August said it came from the network executives. He tried to fight it, but they were having none of it. I have a meeting tomorrow morning with Mr. Folmer, the executive who made the final decision and human resources. They said it can't wait until next week. I guess it was good while it lasted. I had three amazing weeks at work before it all came crashing down on me. Well, at least two average ones and one amazing one."

I put my fingers to her chin. "I'll make sure they retract that publicly."

A shadow of a smile hits her lips. I want nothing more than to kiss her.

"Are you done?" she asks. "We need to talk to Brett, and I'd like to get back to the party before it's over."

"Here." Ozzy hands me a small box. "It works the best if you clip it to the inside of your breast pocket. Make sure you click it on and let me know when you're ready to rock and roll. I'll let you know if they get chatty again."

"I appreciate it." I slide the box into my pocket and take Emma's hand in mine. "Let's get back to the party."

I shake hands with Crew and his team, and Emma and I are out the door of the small farmhouse with Mason in tow. When we get to my car, I open the passenger door for Emma, but she doesn't get in.

She also doesn't look tired or pissed any longer.

She's biting back a smile and looks between me and Mason. "We're not going back to the party, and we can check on Brett later. We have something more important to do."

"I might've been up for egging Molly Minders' house ten years ago, but even I'm mature enough to realize no one gets away with that shit anymore. Those guys in there aren't the only ones with cameras, Em."

Mason laments one of his many first-world problems. "I

have to agree, which is too bad, because we have more eggs at home than we know what to do with."

Emma ignores both of us as excitement lights up her dark eyes. "I cut my conversation with August short when I got another call. It was Deep Throat, AKA Rylan Crawford! He saw the bullshit news bit about me being put on leave. You guys, guess what?"

I lean into the car and drag a hand down my face. "You didn't."

"You told him you know who he is?" Mason asks my exact thoughts.

Emma's smile swells. "I did. He was obviously surprised, but I convinced him this is for the best. We need each other at this point. He agreed to meet with us to discuss everything."

Mason's expression matches Emma's. "I'm so here for this."

"No. I don't like this. He dragged you into a dark alley at the parade. Your dad has an entire team who does way shadier shit than I thought they did thirty minutes ago. Let them deal with Rylan."

"If we send my dad and the guys in for him, he'll freak, and we'll never see him again. You can come with me or not, but I'm going," she argues.

"I'm curious," Mason states. "I'll go with Emma."

I glare at him. "Whose friend are you, anyway? It's taken me ten years to get her right where I want her, and I'd really like for her not to be kidnapped or worse."

Emma's hand hits my abs and slides up my chest. The next thing I know, she's pulling my face to hers, and our lips are molded as one.

I can't take it.

I dip my hand into her hair and plant my other firmly on her ass. What started as her kiss is officially mine. I don't give a shit that Mason is front and center for the show.

Hell, at this point, I wouldn't care if Levi saw us.

Maybe this would be the best way to break the news. It's not like anything is going to change.

Despite my life being turned on its head, I've fallen hard. Hell, maybe my world going up in flames made me fall harder.

Who the hell knows? Not me. The only lessons I've had when it comes to successful relationships is my mom making me watch the Hallmark Channel back in the day.

Those men never ended up divorced or ran out on their family. When times got tough, they ate a cupcake from their plucky little bakery and forged ahead like a real man.

Mason clears his throat. "In the name of love, I'm sorry this took ten years to happen. You two are perfect together. When you guys get married, I'm going to name some chickens after you."

I break the kiss and tip my forehead to hers and pull in a deep breath. "If anything happens to you, I'll hate myself forever."

Emma gives her head a little shake but doesn't pull away from me. "I trust him and have a good feeling about this. It took ten years for you and me to happen. I wouldn't risk this for anything."

I kiss her one more time. "Okay. We'll meet Rylan tonight and I'll talk to Pike tomorrow morning."

"Thank you." Her smile is back, and she pulls away from me to fold into the passenger seat.

Mason reaches for the back door. "This is either going to be epic or the worst idea ever. I have a feeling there will be no in between."

I stand next to my car and tip my head up to look through the barren trees of the forest.

I agree with Mason.

I just hope it's the former, and not the latter.

25

OPEN-FACED SANDWICH

Emma

It sucks to lose control of your own life because someone else is a shallow, ugly-on-the-inside, conniving bitch.

Do I have proof Molly Minders fictionalized an entire daytime TV melodrama about Brett Sullivan and me?

No.

But when a girl knows, she knows.

I watched the newsclip over and over on our way to the city. Every time I pressed play on that sucker, I was more and more convinced.

I could see it in her eyes.

She might've been "reporting the news" but she did it with a smug-ass look. August was beside himself apologetic for not being able to do more, and Ross texted to tell me he knows it's not true and he'll make some calls to do what he can.

At least I have people in my corner who believe me.

And let's be real ... the last time I felt in control of my career was when I was reporting on tornados and bison. Since then, the highs and lows have been so drastic, I can't keep up.

If I'm not high on luck, then I'm down for the count.

Jack puts his fancy car in park, kills the engine, and turns to me and Mason. "We have no idea what we're walking into, so this is how it's going to go: we stick together no matter what. I don't care if you're about to pee your pants, no one breaks up the three amigos, got it? Mason, we will flank Emma. Do not leave her side. No one is nabbing her tonight or ever again."

Mason unbuckles, leans up between the seats, and puts his hand out for the universal *go-team* gesture. "A Homies sandwich. Who's with me?"

I crinkle my nose in disgust.

Jack winces. "Fuck no. You're a bodyguard. Emma is mine. No one is sandwiching her. She's an open-faced sandwich."

Mason yanks his hand back and rolls his eyes. "That's not what I meant, and you know it. Let's do this. I've got to get home before sunup. Jessica is in her last trimester—it's bad enough she had to put the chickens to bed by herself."

We all climb out of the car. "We can't be late. I don't want Rylan to freak out and leave."

Jack claims my hand in a tight grip. "At least he agreed to meet in a public place. A sports bar is fitting."

Mason is on my other side as we walk down the busy sidewalk. "What do you think he's going to tell you that he wouldn't tell you over the phone?"

"I'm not sure. All I know is Rylan Crawford has the answers we're looking for, and in a weird way, he wants to help Brett. We need him to trust us, especially after I told him we found out his identity. And we need to make sure his mom and sister are okay."

My phone vibrates in my pocket. I internally groan when I see the caller. Shit. I connect the call and put it to my ear. "Hey, Dad."

There's a pause. For a moment I think the call didn't connect until my father's low and barely controlled voice hits me. "You do remember that we're tapping your phone, right?"

I stop in the middle of the sidewalk. It takes a half a step, but Jack and Mason follow suit.

Jack frowns. "What's wrong now?"

I give him a small shake of my head as I lie to my dad. "Yeah. I remember."

I totally did not remember. Too many things are happening at once.

Another pause.

A less-controlled Asa Hollingsworth's voice turns into a slight growl. "So you're telling me that you talked the guy into meeting you in a bar by yourself? The same guy who drugged and framed an NFL quarterback who's twice your size?"

Suddenly, I feel like I'm fifteen and back in high school all over again. "First of all, we're meeting in a sports bar, not a bar-bar. And I'm not an idiot. Jack is with me."

Mason holds out his arms and looks offended.

"Sorry. Mason is here too," I amend.

"Oh, well now I feel better," Dad bites with sarcasm. "As long as Mason is there."

"We'll be fine, Dad. The place will be packed."

The sarcasm just keeps on coming. "Right, just like the parade since you were totally fine there. I can rest easy. Have fun. Stay for a drink. Enjoy yourself."

"Don't you have better things to do at the moment? Like keeping Keelie from murdering Knox's cougar girlfriend?"

Dad's exhale tells a tale of his stress level. "Making sure everyone lives through the night is my only priority at the moment—and that includes you. If you wanted this to happen, all you had to do was say the word. I would've sent someone from the team with you."

I don't take my eyes off Jack when I answer. "We'll be fine. I'll even call you when we're on our way back to Levi and Carissa's."

"Even though I'm watching your location constantly, that's nice. It's the thought that counts."

"And here I thought Mom was the helicopter parent. I've got to go. I don't want to be late."

"Call me no matter what," Dad demands. "I want to hear your voice. Love you, baby."

"Love you too." I disconnect the call and turn back to my bodyguards for the night. "Let's do this."

Jack

I open the door for Emma without taking my other hand off her.

The place is covered from top to bottom in Founders colors, still celebrating the city's victory on the biggest stage of the year. Every television in the place has a different basketball game going but one. The big one in the middle is replaying the football championship from last weekend.

I wrap my hand around Emma's hip and put my lips to her ear. "Did he happen to share a selfie so we'll know who to look for?"

She puts her hand over mine as she looks around the bar. "He'll find me. He always has."

"That's the truth," I mutter and lead our threesome to an empty high top in the center of the bar. Emma takes a seat next to Mason, but I stand at Emma's back.

A waiter doesn't waste any time greeting us with his hands full of empties. "What can I get you started with?"

Mason looks at me. "Are we eating? I missed dinner at the birthday party."

I turn to the waiter. "We're not staying long, but I'll make sure and tip you like we were. Four waters."

He must not believe me because he loses his smile and grumbles, "Be right back."

"Please and thank you!" Emma calls after him as her elbow connects with my ribs.

"I'm too tense for manners right now, Em."

"Now that you have his number, maybe you should text him and let him know where we—" Mason stops mid-sentence, and stares over our shoulders. "Never mind. I think he found us."

Emma and I turn at the same time. The guy is barely taller than me, but I've got at least thirty pounds on him. He's skinny and doesn't look like he has an ounce of fat on him even though he's in an oversized hoodie and old jeans that swallow him whole. He's probably in his mid-twenties.

Rylan stares straight at Emma. "Hey."

She smiles.

She actually smiles at him.

"Hi. Thank you so much for coming. It's just the three of us. I know I said Brett's agent would be with me, but this is our friend. We were all together when you called."

Rylan frowns at Mason. "Do I know you?"

Mason shrugs and waves him off. "I get that all the time. You've probably seen me online. I'm the chicken man."

Rylan hikes a brow. "No shit?"

Mason smirks. "Yep."

Rylan is impressed. "Your wife is hot."

Mason's smirk grows into a grin. "I know."

Enough of this. We need to get this party started. "I'm Jack Hale, Brett's agent. We need information to get the charges dismissed. We promise to leave you out of it."

Rylan forgets all about how hot Mason's wife is and turns to me. "Dude, that's not possible. I told you enough. It's your job to figure out how to get him off the hook."

Emma puts a hand out to try to calm the situation. "Let's take it down a notch. This is the main reason I wanted to meet with you. We learned something tonight—something you need to know."

Rylan stuffs his hands in his hoodie pockets and looks around the crowded bar. "It's the only reason I agreed to this."

"Do you want to sit?"

He shakes his head. "No way. Spit it out. This place isn't my jam. I want to get out of here as soon as I can."

Emma shifts on her barstool and glances at me before letting loose. "We know why you're trying to help Brett Sullivan. But the people who paid you to drug him are going to use that against you."

Rylan takes a step back, and for a second, I think he's going to bolt on us.

"They've been trying to contact you, but you haven't answered. Am I right?" I ask.

His gaze jumps to me, but he doesn't confirm.

"Rylan, they said they know where your family is." Emma's tone softens. "They even know where your sister is—down to her dorm room number."

His expression hardens. "The fuck?"

"And that's why you're trying to help Brett," I continue. "Because he helped Renee. She's a recipient from Brett's foundation. You did what you did, and now you feel guilty."

Rylan shakes his head, but not because we're wrong. He realizes Pike and Acosta have him right where they want him.

Emma gives my arm a squeeze. "You helped us. We wanted to help you. You need to know your family and your sister could be in danger."

"Not family. My mom," he bites. "Mom and Renee. They're all the family I have. How do you know this?"

"We know people who can find information. This is even more of a reason to work with us." Anger settles in my gut as I think about Fred Pike threatening this kid's mom, sister, and me. "We're one step ahead of these fuckers. We can let you know what they're doing. But we need more from you. We need evidence to get Brett Sullivan off the hook because you framed him."

Rylan finally comes unglued and takes an aggressive step toward us.

I shift in front of Emma.

But Rylan doesn't get aggressive.

He's as pissed as I am for the same reason.

"You want me to go to the cops and tell them what I did? I'll go to fucking jail for that," he bites.

Emma stands from her stool and moves to my side. "We can find another way. We need to work together, but we're running out of time. What I do know is that to keep your mom and sister safe, keep you off the radar of the police, and get Brett off the hook, we need to expose the people who did this to begin with."

Rylan looks skeptical. "How the hell are we going to do that? You basically got fired, right? It's not like you can just whip up a piece to put on TV anymore."

Emma sets the record straight. "I was not fired. I might have my own problems at work, but that's a separate issue. Once this is taken care of, the world will know I'm not with Brett Sullivan."

I pull Emma's back to my front. "Trust me, she's not with Sullivan. What do you say?"

Mason pipes in and surprises us all. "You seem like you care about your mom and sister, Rylan. It seems to me you don't have a choice. I've known them for over a decade. You can trust them."

"No offense, but I don't trust anyone."

"I get it," I agree. "My list is getting shorter and shorter these days too. I don't know you and you fucked over my client in a big way, but we need each other to dig our way out of this shit."

Rylan gets defensive. "I didn't know who he was, okay? I'm not above doing some shady shit to make some money. When my buddy passed the job to me, all I knew was what they wanted done. He funneled enough cash for a plane ticket to me with instructions. They even told me where he'd be at the last minute. I didn't know the target was the guy who runs that foundation. That scholarship changed my sister's life. She's smart—different from me. I might do some questionable shit, but I never would've taken the job had I known it was him. Hell, I didn't know it was him until it was too late."

"What do you say? Are we going to show the world who these motherfuckers are so we can all move on with our lives?" At my words on moving on with our lives, Emma leans into me further.

Rylan directs his glare at me. "You'd better not fuck me over."

"We would never," Emma assures him.

Rylan looks around the bar, anxious to get out of here, which I agree. "What do I have to do?"

"You can start by answering your phone when we call you," I say. "And call Acosta back first thing in the morning. Make an excuse as to why you ghosted him. Tell him you think you found Sullivan. Get him to talk. The more he says about what went down in Vegas, the better. I'll make sure he pays for masterminding the whole thing."

"What good is that going to do?" Rylan demands. "That won't prove shit."

"Trust me, it will. We're monitoring Acosta's phone. How do you think we found you? Between you talking to him and me handling his boss, which I plan to do first thing tomorrow morning, we'll have all the evidence we need. We have the evidence now, but it won't be admissible."

"You sound like a fucking lawyer," Rylan mutters.

Mason smiles. "That's because he is."

The color drains from Rylan's face, but he stammers his agreement. "Fine. I'll do it."

I feel Emma's relieved exhale. "Thank you. You won't be sorry."

"I'd better not be." Rylan makes a move to leave without saying goodbye but turns back to us. "Does this mean my phone is tapped?"

"Um, yeah." Emma winces. "But not officially. Still, I wouldn't conduct any other ... business on that line."

"See?" I point out. "You can trust us."

"Fuck." Rylan shakes his head, and this time he really doesn't say goodbye. He proves he can move fast and make himself disappear in a crowd for the second time.

Mason smiles. "I think that went about as well as it could have. Please don't tell me we have any other stops to make tonight. I've got to get back to the fam."

The waiter never returned. Even so, I pull a twenty from my money clip and toss it on the table—my way of creating my own karma.

"We're done for tonight. Let's go." I take Emma's hand in mine and dread the fact we're going to Levi's place.

I need to get my house put back together. I need windows, locks, and a new security system so I can have Emma to myself again.

26

END GAME

Emma

I turn the key in the lock of the biggest door I've ever seen and press the handle. "Carissa said she'd leave the alarm off for us."

"Sneaking into Levi's house after curfew," Jack whispers into my ear as he gropes my bottom in a playful squeeze. "Something I've never done before."

I brought an overnight bag with me earlier to the birthday party, but Jack has his slung over his shoulder. We dropped Mason off and came straight here after having a long conversation with my dad about our plan.

A plan that will only work if Rylan Crawford follows through on his side.

That doesn't mean I'm one hundred percent confident he'll do his part. I do think I'm at a solid seventy though, which means I feel better than I did before our meeting tonight.

What I'm not feeling good about is the current state of my employment or the fact a coworker from my company has enough power to put me on unpaid leave. And that they were willing to announce it to the world before telling me or allowing me to defend myself.

Jack and I move through the shadowed halls lit only by the stars shining through the stained-glass ceiling from the third floor. It's the first time I've ever been here in the middle of the night when it's silent and still.

I'd say the creaks of the old wood floors creep me out, but Jack's stomach growling breaks through the quiet.

I look over at him before we get to the grand staircase in the middle of the house. "We never ate dinner."

"You don't need to remind me. I'm starving."

I grab his bag, toss it on the floor by the stairs, and take his hand. "Carissa had enough food to feed an army. Let's grab a bite before we go up."

When we get to the kitchen, I flip on the light over the stove and zero in on the big box on the island. I turn to Jack. "Cake?"

He puts a hand on his abs and smirks at me. "Are you trying to sabotage my six pack?"

I pull out two forks, don't bother with plates, and flip open the box. "Maybe. If I want to keep you all to myself, I don't need the competition. You've always had a trail of females lusting after you."

Despite the fact he's become a health freak, he plucks a fork out of my hand and stabs it into the leftover birthday cake. "Despite my reputation in high school, I'm particular. My tastes are refined."

I take a big bite of cake and talk with my mouth full. "I still can't believe the enchanting Jack Hale is picky. That's hard to believe since it took you all of two-point-five seconds to charm the panties off me."

Jack licks his lips, drops his fork in the cake box, and turns to me. I yelp and have to hold my fork out to keep from poking him since he picks me up and plops me on the island. He even hikes my sweater dress up high enough to spread my legs to stand between them and yanks me to the edge.

The next thing I know, his hands are on my ass, and we're nose to nose with his thickening cock pressed to my sex.

"Trust me, Em, I'm picky. I do not pick up women in hotels, bars, or on work trips. Hell, I don't pick up women … ever. You definitely don't fall into that category."

I forget all about his empty stomach and the decadent dessert next to us. Wetness pools between my legs, and something that wars between excitement and hesitancy swims in my belly. "You categorized me?"

His blue eyes bore into me as he slides one hand between us and lands between my legs. Excitement wins when the tip of his finger traces my sex over my panties. "You're definitely in a category, baby."

I grip the edge of the counter. "I can't decide if that sounds like good or bad news."

His finger doesn't stop creating magic between my legs when I lose his other hand. "Of all the categories, it's a big one."

I force myself to breathe. "That's not good. That means I'm one of many."

I can barely focus on his words, let alone anything else he's doing that isn't between my legs, so he surprises me when he brings his finger to his mouth and licks a huge swipe of icing off it.

Right after he licks his lips, he puts his mouth to mine at the same time his light touch between my legs yanks my panties to the side, and I get his touch.

His real touch.

Skin to skin, at the same time I drink in the taste of him and sweet buttercream when his tongue dances with mine.

He swipes my clit, igniting a low moan from deep in my chest.

I feel how wet I am on his fingers. So when he breaks his kiss abruptly, I'm left wanting more.

Wanting everything.

He's nonchalant when he swipes his thumb through the center of the cake and brings it to my mouth. His stare on me is hot and determined as he teases my clit. "Open."

I do as he says.

My mouth and my legs.

The corner of his mouth tips. He likes that.

Damn. I've never sought approval from any man in my life. I don't even recognize myself. I want everything he's giving me, so I don't wait another moment.

I lean forward and wrap my lips around his thumb.

But this time I lose the appreciation in his features, because my eyes fall shut when he presses two fingers into my sex at the same time. The sugar on my taste buds assaults my senses at the same time he swipes my clit.

I open my eyes when his other thumb presses onto my tongue. "You like that."

Not a question. He knows I like it.

And since there's no way I can answer, I let my teeth sink lightly into his flesh.

That wins me a lazy smile and another swipe of my clit. "Suck, baby."

Mmm.

I suck and think about other things.

His gaze roams up and down my body. "Fuck, look at you."

All I can think about is what he's doing to my body and my heart. He strokes my cheek and my clit as he blows my mind with more than his touch.

I whimper when he gives my clit more pressure and my sex another firm pump.

He leans in and puts his lips to my ear and whispers, "You're the—"

"What the fuck?!"

My eyes fly open when every light in the room kills the magic.

I lose Jack's fingers, but I gain his arms as they cage me to his chest like bands of steel protection.

From my brother.

Jack

"What the fuck?!" Levi yells even louder on repeat.

"Dude—" I start and cringe at the word that came out of nowhere. I haven't uttered the word dude in years.

But Levi doesn't allow me to say anything. "Dude? I just walked into my kitchen to find my little sister sucking my best friend's thumb while your other hand is…" Levi brings his hands to his face and scrubs his eyes like we just threw bleach into them. "Fuck me. I can't even say it."

Emma burrows deeper into my chest. "Oh my God."

I move a hand to the back of her head, hold her tight, and don't take my eyes off my best friend who stands at our sides. There's too much to focus on, like my rock-hard dick and Emma trying to catch her breath since I'm pretty sure I was about to push her over the orgasmic edge of no return.

Fucking Levi.

"I can explain."

Levi drops his arms to his sides and glares at me. He's standing there naked besides a pair of pajama pants. "There's no explanation that will ever make it okay to see my sister sucking on your thumb."

Emma groans.

And not in a good way.

"Shut the fuck up and quit saying that. You're upsetting Emma," I bite.

Levi squeezes his eyes shut as his knuckles whiten. His hands clench and unclench into fists at his sides. "It's burned on my brain."

I stroke Emma's hair as I try to calm the mood. "You should know how to fix that. You are a neurosurgeon."

"Levi, is it the kids?" Carissa's voice joins the party before she stutters to a stop next to her husband. She's wrapping a robe around her as her eyes bug out from the sight of Emma in my arms. "What the—"

"This is exactly what it looks like." Levi interrupts her and points to his sister and me. "No, I take that back. It's fucking worse. So much worse. I can't form the words. I've already tried."

Carissa's expression turns from shocked to something else as she bites back a smile.

"Do not do that. This is not a good thing," Levi warns before turning back to us. "How long has this been a thing?"

"Make it stop," Emma pleads against the skin of my neck.

"Go back to bed," I say. "We'll talk about it in the morning."

"This is bad. So, so bad," Levi chants.

Carissa crosses her arms and doesn't stop staring at us like we're a freakshow at the circus. "I don't think it's a bad thing."

"Oh, for fuck's sake," I mutter.

I've gone over how this conversation would play out in my head a couple of times during the last week.

Okay, maybe just once. It's been a busy week between a kidnapping, a drive-by shooting, my old boss wanting to end my life as I know it, and me dreaming of things I've never thought about before. Like tucking Emerson Hollingsworth away and keeping her as mine for the rest of my life.

And I mean that in the purest, most non-creepy way possible since I don't want to lock her in my basement or wear her skin.

I only want to taste it.

Again, not in a horror-movie type way.

But before that can happen, Levi needs to get over himself.

Emma is my first priority.

I put my lips to the side of her head. "Are you okay?"

"No," she croaks. "Not at all okay."

Carissa moves to stand in front of Levi placing her hands on his chest. "Let's go back to bed. You have to leave before dawn for rounds. Everyone can talk tomorrow."

"There's nothing to talk about," I say. "This is not the way I wanted you to find out, but it is happening."

Carissa turns to peek over her shoulder at us and smiles. "I like it. In fact, I can't think of anything better. If you're both happy, then so are we."

Levi frowns at Carissa, which I don't think I've ever witnessed. "We are not happy. You did not see what I saw."

"Stop talking," Emma mumbles into my neck.

Carissa lifts to her toes to kiss her husband. "It's Jack and Emma. We're not just happy, we're ecstatic. Come to bed. It will all be better tomorrow."

"It will not." Levi winces like he's afraid to glance up at us until his stare lands on the open box. "Holy shit. What the hell did you do to the cake? You know what, never mind. I don't want to know. I'm going back to bed even though I'll probably have nightmares." Levi turns back to his wife. "We are not eating that cake."

Levi leaves but Carissa turns to us with the biggest smile on her face. You'd think she just won the lottery as she jumps up and down and claps.

Emma finally pulls her face out from the crook of my neck to peek at her sister-in-law.

"I'm so happy!" Carissa whisper-yells. "Don't mind Levi. I'll handle him. There are two bedrooms ready for you, so I guess you can pick one. Goodnight!"

We say nothing and watch Carissa skip off after my grumpy friend.

"That was horrific," Emma whispers, even though it's way too late for whispering. "Definitely worse than being put on leave with no pay for doing something I did not do. I didn't think the day could get worse, but I will never recover from that."

I tip her face to mine and smile. "You'll be fine. So will Levi."

She shakes her head. "I'm moving away tomorrow and never returning. I'm starting over. I need a new family. I'm likable … most of the time. Someone will surely adopt me."

I hike a brow. "I like you. And you missed the conversation I had with myself that I plan on keeping you. If you run away, I'm coming after you."

Her thighs squeeze my hips. "You're keeping me?"

"Yes," I confirm. "But not in the basement. I might be a freak, but not that kind, even though I do like it when you suck icing off my thumb."

Finally, I get a hint of her beautiful smile I love so much. "*You* are so *you*, Jack. You've always made my heart race."

I tuck that away for later and pull her tighter to me. "Do you want any more cake?"

Her eyes narrow and her hint of a smile disappears. "Are you trying to give me PTSD?"

I lean to kiss her quickly before I pull her dress down and help her to the floor. "We're going to bed. And I don't care where we are—I'm going to make you forget about everything else in the world but me."

Emma

Stars explode behind my eyelids for the second time.

And, no, the first time was not in Levi's kitchen. That made my head explode.

Jack is generous when it comes to orgasms. In the short time we've been together, I'm pretty sure I'm batting two to one compared to him when it comes to falling over the edge of ecstasy—or whatever the sports metaphor is.

Jack's mouth slams down on mine to quiet my moans for the second time since we got to bed. We picked the room on the third floor and farthest away from babies and brothers and best friends. If it weren't so late, I would've begged Jack to take me back to the hotel.

Jack pumps into me two more times before he comes. Every beautiful muscle in his body tenses as he presses me into the mattress.

He did what he promised. He made me forget about everything but him.

But us.

He doesn't move or pull out. He's spent from his own release and the day. Hell, the week.

I should let him enjoy his moment, but it's killing me. I can't wait another second, and I have to know.

His name is a whisper on my lips as I enjoy the thrum of his heartbeat against my chest. "Jack?"

He exhales before he turns his head to press it against my temple. "Yeah, baby?"

"What were you going to say to me earlier? You know, before I died a thousand deaths from mortification."

He lifts his head far enough to gaze down at me. A smirk plays on his full lips. "Who's the drama queen now?"

"Too soon." I press my heel into his rock-hard ass. "You categorized me. I want to know what column I fall into when it comes to you."

Jack loses the smirk. His hand comes up and brushes the hair from my forehead before he frames the side of my face with his strong hand.

"Baby, you're in a category above and beyond. You made the category your bitch. It's one I've never contemplated before."

I suck in a shallow breath and force myself to breathe. "Jack."

He leans in to kiss me. It's not bruising or possessive and there's no tongue.

It's so not Jack.

But it touches me in that place again—the new one that I only learned about this week.

"You and me ... we're the end game, baby." His blues bore into mine, and my heart skips a beat. "I'm burning the playbook. You're mine."

27

JACK HALE IS IN LOVE

Jack

I take a sip of coffee and look out the kitchen window to nothing but a cold winter morning and dark rolling hills. The sun isn't set to rise for another hour. Levi has rounds this morning, and there was no way I was going to allow this to go on another day.

We're addressing this shit before he leaves. When Emma wakes up, she won't have this to worry about.

I know this house and land almost as well as Carissa and Levi. I spent my last semester of high school sneaking in and out of this place.

When I hear him, I turn and lean my ass to the counter. He's standing in the same spot he was last night, but this time my friend is dressed in scrubs and ready to save lives.

"I need to get to the hospital." Levi drops his bag on the island, crosses his arms, and looks me up and down. "You're up early."

Unlike him, I'm not dressed for the day. I look like I just rolled out of bed after an active night of sex and confessions, which is the truth. I left Emma naked and asleep so I could get this done without her having to deal with her brother.

I'm anxious to get back to her.

I set my mug down on the counter. "I want to talk to you before you leave. Just you and me."

He glances at the trashcan in the corner where I tossed the cake last night before glaring back at me. "There's nothing I want to talk about."

"Are we really going to fucking do this? We've known each other our whole lives. I was your best man. I've always had your back." I hold my arms out low. "You know me, Levi."

He takes a step forward and the only thing separating us is the kitchen island. "Exactly. I do know you. Which is why last night was such a fucking shock."

"Are you kidding me?" I hiss.

"She's my sister, Jackie. That's all that needs to be said."

I am rarely at a loss for words.

In fact, I can't remember the last time I was so fucking shellshocked that I didn't know what to say.

I look to the side so I don't say anything I'll regret.

"How long?"

I shrug and look back at him. "Does it matter? Will it make a difference?"

"I want to know how long you've hidden this from me."

"I'm not sure what you want, Levi. Fuck, do you think I can't take care of her? I haven't seen your tax returns, and even though you literally cut heads open for a living, I know I made more than you last year. There's no way I couldn't have."

"You think this is about money?" Levi spits. "I don't give a shit about that. I never have."

"If it's not about that, then it's about *me*," I thunder. "Which makes it fucking worse, and you know it."

That shut him up.

Well, fuck me. His jaw turns to stone, and his stare doesn't waver.

It's all I can do not to scream the fucking mansion down. "Do you really think I'm going to fuck her over? This is Emma we're talking about. Your sister."

Levi pulls in a breath like he's about to answer, but I don't let him.

"Don't." I hold a hand out to shut him up. "If you actually say what I think you're going to say, we've got bigger problems, man. I might not be a Hollingsworth, and I've never had a father, but that doesn't mean shit. I don't need six months or a year or even a decade to know what I've got. You can hate it. Hell, you can hate me, but I'm not giving her up. If it comes to choosing between you and your sister, I'll pick Emma every fucking day until the end of time. And if you do anything to give her shit about me, we will go to blows. You will not upset her. Got it?"

"Holy shit." Levi rocks back on his heels and crosses his arms. His head tips to the side to contemplate me. "This is real. You love her. You actually love her."

It's my turn to ponder that thought.

"This isn't casual," Levi adds.

"You know, *fucker*." I stress that last word with zero affection for my best friend. "The only reason I'm not hurdling this island to punch you in the face followed with a knee to your balls is because that was a statement and not a question."

Levi's lips twitch in the corners. "You wouldn't dare."

"I've never in my life wanted to punch you before last night. But I will if you insinuate one more time that what I have with your sister is casual. Good luck cracking heads open with one eye while doubled over with your balls lodged somewhere near your… I don't know, kidneys? I only know the female anatomy—not all that other shit."

Levi shakes his head again. "Jack Hale is in love with my little sister."

"What?"

Levi does a quick one-eighty.

My insides clench.

Emma stands on bare feet behind Levi wearing the T-shirt she stole from me at the beginning of the week. It hits the middle of her thighs. Her arms are crossed, hugging her middle, and she looks like me—thoroughly fucked in the best way possible.

She's beautiful.

And she's mine.

But the only way I'm letting her keep that T-shirt is if she agrees to major life changes.

That's a conversation for another time.

Maybe I'll get a tub of icing to convince her.

I move around the counter. And just because he dragged me through hell the last five minutes, I give Levi a hard shove to the chest when I pass him.

He has the nerve to laugh.

Emma ignores her brother stumbling back two steps and bites her lip as I claim her face.

She lifts to her toes to meet my kiss. This isn't how I thought this moment would go.

If it backfires on me, I'm definitely punching Levi in the face.

When I finally tip my forehead to hers, I pull in a deep breath. "Baby, in a weird way, I think I've loved you since I kissed you the first time in the barn when you were fifteen."

"What the hell?"

Well.

Levi's good mood didn't last long.

We ignore him.

Emma's eyes glass over as she smiles. "I've compared every single man I've met to you. If that's not love, I don't know what is."

I don't look away from the woman I'm going to take shopping for rings as soon as we fix our problems.

I don't see it, but hear Levi grab his bag and stomp toward the garage. "Don't mind me, I'll get coffee on the way to the hospital. I'm leaving before I learn something else I don't want to know."

Since we're by ourselves, I yank her T-shirt up to cup her perfect ass. "I love you. If you want to keep that T-shirt, you have to move in with me as soon as I have windows."

She slides her hands up the back of my sweatshirt over my bare skin. "I thought I was lucky you were my first kiss. The fact that you'll be my last is a dream come true."

I brush her cheek with my thumb. "I plan on being your last everything. What do you say we start the rest of our lives with shower sex?"

She licks her lips before she smiles. "I think I want something more than icing."

All my blood rushes to my dick.

Yeah, I'm definitely in charge of my own karma, thank you very much, universe.

I just had no idea it would start in a barn full of goats and end at the Nebula Black Resort in Vegas.

Emma

He loves me.

I'm his end game.

The sarcastic, larger-than-life man who threw frogs at me

when we were little has proved he can turn me to mush in a heartbeat.

Mush isn't the sexiest look on my part, but Jack seems to get off on it.

He did in the shower this morning.

We had breakfast with Carissa and the kids, but Jack spent most of the time on the phone with Brett Sullivan. Brett's more than ready for this to be over, but when he found out who Rylan Crawford was, he was as surprised as we were. He still keeps in touch with Renee.

That's when I learned he stays in contact with all the recipients of his foundation. They're not just for PR. He cares about them.

Brett Sullivan is a good guy. He's ready to clear his name, come out of hiding, and enjoy his MVP and victory.

If Jack and Rylan do what they need to do today, that might happen sooner rather than later.

Jack kissed me in the circle drive in front of Levi and Carissa's house so we could go our separate ways. I was on edge when I said goodbye. This is one of the few times we've been apart since we got together.

But things are going down today.

Ozzy called to let us know both Fred Pike and Gary Acosta plan to be at the Pike Agency even though it's the weekend. They have meetings scheduled all day about contract renegotiations that are on the up and up and blackmailing anti-heroes, which are totally on the down low.

Jack is on his way there now.

Hopefully Rylan is going to follow through on his promise to call Gary Acosta.

And I have to go to work.

But not work-work. There will be no working for me today, or in the near future unless I can get this figured out. I might be on edge, but it's being fueled by nothing but my red-hot anger.

I'm about to go into the station for my meeting with Mr. Folmer and HR, when I get a call from Ozzy. And what he says to me blows my mind.

"Emma, did I lose you?"

I sit and stare at the parking lot of the station and glance at the clock in my car. Damn, I'm late. "Sorry, I'm here. I shouldn't be surprised, but I am. I'm late for my meeting."

"I'm sure that will go a whole lot differently than it would've. You going to be okay?"

I force myself to move. "I have no choice, right?"

"Texting you now. Do what you want with it. But if I were you, I'd go for the jugular."

I beep the locks on my car and double-time it to the front doors. "And that's why you work with my dad, and I report the news. I don't do *jugulars*, Ozzy."

I hear a smile in his tone right before I get the notification for a text. "I saw you run out onto that football field. Work with me, Emma. At least make me proud and aim for a kneecap."

I use my ID to buzz into the building, surprised it hasn't been deactivated. "I'll do my best. I've got to go."

I stop inside the door, open my texts, and try not to allow my eyes to bug out from what I'm looking at.

Dang.

Ozzy is good.

There's an audio file, too, but I'm interrupted by someone clearing their throat.

I look up to Sadie, the receptionist. She's been nice and welcoming since I started here but not anymore. Her expression is bland with a touch of judgy as she stares at me. "You're late. They're waiting on you in Mr. Folmer's office."

My smile is fake with a touch of bitchy. "So sweet of you to point that out. May I see myself in, or do I need to be ushered?"

Her expression falters. She has no idea what to do.

"It's okay," I go on. "Since I haven't done anything wrong, I feel good about walking in there by myself."

I hike my purse up my shoulder and hold my head high as I walk through the halls to the executive producer's large corner office. The few weekend reporters are staring at me, and not the way they did when I returned from Vegas after chasing down the most coveted interview in Sin City.

The open-concept workspace will allow them a front and center view for what's about to go down. Mr. Folmer's office might be soundproof, but the modern layout is made of glass walls. This could be like a silent movie playing out in technicolor.

And, of course, Molly Minders is perched on the edge of a desk talking to another member of the weekend cliquey club. Her cubicle isn't anywhere near here. I'm sure she was circling like the vulture she is.

"Emma." She feigns surprise to see me. "How are you?"

I decide to focus on all the good things in my life at the moment like Jack, love, and the multiple strings of orgasms he seems to enjoy giving to me as much as I enjoy receiving them.

Even though I'm late, I take a moment and stop to talk. "I'm great, thank you for asking. I think the bigger question is … are you okay?"

Like any good reporter, she schools her features perfectly. "Why wouldn't I be okay?"

I tip my head and study her for a moment. "You look tired. Maybe you're coming down with something again?"

She shakes her head. "I feel amazing."

"Glad to hear it. Maybe it's just a lack of sleep. You should really focus on getting a full eight hours. Then again, that must be really hard while managing your schedule."

She loses the smile altogether. "At least I have a schedule."

The door to the corner office opens, and Mr. Folmer pins me with a frown. "We're waiting, Emma."

I toss him a smile. "Sorry, just catching up with Molly." I turn back to the woman who is now standing straight on spiked heels, and I lower my voice to a whisper this time. "Mr. Folmer looks tired too, don't you think? But I guess that happens when you're out all night and not at home with your wife."

Despite the heavily contoured angles of her face and expertly applied bronzer, Molly's complexion pales.

"Hey, try magnesium glycinate. It's good for your heart and helps you sleep."

I turn for the office door.

"Wait—" Molly calls, but I'm already halfway through the threshold.

I smile and wave through the glass before she turns and hurries away.

She should really choose more sensible shoes. You never know when a career-changing opportunity presents itself. She'll never make it in those shoes.

I shut the door, move to the small conference table in his office, and take a seat across from the three superiors. Mr. Folmer, August, and a woman whose name I can't remember, but she did help me sign up for my insurance, are sitting across from me.

The station executive big-wig and two witnesses.

Someone is going to regret that decision.

I set my cell on the table next to my purse. "I'm sorry I'm late. I had to take a call about something work-related."

"You've been put on leave," Mr. Folmer reminds me. "You are not to be working or representing WDCN in any capacity until we make a final decision about what to do about your situation."

I pull in a deep breath. "Yes, my situation. I'd like to talk about that."

August leans forward and looks like he's throwing one of those flags like they did in the football game to stop the aggressive play. "We're here to talk. No one is making decisions about anything today."

"There's a process we need to follow," the woman says.

I look at her. "You mean, you're checking off your list before you can officially fire me?"

She gets defensive. "That's not what I said. The process is to protect everyone involved—including you, Emma."

"Great," I say. "Then I'll start. I'm not sure where you came up with the story that I am somehow involved with Brett Sullivan from the Founders. I never met him until I interviewed him after the game."

Mr. Folmer taps the tips of his fingers on the table as he glares at me. "Interesting. We have conflicting facts."

I hold Mr. Folmer's condescending gaze. "Your *facts* are wrong, which means your source is not credible."

"My source is very credible," he counters and licks his lips before leaning forward to rest his forearms on the table. "Emma, I'm not sure how things worked at your previous networks, but this is the Capitol. We might be an affiliate, but we have a broad viewership, as you know since your initial interview with Sullivan was seen far and wide. Every move we make is scrutinized, not only by the entire country, but the world. August made the decision to release your private interview with Sullivan before pushing it up the channels. It's more than suspect that you're the only one he's chosen to speak with, and he's gone missing."

The woman from HR scribbles copious notes so she can

check all her boxes while August looks more and more nervous as the moments click on.

August tries to turn the meeting in another direction. "How did you land the second interview, Emma? Maybe that will ease some worries."

"I reached out to his agent." That's not a lie.

"That's it?" Mr. Folmer bites. "And of all the broadcasters across the world, he picked you?"

I smile, because nothing could be more truthful than that. "Yes. He picked me."

The woman looks up from her notes that are being formulated to take me down. "We're going to need more than that. Records would be good. Emails? Texts?"

I have enough texts from Jack to write a novel, but nothing I'm going to share with them. "No. We spoke on the phone."

"I hope you can appreciate that we need proof," she explains.

I lean back in my chair and counter. "You said you have proof I'm involved with the subject. I'd like to see it."

"It's employment at will. We don't need proof," Mr. Folmer points out. "Using your personal life to further your career is unethical."

I lean forward and stress my words. "That is extremely unethical. Finally, something we can agree on. But it sounds like you've made your decision."

Mr. Folmer hikes a brow.

"No, no." August tries to make me feel better about my impending termination. "Not yet."

"If that's the case, I think I deserve to know your source. I can only guess it's Molly Minders."

The nameless HR woman fidgets in her seat.

August's gaze drops to the table in front of him.

Mr. Folmer proves he's an adept liar. "You would be wrong."

"I guess we'll never know," I say. "But I do want to make sure that all WDCN employees are being held to the same standards. It would be a shame to find out that others are using their personal lives to further their careers when I was fired for it."

"Of course, we hold everyone to the same standard," the woman explains.

I turn my gaze back to Mr. Folmer. "I don't think everyone is held to the same standard."

He leans back in his chair.

I lean forward. "I never laid eyes on Brett Sullivan before the game in Vegas. I can count on one hand how many times I've spoken to him. I will not allow you to manipulate me or my career. I want a retraction, and I want it done by Molly Minders."

Mr. Folmer leans forward and speaks through a hiss, but something about him seeps desperation. "That's not going to happen."

"Please. Can we talk about this calmly?" August begs.

I look to my producer who I like and have respected since the first day I met him. "I am calm. And I'm sorry you've been dragged into this. You've been nothing but kind and supportive. You don't deserve this headache."

"We're done here." Mr. Folmer stands so fast, his chair rolls back and hits the wall. "You're fired. No entry level field reporter is going to talk to me like this. Dawn will get your final paperwork to you."

Dawn. That's her name.

"One more thing." I pick up my cell to unlock it and tap on the photos app where I saved the pictures and video Ozzy sent me. I bring up the one that is zoomed in on Mindy and the executive producer who's trying to ruin my career that was taken by someone on Crew's team last night.

Mr. Folmer and Molly.

They're standing next to a luxury car in an embrace.

I turn the cell around and set it on the table for all to see. "I haven't had time to study all of these. But if I'm not mistaken, this looks like someone using their personal life to influence their career." I glance across his office to the credenza behind his desk to a picture of a family photo. "This doesn't look like your wife, Mr. Folmer. In fact, it looks like your *credible source*, if I can use that term loosely."

Poor Dawn gasps. "Oh my."

August winces.

"Fuck," Mr. Folmer hisses. "Where did you get these?"

"Does it matter?" I flip through pictures. More embraces. A kiss. A grope. Walking arm in arm into a condo in Falls

Church. "I doubt this is your house, right? These were taken last night. Not that it matters what day of the week it is that Mindy uses you to influence her career."

Mr. Folmer falls into his chair. "You followed us?"

I'm not about to let anyone know I have access to an entire team who specializes in information and does it through a global satellite system. I ignore his question and pick up my cell. "There are more. I'll email them to you—all of you—so you'll have a copy for your records. You know what? I'll add Molly, just in case she wants a copy. Memories."

"Wow," August whispers.

"I … I don't know what to do," Dawn admits.

"A retraction read by Molly," I repeat, as I stand and slide my cell into my purse. "On the evening and nightly segments, or you'll hear from my attorney. We'll go from there."

When I glance up one more time, August has a smirk on his face. Dawn looks constipated. And Mr. Folmer…

Well, I hope he doesn't pop a vein.

I wouldn't want that for anyone.

On my way out, I wave sweetly to the receptionist. "It's a great day for a retraction, isn't it?"

She frowns.

I don't wait for her to say anything, because my cell rings. I can't help but smile when I see who it is and answer. "It's Saturday. Shouldn't you be sleeping in late?"

"There's too much going on to sleep, even for me. I'm hiding in my room so no one hears me before I go downstairs. I can hear them fixing breakfast," Saylor says. "You haven't answered any of my messages or calls."

"Sorry. I've been going through some stuff. Please don't tell me your mom killed the cougar."

"It was so stressful, Em!" Saylor exclaims. I start my car up and transfer the call to Bluetooth. "Ricki was all over Knox during presents and cake after you left. I thought I was going to throw up. It was all Dad could do to keep Mom calm. At first, he kept filling her wine, and then I think he realized that wasn't a good idea. You know she gets loose lipped, but it was too late. Things finally fell apart when Mom asked Ricki if she's perimenopausal yet."

It's my turn to gasp as I turn out of the parking lot. "She did not."

"She did. Emma, I don't even know at what age that happens, but I don't think Ricki is that old."

"Did you find out how old she is?" I head for Alexandria. I told Jack I'd call him right after my meeting, but the cougar news is too good to put off.

"Guess!" she demands.

"You know, I've got a lot going on right now to play the guessing game."

"Fine. She's thirty-two. She's been divorced, not once, but twice! You should've seen Mom when that little bit of information was dropped when we got home from the birthday party."

"Knox just turned twenty last month. What is he thinking? Is it his mission to give Keelie a heart attack?"

I glance at the screen on my dashboard when a call comes through.

Shit. It's Ozzy.

"Saylor, I've got to go. We'll pick this up later, okay?"

Typical Saylor. She ignores me and keeps talking. "You should've seen Dad. He was trying to keep the peace. I saw him pull Knox to the side. I have no clue what was said, and he was too tense for me to ask him. That's why I'm calling. Can you call him and snoop around for details?"

"Sure, I'll call later. But I've got to go."

I'm about to hang up on her when she states, "I think Knox is having an existential crisis."

"Saylor—"

"Shit," she whispers. "I hear someone on the stairs. Gotta go."

After all that, she's the one who hangs up on me.

I click over as fast as I can. "Hello? Ozzy, are you there?"

Dammit. I'm about to return his call when I get another one.

This time it's Crew.

I answer immediately. "Hey, what's up?"

"Are you by yourself?" he bites.

"Yes. I'm leaving the station. You should've seen my boss's boss when I showed him the pictures Ozzy sent—"

Crew interrupts me. "Where is Jack?"

I pause, because I've only heard Crew speak in this tone once in my life. It was during the nightmare my freshman year of high school. "He's surprising his old boss this morning. We're meeting after at his place in Alexandria."

"Fuck."

Panic bubbles inside me. "What's wrong? Is everything okay?"

"No. Everything is not okay. We're not the only ones following people."

28

SHRIVELED PEAS

Jack

"Um, but you don't have an appointment."

I slide my hands into my pockets. It's all I can do to keep my cool when I think about all the ways this agency has tried to fuck me and my client over.

I had plans to come here today and fake it like a depressed person with a shitty lover, but when I woke up this morning, I couldn't look myself in the mirror and do it.

I've been trying to get hold of Rylan Crawford ever since I kissed Emma goodbye. He's not answering my calls. Even worse, Ozzy said his phone is dead.

The last time it pinged a tower was about an hour after we left him at the sports bar last night.

My gut tells me the guy did not get cold feet.

I stare down at the receptionist who looks like his nerves are shot. Pike goes through receptionists like dirty underwear. He promises them an in to the industry and proceeds to work them to the bone. Case in point, this guy working the desk on a weekend. "If you could let him know I'm here, that would be great. I have a feeling he'll see me."

The guy stumbles on his words as he reaches for the phone. "I'm not sure. Let me check with his assistant. He doesn't take walk-ins. What team are you with?"

"Yeah, I'm not that kind of athlete. I used to work here. What's your name?"

"Easton. You worked here?"

"Unfortunately. You should rethink your employment choices too." I put my hand on the receiver and push it back into the cradle. Barely stepping through the entrance reminded me how much I hate this place and there's no way I can go in there and fake anything with my prior asshole boss. "You know what? No need to announce me. I think I'll surprise him."

Easton juts up from the sleek office chair. "No. You can't do that."

"Watch me."

There's no security or locked doors. When I walk around the corner and down the hall, it brings me back to the stressful, and quite frankly, shitiest time of my career.

Flipping off the Pike agency was the best thing I've ever done.

Other than chasing down Emma Hollingsworth in Vegas. Now, that is my best move yet.

"Sir. Sir. Sir! You cannot go into his office unannounced. I'll lose my job. Wait!"

I hold my hand up but don't look back. "The sooner you find another job, Easton, the better off you'll be. Trust me."

Being a sports agent isn't for the faint of heart. I bet I log as many hours as Levi. The best deals are not brokered Monday through Friday between nine to five. Agents have to strike while the iron's hot, and that's often on the weekends.

Easton and I are turning heads left and right as we walk by offices and cubicles. When Gary Acosta sees me, he almost spits out his coffee. "Jack?"

I point to him, but don't stop as I head to my target. "You're a weak, weak man, Acosta. When this is done, your clients are going to be begging me to represent them."

His beady eyes saucer as he sets his coffee down and moves toward me. "What are you doing here?"

I make the last turn to Fred's office. "You know what I'm doing here."

"Please, let me ask if he can see you," Easton begs.

The moment I push through the door, Fred swivels in his chair. His eyes narrow when he sees me and the commotion that's hot on my heels.

Easton is out of breath. "I'm sorry, sir. He wouldn't let me call first."

"I'll get back with you." Fred sets his cell on his desk and spears the receptionist with a what-the-fuck look. "I'll take it from here, West."

"It's Easton, sir."

"Whatever." Fred dismisses him like last week's trash. "Shut the door on your way out."

Gary follows me in. The moment I hear the door click, I cut the space to his desk and slam my hand on it. "Where the hell is Rylan Crawford?"

Fred leans back in his chair and steeples his fingers like he's a Godfather in a mafia movie from decades ago. "You have a lot of nerve barging into my office."

I ignore that. "Where is Rylan?"

He has the nerve to shrug. "I have no idea who you're talking about."

I want to yank his ass over the desk and throw him through the window. "Let me refresh your memory. He's the kid you hired to drug and frame my client to get back at me for being successful because your balls are the size of shriveled peas."

"You know nothing about my balls." Fred glances at Gary. "It seems the popular guy who everyone wanted to work with a few weeks ago is down on his luck."

"I'm hardly down on my luck. You've fucked with the wrong guy, Pike. I've got proof, and I'm willing to share that shit far and wide."

He tips his head and narrows his eyes. "You don't have shit. What you do have is a superstar who's looking at prison time. Drugs or guns on their own are swept under the rug every day. But together? He'll go down as the quarterback who had twenty minutes of stardom until he fucked his own career. And you were the agent who let it happen." Fred looks back to Gary. "Has that ever happened to us?"

I'm pretty sure I hear Gary audibly swallow over a lump in his throat. "I don't think so."

"No. The answer is no, that's never happened at Pike. Athletes will see you're running a one-man show and can't protect your clients."

When Rylan fell off the grid overnight, I realized I don't give a shit what's admissible in court. Rylan Crawford might've made some poor choices in his life, but he took a risk to help Brett.

And I'll die trying to help him.

I pull my cell out of my pocket, pull up the illegally obtained recording, and press play.

It doesn't matter how many times I listen to the vile shit that Fred and Gary orchestrated, it makes my stomach turn every time. The way they tried to crush all my blood, sweat, and curse words it took to build my own business over the years only makes me more determined than ever to fight harder.

Be better.

Win.

"What the—" Gary mutters in shock as he listens to himself make excuses why he can't do more to fuck me over.

Fred reacts completely differently.

He's not shocked.

Anger pulses through him.

Literally. The vein at his temple pulses at a rate that cannot be healthy.

If this fucker dies on me before I can prove what he's done, it'll ruin my week for good.

I wait … and crickets. Fred seethes and says nothing. Gary stutters and fills the silence.

The whole damn time, I have to dismiss about one hundred and fifty notifications from my father-in-law-to-be's associates.

And my father-in-law to be.

Now I'm really on edge.

I slide the cell back into my pocket and stare eye to eye across the desk at Fred. "You've got thirty seconds to tell me where Rylan Crawford is. And if you've fucked with his mother or sister, I will make sure the world knows the kind of man you really are."

Gary doesn't give a shit about covering their asses. He flips out. "How did you get that recording?"

"Shut up," Fred warns.

I look at Gary. "You want to know how? The fact I have a recording of one conversation should make you wonder what else I have and what I'm capable of. Where is Rylan?"

Gary turns on his boss and thunders, "I told you this was a bad idea. I am not going down for this. I'm especially not going down for you!"

Fred comes around the desk. But he doesn't come for me.

He bunches Gary's dress shirt at the neck and slams him against the wall. "I said shut up. Don't say another fucking word, got it?"

Gary grows a pair. Finally.

And I'm not sure this could've worked out better.

For me. Not for Fred.

He goes flying back into the edge of his desk. Gary follows and puts a hand to his neck to keep him there. "You've done some bad shit in the past but nothing like this. If you did anything to that kid or his family, I'll go to the authorities myself. I did not sign up for this shit. Where is he?"

The bulging vein at Fred's temple earlier was nothing. His face is beet red. Since he's the only one with answers, I wonder if I'll be forced to step in and save him from Gary.

"I had to take matters into my own hands since you wouldn't do your fucking job!" Fred croaks.

"Where is he?" Gary demands.

Fred pries the hands off his neck and gets enough space to stumble to the side. He puts his arm out to keep Gary away and gasps for air. "That asshole was working with Hale and his little girlfriend. That couldn't happen. I had to put a stop to it since you wouldn't."

I pull my cell from my pocket and press go on one of the many missed calls I've had since I walked into this office.

Ozzy answers before it can ring through once. "Answer your fucking phone."

I get right to it. "Rylan didn't get cold feet. Pike did something to him. I'm trying to find him, but they won't tell me where he is. Have you tracked down his mom and sister?"

"I've been listening to the whole thing on the wire. Jack,

something has happened. I don't know how to tell you this."

I tense. Ozzy's tone is grave.

"What?" I bite.

"There's been an accident. Emma's car was hit on her way from the station to your place."

I forget all about Fred and Gary. I open the door and am in an all-out run. "Is she okay? Where is she?"

"Crew was talking to her when it happened. We..." His words trail off.

"Where is she, dammit?"

I'm almost to my car when I hear the words I'll never forget.

"Jack, she wasn't just hit. She was targeted. They took her."

29

SEVEN DEGREES FROM DRAMA

Emma

Who knew a drive-by shooting wouldn't be the worst thing I'd endure in life?

Don't get me wrong, that hellish moment might've been over a decade ago, but it was bad. I can still close my eyes and hear bullets hitting metal.

But something as innocent as a fender-bender turning into a carjacking is pretty damn bad too.

When I got out to see the damage to my bumper, I was greeted with a gun in my side. I was still on the phone with Crew at the time. He heard everything.

Before he forced me back into my car and slammed the door shut, my cell met its untimely death in a million pieces on the pavement.

He's not that much taller than me, but wide and strong. I couldn't see his face. He had on a ski mask and didn't even look like a criminal. Damn the cold weather.

I fought and screamed. Trust me, I did my best. I thrashed and punched and kicked, but I was no match. It wasn't much of a scuffle for him. When he fought to restrain my arms, the bracelet my father gave me was ripped off.

The tracker and my phone.

They're gone.

After the last week, I've decided that if running onto a football field and fighting off carjackers are career hazards, I either need a new job or a gym membership that comes with a personal trainer.

I am not cut out for the lifestyle I have fallen victim to.

I have the bruised ribs, cut on my chin, and zip tie around my wrists to prove it.

And even through it all, I wasn't completely freaked out, because my dad is Asa Hollingsworth. My adoptive uncles are badasses. Hell, one of them is even a CIA officer.

Dad might not be a helicopter parent as much as Mom, but I know for a fact he has a tracker on my car. He has since he handed me the keys to my first one in high school and didn't try to hide that fact.

So as long as I was in my car, I knew I'd be okay.

That lasted less than ten minutes.

It didn't matter how much I screamed, kicked, or thrashed —the guy managed to park my car in the lot of a deserted building. I was yanked out and thrown into the back of an old conversion van.

That is when my freak out hit an all-time high.

The Playbook of Emma

There was a driver waiting in the van.

Two against one.

The man who took me slapped duct tape over my mouth and wrapped it around my ankles.

I had no chance against one. There's no way I'll survive against two without a way for my dad to track me.

And Jack.

If he knows yet, he's got to be beside himself.

We've been driving for almost an hour—or at least that's how it feels. The road turned bumpy and rough a while ago.

One more mark against me getting out of this mess on my own.

I've barely heard what they're saying. They turned the music up to decibels that would rival any throwback hair band concert.

My body aches more and more with every bump and turn. But never as much as when I'm thrown into the wall of the van as they come to a quick turn before an abrupt stop.

Shit, that hurts.

The silence feels deafening when the car shuts off. I can finally hear them talking.

"Let's dump her. I want to get out of here."

"No shit. From now on, no more jobs that touch high profile targets. This is bullshit."

I tense when the back doors of the van open. Frigid air

floods the space, and I'm forced to blink away the bright sun.

Both men are wearing masks. When the same one who carjacked me reaches for my bound feet, panic fills me from the bottom up.

My screams are muffled and desperate. Tears streaking my face feel like ice in the wind when they yank me from the van.

We're on a dirt road in the middle of bare trees. Dead leaves crunch under their feet as they drag me around the vehicle to a small cabin. Under any other circumstances, I'd think it was quaint and cute. There are cobble steps leading to a covered porch and empty flowerpots on either side of the door. Hell, there's even a welcome mat.

Hypocrisy at its finest.

My feet drag behind me like lead as they pull me through brush and twigs, up the stairs, and to the door.

When one of the guys pushes it open, I gasp at what I see. Or *who* I see.

Rylan Crawford.

He's tied to a chair in the middle of the family room. It looks like it takes all his energy to lift his head and open one good eye since the other is swollen shut.

It flares wide when he sees me. He thrashes in his chair and almost topples over.

"Why her?" he screams. "Your beef is with me. Let her go!"

"Trust me. Not our choice, man."

They pull another wooden chair from the kitchen table and force me to sit.

They weren't kidding when they said they wanted to get out of here. They make quick work of the duct tape. My chest is wrapped to the spine and my bound legs are taped to a chair leg.

But they show some mercy, if you can call it that. I cry out when they rip the tape from my mouth, feeling the blood trickle from my raw lips.

I heave deep breaths through my mouth and turn to look at Rylan but say nothing. His face and body say it all.

He fared worse than me. Dried blood covers his swollen eye. There's a gaping cut on his forehead.

He had more of a fight in him than I did, or they did this to him after the fact.

The guys take one last look at us before turning for the door.

"Good luck," one offers.

The other finishes his thought. "You're going to need it."

And with that, they're gone.

Rylan winces through his pain. "Why the fuck would they drag you into this? You okay?"

I nod and force myself to get it under control. My words are hoarse. "How long have you been here?"

Rylan heaves a deep breath. "Since last night sometime.

They got me coming home from the bar after meeting you."

"Who are they?"

He winces when he tries to wet his dry, busted lip. "I don't know, and that's fucking unheard of. I know everyone in this town who'd be willing to do shit like this. Not nab me—they could find a million people to do that. But you?" He shakes his head. "No way. No one wants that kind of attention. These people are no joke and have a shit ton of money to dump to make their problems go away. We've got to get out of here."

I pull at my hands and feel the tension in my shoulders. "There's no way I'm getting out of these binds."

"I can, but I need help. I need you to tighten my zip tie."

"Tighten it?"

It's like he's gotten a second wind since he's not here by himself. He rocks his chair the four feet that separate us until we're back-to-back. "Tighten it as much as you can. If it's loose, I can't break it."

"If you say so. This seems counterproductive, but I've never been zip tied before. I've also never been carjacked or kidnapped."

"These motherfuckers do not mess around. Hurry up," Rylan demands.

I have to use all my strength at this angle, but I pull on the plastic as hard as I can. "Did that do any good?"

I can't see him, but I can hear him. He rustles as the chair rocks on the hardwood.

"Fuck," he grits.

"I can try again."

And then…

Snap.

He groans with relief.

I crane my neck back and see him wiggling his arms within his own duct tape. "Can you get out?"

That's when I hear the rip of tape and his chair crash to the floor. Rylan comes my way and rips at the tape around my legs and chest. "If that fucker touches my family, I'll kill him myself."

"Pike?" I ask.

When he finally rips the tape away from my body, he rushes to the small kitchen on the other side of the room and bangs through kitchen drawers until he produces a knife. "Turn around."

The moment he cuts the plastic tie from my wrists, the blood rushes back to my hands and fingers. I shake my hands out and rub the welts on my wrists as he frees my legs and ankles. "Are you talking about Pike?"

"That's who I thought was the mastermind, but I heard those guys talking. Pike only coordinated this shit." He shakes his head as he rips his hoodie off over his head. "Here, put this on. It's cold, and you don't have a coat."

I take the hoodie thrust into my hands. "But now you're in just a T-shirt."

He rushes to the kitchen to dig through more drawers. "I'm fine. Put it on. We need to get out of here."

The last thing I'm going to do is stand here and argue over a hoodie, so I pull it over my head. "If Pike isn't behind this, who is?"

He slides a switchblade into his pocket and digs through another drawer before dumping a few things on the counter. "I can't fucking believe it. There's only one person who wants Sullivan out of the picture more than anyone."

I stuff my hands into the front pockets of the hoodie. "Wait, I thought this all started because Fred Pike wanted Jack's clients. That's what they said on the wiretap."

Rylan goes to the back door of the cabin and peeks out the curtain before looking back at me. "Look, before I found out it was Sullivan, I didn't give a shit who wanted who out of the picture. Hell, I've never given a shit about anyone but my family—look where it got me. On my way home last night, I got a call from the guy on the streets who hooked me up with this job. Turns out, Pike coordinated the whole thing for his client who wants to stay seven degrees away from the illegal shit. But they followed me and saw me meeting with you and your old man. When I got home last night, those assholes were in my house and jumped me."

"Wait." I pause to put it all together. "Are you saying it *was* the quarterback who Brett replaced? Mark Morse?"

Rylan tucks a meat tenderizer into the pocket of his baggy jeans and stalks across the room to me, forcing a hammer into my hands. "I was just as surprised as you, lady. They want Sullivan and your man out of the picture. And the fact that we're standing in a cabin in the middle of BFE proves they're willing to do anything to make it happen."

My mind is blown.

Rylan grabs my arm and pulls me to the back door. "I hope you like to run."

Well, shit.

30

A PLAN ... ISH

Jack

"You're sure this is it?"

"I'm watching you on the satellite cameras, Jack. Do you really think I'm going to tell you to go south when they took her north?"

"Offending you is at the bottom of the list of things I give a shit about right now. I do not have time to make a U-turn. How far out am I, Oz?" I demand. "I just crossed into West Virginia."

"About seven minutes. I'm following the van that just dropped her off."

Ozzy spun his magic. Everyone is on this line, but no one speaks unless they're needed.

Other than me.

Chasing after the woman I decided I want to be with for the rest of my life after she was taken is something I never thought I would do once in a lifetime, let alone twice in one week. If I question Asa's badass team, they can get over it.

"We're ten minutes behind you," Asa growls. "Someone had better get the guys who touched Emma in cuffs and in the back of a squad car before I get there. If I get to him first, we're going to have more shit to cover up when this is said and done."

The static of a radio crackles over the line. It's Jarvis. "I've got a highway patrol unit a half mile behind the van. They're waiting on backup before they pull them over. We've got them in our sights. I don't think we're going to have to hide any bodies tonight."

Any other time, that might make me question the family I plan on marrying into.

But not today.

Today, I don't need an invitation to join Asa in first-degree murder.

"What's the status on Bella?" Crew asks.

Cole and Bella Carson joined in on the effort at the last minute. They're freaks, because they even brought their kids. "I've got eyes on Bella. She's walking into the Pike Agency as we speak. You know my wife, she can talk for hours. She'll keep them there until my contact can rush through the arrest warrants. I wish this was under different circumstances, because it's been a long time since I've worked with my wife. I've got the kids in the car since we came straight from the airport. Grady is on his way in case she needs backup."

"I'm getting there as fast as I can. Tell Bella to keep them confused with her Britishisms. I'm still fifteen minutes out," Grady says.

"Jack, you'll get to Emma first. What's your plan?" Asa demands.

"My plan is to get to the fucking house and take her back. If I have to bulldoze the door down with my car, I will."

Ozzy butts in with an update. "You're six minutes out, Jack. You're going to come up on a turn in about a mile. It's your next right—take it."

Crew reminds me of the obvious. "You're unarmed, so you need a plan. The guys in the van left her there, but we don't know if anyone was in the house to begin with."

I drag a hand down my face and press on the gas. The engine of my Porsche Panamera purrs as I speed down the two-lane country highway. "I don't have the luxury of time to formulate a plan. We'll see what happens when I get there."

"You're not used to this, Jack," Asa says. "There's nothing I want more in the world than to get my daughter back, but you could make things worse. Much worse. Do not park close to the house. Oz will tell you when to stop. Approach on foot to surveil the situation. If you can get close enough to look in the windows, do that. But do not go in without our okay."

I white knuckle my steering wheel and hold my silence. What I do not do is make any promises. Asa is the least of my worries. "We'll see."

"Fuck."

I have no idea which badass that was, and I don't give a shit.

"Change of plans," Ozzy clips. "We have an unknown vehicle in the mix. A black SUV that just turned into the drive. It approached from the opposite direction."

I slam my steering wheel. "Dammit!"

"That's it. Do not approach until we get there," Asa orders.

"They're pulling up to the house." Ozzy continues to report the live events that are nothing but a real-life nightmare. "Oh, shit."

"What?" I demand.

"I've got sight of two people exiting the back of the cabin. They're on foot."

Asa sounds as unnerved as I feel. "Can you see who they are?"

"I'm zooming in as far as I can." There's a pause before his next words make me feel better … or not. "Looks like one male and one female. I'd put my wife's fortune on it—that's Emma. I don't know who she's with, but they're on the run."

Emma

"Do you hear that?" I hiss. "It's a car."

Tires on gravel come to a screeching halt as Rylan opens the back door.

Our gazes jut to the front of the cabin and through the windows.

"I don't know who that is, but I'm not waiting around to find out." Rylan opens the back door at the same time we hear car doors slam.

He doesn't have to pull me. My adrenaline kicks in, and I'm grateful for my love of comfortable shoes. We're on a full out run through the forest—through brush, sticks, and piles of left over snow from the last storm. Rushing out onto a football field was a breeze compared to this.

Someone yells from the house.

I look back just as my foot catches on a dead limb.

I go down on my side, landing hard on an iced-over pile of snow.

"Fuck me," Rylan growls in a low tone. "It's him."

A pain shoots down my side to my hip when I see them coming at us.

I have no idea who one of them is, but I know the other one. The echo of his voice bellows through the desolate forest. "There they are!"

I might not know the intricate rules of football, but I am detailed when it comes to research. I memorized every first, second, and third string player on the Founders, so I recognize him.

A quarterback controversy is a professional sports version of a Bravo reality show.

And Mark Morse is heading straight for us.

"Get the fuck up, Emma." Rylan doesn't wait for me to get up. He yanks me to my feet.

We run.

And that's when my mind takes me back to another time that was no less horrific…

Gunshots.

31

RED ZONE

Jack

"Fuck!" The word rings through my car.

Shocker, I do not do what Asa says. I pull up next to the black Defender with personalized plates that insinuate the driver is a number one quarterback.

I'm at the Founders headquarters and stadium enough to know that car.

Number one, my ass. If I have anything to do with it, he'll be the number one bitch in a federal penitentiary.

I grab my cell and put it to my ear as I kill my engine and race to the house. "Did you hear those gunshots?"

"Two males entered the cabin and exited out the back door. They're following Emma and whoever she's with," Ozzy continues to commentate. "Emma is up and running again. They missed."

"We're close," Asa bites. "Can you trace them through the forest, Oz?"

"For the most part. Emma and her partner are headed straight north but won't be for long. They have no idea where they are because they're headed for an overlook. They're going to run out of land."

I don't bother with the cabin and move around the side of the house.

"I see you, Jack. Slow down and be quiet. They're armed, and you're not. Stay behind them," Ozzy orders.

"He's not shooting at Emma again," I growl.

The moment I round the back corner of the house, I barely catch sight of Emma's dark hair trailing behind her before she disappears into a dip in the earth since we're going downhill.

Mark raises his arm that he usually uses to throw a pigskin. Instead, he's gripping a handgun.

Another bullet ricochets off a tree.

I come to a stop next to a cluster of trees that are so big, they look like they're decades old. "Morse!"

"Shit," Ozzy mutters.

"Dammit, Jack," Asa yells into my ear. "What did I tell you?"

Mark Morse stops in his tracks with another man I do not recognize.

I keep talking to keep his attention. "You could've been traded and ended your career throwing for a mediocre team. Instead, you were salty and chose felonies. Not a good choice."

The moment our gazes meet, he freezes for a split second before he starts to raise the weapon toward me. No more than twenty yards separate us.

The red zone.

Even though I'm holding my phone, I hold my hands up to reveal the fact I'm unarmed and very fucking vulnerable.

But he's not focused on Emma, and that's my only goal in life at the moment.

My voice carries through the woods before he can train his sights on me. "I wouldn't do that. We've got cameras on us. You shoot, and it'll be breaking news before you can figure out what your next move is."

Mark glances at the guy next to him before glaring back at me. But he does lower his arm. "This is my property. There aren't any cameras out here. And the way I see it, you're trespassing, Hale. I have the right to protect my land."

I don't move, but I do keep my cell connected to the call. Ozzy might be able to watch from space, but I have no clue if he can hear. "What you don't have a right to do is kidnap people and keep them hostage. Guess what? We have that on video too. You're racking up the charges as we speak. Toss your gun and cut your losses while you can."

The guy with Morse mutters something I can't hear and starts for me.

When he does, he reaches behind his back and produces his own weapon.

That's when I hear her. Emma screams from somewhere in the woods. "No! Jack!"

I barely have a chance to shift behind the trees when I hear two quick, concurrent shots.

A moment passes when another sound comes from the opposite direction.

It does not echo through the forest.

It's so faint, I have to do a double take to make sure I actually heard it.

Pop.

A silenced gunshot.

Then, a thud.

"What the fuck?" Morse yells. "Who's out there?"

Feet hit the forest floor. Twigs and dead leaves crunch quickly under heavy feet.

My heart races, but I take a chance and peek from behind the tree I'm using as cover.

The guy that was running for me lays on the ground bleeding from his head.

I put my cell to my ear and whisper. "Please tell me Asa and Crew are here."

"Fuck you, Hale!" Morse bellows. "I will take you down if it's the last thing I do. Your fucking client and little girlfriend won't be far behind!"

Emma

"Jack!" I scream for the second time.

Rylan pulls me back to the ground to hide behind a berm. "Shut up."

Tears run down my cheeks. "He's shooting at Jack."

"There's someone else here. The guy with Morse is the one who hired me to do that job. He's dead. Who the fuck has a silencer?"

I'm not about to tell Rylan I know who that is.

But I know.

Jack and my dad are working together.

I peek over the ridge and see Mark Morse's back is to us. His body language is easy to read.

He's agitated and restless. Those dispositions do not mix well.

Beyond him, Jack appears slowly from behind a group of trees so wide, they make up a wall. My heart catches when I see him face the man who shot at us running through the forest.

"Drop the gun, Morse. You're in a lose-lose situation."

Morse shakes his head. "I wasn't a loser at anything until you got the GM to bench me so your golden boy could have his day. Don't tell me you didn't."

When Jack shrugs, it hits me in a deep place. It's confident and casual and so, so *him*. How many times have I seen him do that with those beautiful blue eyes focused only on me. "I'm flattered you think I have that much power. It just so happens I represent the more talented player."

"Why is he baiting him?" I whisper.

"To save your ass," Rylan mutters. "Which means, I'm sticking with you."

"You fucker," Morse growls.

Jack has the nerve to hold out his arms like he's throwing a dare at Mark's feet. "What are you going to do? Look at your buddy over there on the ground. The moment you raise that gun, you're done. You might not see anyone else, but you're surrounded. You're one bad move away from going down."

Mark shakes his head like he doesn't believe it and scans the area. His gaze finally settles back on Jack.

That's when a hand wraps around my mouth.

I let out a muffled scream until a familiar, whispered voice pulls me back to his chest.

"It's me, baby."

I flip my head around and gasp. "Dad!"

Rylan jerks in surprise and falls to his ass.

I start to throw my arms around his neck when I hear Mark Morse.

"Who was that? Is that you, little Hollingsworth? The woman who ruined my entire fucking plan?"

Dad puts a finger to his lips and spears Rylan with his best *shut up* look before he pushes me behind him.

He pulls a gun from his jacket and peers over the edge of the hill before he puts his cell to ear. "I'm with Emma. Put an end to this shit, Crew."

Jack

"Look at me, Morse," I demand.

Mark turned away from me when Emma screamed. He ignores me and stalks toward the spot I saw Emma disappear. "Shut the fuck up, Hale. If I never see you again, it'll be too soon."

There's no way he'll touch her. Ever.

I'm at an all-out run. "Morse!"

Morse pauses, turns, and raises his gun at the same time. "I said shut the—"

Two shots.

One loud.

One silenced.

"Fuck." I fall to my knees.

Morse hits the ground.

And Emma screams.

Emma

"No!"

Jack falls to the ground.

"Emma, stop!" Dad yells.

"Shit," Crew bites.

I pull out of Dad's arms and stumble over wet, cold ground to get to Jack. I trip on a pile of icy snow and fall to my knees beside him. I lay my hand on him where blood starts to seep through his clothes.

"You were hit. Holy shit, you were hit." Tears stream down my face as his blood covers my hands. "Dad! Call someone!"

He's already on the phone. "I don't have an address, but I'll send my coordinates. We have a gunshot wound to the thigh." Dad comes down to one knee on the other side of Jack and presses two fingers to his neck. "The victim is conscious. His pulse is a little low. We also have two fatalities. You'll need more units."

Jack pushes my dad's hand away and tries to sit up. "I'm fine. It's just my leg."

I put my hand to his shoulder, push him back to the ground, and repeat for the third time like anyone here needs me to declare the obvious. "You were shot, and you're bleeding. Don't move a muscle, Jack Hale."

Crew and Rylan join us.

Crew is holding a rifle and wearing an expression that bleeds guilt. "Fuck, Jack. I was a split second too late. I had to wait for him to raise the gun on you before I could shoot. As high profile as this is, this'll be all over the news. We have everything on video to prove it was self-defense."

Jack winces and finally gives in. His head falls to the ground, and he squeezes his eyes shut. "Hey, better late than never. If the drive-by didn't get me, something was bound to, right?"

Dad moves my hand to study Jack's leg. "You're going to need surgery. But it looks like it just caught your flesh."

I push my dad away and press lightly on his injured leg with one hand and frame his face with my other. "You're going to be okay. You have to be." I turn to Dad. "Call Levi. Make sure he has the best surgeons on his case when we get to the hospital."

Dad gives me a chin lift.

"I need to call Carson. We're going to need some creative report writing to cover this," Crew adds.

Jack grabs my hand and pulls me to him.

I go willingly.

I don't want to be anywhere but with him.

He tags the back of my head and holds me to him when our lips meet. It's a kiss brewing with equal parts desperation and relief.

We're alive and together.

Our kiss lingers for another moment, but I don't pull away. My forehead rests on his. I'll never take for granted his beautiful blue eyes staring at me so intently, I swear, he can see my soul.

"You're moving in with me," he grits through the pain.

I nod, barely able to control my tears. "Yes, I am."

"You did well, Jack."

I press my lips to his once more before sitting up to look at my dad.

Dad keeps talking. "You got to her, and you did what you needed to do. I'm grateful."

Jack doesn't look away from me. "I'd do it again."

"Let's hope that won't be necessary," Crew says as he puts a hand to his ear. I realize he's wearing an earpiece and is on a call. He nods. "Good news. Keep me updated." He looks down at the rest of us. "Bella did what she does best and controlled the situation at your old agency until they got the warrants. Carson said both Acosta and Pike are being read their rights as we speak. The guys who carjacked you have been detained. They can all hang out in jail tonight."

"Thank you, but when will the ambulance be here?" I'm glad Dad and his friends are handling the bad guys, but all I care about is getting Jack to the hospital.

"Shouldn't be long, baby," Dad assures me.

"It shouldn't be long at all," Crew adds. "Ozzy contracted for a private life flight."

Jack pulls in a deep breath. "If I didn't care about bleeding on my leather, I'd say throw me in my car and drive me there. I hardly need a helicopter."

"That's on me," Crew says. "Like I said, I had to wait until the last second. I feel like shit that you caught a bullet."

Dad shrugs. "It's nothing the rest of us haven't done."

"Who are you people?" Rylan has been standing back and taking this in as an outsider. "Creative reports, private helicopters, and talking to nine-one-one like you ball with them every weekend."

I shake my head. "They're connected."

Crew does some clickity-clack thing with his gun before resting it on his shoulder and pointing it to the sky. "By the way, your mom and sister are just fine."

Rylan crosses his arms and rocks back on his heels, not looking the least bit cold standing there in his T-shirt and jeans, but he does breathe a sigh of relief. "Any other day, I'd question how you know that. But after what I saw play out here, I'll take your word for it."

We all look to the sky when we hear it … the whirling of helicopter blades.

When I look down at Jack, he's not focused on anything or anyone but me. "I can't wait for this shit to be over. I'm ready to live our big, fat, fabulous lives. We're going to live large, baby. All we need to do that is each other."

With that, my tears form again.

After what we've been through, most people would want a normal, quiet life.

But not Jack.

My larger-than-life Jack. He'll demand nothing short of fabulous.

With me.

"I love you, Jack Hale."

"I love you, too, baby." He yanks me down to him once more when the helicopter starts to whip the cold air into a frenzy around us. "I love you too."

32

SPONGE BATH

Jack

I drag my eyelids open. They're heavier than the pressure I put on myself to pass the bar years ago.

And that was some heavy shit.

The last thing I remember is my mom talking to my grandma on the phone. The pain meds must have knocked me out. Either that or my body shut down in a pure defensive mechanism to block out my mom's frenzied pacing.

What I do know is before I fell asleep, it was just Mom, Emma, and me. That's not the case now.

"You fuckers have the most boring lives if all you have to do is sit around and watch me sleep." I lick my dry lips and shift in my hospital bed, scanning the room until I find Emma. "Everyone but you. You can stare at me all day long. I've stared at you plenty while you sleep."

She's the closest to me and stands as soon as our eyes meet. She takes my hand in both of hers and leans down to kiss me. "I talked your mom into going home and getting some sleep. She'll be back first thing in the morning. I'm not leaving you."

"As long as we both fit in this hospital bed, I'm good with that."

"This is going to be the rest of my life, isn't it?" Levi complains.

Carissa stands from where she was perched on his knee. Apparently, I'm so popular that it's standing room only in this place. She moves to the foot of my bed and crosses her arms. "Levi is happy. He'll get used to you and Emma being OTT with your PDA."

Cade rolls his eyes before he throws a glance at his brother-in-law. "Like you and my sister were easy to be around."

Mason smiles. "I'm happy for everyone. Now we just need Cade to find someone—"

"Whoa." Cade puts his hand up to Mason. "After what happened with Mom and Dad, I'll never get married."

"And that's okay," Carissa says. "You don't have to be married to be happy."

Mason keeps looking on the bright side. "At least we're all together again."

Cade shrugs. "I had to make sure Jack was alive, so I stayed an extra day.

I push the button to incline my bed and wince when I shift my leg to sit up. "I appreciate that."

"But I do have meetings tomorrow. I need to get to the airport," Cade adds. "Seriously, I've been where you are. Glad you're okay."

Emma puts the arm of my bed down and sits on the edge next to me. "You'll be back to wheeling and dealing before you know it."

I put my arm around her even though I'm tangled up in this damn I.V. "Sooner than that, baby. I've got to act fast while Brett is still the golden boy."

Emma turns to me. "He called me again while you were asleep. There's no way he can get to the hospital or go home with the news. He met with his coaches today and went back to Whitetail. He said he'll see you when you're discharged."

Levi stands and comes to his wife. "I've been following the news all day. He'll be the golden boy for a long time. I'd say wheeling and dealing might be like driving a car. You might not trust yourself to draw up contracts while you're on pain meds. Your doctor said you should be discharged tomorrow."

"I have the main floor extra room ready for you," Carissa adds. "There's no way you can hobble up to the third level."

I look around the room to my friends who have been in my life for what feels like forever. In Levi's case, it is forever. "You guys have taken care of everything, huh?"

Emma smiles. "Of course, we have."

I return her smile with a smirk. "Does that mean you're going to give me a sponge bath?"

"Great. This *will* last the rest of my life. We've got to get Cade to the airport." Levi's sigh sounds like an old man, but he comes around and holds up a fist. I give him a weak bump. He doesn't look like he's sick of me any longer. His expression is serious. "Glad you're okay, man. It would suck to lose you as a brother-in-law before you officially hold the title."

Emma sinks deeper into my side.

I give Levi a chin lift. Now isn't the time to ask him to be my best man since I haven't even proposed yet.

Cade gives me a low wave. "I'm sure you'll be kicking ass before I return for another birthday. I'll keep up with you in the text group."

"Homies for life." Mason hops down from where he was sitting on the windowsill. "I will see you soon. Jessica is making you dinner and a cake."

I hike a brow and glance at Emma. "I do like cake."

Emma laughs.

"Okay, now you ruined the moment and pushed me over the edge. I'm out of here." Levi fakes a gagging noise and pulls the door open while waiting for his wife to exit. He follows her out.

"See you tomorrow, roomie," I call to his retreating back as they file out. I wait for the door to shut and focus on the only person I want to be with. "Finally. I was not expecting to wake up to that."

Emma stretches out long and presses herself to my side opposite the leg they dug a bullet out of. I'm going to have one hell of a scar. I rest my head on the pillow and do everything I can to focus on her and not the throb that's growing by the moment. "I finally have you alone."

Emma's hand comes to my abs and slides up my chest. "Don't get any ideas. I'm going to snuggle with you until your next pain pill, then I'm going back to the chair to let you sleep."

I put my hand over hers and press it over my heart. "You do know I'm naked under this sexy-as-fuck hospital gown, right? All commando for you, baby. I was not kidding about the sponge bath."

She tips her head and presses her lips to my jaw. "I'll definitely do that. But not tonight. You need to sleep. And it's not like I have a job."

"Tell me what happened at work before you were kidnapped—for a second time." I close my eyes to push away thoughts of what could have been and hold her tight to my side.

"It doesn't matter right now. I don't want to talk about it."

I give her a squeeze. "Tell me."

She sighs. "It feels like a million years ago even though it was just this morning. It went how I thought it would go. I'm pretty sure after showing them the pictures that I'll get my job back, but who knows."

"I'll sue them."

Her hand presses lightly on my chest. "You don't have to—"

I bring my hand to her hair and give it a light tug for her to look at me. I've got my second wind, relatively speaking. "You're in this position because of me. You can bet your sweet, perfect ass that I'm going to file suit on your behalf. There are benefits of being right here besides the life-altering orgasms. I can argue in a courtroom as well as I can negotiate a contract. They're going to pay for what they did to you."

"I guess that will be the deciding factor on if I have a job in the District or not."

I lean back on my pillow and close my eyes again. "Baby, I have a feeling after this week, you can write your ticket anywhere you want."

"Please, Jack. Today has been too much. I don't want to talk about anything else stressful."

I turn my head to press my lips to her forehead. "Okay, baby. Whatever you want."

And I realize, that's the way my life will be from here on out.

Giving Emma whatever she wants.

And I wouldn't want it any other way.

Emma
Two months later

I'm bent over Jack's bed. Jack stands behind me with his hand between my legs, teasing me mercilessly.

"Jack." I'm breathless and needy. I try to rock back on his

fingers for more, but he squeezes the globe of my ass to keep me where I am. "Please."

"Do you know how beautiful you are?"

I fist the messy sheets beneath me. I have an early morning meeting. On the scale of zero to life-changing, it's right up there at the top.

I'm so nervous, I barely slept last night.

I was about to get in the shower when he pulled me back into the bedroom, made an event of stripping me of what little I had on, and put me in this position.

"You need to relax, baby."

"You know that telling a woman to relax does the opposite, right?"

My clit gets a flick.

I moan.

"Baby, that's like throwing a dare at my feet. When I say relax, I mean be here for the experience. I'll do all the work."

I get another circle.

More pressure.

I lift up on my toes and arch.

"Now you're cooperating," he drawls.

That wins me more. So much more.

"Yes. That. More of that," I beg.

"I fucking love that, Em. Love you."

He finally gives it to me. He gives me everything.

It doesn't even take a minute. I come hard. And he doesn't let up. He holds me where I am and squeezes every ounce of my orgasm from me before he slams into me from behind.

He doesn't take his time this morning like he usually does. He angles his hips and slams into me over and over.

Every time we come together, his breath speeds. His fingers dig into my hips when I thrust back to meet him.

"Yes," I groan. I love this. His power. Every time we're together it's better than the one before.

Jack had six weeks of physical therapy after surgery. He's not running marathons yet—not that he ever would ... we both hate running.

But he's back and better than ever.

When he slams into me the last time, he groans and bends at the waist to envelop me.

He kisses my bare shoulder. "Are you relaxed?"

I exhale and sink into the mattress that has become ours. "If I'm so chill I look like I don't give a shit for my interview, I'm holding you responsible. It will be your fault I'm still unemployed."

"More time with you. Do not tempt me, Hollingsworth."

He presses into me once more before pulling out. I hurry to the bathroom as he picks up his cell.

The man gives busy a new definition.

After he got out of the hospital, he quickly renegotiated Brett Sullivan's contract. I can't keep track of all the endorsements he landed.

That's when they started knocking on Jack's door.

Metaphorically, that is.

And by *they*, I mean professional athletes. The story of what happened at the Pike Agency spread far and wide. Fred Pike and Gary Acosta have been charged with being an accessory to a laundry list of things. Athletes quickly realized they want what Brett has—an agent who gives a shit about them and not the dollar signs attached to them.

Loyal.

That's Jack, through and through, in every aspect of his life.

So I'm not surprised he has messages waiting for him before six in the morning.

When I walk naked to wash my hands and flip on the shower, Jack is standing there as naked as me.

This brings me back to our first morning at Nebula. Jack is confident in his skin. He's the same today as he was then, plus one pink scar on his thigh.

"Are you okay?" I ask.

"That was about you."

I stop in the middle of the bathroom. "What about me? And I can't believe we're having this conversation naked."

His lips pull at the corners. "I'd have every conversation naked with you if I could."

I cross my arms. "Tell me."

He pauses before he speaks. "That was the attorney representing WDCN. They settled before we could go to court next week."

It's my turn to pause as it all comes back to me. "What does that mean?"

"It means they knew we had them by the balls. Their retraction was shit, and they didn't offer you the same position when they tried to make it better. Their attorneys finally convinced them to see that a judge would never side with them. It's a good offer, baby. The only stipulation I want added is that there's no NDA. The deal should be able to be made public. That will be all the retraction you need. Not that your followers need that. You're more popular than anyone at WDCN."

I lean into the counter and feel like I just shoved the anvil off my chest that's been weighing me down for weeks. Even though Molly Minders is still at the station, the last I saw she's not anchoring the weekend desk anymore. She's back to being a field reporter.

A demotion.

I wonder if she wears more sensible shoes.

I don't need to think twice. "I'll take it."

Jack's brows crease. "Don't you want to know what it's for?"

I shake my head. "It doesn't matter. I'm not going to keep the money. I'll donate it to Brett's foundation."

His expression softens as he moves across the marble floor to me. I'm in his arms and our bare bodies are pressed together. "You don't have to do that. They put you through hell."

"I don't want their money. Which means I really need to get this job today. I've been mooching off you for two months."

"Best two months of my life, the physical therapy notwithstanding." He leans down to kiss me before he lifts my left hand between us. He fingers the ring he put there last week when he got down on one knee and proposed. It was after he took me to dinner and we walked arm in arm down to the pier in Old Town.

It was romantic and perfect, just like him. I even have pictures to remember it forever, because he thought ahead and hired a photographer.

The diamond is huge, but the band is dainty. Bold and feminine—just like the two of us together.

It feels so good, I haven't taken it off since he put it there.

"I'm not sure how many times I have to tell you, this is us now. Get a job or don't. I don't care. All I want is you." He lifts my hand to kiss the knuckle of my ring finger before he smirks. "That being said, I have a good source who told me the interview is a formality. You're really going to have to fuck it up to not get this job."

I plant my face in his chest. "That makes me even more nervous."

He takes my hand and pulls me to the shower. "Let's get ready. Big day, baby. A cable sports network with a family of streaming channels. You don't get any bigger than that in the industry. And here I wanted to be the popular one."

I step under the steaming hot water with him and go right back into his arms. "Luck. It's all luck, and you know it."

He shakes his head. "We don't need luck or karma. This is the House of Hale. And you'll be Emma Hale as fast as I can get your mom to plan the wedding. My only requirement is that we say I do before football season. The sooner the world knows their sports darling is mine, the better."

I lift on my toes. "Mrs. Hale. I love the sound of that almost as much as I love you. The sooner the better. I wanted to be yours since you kissed me the first time in a barn with a slew of goats."

Jack puts my back to the marble wall and claims my face with his big hands.

He kisses me.

He was my first kiss.

He'll be my last.

My forever.

EPILOGUE

Jack
Seven years later

The Hollingsworths have proved over the years they have no chill.

No fucking chill.

And today supports my argument more than anything.

When I said this to Emma, she actually laughed in my face.

After she finally calmed down, she stated I have no room to talk. Then she kissed me, said I have less chill than anyone she's ever met, and that she wouldn't have it any other way.

I told her she was crazy.

Then she reminded me how I announced that we were expecting the first heir to our throne.

That shut me up.

But it's not my fault that my sperm is just as obsessed with her as I am. That's exactly what I told every person who would listen to me. And since I have a way of demanding attention, that was pretty much everyone I knew and even those I don't since I posted that shit on social media.

I can't help it.

When we found out she was pregnant seven months ago, I did it all over again with the added reminder that Emma and I are genetically created to produce perfection. I might've announced that with a picture of my hands on her bare belly.

I never had a dad.

Before I saw my opening and forced myself back into Emma's life, that was my only apprehension in the world.

I kept that fear to myself. I never told my mom, Levi, or even Emma—and I tell her everything.

I knew I wouldn't be a shit dad, but I had no fucking clue how to be a great one. And when it comes to the stuff in life that matters, I don't do anything half-ass. It's a compulsion. I can't let people down.

I'm not an idiot. I know it comes from being unwanted by my own father. I've tried to control it, but I can't.

When Emma was pregnant with Max, I experienced inner conflict for the first time in my life.

Pure happiness laced with uncontrollable fear.

I was consumed by it.

When I held him in my arms for the first time, I cried.

I don't remember the last time that happened. Not even when I promised to love and cherish my wife in this very spot seven years ago. Making the commitment to Emma was easy. I knew I'd kill it as a husband.

But as a dad?

Fuck.

Yeah, I cried that day.

And every day since, I wonder how any man could walk away from something as perfect as their own child. My inner need to not let anyone down reached new heights.

I'm a damn good sports agent. My clients receive the best in the business no matter where they are in their career.

My friends will never have anyone more loyal at their side.

My mom and grandmother will always be taken care of.

And Emma will know nothing but love and support. No wife on earth will ever have a bigger hype man and protector than me.

But my kids?

They'll have the best fucking dad on earth.

I watch my wife walk down the aisle carrying our second perfect creation. Seven more weeks until I can hold Sloan in my arms. I tell Emma every day how envious I am, which explains the photo that went viral on her socials. Even Mason's chickens laid green eggs—they were that jealous. I can't keep my hands off my growing daughter in Emma's swollen belly.

I wink at my wife. Curvy, beautiful, and hotter than ever.

She returns my wink with the smallest air kiss on her perfect, puckered lips.

I can't take my eyes off her as she stands next to the other bridesmaids in her number one position of matron of honor.

Then I turn and can't keep the stupid grin off my face. Max is paired with his cousin, Juliet, Levi and Carissa's youngest. Carissa announced that they were stopping at four kids. But if my best friend has anything to say about it, I wouldn't put my money on that. My son is looking like a miniature badass in his tux and custom sneakers I had designed just for this occasion. There's only another pair like them in the world, and I'm wearing them.

Having contacts at the big swoosh has its perks.

I did make my three-year-old son promise not to run in them until the reception. They'll be scuffed to shit by the end of the night.

Max is hell on wheels.

I love it.

I don't really care if he breaks that promise. I doubt the bride will either. She's given this family a run for their money over the years. I'm pretty sure it brings her joy when her nieces and nephews give their parents hell.

I've got to give my son credit. He makes it all the way to the second row before he starts to skip and hop to his mom.

He's standing on the wrong side, but no one cares. Emma wrangles him and her bouquet as best she can while everyone else turns when the quartet transitions into the bride's music. At least my son didn't spike the ring bearer's pillow like a football. I breathe a sigh of relief and call it a win.

The Hollingsworth family has grown over the years.

Knox dumped his cougar girlfriend the month after he created drama at Hudson's birthday party. He continued to live his best fraternity life until his senior year of college when he was shot through the heart with cupid's arrow. She was quiet and shy and a brainiac. So basically, the female version of Knox before he broke out of his shell in college. She was also two years younger than him.

I swear he stayed in college to get every degree he could collect just to stay with her.

They were married in this exact spot last year.

He might not be a legal Hollingsworth, but the family has claimed Cade. He's as official as anyone and kept to his word that marriage is not for him. That doesn't mean he's alone. We don't even call her his girlfriend anymore, because they're in it for life. Cade and Hallie are happy the way they are. They haven't announced it to the world in the same fashion I did, but she's pregnant. I've never seen Cade happier.

And now it's Saylor's turn.

She continued to keep her parents on their toes throughout high school and college.

Or what little college she attended. She's proof a degree isn't needed when you're willing to be creative and work hard.

Saylor took a lesson from Mason's chickens and found success on social media. Her online boutique has grown so much over the last couple of years, she bought her own piece of land in the middle of nowhere and built a warehouse where she runs her up-and-coming dynasty of fashion.

Saylor is a lesson in opposites can attract, because she fell in love with her accountant. The rest was history. He promised Asa he'd love and protect her and keep her out of tax jail.

What more can a dad ask for?

I do wonder if he knows what his new father-in-law does for a living.

I found out the hard way.

I hope he doesn't have to.

When Asa walks Saylor to the altar that's gotten a lot of use over the years, it's hard to focus on what's going on right in front of me. All I can think about is the day I watched Emma walk this same aisle straight to me.

And here I am watching my entire world stand in almost the same spot.

Yeah.

My life is fucking fabulous.

Emma

Jack walks into our room in nothing but a pair of athletic shorts. My husband looks as good as he did the day he chased me down in a posh Black Resort.

I'd say he looks just as good as he did when he gave me my first kiss, but he doesn't.

He's better in every way possible. He's more than a dream. He's my universe.

Every beautiful muscle is on display as he stalks toward me. There are times like this when I wonder if I can be more in love with him than I am right now, but then another day goes by, and he gives my heart another reason to pour over with love.

"Did you put the house to bed?" When I found out I was pregnant with Max, Jack announced we needed a big house with a yard and, I quote, a white fucking picket fence.

Our house is big, but there's no picket fence. There is a security gate and enough land and trees surrounding it that we have plenty of privacy in the summer, especially around the pool. And we're only ten minutes from downtown. And since I travel most every week to a different game, it's nice to be near the airport.

I got the job all those years ago, and Jack is my biggest fan. If he's not with his clients, he's watching me on the field. He invested hours teaching me the intricate rules of football before moving on to basketball. I've been back to the big game every year. This year I was barely pregnant and thought I was going to throw up the whole time. It was a blowout, so at least I didn't have to run to get an interview.

Jack's agency is booming. He has an office with a small staff. Brett Sullivan is still his number one client and also a good friend. Even Rylan Crawford is thriving these days. After a year of friendship between Brett and Rylan, Brett hired him to help run his foundation. Brett said he's never had anyone so committed to his philanthropy.

"Keeping you safe, baby, one day at a time." He climbs up the bottom of the bed, yanks the covers off me, and pulls my right foot into his lap. "You were on your feet too much today."

"It was worth it. It was a great day. Max danced with your grandma until her knees were swollen. I can't lie, I'm so happy your mom and Pierce took Max home to spend the night. I might sleep until noon."

I relax into my pillow as his strong hands start to put pressure on the balls of my feet. Not exactly orgasmic, but it's a close second.

Jack reaches to push my tank over my belly and leans up to kiss our daughter before moving onto my calf. "All the Hollingsworths are married. Time for your dad to retire the altar."

I rub my belly. "I know. How is that possible? Saylor is almost as young as Levi and Carissa were."

He switches to my other foot. "My only regret in life is that I didn't force you to love me sooner."

A small smile plays on my lips. "Like you'd ever have to force me to love you. Loving you is the easiest thing I've ever done."

He drops my foot and crawls up my body before fitting himself to my side where he props himself on an elbow.

His other hand smothers mine over our little Sloan. "Just think about how many more babies we could've had if I would have stayed in that barn with you all those years ago."

I look up at him. "I think I've got one more in me. We'll have to go to a zone defense though."

Jack leans down and puts his lips to our baby. "You heard it here first, Sloan. You're going to be a middle child. I'm going to hold your mama to it."

Sloan kicks.

I smile. "She approves."

"Or she doesn't. Who knows?"

"I think it's your voice. She loves her daddy already, just like the rest of us."

Jack nudges me to my side and fits himself behind me. I give him my weight and savor his warmth and strong chest supporting me. Us. Just like he does our entire family.

He presses his lips to my head. "Go to sleep. We can sleep in and have morning sex like the good old days."

I close my eyes. "Something to look forward to."

"Love you, baby."

"I love you too." I pause and feel my body get heavy but need to say one more thing. "Jack?"

His voice is as heavy as mine. "Yeah, baby."

I don't tell him this often, but there are times like this that I love to remind him. I've been doing it ever since I watched him hold Max for the first time. "You're the best dad. Our babies are lucky. I'm lucky to have you."

He buries his face in my hair and holds me tighter. "Em, you know you break me when you say that."

I close my eyes and allow sleep to take over. "It's my job to make sure you never forget it. I'll tell you forever."

"I'll hold you to that, baby. Forever."

Thank you for reading. If you enjoyed *The Playbook of Emma*, the author would appreciate a review on Amazon.

Read more from the Killers and Next Generation
The Chemistry of Levi

Read Crew and Addy's story in *Vines*
Read Grady and Maya's story in Paths
Read Asa and Keelie's story in *Gifts*
Read Jarvis and Gracie's story in *Veils*
Read Cole and Bella's story in *Scars*
Read Ozzy and Liyah's story in *Souls*
Read Evan and Mary's story in *The Tequila – A Killers Novella*

ALSO BY BRYNNE ASHER

The Agents

Possession

Tapped

Exposed

Illicit

Winslet

Winslet

Killers Series

Vines – A Killers Novel, Book 1

Paths – A Killers Novel, Book 2

Gifts – A Killers Novel, Book 3

Veils – A Killers Novel, Book 4

Scars – A Killers Novel, Book 5

Souls – A Killers Novel, Book 6

Until the Tequila – A Killers Crossover Novella

The Killers, The Next Generation

The Chemistry of Levi, Asa's son

The Playbook of Emma, Asa's daughter

The Carpino Series

Overflow – The Carpino Series, Book 1

Beautiful Life – The Carpino Series, Book 2

Athica Lane – The Carpino Series, Book 3

Until Avery – A Carpino Series Crossover Novella

Force of Nature - A Carpino Christmas Novel

The Dillon Sisters

Deathly by Brynne Asher

Damaged by Layla Frost

The Montgomery Series

Bad Situation – The Montgomery Series, Book 1

Broken Halo – The Montgomery Series, Book 2

Betrayed Love - The Montgomery Series, Book 3

Standalones

Blackburn

ACKNOWLEDGMENTS

Writing Jack and Emma's story was like going home for a holiday. A family reunion. Like a big, warm hug that gave me all the feels.

I was talking to my best friend about where I started. She and I were sitting in my driveway, watching our kids play, going through a church directory to find good character names. That was over a decade ago.

My Killers have come a long way. Crew's fucked up family has become something of fictional magic. Writing the next generation might be even better.

Jack and Emma's love story was nothing short of epic. It was fast and furious and full of emotion. There's no way I could've written this book without the support of my family and friends.

Did you know the Black Resorts are really a thing?

Okay, it's a fictional resort.

Thank you to my author bestie, Layla Frost, who allowed me to set Jack and Emma's epic one-night stand (fictional!) at her resort, Nebula, from her Black Resorts Series. If you haven't read ***Little Dove***, do that now! Not only does Layla loan kick-ass fictional resorts, but she's also the best author friend I could ask for. She's the decadent cupcake to my tangy sauvignon blanc.

Annette, thank you for keeping me organized, on track, putting up with me, and being the sweetest friend. We talk almost daily. I don't know what I'd do without you.

Hadley, my editor, my friend, and my early morning sprinting buddy. Thank you for always having my back and making my words pretty and perfect. You're a precious friend.

Cindy, thank you for stepping up at the last minute and reading for those tiny details and timeline consistency. I appreciate you so much and can't wait until we can hang out in bourbon country again!

Carrie and Beth, thank you so much for your eagle eyes. Having you as final proofers means so much to me.

Bex, thank you for always being there for me to bounce ideas off of. You're a beautiful, supportive friend.

Thank you to my review team who grew leaps and bounds before this release. Your support and love for my books continues to overwhelm me.

Thank you to the Beauties for hanging out with me daily. In a world of social media that can be sketchy at best, our little corner of the internet is a sunny, bright spot. You encourage me to be better and give you fresh stories.

And to the love of my life, thank you for encouraging me and being my biggest hype-man. There is no way I would be able to do this author gig without you at my back. I love you.

ABOUT THE AUTHOR

Brynne Asher lives in the Midwest with her husband, three children, and her perfect dog. When she isn't creating pretend people and relationships in her head, she's running her kids around and doing laundry. She enjoys cooking, decorating, shopping at outlet malls and online, always seeking the best deal. A perfect day in Brynne World ends in front of an outdoor fire with family, friends, s'mores, and a delicious cocktail.

- facebook.com/brynneasherauthor
- instagram.com/brynneasher
- amazon.com/Brynne-Asher/e/B00VRULS58/ref=dp_by-line_cont_pop_ebooks_1
- bookbub.com/profile/brynne-asher

Printed in Great Britain
by Amazon